I MUST HAVE YOU

a novel

I MUST HAVE YOU

a novel

JoAnna Novak

Skyhorse Publishing

For my Mom and Dad—now, then, and always

Skyhorse Publishing books may be purchased in bulk at special discounts for sales promotion, corporate gifts, fund-raising, or educational purposes. Special editions can also be created to specifications. For details, contact the Special Sales Department, Skyhorse Publishing, 307 West 36th Street, 11th Floor, New York, NY 10018 or info@skyhorsepublishing.com.

Skyhorse® and Skyhorse Publishing® are registered trademarks of Skyhorse Publishing, Inc.®, a Delaware corporation.

Visit our website at www.skyhorsepublishing.com.

10 9 8 7 6 5 4 3 2 1

Library of Congress Cataloging-in-Publication Data is available on file.

Cover design by Erin Seaward-Hiatt

Print ISBN: 978-1-5107-1941-5
Ebook ISBN: 978-1-5107-1942-2

Printed in the United States of America

I thought about saying just two words: "I'm gone."

—Michael Jordan, January 13, 1999

THURSDAY

THURSDAY

1 ·· ELLIOT

I WAS IN THE GIRL's bathroom forever. Marissa was being
a putzy stripper. Over winter break, the stalls had been
repainted dusky blue, and that masking-tape-lacquer smell
lingered, even with the Sharpied Savage Garden lyrics and
trains of hearts and smiley faces *see ya, adios*. On the back
wall, across from the handicapped, there was a poster, a
close-up of a grody penis flecked with squinty sores oozing root-beer-colored pus. The caption? STDs DON'T CARE
ABOUT YOUR BOO. I'd studied the image a million times,
trying to understand why *that* species appealed to Lisa. For
two months now, since Thanksgiving, she'd been too busy
dating Junior Carlos—and not just middle-school dating,
but weeknight R movies, no parents dating—to be my best
friend. I'd only seen one other wiener. Penises didn't exactly
call my name.

"Elliot. Do I seriously have to do this?" Marissa looked
like she'd swallowed a stick of Juicy Fruit, ten calories that'd
linger in her stomach for seven years. She'd lost twenty
pounds since we started, but her lips were still fat. "Can't we
wait?"

My thoughts echoed off the quiet. I didn't need a Marissa
Turner problem.

"Why *weight*?" I winked. She didn't get it. "I mean, why wouldn't you want your picture in there? Everyone does. That's the best part of *Real Talk*."

"Yeah, I know. You gave me the last issue." With a wooden-heeled clog, she kicked her ketchup-red backpack. All the zippers were festooned with Backstreet Boys key chains. "I can show you. I don't wanna wreck this, though, when I could lose . . . whatever. I could lose a lot more. I'm so pretide today."

Her mouth stayed open: her tongue lolled like a dark purple slug, as if she'd sucked a Blue Raspberry Blow Pop. Maybe she'd been cheating.

"Hey! Amy Heckerling represent! Crimson *wave*, not *tide*. Big dif! Also: I know what I wrote. You don't need to prove anything. Girl! You hit a goal! Show that stuff!"

"What stuff?" She planted her hands on her waist, like a challenge.

"Let me look."

I grinned and glowered. With my arms crossed over my chest, in my black turtleneck and black leggings, I felt like Miss Petite Sophisticate, model of muted glamour. My dark brown hair was shellacked with my dad's mousse, the lank strands bunned so flyaways wouldn't interfere with my ferocious mind. Critic, gamine, beatnik: I could've passed for Susan Sontag or Audrey Hepburn in *Funny Face*, but I was an eighth grader, a wannabe writer in French ballet flats. Someone whose mother thought sequined clothes bled cheap.

Marissa wore lint-blue overalls from GAP. She was rubbing the metal hook and eye with shaky hands, her nails painted metallic red and glitter-mob gold. A few months ago, she'd been spready, a bus driver in the butt (when she crouched, the fabric pinched into crow's feet). Now those overalls sagged. I nodded. A smile gripped my face. I didn't need to look at Marissa to see her. I knew her numbers, her form: every day I monitored her. The way Anna, my mom, practiced writing poems or doing yogi moon salutes, I studied my clients' bodies: I knew every sliver of flesh, every ounce, every wax and wane, every eclipse of bone.

No, *I* didn't want her bod, but *most* girls would be green-eyed. I was proud.

"You'll be an inspiration. Forget Calista Flockhart."

"Who?"

"Ally McBeal?"

"Oh, that creepy dancing baby? Yeah, Ethan Suva brought in a tape for Ms. McMahon to play in LA, when we were, like, talking about imagery or something, and then she had to turn it off 'cuz she started crying."

Park Junior High's edgiest were boys: this depressed me. I fantasized about using the plastic cutlery I filched from the caf to saw my wrist and disrupt the system. No Doubt, Melissa Etheridge, Veruca Salt, Tori Amos: girl power and riot grrrl anthems and Take Your Daughter To Work Days were over-obvious efforts to convince girls they weren't just girls, as though girlhood were so intrinsically limiting that it could never be synonymous with power or riot or even professionalism. Eighth-graders proved this. They were cowed by difference; they were boring, normal, good, predictably bad. That was another reason Lisa's horn-doggedness worried me. Recovery had ruined her.

"Get out. That's brilliant. Ethan's so right brain, it's, like, whack."

"Huh? I heard he was bipolar."

"You know Ethan's a savant, right? Well, he's left-handed, which signals throttled creativity, and a sensitive constitution . . . artistic genius. Maybe he tapped into Ms. McMahon's repressed feelings or, I don't know. Do you think she had an abortion? Wait—didn't your sister date one of his brothers?"

"Yeah! God, that one really was a psychopath! How'd you know?"

Don't blow this, Elliot. Marissa and I were sorta becoming friends. When she called for pre-dinner advice, we talked about more than how to make a baked potato disappear without admitting a bite. I'd been chill, but in the bathroom's Gak-green lights, I was flashing my uncool, like how I always mis-sang Spice Girls, shouting one more, "If you wanna be my lover," as Mel B. rapped, "So here's the story from A to Z."

"You told me at Befores? No clue. Sooooo . . . Afters!"

I unzipped my soft black pencil case. I took out my camera, a Polaroid Spectra, boxy, easy, point and shoot. It had been a gift from my mom two years ago when, propped on the platform heels of *Now and Then*, a '60s revival had swept Park Junior High's sixth grade. I'd eschewed peace sign necklaces and lime-green tube tops and the aural malaria that was The Archies's "Sugar, Sugar," but I loved my throwback camera: it had helped me get Lisa *flaca*, and I'd been coaching other girls' weight loss ever since.

"Can I just keep my clothes on? Or, like, my shirt?" Marissa said. "Is my face gonna be in this? Can I do my lip gloss?"

"After pictures don't have faces. This is a focus on bodies. Don't worry about your lip stuff. You know there's calories in those."

"But my lips look like death."

"Hey! B Lunch is almost over. We have to do this. I've got to get to the library and make photocopies."

"I just don't think I wanna. You can't make me."

I watched her. She was a mannequin, rigid and melting under shop lights, thirty-five pounds heavier than me, but I could've blocked her if I had to, if she tried to bolt. I held the straight-arm hang record in PE. Anna, mommy-plus-one-glass-of-chardonnay, called me *Tenacious, Acquisitive, Tireless*—Walt Whitman's way of saying I was a fighter. I checked: the bathroom door was locked so no one could burst in from the Fine Arts wing. I didn't need Ms. Washburn here wringing her oil-pastelly hands. I needed Marissa Turner to undress and let me take her picture.

I took a ujjayi breath, like Anna had taught me. When I inhaled, my ribs accordioned and I greeted every knot of my hunger. That was comforting. My stomach growled to my volition, which said in signature Spanglish: *handle Marissa*: *ella es una* simpleton. *Marissa=distraction. Postre. You don't miss tu amiga mejor; Lisa's sick.*

The truth was Marissa wanted to be coerced. She wanted me to applaud her, celebrate her, Fatboy Slim praise her. And, she wanted my attention, even though my compliments meant zip. Once I gave a girl a goal, she wrote her own story. That's why Lisa was special: she'd become such a whisper of herself, she almost died.

"If you want to leave, there's the door. Unlock it and go. Take that skinny butt to the APR. Have a taco salad or a flippin' slice of pizza. Do it. Like, don't even blot the grease. Wash it down with a chocolate milk. Have two cartons. As if I care."

"Elliot, you're a jerk."

I unzipped my black Five Star Trapper and flipped to the last tab where I kept client notes and the draft of *Real Talk: Meal Talk*. Let Marissa feel ignored. I paged through mock-ups of next week's issue: eight pages, folded hamburger style. 1999 was only fifteen days old. We were still in resolution season. I'd written purifying recipes to inspire my girls to replace their Mr. Pibb and Snapple and Hi-C. Celery water, Lemon Fizz, Cucumber Spaaaahh. "Scooch the Pooch" was a cartoon stick figure doing reverse crunches to blast her lower abs. On the back cover, a Polaroid-sized box, penciled with an X, waited for Marissa.

My clients loved the Afters so much I was starting to believe my mom's complaints: kids won't read. (*Not* can't, *El, but* won't *when given a choice*.) My audience would grow up to be her students. They wanted gospel and testament, smack-you-in-the-face pictures, obvious proof. Sure, in Health, cockeyed Ms. Cummins lectured about the sorcery of magazines—complexions smoothed, boobs boosted—but those computer programs were out of our reach. We had snapshots—like the one of me and Lisa taped in my locker that verified we really had been best friends: Only a year ago, on a field trip, we'd used our good-girl cred to ditch the Navy Pier food court and wander the boardwalk's bazaar, buy each other red rope bracelets from Guatemala, blow our lunch money in a photo booth where we mugged for the flash and traded reasons it was stupid to waste life chewing.

"You know I hate this, right?"

I looked up from my binder, feigning shock. "Be thankful you're getting thin?"

"Yeah right. *Sooooo* thin."

Marissa sighed, frowning in the mirror. She tucked her wavy black hair behind her ears. She stepped off her clogs and closed her eyes.

With the grace of a zombie, she unclipped her overalls. The denim slipped over her hips and slid down her legs, eddying at her feet. She pulled off her daisy-printed Henley. She was teen-girl naked, in a buttercup bra-plus set I recognized from the dELiA*s catalog. The underpants sagged. Her hipbones pestered the cotton.

I turned away. Leaning into the mirrors, I scratched a shriveled pimple off my nose. I tried to only see that zit. Nothing was worse than mirrors—especially skinny ones. Mirrors thickened your thighs and widened your waist. They tricked you into believing under-eye shadows spelled weight loss, coerced you into safety so total they'd practically scoop your Rocky Road. I didn't need a reflection to tell me I wasn't a pretty starver. I wasn't a Lifetime movie, seed-bead printing, pipsqueak voice, Hard Candy nails, Clara in *The Nutcracker*, first-chair flute—I was Park's only decent eating disorder book, *The Golden Cage*: a young woman, ascetic, brittle, recalcitrant. Not that I was jealous. Insecurity was a dog I sent to the pound when I got *flaca*.

"Ma*rissa*! Gorgeous! Call Ford. Let's get you an agent." I didn't pedestal clients, but Marissa really was super pretty. Park girls would kill for her parts, like pieces they lusted over in *Seventeen* or *YM*: concave abdomen with the merest comma of navel; licked luster of protruding ribs; inner thighs that evinced commitment to the hardest leg lifts. "You're, like, famine-hot. Everyone's gonna want your secret."

"I doubt that." But she stood still, ready for me.

I looked at her through the viewfinder.

"Don't smile. Remember, I'm only using your body—'cuz, your body *is* the smile, metaphorically, after all that hard work. I'll crop out your head."

"It's anonymous, though, right? Will there be other girls in this issue?"

"No." Idiot—there were never other girls. "*You* deserve kudos—like, props, *not* the granola bar. You worked hard: own that! Love your effort. Say skinny!"

"Skinny."

She forced a wan Picture-Day smile.

I clicked; the Polaroid spat. Marissa's Before from three months ago was filed in my Trapper: in it, her boobs were up in her clavicle's biz, a mini-muffin top gabled her waist-band, her belly was a mango. I mentally patted myself on the back, vertebrae clunk-clunk. I'd requested Marissa wear the same bra-and-panties, so you could totally see how she'd become Tyra Banks' gangly kid sister.

"*Perfecta*. That's that!" I said, shaking the film. "You can get dressed."

"Elliot, can I ask you a favor?"

"That's what you hired me for."

Marissa glared at the floor, twelve-inch square tiles, white with navy spangles. Not including the three half-tiles in the handicapped stall, there were 180. Ever since getting *flaca*, I'd loved to count: if pandemonium ever erupted, I'd have mastered my environment, the way my hero Michael Jordan envisioned the court, eyes in the back of his head. Marissa probably just thought it was gross to be in the bathroom, barefoot.

"Can you take a picture with me? Like, in the mirror?"

I was flattered, but not 100 percent. I was anxious, too. I hadn't taken a picture with a girl since Lisa—I couldn't repeat that mistake. Her mom had found graph paper where Lisa had compared us, measured our bodies in the photo and calculated their proportions, Lisa's arm X-times bigger than mine, our knees and thighs, our necks. At the end of last school year, when she was sent to in-patient, her mom pulled up while I was waiting for the bus and handed me an envelope. Inside was a photocopy of the computations, smacked with a Post-It: *leave Lisa alone.*

I fanned the Polaroid, pretending I'd misheard. "What?"

"Take one with me." She was a yeller, a cheerleader who stood on a lunch chair, chanting. Now her voice ducked. "You undress. I wanna see. Can't you?"

"That's a no. Total no."

"What's the big deal, Elliot?"

"Well, it's weird," I said. "And sick. Plus, I don't like to be in pictures. And if I do this for you, everyone's going to want me to hop into their shot."

"We're the same height, aren't we?"

I didn't know how she knew this, but I liked that she did. "So?"

"So it's hypocritical to make people do something you hate. *You're* my goal."

"Don't go there, hon. You don't want to be like me." I was foxtrotting around a feral cat. "Are you a lesbo?"

"Excuse me?"

"Your body is never going to be mine and vice versa. I know it's hard—I mean, inspiration is important. But focus on yourself. Unless you've got, like, a crush. In which case, cool—but I'm not into girls. So, like, why do you want to see *me* naked?"

"Who said anything about *your* naked bone bag? Sicko! How rude!"

"Original, hon. *Full House* called. Stephanie wants her catchphrase back. Watch your mouth. Remember: you talk dirty, you eat dirty."

"Give me the picture, Elliot. I don't want to be in fucking *Real Talk*."

"No way. The photo's mine."

"Well, the body's mine."

"Well, I bought the paper."

Marissa snorted. As she pulled her overalls, her stomach bunched. In the After, her body was a slim brown column. I should print this issue in color, at least the photo, to show off her collarbones. Or circle them, draw a dialog-bubble: ALMOST!

I didn't notice her wind back her arm until her fist was coming toward my chest. The thud trounced me, like I'd been lobbed with a dodge ball. I staggered, saw stars, huckleberry blackness. Neon rhombuses. I was a fucking baby! I leaned against the wall and drove a fist into my stomach and winced: Lisa-one, Lisa-two, Lisa-three, Lisa-four.

"Did you just punch me in the boob?" I sputtered. "What the hell? Ho bag."

"What boobs? Bony freaky." Marissa had the picture. She pulled open the bathroom door. There was the hallway—green, green, green, the milky smell of puberty, beige.

"Marissa, c'mon! Don't act like a twat!"

The lunch bell trilled. This was when I missed Lisa the most. When I realized I was nothing. I needed her. I was desperate. I held out my hand, ready for the Polaroid.

"Elliot, c'mon." Marissa had a playground expression that sang, *Na-na-na-boo-boo.* "No wonder Lisa's over you. Stop acting like you're the only girl who can be anorexic."

..

C Lunch had begun, but I stayed in the bathroom. Being near the toilets curbed my appetite. If you wanna lech up, if you're fetishy for ana + brunette, I was into touching my swallow—one hand around my throat, my grip hugging my jugular: it made survival sexy. Kinky, even: my *gorge, mi garganta* cupped by the glabrous curve between my left pointer and thumb, that webby patch of striation I could never slather with enough Frosted Snowdrop. I kept this from my clients: starving gives you dry skin.

I counted my slivers of Red Delicious, browning at the cut. My mom didn't monitor the fruit; she just bought it. I fixed lunches.

I chewed with my molars and tried not to taste. The flesh was wintersome. Mealy. Not good. I didn't want to like food, anyway—I wanted to be adult—Pinter one-acts, Shostakovich symphonies, self-staged orgasms, a body above puberty's stupefactions.

I spat the chewed-up apple in the sink. Marissa's Eyeore 'tude, her bratty snark enraged me. I should've punched her in the ribs. She was a spineless version of Lisa: she didn't deserve me. *Ef eating, get to the library*, I told myself. *The Xerox is slow. Like Marissa!*

I chucked my apples across the bathroom. The fruit scattered on the floor, ear-shaped splotches. It reminded me of spooge on the girls' faces in *Terrible Twos and Twisted Threes*, the video Lisa and I'd watched the last time I saw her outside of school, a few weeks ago at a sleepover before Christmas. It was her dad's tape: Mr. Breit was freaky.

Truth or dare?

Truth: Ever since watching it, I'd been a touch traumatized.

The movie had me wondering: Did my own dad, Rolf, amuse himself with stuff that sick, all these weeks he'd been in Europe, on business? What would a human dick look like in real life? What if confronting the organ ruined the one boy I like-liked, Ethan Suva? What if some day he wanted me and I'd been repulsed forever by a porn penis: Barbie-tall, pink, foldy like Jabba the Hutt? (Hidden in the vaginas, it hadn't been so bad, like the penis was a potato replanted in earth.) Ever since that sleepover, XXX images thaumatroped across my brain, sex and girls; girls, sex; Lisa, me.

Daddy, make me a juice box, one porn sister'd said. When Lisa was too grossed out to watch, her fingers latticed across her eyes, I'd relayed to Lisa how wide and wet and gummy a mouth could be, exhausted from blow-jobbing, how *his* stomach heaved like a woodchuck; the way *she* sucked him, lovey-dovey, like she was unclogging a milkshake straw. After all that, she wouldn't return my phone calls. She avoided our trophy case meet-up spot. Today, she hadn't been in science.

I slid off the counter. My blood pressure painted my head with highlighter fluorescence, radial midnight. What did Marissa know about me or Lisa? I was tired of waiting for our friendship to heal itself, for Junior Carlos to break up with her, for Lisa to go back to being super skinny.

I checked the bathroom mirror. I gave the flaky zit one last scratch. I smoothed my bun. I didn't want to be like my clients, bruising my knees for a breakthrough. Sometimes I felt like the only girl who tried, the only Park girl who wasn't slouching through life; I paraded like coronation was imminent. *One day I woke up and I was different,* I'd written in *Real Talk*: girls needed to believe they had the power to reset their own lives. Maybe I needed the same wake-up call, too. I needed to listen to my own advice. *Puissance,* my mom had taught me—and Anna was always right—power was something you orchestrated yourself. I shook my Trapper: two quarters, one phone call. It jingled.

..

In my black turtleneck covering my black training bra hiding my black xiphoid process and my black-blooded, Lisa-lusting heart, I headed to the payphone. Low Mozart issued from the choir room; a struggling modem whined.

I turned down an elbow of hallway, where last quarter's best artwork hung. Dawdling predated my diet, but hunger helped me fantasize. Adolescence is one big detour. Now, I imagined I wasn't at Park, but Manhattan two summers ago, with Anna. Anna said imaginative play, *gambols or gambles,* could be *profitable*; school should be less structured, more sympathetic to *individuals' constitutions*. I shouldn't miss a chance to hop a train of thought. Trusting her made me strange, but I relished every breath that separated me from Other girls. Other girls hated their moms and feared the unknown; their skinniness was one more attempt to smite the womb. When those girls visited NYC, they flashed peace signs in Times Square, caught the fatuous Broadway shows that came to Chicago. I'd been to Soho—according to Anna, *rejuvenated by the muse.* For a month, I'd wandered in my mom's wake, prettied by her company, maître d's sending us champagnes and Shirley Ts. I'd sat in a diner with black coffee, a leatherette notebook from The Strand, trying to write stories and plays and poems surrounded by burnt bacon butterscotch milkshakes hazelnut coffee toast, heady conversations, micro-dramas and epics; harangues, squabbles, jokes. Anna was right: everyone hung out in someone else's aisle. She'd taught me *how to look*—not just at a Jeff Koons, but all over—to see art anywhere: steel drumming muzzied with pot in Washington Square Park, needle-heels lisping across Bergdorf carpets. Art was what to eat (an onion bialy, we chewed and spat in paper bags) and how people behaved. Once, we'd rounded a blind corner onto a gust of cigarette smoke that materialized into a scruffy man, who unleashed a legit Brit lexicon: *pardon me, loves*. Anna went soft as spoiled fruit. Farther down Mott, she'd said, *El, that one got me throatily.*

In Park's glass cases, each pinch pot looked wormier than the next; linoleum prints stood on easels, placards whorled with the calligraphy Ms. Washburn used to make everyone's name seem special. I stared, bored. Arms over my chest, lips pursed: my reflection was *so* gaunt I couldn't see my whole self, only parts. In Soho, there hadn't been a mirror in our sublet, just jungle-green walls, so my mom and I roamed the city, where a single color couldn't asphyxiate us.

I walked on. The framed watercolors were big as bedroom posters. When I saw my own, I gagged. My portrait was a black-and-white of Michael Jordan and Spike Lee: it sucked. MJ's eyes looked meaner than in the Nike ad, like Tim Curry in *Home Alone 2*. *It's* bad, *don't hang it*, I'd said to Ms. Washburn; I'd felt guilty, especially after she'd told me not to be a *brown-noser*. Well. I wasn't good; I wasn't like Mike. He'd been my idol since the Flu Game when, parched, nauseous, dizzy, he'd led the Bulls to victory against skeeze-bearded Karl Malone and the Jazz. I'd watched with Rolf, who cried as Scottie Pippin slung MJ's arm over his shoulder. *That's teamwork. Exceeding your capabilities when you're surrounded by people you trust.* My dad dabbed his red eyelashes with a monogrammed hankie; he was more emotional than me and Anna combined.

..

A punk had plastered a Mustard Plug sticker around the payphone receiver, but the mouthpiece wasn't covered.

I fed my quarters into the slot. They were my assertiveness fund, a tool I used with clients. *Go on*, I'd say in the Park Snack Shop. *Make the right choice.* Yesterday, I'd nearly depleted it, coaching Rocyo, my newest girl, at our trial: I'd walked her to the line, given her a dollar's worth of coins, told her *order wisely. Dunk-a-roo con fresas?* she'd said. I'd frowned. *Fresa* frosting. *No.*

I dialed. Park was quiet; the ringing went on for a week—could time stop and forget me? I saw the Orlowski-Breit's phones lighting up, rattling on their receivers, the black cordless in the living room, the furry pink princess from Limited Too on Lisa's nightstand, the UFO-shaped speaker-answering machine combo in the den. If I got the machine, I'd wait. Phone calls meant hope. Lisa could call back. I pictured her in the ratty blue-green flannel pants she'd worn the last time we hung out, when we'd exchanged presents and watched porn, dozing on the L-shaped black leather couch. Sick, sniffles, a cough. Sneezing like Betty Boop. Blowing her nose rosy, raw. Hoarse. I felt like a mom:

I hoped she didn't have to be alone, that someone was taking care of her, straining the noodles from her Mrs. Grass so she could score a sick day slim-down.

I'd never ditched, but if Lisa needed me, I would. If, before wind chill, the temperature was negative thirteen degrees; if, like this morning, I had to hop on one foot to keep warm, waiting thirty minutes for the bus because black ice made the route run on the inclement schedule and my mom was too late to give me a ride; I would find a way to Lisa. Frostbite could have my fingers.

The ringing stopped. I heard her open her mouth, Angelina Jolie lips. "Hello?"

She didn't sound at all sick. She sounded fine, a little husky, mature. More beautiful than ever. My pulse snagged. I couldn't speak.

"Who is this?" She cleared her throat. Coughed.

"Hey! It's me. So! Random question: Marissa Turner. She went postal during a photo shoot. Like, when she finally let me take her pic, she wanted one together and I wouldn't and she flipped out, and acted like a total nut, and said something's up with *you*. Do you have Lisa Logic? What's her dealio?"

Lisa exhaled a craggy sigh. "Ugh. Who *are* you people? We don't want what you're trying to sell. So, like, why do you keep calling?"

"What? Wait—Lisa?"

Her voice lowered. "Listen: I'm not talking to you unless you get help."

I felt like my brain had been dunked in Jolt. "What?"

"El. You. Need. Help. You know what I mean."

She hung up. I stared at the black receiver, streaked with hand grease. There was no misunderstanding Lisa. Clear, blunt, honest, real Lisa, at home, a victim of Junior Carlos's menticide. *Idiot*, I thought. *Trying to fatwash me.*

2 ·· ANNA

How many fuck-ups do I get? How many occasions to make the wrong choice? Amendment: how many occasions to *knowingly* make the wrong choice, to court the wrong choice from across the dance floor, to buy the wrong choice a rum and diet, to engage in light banter with the wrong choice in the trance of house music, to let the wrong choice cup my hips and steer my engine, to despise dancing but hatefully dance, hard and wild as a hartebeest against the wrong choice's hot heart-center, to get in the wrong choice's roadster and ignore the wrong choice's slurring stanzas, to close my eyes and listen to the wrong choice sing-along to Eurythmics, "sweet dreams are made of this" wrong choice, not-breathing-and-so-not-in-my-body wrong choice, wrong choice of Sauvignon blanc and seltzer, wrong choice of knees in the seat and feet out the window, panties on the pavement wrong choice, wrong to want this wrongness, wrong to wrong the wrongness and not just witness, wrong to unzip the wrong choice's pants, to choke on the wrong choice?

The right choices are few and far between. I savor them:

1. I have not given up the code to the faculty bathroom. This is good. The faculty bathroom is a Glade-scented haven where I don't have to worry about running into

students or colleagues. I really don't like anyone. The faculty bathroom is adjacent to the faculty lounge, which is across from my office. You punch *678 on a metal numerical keypad to gain entry. Oh. Shit.

2. I have confiscated Carlos Rottingham Jr.'s cocaine. Me. His last-semester ENG 101 Professor. Not Tory La Fraga, cowgirl chief of campus police; not Alicia Aurelio, Dean of Liberal Studies' shoe-obsessed secretary; not Glenn Decklin, Building 13's whiskey-haired guard, with whom I swap *Seinfeld* jibes. I, Anna Egleston, knocked on the frost effloresced driver's side window of Carlos Rottingham Jr.'s emerald BMW at nine a.m., and said, with nary a quaver, *why are you sitting out here in the Antarctic and what the fuck is that in the cup holder? Excuse me, hey, you, didn't we talk about this? Yeah, I don't know,* he mumbled, proving even a graduate of the best high school in the state of Illinois and the progeny of two émigré moguls, one Irish and one Italian, a kid fluent enough in Spanish to volunteer at the Picasso Museum in Barcelona last summer but a self-professed "ghetto geek," a counterculture wunderkind, can be a cotton-mouthed slacker with the ability to lose all sense of eye-contact-based decency on a dime.

Slavering for inconspicuous suicide. Not wanting to live, but being too apathetic to die.

Like, the horror.

"Give me that," I said to Rot, motioning toward the plastic bag. He was all cheekbones and blue metal eyes, black hair parted in the center and framing his forehead like parenthesis. And I was too

too-much—too cold, too hungry, too angry, too revved from my run—to pause and ask myself why I cared so much, to hold a mirror to my heart and ask of it, what are you doing, Anna, and shouldn't you be minding your rosters and advisees, couldn't you be writing? Instead, I snapped at Rot, like I would never even snap at my own daughter. I snapped at him like he had spurned me, lover.

"What did you tell me about this?" My head was in the car: had Rot not been reclining, my lips would have brushed his cheek, streaky pink, my Black Honey pucker marking that flushed cheek, which, coupled with my power, my position, my tits nearly shoved in his face and my nipples bullet-hard beneath my black coat, a lace bra that itched when the heat in my office went into overdrive. All of this made me feel tingled up, vaginally alive, my being was thrival, thrum of an electric shaver in my grip, somewhat unwelcome, on this occasion, in this most public place, the College of Cook County campus, in the oceans of concrete we've all been singing about for the past it-seems-like-three-thousand decades, next to a gray Plymouth Voyager with the passenger side collapsed and a Chicago Bears decal flapping off the bumper, in Commuter Parking Lot D.

"I said, what the hell did you tell me about this?"

"I wasn't going to, fucking, supply you," he said.

"Give me that," I was lunging a little, leaning with attitude. I think that constitutes narc status. I saw a bumper sticker on one of my colleague's Volvos:

[Anytown]: WHERE THE COFFEE IS STRONG AND SO ARE THE WOMEN.

Rot squeezed the bag in my hand. "What the hell, *professor?*"

I ignored that last word. I ignored his resemblance to Jared Leto, the grottos of shadow that give a well-built face such a sexy, suck-out look. I pocketed the drug and walked back to the building, concentrating on my ass.

3. Thirteen years ago, I ignored my thesis advisor, Arlene, that *Luftkopf*, when she said, *a PhD or motherhood, hm*. I have never been an either or. I'm always both.

4. And Rolf, my husband, from the Ritz-Carlton, Vienna, even this morning, has again assured me he loves this: how I take freedom by the reigns, all the right choices I make. Like no breakfast. Like afternoon coffee with a shot of espresso, an indulgence for which I absent myself from campus. Like trysts. And the declension of our monogamy, more subversive than divorce. This subversion reminds me why I fell in love with Rolf to begin with, which really dumps coffee grounds and motor oil and banana peels in the proverbial water. O Rolf and the acceleration of our cyber messaging, its familiar *froideur* over AOL! How he loves our daughter Elliot's independence—independence, he writes, in no small part fostered by her mother. Her mother's lust for life. Her mother's—my (so easy to be subsumed by a role)—predilection for working through lunch. For not concerning herself with the stupefying chores of home.

5. Microwave popcorn.

..

The faculty bathroom is private. The fake geranium is carnelian blossomed, the purse rack teal wire. There is usually a back-up stack of brown paper towels—today there is not. There is a full roll of single-ply toilet paper. The floor is shades of honeycomb and caramel, rectangle tiles the size of dominos that run both perpendicular to and parallel with one another.

It is an unnecessarily busy floor. My head aches to look at it now, with my blood galloping and my brain aroar. The floor, the soles of my boots click against. The floor is always sticky. Piss? Soda? Lotion? And yet the room is an icebox: shouldn't whatever's tacky freeze away?

Faulty logic, I think. But I flounder when teaching argument, too. *Poet: doesn't know it*, per my department-meeting repartee.

The toilet is white enamel like the sink, minus the hairline cracks. I twist the hot and cold, and the water surges. There I am in the mirror. *Silver and exact.*

The pedant in my brain hates me: *which to enjoy is not to consume.* I have become a woman that memorizes Sylvia Plath.

A woman heaving in the bathroom?

It is surprisingly easy—though I'll be vaporized after.

Butter Blasted was my lunch and now my mouth tastes malolactic. My lips are slippery. The center of my tongue, raked into numbness. Marauded by my congestion, the bathroom smells like dander. The moment is pixelated by sensations. Mountain Dew coruscation of over-sink light.

Peals of girl-squeal through walls. Smudgy dun of the faucet. Glossy white paper towel dispenser and its jack-in-the-box crank.

Thank hell I ran first thing this morning. I used the college's cobbled-together fitness center, pounded the shaky treadmill with the ribbed belt closest to the indoor serenity pond—really, a flotilla of rafted plants the color of soggy green olives—five miles, forty minutes. I'm not fast; I don't aspire to be fast: I want constancy and consistency, the steady pummeling of chronic, unflagging, devotional, genuflectory dedication. It's so much easier with my body than my head or my heart. On treadmills. At the gym, for which I am grateful, especially today, when this morning, I couldn't handle outdoors: the roads have been agony, black ice everywhere, an inhuming, already, too much, this winter; and El was out the door, satchel and apples, black mantis-legs sticking out from her black parka, early for the bus.

There's an alternate schedule, she told me. *For inclement weather, which I'd say this constitutes. Oh, weird one: is there dew point in winter? Mom? Anna?*

And I was pulling on my running tights and slicking back my hair, mind hiding in a thousand corners, finding my papers and filling my water bottle and considering calling Rolf—whose cheer and dogged optimism, even after factoring in the seven-hour time distance, when all reasonable men would be further day-calloused, can sometimes make teaching tolerable, minor, detourish, and petty—and deciding against calling Rolf—whose same cheer and dogged optimism can other times make teaching an insurmountably dire indentured servitude, a schooling. Then opening the crisper and finding there weren't salad mixes to bring for

lunch. Entertaining whether or not I avoided grocery shopping in order to tempt the Butter Blasted fates (did I have
a postprandial agenda even then?) and cramming apples in
my tote.

What, El? I said before I realized my daughter had already
gone.

The invisible fan cycles on and the faculty bathroom gets
colder. Everything metal hums. I pull my black sweater up,
over, my hair statics, my sweater hugs my crown, head, off,
over, on the hook. I wear a black lace balconette bra. Under
my black wool pants, a black lace G-string. My husband has
been in Austria for two weeks, but it feels longer because this
trip is one block in a tower of business travel. Jenga, we used
to play with Elliot, listening to a tape of *The Magic Flute.*
Which one of these timbers will cause the construction to
topple? Another outcome: how high can the shaft grow
before you all grow bored and start deciding who deserves
the nickname *Piccolo*?

In the meantime, I refuse to frump.

I am not a math person, though I feel a kinship with
statisticians, who deal in factors and odds, probabilities,
curves and formulas, outlier conditions: isn't that a poem?
The most I bandy with numbers is when I sestina (soused,
it's been known to go down). Still I can't account for the
calories in microwave popcorn. I won't even try to gloss the
nutritional label. There are popped and unpopped calories,
grams of sodium and saturated fat. Servings per bag, servings
per box. Total mindfuck.

All I know is, whatever I ate, it's too much.

My emesis is left-handed, my mimesis right. But seriously, I use my left index and middle finger the way a pitcher,

off-duty, relies on the dud. *Baby the moneymaker*—that's a Rolfism, something he mockingly reports his colleagues say about golf.

I hinge at the waist and close my eyes as the black nails disappear inside my mouth, wet and sicky hole.

I've chosen an ugly hobby—and a fuck up of a student. Rot. Three months of serious eye contact, hardcore finger-tip brushing when homework changed hands, bracketed moments in class discussions when I felt myself talking to only one person in the room led up to the Wednesday before Thanksgiving, when I held all-day office hours since Park Junior High is the only school in the district that doesn't allow for a civil holiday recess and what would I do all day at home when at work I might test my luck? That day was exciting and desperate. I'd arrived to find the sign-up sheet Scotch-taped to my office door a field of blanks until the last one—my 3:15 slot belonged to Rot. He wrote in left-slanting cursive. He'd shown up two minutes early.

Bending over the toilet zings me. I'm always frightened initially, the terror that mounts as a roller coaster ascends: how many more inches before the bottom drops out? Before I start, when there's no way in hell I'll be backing down, like a plane taxiing down the runway, about to take off: I'm onboard, knee shaking in time with my pulse, wondering why beverage service isn't a right away sort of thing so I can be at least holding a glass stem as I wonder if the engine will explode, when I fantasize about yelling, *let me off, mother-fuckers! Let me off*!

In other words: will this be the purge that kills me?

Ah, but you're a writer, Anna, I tell myself. *At times of upheaval, huzzah! Cling to your identity. Relish the risk.*

I jam my fingers further, find the place where mouth becomes throat. The first physical effect is coughing. It's genteel, clipped, a mealtime hack, raised hand, sip of water, *no, no, it's okay—wrong pipe*. Nothing frightening. Nothing that would turn gourmandizing heads in a loud restaurant, nothing that would interest nosy students in Building 13's halls or the lounge's college-hour occupants, faculty microwaving smelly chicken potpies.

I feel supernatural, rational, brilliant: removing my own food? Mastermind. I am an adult woman, engineering—organically, sans substance or serum or chemical, snorts or injections or charge cards—an altered state.

Then the coughing becomes ugly. I'm not a math person—I'm not a biology person either. I don't understand the mechanisms that usher cough from hack to expulsion—I only know the distension wrenches my cheeks. They puff—*terrible fish*—and I spit a dribble of clear oiliness into the water.

But not Sylvia Plath, now, more . . . Linda Blair-ish.

Have you ever licked a finger and rubbed the buttery salt out from the inside of a bag of microwave popcorn? Harsh fake flavor?

I pause. Tension vises my head, like it's caught inside an ambulance strobe, red and loud and unavoidable. For a second, I remember why purging frightens me: it's the only time my mind is wordless.

But my stomach bulges from black coffee and Butter Blasted. There's no going backwards. Every so-called regression is merely an unfortunate step forward.

The popcorn comes up in three hay-colored hurls; it looks like coarse-ground cornmeal. The sound splats on itself in the toilet, like coital smacking: ass and cock, gut and gut. The sound emanating from me is a whelping howl.

Now I feel nothing.

I'm a body, a vessel, a husk.

Could this be death?

My mother passed with vomit: a pond of it in her lap.

My eyes burn. My fingers are cold: two of them are coated in half-digested snack. I'm shaking. Mirror-me is splotchy skin and gross, especially the cheeks. I vacuum them in, try for pinched. Then I relax. Are they normal? Am I mussed? I don't think so. I don't have to touch them to feel they're sticky. My itchy eyes find my gaze, register some flintiness— shame, satisfaction—wander off.

After I purge, I savor improvidence: pump so much pink soap it pools in my palms.

Actually, I take perverse glee in wasting all the college's resources: photocopying submissions; filching good envelopes; green, felt-tipped pens.

It's just one of those things.

I shut the tap. Reaching over to flush the toilet, I feel something, a nothing, the shiver that passes over you during a perfect sentence. There's a plunk. So small a sound, if the bathroom weren't the size of a phone booth, I probably wouldn't hear it at all. If there'd been multiple stalls, I would hear, first, the rub of wadded toilet paper over some woman's ruddy crotch. An ornery zipper.

I look around. On occasion, three or four times a week, for the past few years, I've been ralphing lunch. The atmospherics of afterward are trauma in miniature: How I am fine. How I am shaken. How I am haunted—as if by a churlish physician or a beggar-wraith scrambling for food or my more-sensible self, and yet there is no one in the room. How I deny the purge and replay it, and the binary of avoidance and repetition is not lost on me. I peer into the toilet bowl.

There is my wedding band, diamond diamond diamond, atop a float of masticated popcorn. *Something with some sparkle*, Rolf had said ten years ago, parading me like a Saratoga mare around Cartier. His effusiveness is so unconditional; he'll come home with souvenirs for El, and gifts for me, deckled diaries, gold-edged agendas from stationers in Paris and Hamburg and London, ever since he's been traveling. He's FedExed silk robes, powder-blue tap pants, chiffon nighties, hand-tatted garters. All the affection is intimidating, when my feelings for him mute so easily, for whatever isn't immediately before me. I'm a bad mother, and, wifely, a lackluster philandering Eve, and moreover, I find Rolf, his showiness, compensating, cliché, as though I am so provincially-minded that I won't love him without parochial displays of materialism.

Still, panic burrows in my heart when I see the ring in the toilet. Rot aside, I don't want to be an unwed woman. The ring is valuable. I have reached the highest salary step. I'm too old to radically reinvent myself: slowly, my habits either will or won't erode me. I don't want to be alone.

"Unbelievable." I mutter it to make sure: first, that I haven't died; second, that, provided I'm alive, I'm not overheard. I find it comfortingly uncomfortable to talk to myself. "Fucking brilliant, Anna."

I asked for an epidural with Elliot. Ears, nose, tongue, et al.: I am unpierced. I won't accept Rice Krispies treats prepared by colleagues for fear of *Salmonella*, *Listeria*, errant hairs, flea-flecked fur of cats and dogs. This is to say: I exhale with relief and pluck the ring from the toilet, lest it sink further.

My fingers are barfy. I am not repulsed by what I disgorge, which isn't really so much. It goes down with one flush.

I rinse off the ring. Through the stream of water, the gold's shape warps. My fingers are too cold-shrunk to put it back on. I slip the band in my back pocket and that's when I remember the baggie I took from Rot. I pat it through the fabric; it feels like—how I imagine—a hemorrhoid.

In a flash, I see myself on a closed-circuit monitor: a top-less woman in business-casual black, fishing around the toilet, talking to herself, tapping her own ass.

I check El's third grade Casio, the only watch that works with my wrists. They have always been small. I have not purged myself into thin wrists. The minute and the hour hands refuse to stop waving. I pinch the bridge of my nose, squeeze my eyes, try again. There: five minutes, and I teach.

How should I handle Rot's coke? If I were teaching cre-ative writing, this could be a prompt: Invent a character. Interrogate someone who must decide whether or not to keep something she's shoplifted. Write a vignette that stems from a middle-aged woman asking herself this. But I'm not teaching creative writing. I'm teaching Comp. My coke is intro paragraph, body, body, body, conclusion. Thesis reiter-ated throughout. And topic sentences, please. How I handle the coke is mine alone.

I have options. Time. My classroom is around the cor-ner, down the hall. A professor has permissions, allies, occa-sions to be late, ways to make covert phone calls, last-minute options. A professor always does, but an attractive, female professor has more means of recourse. Men. Procedures. Handouts on mandated reporting inside plain black binders that sit unopened on the bottom shelf in an office. I could consult the protocol, never as juicy as the term's opacity. *Surrender the contraband. File a report.*

I could go rogue, police on my own: flush the baggie, forget Rot. Lift the rug and sweep, sweep, sweep.

Third option: let's call it the Sartre. *Nothingness lies coiled in the heart of being—like a worm.* Nothing is what I decide to do. In this way, I will tempt danger. The bag could rupture, the powder seep through the fabric, into my skin: farfetched, not absurd. Absurd is Russell Edson—a poet who'd imagine a situation to an unimaginable end. What's so terrific about fantasy? Every three years, in Contemporary Lit, they go gaga over Edson, poetry's kooky Tom Hanks. Am I spiteful? Only afraid to abandon myself to my own writing. That's what I'd discovered that Soho summer with Elliot.

My sweater's hem covers the pocket's bulge. I'll keep the baggie close. I've known Rot since I called roll last August. He corrected the roster: "My name is mad pretentious. Carlos Rottingham Junior? Douchebags and douchebags. Call me Rot." Rot will come. It's been since Thanksgiving that we partied. Too long. He'll be looking, for me, his coke. In his first essay last semester, a personal narrative in response to the question, "What drives you," Rot submitted a two-page response another professor would've interofficed to the Dean of Students. Rot wrote about the chase. That's when I knew I wanted him. Alone in my office, my green pen hovered over his words: how he was always searching for the next high, the one that would put every one preceding it to shame, the one "deleterious enough to destroy him."

Oh baby, I thought, feeling motherly and uncapped. I dropped my pen. *Me too.*

3 ·· LISA

"I don't rely on mirrors, so I always take Polaroids."

The line has been racing like Sonic the Hedgehog through my brain. Now it clicks. My hand is still hot from the phone. My parents totally need to upgrade their portables: this one practically sweats.

Sweats, like, behind my knees and under my arms and between my legs when I heard and then hung up on Elliot, sweats to infinity when I realized why *Clueless* was ringing weird bells, sweats to infinity times infinity when out of nowhere I worked up the nerve to curveball an ultimatum. But I'm done concerning myself with Elliot's effluvia (vocab points?). My sick day has become *so* sick: no parents, just me with my smoky, snagged-up voice and Junior Carlos chilling, villainous, on the couch.

Elliot Egleston does not know what's best for everyone.

Junior Carlos puts down his pager. He seems distracted, somewhere else. He needs to work on his resting face: his eyes kinda cross. Otherwise, he looks like Brad Renfro in *Apt Pupil*, but taller and with shoulder muscles like T-bones and chiseled-out cheeks and eyes like highlighters, the rare blue shade.

"Was that your mom?" he says. "How's your grandma?"

"Denial," I say.

"Denial?"

"Negative, I mean. No, not them. No one."

I'm shaking, sweating. What's wrong with me—I haven't *really* been thinking about my grandma. She has congestive or congenital heart failure, needs fluids but also has edema. In a hospital room, my mom is sitting with her at this very moment. My grandma is legit going to die.

My terror is so big I can't think about all its parts: it's like dumping a pouch of marbles in a dark room and trying to tiptoe. I can accept death, but not without my brain cramping, not without having to gulp for air. I really don't want Junior Carlos to leave. I want to be normal enough, recovered enough, that I can grow up and spend all day with him, forever. I really don't want to be alone.

I'm on speech team, though, so my face is good at transforming. I relax into a smile. "You can press Play."

Alicia Silverstone's voice returns, inviting and girly, a sequined armchair in the living room. Junior Carlos holds down Volume, and the sound increases: a half-way blue bar on the TV screen gets bluer and bluer, like a cartoon thermometer about to explode. An explosion. That happened once: my mom and I were arguing over Lifetime—by arguing I mean having the silent-movie version of what junior high boys call a *cat fight*—which was me on one half of the leather sectional, her on the other, each of us with a remote, and she was turning *A Secret Between Friends* off and I was turning it on and we went back and forth, until the bulimic girl-buds were swallowed up by a black hole and the TV *pffed* like candles blown out on a birthday cake, then a low, zangy hum. My dad was at the station—I think it was March of sixth grade, when WBEZ did big coverage for the Domestic Partner Ordinance, which, like all gay matters, divided our family. My mom thought equal rights were an honest-to-Christ sin and my dad thought they were only fair and I thought something, like, it's up to each person to do what—or who—they want.

That one channel battle is emblematic of my relationship with my mom: I'm not budging and she's not budging, and polite as we may be in public, at home neither of us will even think about backing down. Sometimes I try to imagine the sadness I'd feel if my mom died: Would I talk to her portrait the way Cher talks to her stunner mom, aka the total Betty, she of the '70s hair? Would I feel guilt for not conceding more, for all the fights I picked on Dr. Ogbaa's fainting couch? (*It's a divan, Lisa,* Dr. Ogbaa always told me, tapping her manicured nails on the mahogany arm.) Would death repair my relationship with my mother, the way the threat of it seemed to with *her* own mother? As if.

..

Here's *Clueless*: Cher has worn her yellow-jacket plaid blazer and miniskirt; Travis has left his Cranberries CD in the quad; grades have been argued, and Cher's father is proud, very proud; Cher wants to be five ten like Cindy Crawford, so no delicious Italian brew, thanks; Josh has read Nietzsche; Cher and Dionne and Murray and Elton and Tai and Amber have partied in the valley; Amber has worn Cher's yesterday maroon dress. Murray has cut his hair. Dionne's grandchildren will be horrified by his yearbook photo. Tai has rolled with the homies. Cher has wrecked her Alaïa and been mugged and rescued; she's schooled that Alanis Morissette lookalike hanging out with Josh about Shakespeare via Mel Gibson.

It's my fifth absence of the year. My mom is being extra-compassionate, letting me stay home with just a ninety-nine-degree fever. I know it's because of my grandma; I know I should appreciate that, but my mom aggravates me. I acknowledge my bias.

It hurts to swallow: my throat feels like a Brillo pad. Junior Carlos is *not* legitimately sick—he's legitimately sweet. He rushed to his nine a.m. at College of Cook County and then turned his Bimmer around, called me from the car phone, asked me what I wanted from Blockbuster, or more specifically, did I want anything else besides *Clueless* and did I have enough blankets and if so were they warm enough or the annoying scratchy kind and did I like down quilts because he always keeps one in the trunk, and most importantly what snacks would help me feel better: ice cream, ice cream, sherbet, or ice cream.

OJ, said the sensible, recovered-but-not-quite part of me, the girl who'd spent summer in in-patient treatment for an eating disorder. But then, when I heard him use coo and baby talk, I remembered that I didn't need to use a sick day to lose a couple pounds. I was done being Elliot's little side-kick. When Junior Carlos said, *Lee-Lee, you need a lil' som'n som'n*, the lover-of-all-treats-frozen inside me perked up at his wannabe gangbanger slang. *Dreamsicles?*

Your dream is my command.

I've eaten one Dreamsicle. I was contemplating a second before Elliot called. Before the phone rang, I was snuggled next to Junior Carlos, the two of us bugs in a rug under the heavy, knit Last Supper blanket; his arm around my shoulder the way the snake trainer at Brookfield Zoo wore a viper like a shrug.

Now, though, after lying to Elliot, I'm shivering and sticky and witnessing myself, beyond myself, disassociated, out of it, whatever you want to say, sweaty, hot, the swamp girl from Alaska, freezing in my flannel pants, still as a statue by the phone.

I mean, look at me: dirty-blonde hair alligator clipped in a side ponytail, puddle-blue eyes rimmed in lots of black. I'm wearing a cute tank with adjustable lace straps, with the plastic clippies like on a bra. You'd think in a state like this I'd be self-conscious about having V-town visitors, but Junior Carlos is persistent, demandingly kind, just the sort of aggressive I like, which, in an adult man (which, technically, he is), if *Cosmo* is right, might be called *take charge.*

In a girl, that's *bossy. Ambitious* or *aggressive.* But I don't care what I'm called—my recovery mantra is about piling my confidence so high you'd need a helicopter to peep the top.

I. Do. What. I. Want.

And if what I want is to cease communication with Elliot Egleston, that's my prerogative. And if what I want is to eat Dreamsicles all day, drink Strawberry Crush floats all night, and meld my bodily soda with Junior Carlos's, so be it.

Cher is offering Christian, the James Dean lookalike, some wine. Junior Carlos snorts at Christian's deflection. And even though I'm sick, I'm the one standing, and what I want is to be hospitable. It's the least I can do.

"Do you want a drink, babe? My throat feels like a . . . a bad thing. Hitler!"

"Hitler? Who are you?" Junior Carlos laughs. "V and S, if you've got it." He pauses. "Hey, straight up—wouldn't you be all over Cher if you were Christian? I mean, he's gay, but like, even the faggiest fag—"

"Hey!"

The kitchen is separated from the living room by an island. There are cabinets on the kitchen side, and I get on my hands and knees in front of the first set of doors. I move aside my mom's Grape Nuts and my dad's Sugar Smacks, a weird number (five?) of canisters of oatmeal, white and brown sugar in cloudy Tupperware tins before I find the Smirnoff. I fill two tumblers with ice, make one mostly vodka and the other just a splash.

"Okay, even the gayest gay—I didn't mean it, like, bad. You know I'm a friend to the closet. Have you met my cousin?"

I fill the glasses up with Squirt. "I have met your cousin."

Cenzo is bi. He was in eighth grade at Park last year, and I didn't really know him, but if you had eyes you *knew-knew* him: he was District 107 infamous because he'd had to wear his gym uniform every day for all of October, after insisting on celebrating Gay History Month by coming to school in a vintage Laura Ashley party dress. With leg o' mutton sleeves. And a metallic sash. Hard to miss.

"Twerpy little fag stick. And I say that with, like, so much love."

I walk back to the couch. The liquid in the tumblers doesn't even move. In fifth grade, my mom made me take finishing classes—I've legit walked around with a dictionary on my head. I am exceptionally balanced. "What were you saying before you started talking smack?"

"Would your sexual orientation preclude you from getting it on with Alicia Silverstone?"

I hand Junior Carlos the vodka-y cup. "*Clueless* Alicia?"

"That's who I'm talkin' about. Wouldn't you be into that?"

"What do people say, white on rice?"

"And what is this?"

"Sprite on ice?"

"Sprite?"

"Squirt."

"Just a little squirt for me, babe, please . . ." He sets his drink on the coffee table and reaches toward me, wiggling his fingers like Creepy Crawlers. For someone who had woofers or whatever installed in his car, he's such a dork.

"You're sick. Use a coaster or my mom will slay me. Okay? They're by the phone."

I point to the stack. They're cork, printed with Catholic saints. That's my mom for you: three mornings a week, she's at 6:30 Mass; she made me return the Joan Osborne cassette I bought from Hot Rags, where I've had a neon orange slip of paper entitling me to an $8.50 store credit ever since; and yet she doesn't find it at all blasphemous to buy religious iconography from Pier One.

Junior Carlos flicks two coasters like Frisbees. He sets his cup on St. Elizabeth of Hungary, her robes peeled open, revealing white and red roses. I plant my drink on St. Kevin— his left hand hovering over his heart, his right, a perch for a blackbird—and flop dramatically onto the couch. I have another four months of CCD classes before I make my confirmation, and I guess I should feel guilty being duplicitous and premaritally sexual—having my boyfriend over when I'm theoretically pooped-out on the couch; lying to the Elliot, who, really, is a pathetic creature, with no friends but me, and who, according to Dr. Ogbaa, has problems on top of problems—but I don't. I don't feel one gram of guilt. I do what I want. I cross my legs, and Junior Carlos grabs them and straightens them across his lap.

"Do *you* think Alicia Silverstone is hot?" I ask.

We consider the screen, where Cher sits in the backseat as Di practices driving. They're about to accidentally get on the freeway, where Dionne will be overwhelmed in that weird crocheted swim cap thing and Murray will be keeping her calm and Cher will get all introspective. For now, though, Cher keeps popping her head between the driver and passenger seats. It's not her most flattering moment: she's wearing a blue-flowered choker, a scrunchie. She has that weird mollusk mouth. And even though her legs are sometimes good, when she's in her gym uniform, with the tank top over the T-shirt, her boobs are all Nerfy. I don't think she's hot, because, above all, she's fat, especially her upper arms.

Wrong! She's not fat, Lisa. By no standard is she fat. She is a young woman. An actress. A daughter. Even if she were overweight, she wouldn't be defined solely as fat. I don't know if I believe cognitive reframing but Dr. Ogbaa has me doing it whenever I have a behavior-y thought. Now it's as automatic as wash hands after flush. *Think of celebrities known for fatness. She's not Roseanne or Whoopi.*

"Um, yes." Junior Carlos takes his drink from St. Elizabeth. A wet ring haloes her torso, circling the roses, her miracle, a sacrifice. He gulps and the dark stubble on his neck/throat prickles as he swallows. "I think she's very, very hot."

"How hot?"

"I mean, very, very, *very* hot."

"Like, what would you want to do to her hot?"

He laughs. His blue eyes darken and wander up, like the answer to my question is threaded through his black hair. He's a secret geller, which taught me that some things junior high boys did weren't inherently awful; hair gel and pants sagging just look better mature.

"I feel like you're selling me something I shouldn't buy. What are you saying, Lee-Lee?"

I dip my middle finger in my drink and suck it. It fizzes in my mouth and the alcohol—half a shot, half of what I put in Junior Carlos's drink—stings my sore throat. I really love how I can ask one question and completely change the afternoon.

"Wanna pretend I'm Alicia Silverstone?"

Boys are amazing. I forgot this, spending so much time with Elliot, talking with girls in the hospital and the Monday night LoveThySelf support group. Girls' bodies are about hiding, erasing, minimizing—i.e., wrinkles. Or overemphasizing—cleavage—so everything else recedes. This is why I can't have E.'s negativity in my life. I don't want secrets. I don't want to apologize for eating cereal for breakfast, bowl one or two. I don't want to hide my body if it's tiny or if it's normal or—God forbid—fat. I don't want to care if I look pretty or ugly. Boys get to be out there! All whatever! Under my legs, electricity flexes through Junior Carlos.

"Are you going to make me be criminal?" Junior Carlos says. This game. "How old are you? I'm starting to think you get off on playing jail bait."

I reach my hand into his lap, feel around the Last Supper, where Jesus is holding up a chalice over Junior Carlos's crotch. Then I bend over and plant my face like I'm bobbing for apples. I find one. He's got an erection. I feel an unbelievable sense of accomplishment, like I've figured out how to control matter, transform liquid to solid, make ice, fit my hand inside a sock puppet.

"All right, Fiona," I say. "Let's get criminal. How old am I . . . meaning Lisa or how old am I as in me-being-Alicia Silverstone?"

I turn my head so I can look up at him. Now my ear is on his boner. Through the blanket and his pants, I listen for a pulse. Nothing. Maybe it's dead. I swallow a cough. Then the boner grows. It reminds me of when an earthworm scoots. Junior Carlos has big fingers, but the nails are always trimmed and his skin is soft and smooth, and all parts of him smell good, even his crotch, which smells like Acqua di Giò, and he has zero acne, unlike Park boys who need to be Oxy-cuted. Junior Carlos traces a finger around my mouth. He touches my lips. His skin rubs my skin, paper and paper. Electricity rushes through me: is that osmosis?

"You have a sore throat, young lady. Don't tempt me. I'm not into playing evil doctor."

I open my mouth, gum his penis through his pants. Boys like silly, I learned from an interview with Cameron Diaz. My mom—for real? She still subscribes to *InStyle* and *Jane*, even though Dr. Ogbaa told her keeping fashion magazines in the house isn't prudent. (When I told Elliot about that, she said it would be like giving pyros firecrackers.) But hey: screw prudence. I do what I want.

"I'm fourteen," I whisper into the fabric, muffling a cough. "But I still fit in the kids range for Dimetapp."

He laughs. "How are you fourteen?"

"How are you nineteen and knocking out your Gen. Eds.?"

"I flunked first grade?"

"Cuuuuute."

"Statuuuuatory."

I sit up like a whisper. "Be still, Statue." I head for his mouth and then start hacking up thick green phlegm.

Junior Carlos grips my shoulders. I don't feel, like, very thin most days, but when he holds me or lifts me up, I do. He's not so huge, either, so it's not a given that he should be able to pick me off the floor with one arm. He's five eleven and in high school he was a swimmer. Now he coaches kids in the summer for their adorable IM relays: 100 yards. Who knows what he weighs? Yeah, I've wondered. But men's weights make as much sense as Illinois's laws about age of consent. Those declare our relationship literally illegal.

"Hey, Coughy McCough Cough, I'm not getting sick. I've got a physics exam tomorrow. Believe it or not, there are classes I actually care about passing."

I doubt that, I think. "What's physics even, anyway?"

Junior Carlos laughs. He has a nice laugh. A really nice laugh. It lands once loudly and then trails off, like a basketball dribbling across the court, unmanned, losing steam. The sort of laugh that makes me consider extreme, highly unlikely, semi-charmed scenarios: Do relationships begun when one party is still in junior high have a shot at success? What would success even feel like? Is life so long as it seems?

"Oh to be in the paradise of junior high. Lisa, Lisa. Wait until you meet Mulderink. Or any teacher that doesn't care if you pass or fail, for that matter. College. Then ask me about physics."

"Mulder, like X-Files?"

"You're one in a million, you know that? Mulder*ink*, physics sphinx. So brilliant he left Hampshire High and started teaching at Cook Count. The guy has, like, patents. Okay, he's a supreme a-hole, but, yah know, smart as fuck."

"Fuck?" I wink.

Junior Carlos slaps his forehead. "Don't you feel like you should be less horny, with your grandma sick and all? Who was that on the phone?"

"Keepers of the fuck, wondering why you haven't been fucking."

We have fucked. Twice. It felt like being snowplowed in a well or being rolled up into a carpet and pushed off the Dan Ryan. And, according to Junior Carlos, it's only going to feel better and better the more we do it. Which, even though I'm sick, is the only thing I want to do. I want to kiss and kiss and kiss until my face is hot pink with kissing then fuck fuck fuck.

"I want to fuck fuck fuck," I say.

Junior Carlos pushes me off his lap and the blanket off the couch. It knocks over a cup. This is what I love: how quickly he goes from respectable to rough. Fuck my mom for hating on the sheer idea of me having a boyfriend. Fuck Elliot, too, for being creepy and possessive. I do what I want. Junior Carlos pulls down my pajama pants and throws them on the floor.

"Well, then—where's the pussy?" He starts sucking my hipbones hard, scraping his teeth across my skin, trying to gnash my bones.

"I don't know, Ace Ventura." I sigh. "Keep looking."

I sit up, like I'm about to crunch. I don't do those now. No more eroding the skin off my tailbone doing fifteen hundred sit-ups a day. Futile! Spot correcting is a no-go without proper nutrition. Despite Elliot's admonishments, I don't miss all-nighter workouts any more than I'll miss this sore throat. My poor stomach, the one I forced to contract, the one I can't even see now, covered by Junior Carlos's head.

I wonder if my grandma watched.

I'm wearing new navy-blue striped boy shorts from Victoria's Secret. I changed out of my Jockeys before Junior Carlos came over. My Jockeys are still from sixth grade, except now my butt fills them out. My Jockeys, I wore when Elliot took my picture. The Before. The After was only mirrors. Mirrors and mirrors. Me in my underwear, diving into the mirror. I swear, I don't miss that emptied-out me. Gutted-me in my Jockeys—white cotton. I'm better. I do what I want. I wear cute panties. These: they have glitter woven through the blue parts. They itch. I'm glad when Junior Carlos pulls them off.

4 ·· ELLIOT

THE ONLY THING TO DO was work. "25 Things To Do Instead of Emotionally Eating" would be a cool *Real Talk* piece. I added it to my queue of article ideas.

The library was empty except for the aide, Miss Nancy. She had red, crimpy hair and gelatinous skin, like cold Play-Doh, and a wheedling way of flirting with Mr. Tim, the janitor who drove a razzmatazz Ferrari. She was labeling CD-ROMs at the Computer Ed desk. She only pursed her lips when I walked through the security sensor gates.

Don't think about the phone call, I told myself sternly. Yet how could I forget? Days contained limited interactions. Mine with Lisa were always red-lettered. And now, she'd dissed me. I was angry, with no one to spar with but myself. When you're lacking in the friend dept., devils and angels perch on your shoulders. I assessed the facts. Lisa threatened me: Shouldn't I say *something*? Or would saying anything lead to an even worse situation? At the same time, Junior Carlos could've been holding cue cards, forcing Lisa to read. *Loca*, said my volition. The truth was we needed to talk, faces mouths lips breathing the same air, not overanalyzing the words. I felt like a loser. A has-been. Pathetic. Desperate, stressing in a sarcophagus of books. My emotions were mosquitoes I couldn't slap fast enough; today, I was being eaten alive.

At full capacity, Park housed three hundred bodies; the library held one-tenth of them. Kids didn't check out books. They liked researching on the computer, where clip art dripped with clean lines and uniformity, where, bored, you could Microsoft Paint: draw a stick figure with bazoombas, dump a bucket of black over the whole deal, erase.

I moved like a ghost solider, eyes on my destination, the Xerox (not on the booger-green carpet). I needed to copy *Real Talk*. The library smelled like a warm blueberry muffin. The normal world aureated with my spaceyness. There were circular tables for group work. A grandfather clock, with its freaky pale moon face that reminded me of a pedophile. An L-shaped accumulation of books—fiction here, nonfiction there—challenging my intellect: the space of this room is wide open, ready for *your* contribution, Elliot. And, across from the circulation desk, an oak card catalog, the piano of furniture. The drawers had been opened so many times, they slid soundlessly, like hands into gloves. I'd thumbed my share of blue index cards in that catalog—*eating disorders*; *anorexia nervosa, fiction portrayals of*; *self-starvation*; *fasting, history of*—spent hundreds of lunches starving sans hunger as I gobbled words in place of food, which wasn't even permitted in the stacks. Adults didn't bother bookworms—as long as they weren't bingeing on *Goosebumps*.

I stopped at the shelves of burgundy encyclopedias and opened one, the second "C" volume of Britannica. I searched for "Concentration Camp," scanning the index words at the top of each page. I could get a picture of a truly emaciated person, someone who'd survived Auschwitz, and paste that in place of Marissa's After. Unfortunately, the only images were of crematoriums.

I stationed myself in the Copy Corner. On the Xerox, there was a random newspaper; "PERJURY UPON PER-JURY" read the headline. Underneath, in a grainy picture, Bill Clinton looked like he wanted to suck his thumb. Monica Lewinsky, Kenneth Starr, Paula Jones: last night, when those names came on TV, my mom finished her big glass of wine in one sip. *Our country is flushing away the integrity of a private life*, she'd said. *In favor, I should add, of* Private Parts. *Not that Howard is to blame, but—he hasn't helped.* In the corner, a blip about Michael Jordan: he'd announced his retirement.

I tossed aside the paper. I couldn't handle any more depressing news. I had twenty *Real Talk*s to print. The Afters I'd add, in color, from Walgreens. The next issue would be delivered to my clients, even Rocyo the new one, next week. *You are an all-star,* I chanted. *You're fine. You need to talk to Lisa. There's always something you can do.* I slid my work into the rickety, gray plastic feed, and hit start.

The copy machine creaked. I did calf raises. *Waiting,* I wrote in my clients' plans, *is an opportunity. There's never killing time. Only making every minute count.* Deep inhale, four holds, exhale: my toes cracked, my ankles stretched. Through the glass doors, I saw the courtyard, gray concrete, muddy snow. Once, in the fall, ditching lunch in that very courtyard, I'd mistaken a dead sparrow for a leaf.

In sixth grade, I'd told Lisa how to exercise without peo-ple noticing. We were in the girls' bathroom, and while she was brushing her goldilocks I'd gone into double jacks. Lisa's diagnosis was nowhere in sight: she'd arched an eyebrow, watching my jumping like I'd come to the Park Sock Hop in Zubaz. But lunges in the shower, crunches in bed. Leg lifts on the pediatrician's table. Butt clenches anywhere—in line at Blockbuster, sitting through *The Voyage of the Mimi. Point your fingers and flex your triceps when you raise your hand*, I explained. *It adds up.* Her blonde hair satin. Her lips glittery. A heart-shaped lilac jelly ring around her thumb. *That way you're making progress, your secret, your terms*, she'd said. *I love it. Your brain is perfect, El.*

Outside the library, a gust of wind sprayed snowflakes like confetti. I stopped calf raising. Lisa had loved my brain—now what? I wasn't Junior Carlos, I'd never be.

On top of the Xerox, built-in compartments held paper-clips and staples. The staple spot was empty (except for an image of a staple, raised in plastic), but thirteen paper clips catcalled me in a shining, practical way, like the birthstone post earrings I'd ganked from Claire's. They were small, silver with variegated bodies.

I checked for Miss Nancy. (She'd use library footsteps and suddenly be all about your personal space.) The library was empty: the Encarta CD-ROM set was up for grabs. I rolled up my sleeve.

I unwound a paper clip. It was a fraction of cold, like a thumbtack. My left arm was pale, grayish and creamy: sand dollar, vanilla wafer, scallop. I liked how the parts of my body showed me my viscera, the cat's cradle of veins on the inside of my wrist, contusion purple and storm blue, close and usual as postage stamps.

I stabbed into my wrist with the paper clip, right where the channel between two veins ran parallel. It hurt. Instant, luxurious—not painful. Not painful enough. The Xerox machine squealed. I clenched my jaw as I pulled the metal across my skin. I could exercise, I could eat crumbs (my day was on course for five hundred calories), but I couldn't promise Lisa I'd get help. What was help? Help enrobed you in fat. Turned you into a traitor against your best friend.

Harder harder harder harder. I wanted to sever the soft wrong stuff smothering my veins, gloppy blood vessels, sinuous muscles, the gritty particles of my unlikability, the pestilence. What Lisa hated. What made me me.

The Xerox machine was spewing its last copy. Though I'd gauzed my wrists to be suggestive, I'd never actually cut. The pain felt like nothing. I wasn't even good at self-injury. Twisting, drilling a hole, I tried one last time. I winced at the thought of my veins roiling, a chef's knife cutting off my toes, my body, the bones highlighted like words on a computer screen, spread eagle, swallowed by flames in front of Lisa. *Stop, Elliot!* She'd cry. *Ellie.*

The paper clip's damage was no worse than biting your own arm.

This was my wrist: scratches circled with pink covered my veins; in two eyelash-sized places, blood. I sheaved the *Real Talk*. The words—my handwriting, my plans, my words— marched across the page like ants. I bent the paper clip back into shape and replaced it in its compartment to pass on my skinny germs.

"Elliot?"

I spun and got dizzy—the books in the library were slanting, tumbling off their shelves. Right there, Ethan Suva was ticking the scuffed red wheels on his skateboard, which stood beside him like a dog on two legs. Its owner wore a baggy Pearl Jam T over a gray Henley and black jeans cuffed with sidewalk salt.

"Whatcha doin', mang? Writing Dave Grohl a birthday card?"

His proximity and his lax address made me bashful. I looked down. He was barefoot. His toes were very clean, the color of a peach crayon. Mine were lavender, from crumby circulation. I was grateful for shoes. Had he seen the *Real Talk* cover? Had he heard the paper clip, excoriating like a secret, the residue of how much I knew about him, Suva the Youngest, brother to two gerbil-nukers? He'd been a vegan since forever and loudly declared it, throwing a skinny, blonde wrench into first-period advisory doughnut parties; he honed a grungy style, band Ts, the grinning Nirvana one I especially loved, riddled with Pog-sized holes.

I collected my *Real Talk* from the tray. "Who?"

"Dude. Negative snaps." He laughed to himself, and a smile rippled over his face. "So what *are* you doing?"

I pulled my sleeve over my wrist.

"Working on a thing. Just . . . makin' like . . . copies."

"Der dud der. Makin' copies. Makin' copies, with Elliot-meister. Elliot-a-rino?"

"What?"

"I can't *actually* fault you for not knowing Rob Schneider, but dude."

My heart was somersaulting. I couldn't stop seeing his feet. "Yeah?"

He raised an eyebrow, Jack Nicholson's Joker. He bunched up the sleeve of his Henley and tapped a finger on his wrist, at the spot where I'd paper clipped. Then he reached over and tapped the same place on me.

"Slice and dice?" he said under his breath.

My hand dove into my pocket. I stared at his wrist. I didn't have boy-clients. Ethan's body was another city. In Spanish, I'd noticed the three Xs he Sharpied on himself, but I'd never been this close. I could see faint outlines on his flesh. He'd scrubbed so hard it looked like a swipe of pink highlighter. "It's cave girl, all right?" I started walking. "Primitive coping. Whatever, it's my first time. Verdict's out. It doesn't close the curtain, but it gets the actors on stage."

"Well, what play? Romeo and Ghoooooooul-iet?" he said.

"You can use the copier now. Sorry."

"Dude, why are you sorry? I'm in no rush. You wanna finish up?"

My eyes suddenly felt too big for my skull. I didn't know where to look when I looked at Ethan. He was sorta smiling, half at the floor, half at my feet.

"No, it's . . . um. All yours," I said. I kept walking. "I'm done."

Out of the library, I sighed so hard I made a sound. Anna called breathing like this *prana*. For the past three and a half years of junior high, I'd had a crush on Ethan, but I'd never been brave enough to even pick him for my team when we played Taboo in Headways, Park's gifted class. I wished Lisa weren't sick so I could meet her at her locker and tell her. He'd touched me—that was nothing I'd ever day-dreamed. I'd imagined a whole saga: us getting older; having the same AP classes in high school, the good ones, Psych and Art History; one day becoming friends who rode the Metra downtown, hoofed it to Michigan Avenue and walked around the Museum of Contemporary Art, bumping ulnas in front of Andy Warhol's *Jackies*. We'd joke little, talk less. In my fantasy, my Uncle Marky and his partner, Fernán, were out of town, and I was housesitting for them, and Ethan and I would cab over to their West Loop loft. *No big deal*, I'd say, when I unlocked the door and led him down four steps to the sunken living room, where I'd float onto the deep, velveteen couch, my ribs peaking like the remains of a spiny prehistoric creature, and prepare for him to smother me.

5 ·· ANNA

With few exceptions, I don't remember students. No one from last semester, save Rot.

When I began, I didn't expect to forget so instantly. After all: Ms. Urben, Mrs. Cross, Ms. McCarthy, Mr. Brady, Mr. Eldrige, Ms. Atwater, Ms. Friefel, Mrs. Gorman, Mr. Slade, Mr. Smith, Mrs. Lanthrop, Mrs. Cook, Mr. Richie, Mr. Reid and Mrs. Reid, Mr. Murphy, Mrs. Connor, Ms. Matusiak, Mrs. Koenig, Mrs. Sharma, Mr. Jaffe, Mr. Brown, Mr. Page, Mrs. Singletary, Mme. Blanchot. I could go further: Dean Andrews, Professor Kasser, Professor Macal, Dr. Greenberg, Dr. Javadi, Noel, Peter, Haivan, Hannah, Annemarie, Annalise, Arlene, Jim.

I could tell you more, about any of them, at random. Here: Ms. Matusiak, sand-blasted, after her Peace Corp years Jeeping through the savannah. The Dixie plates she gave us to draw sine, cosine, tangent guides. Her son, newly brain-dead. Second grade: I filed papers for Mrs. Sharma (Dorothy Hamil hair, schnauzer named Butchie). College: Noel paid me for some light cat sitting, taught me to make *arancini* stuffed with cubes of smoked mozzarella.

No, the transitive property doesn't apply to teachers and students. Just because you remember someone doesn't mean they remember you. A rule of love, too. One party's feelings don't guarantee reciprocity. But this was news to me, especially the first couple years of my career, when I wasn't even certain what I was doing—having survived college with a transfer out of an authentic Ivy to an almost in the Midwest; having—solely on the empowered heels of receiving an A and effusive marginalia ("this is why I teach") on my *To The Lighthouse* term paper—applied to graduate programs in English literature in a spirit of *I write poems in my diary* and *why not*. When I wasn't certain of anything, let alone a career or whatever being a teaching assistant in a lowly master's program foretold, I was so stunned to be the body in what I thought was an adult chair that I couldn't fathom forgetting my students. (Now I realize it was no different than any other chair—it was only industrially upholstered.) They were humans! With real, albeit tentatively founded, beliefs and occasionally surprising backstories! They broke out in sebaceous cysts and poison ivy, dyed their hair and angled their bangs and whispered during class. They wrote odes to the same idols they bore on their T-shirts or sewed onto their backpacks, patches, Depeche Mode and U2 and Kraftwerk and The Smiths and Lou Reed—they really liked music. They sat on the same side of a table as me, in Holmes Lounge, so together we could inspect, dissect, and resurrect their poems. And back then, I was not so different from them: twenty-three to their eighteen. I had a shoebox of mix tapes in the backseat of my sky-blue Nova. I still smoked, feverishly. My exercise didn't go beyond drunk Thighmastering. That first year, I'd had a senior, Priya, pre-med, her last semester, finally allowing herself one "fun" elective. I was her teacher: six months her junior.

Now, for ENG 101, spring semester 1999 (dolt suburbs: last week we started on-schedule despite a foot of snow and temps of -13°F and sixty-some reported deaths), I am delusionless. I'm whatever's between jaded and ardent. Realistic?

Some of my colleagues really adore teaching; this is news to me, bad news, every time I hear it. My poor colleagues, so ready to give away themselves, so ready to see only good. I don't subscribe to the gospel of specialness or youth. Mostly my spring students are repeat offenders: they didn't pass ENG 101 in the fall. Some are adults, whose college careers didn't begin right after high school: children, almost always children, diverted their lives. Take Barbara, this semester, the one student older than me, and older by a lot: she must be sixty. She had her first baby when she was sixteen, she told me, in her Literacy Profile. Now she's a grandmamma. *Okay, honey,* she says, when I announce homework. Like that, in the middle of class: *okay, honey.* Her tone—patronizing, servile, buttery—aggravates me.

Also, she's fat. A circus act. Big Bertha.

As I approach the classroom, I hear voices. A girl groans. A boy yells, *Can it.* Someone, mirthfully, idiotically, says *don't be gay.* A pen zips along the corkscrew binding of a spiral. Maybe Barbara is reviewing her blue ballpoint notes, a wobbly and old-fashioned cursive. The hallway is copy-toner and apple-cinnamon scented something. My heart louds. Nervous isn't the right word; self-conscious isn't either. More, I feel as though my face has been replaced with a fishbowl of vomit, my pants dusted with coke. Is that disgust or revulsion? The real me?

See Sartre: "I have it, the filth."

So I go. I pause outside the door, cringe—and enter.

And, like that, they shut up.

Silence in a classroom is a physical thing, inert but infectious, like gas. (Chemistry, too, not a strength.) Silence in a classroom is different than silence in my home, where Elliot and I are often contemplative or occupied, where silence allows the air in the living room to circulate more freely, a mesh for our thoughts, a well-stretched muscle, limber and lean. In a classroom, silence barricades distractions; silence is militant; silence is order, ridding rascals from the ranks. Well. I do not intend to be imposing, but my degree and title and tenure must affect my comportment. That, and my all-black: wool suiting pants, licorice loafers, chewed nails.

The left index and middle's polish, I've already touched up, the minute I had in my office. I collected my roster and blue books, did a quick re-lacquer. *Still wet*, I think, as I walk across the room. I feel student eyes on me: I want to bat them off. I remind myself not to do anything with my hands.

"Attendance," I say. "It's as much for you as for me. Meet one another. Become acquaintances. After all, this classroom is a writing community."

No one snickers—at least, not out loud. Some of these words are familiar to students; all of them are familiar to me. I've been teaching nearly fifteen years: I could write a script.

"Of course today you'll work independently, but, in future discussions, I prefer you use each other's names."

It's only our fourth meeting, I remind myself, the second week of the semester. They're not watching me, expecting fireworks yet. Oh sure, they're still *watching*: teachers are celebrities with training wheels. All students begin with some misguided thought about their professors. That's why they watch: they're watching my legs cross when I sit atop the desk in the front of the room, they're watching my breasts when the thermostat is wonky and my nipples protrude, they're watching me watch them—how long will my eyes hold contact with theirs? Do I have a lazy gaze, a sniffling problem, a tendency to lick the corners of my mouth with my tongue—something to mimic, pounce on, taunt? They're still figuring out my sense of humor, my chalkboard hand-writing, my interest in conversing after class. Barbara, for instance, I've tried to mentally tell, *buzz off.* Will I acquiesce, linger on a cinderblock just beyond their temples? They're not watching my technique; they're watching my body, my person: I am still a new specimen to them. They're watching to prove themselves right or wrong.

I'm still figuring them out, too. That's why today, after attendance, now that I've spent a day reading over the syllabus and another day facilitating introductions and another day proctoring the mandatory Nelson-Denny reading test, I distribute the standard-issue blue books and a half-sheet of paper with a simple, reflective prompt.

"I'll read this out loud."

I pinch a prompt with my dry hand. Of course I don't tell my students that even this act is a gift: in case anyone is illiterate, here's their chance to know what they should be writing about. I clear my throat (still foul-tasting). I feel world-weary and bored, but I try to sound fetchingly blasé. I think about the coke in my pocket. I think about Rot, sitting in the back right corner where, all last semester, he watched me.

""The pressure essay is the first entry in your writing portfolio, a collection that will grow during your time at COCC. By the time you graduate or transfer, you'll be able to observe trends in your writing, as well as, hopefully, celebrate improvements. This essay also constitutes your first grade in ENG 101. It's worth fifty points. Describe a place where you experience total contentment. What makes the place special? Is it a physical or emotional place? Is there a story behind it? How do you get to this place, and do you already feel content when you arrive there or does the location itself calm you down? Use evocative details to show your reader this place and use reflection to explain its personal significance.' Does anyone have any questions?"

It is a simple task, one I stole from a fourth-grade assignment of El's.

Barbara, unsurprisingly, raises her hand. In front of her, a bag of Flamin' Hot Cheetos. Already, there is a damp circle, the size of a pie tin, in the ivory polyester covering her armpit. The room is not hot. It is not nipple-hardening cold, either, but it is brisk. Cook County: cheap old dive, a community college, with barely a budget. Environmental comforts are not a priority.

"How long should it be? I think your sheet forgot it. Did you say, hon?"

I clear my throat. None of my evaluations have mentioned favoritism, though I pick and choose. It is like paging through a catalogue: want, want, no, no, maybe, hell no, murder me. I disapprove of Barbara's manner so much that I'm bluntly evasive.

"As long as it needs to be."

Her chuckle sounds like clucking. "Well, I don't know quite what that means."

"Write as much as you'd like to complete the prompt. I'm not going to say something prescriptive like five paragraphs or six paragraphs or nine. That's arbitrary."

Now that she has the floor, she no longer raises her hand. "What do you mean by arbitrary, hon? We're simple humans here. You can speak to *us* in English."

I smile tightly at Barbara, trying not to grow frustrated. I've experienced worse. Two years ago, another older student, Griselda, slicked-back ponytail and jeans with fringe at the flared cuffs, stood up in front of all five students in the smallest section of Developmental Writing I ever taught, and went on a fifteen minute tirade, the thesis of which boiled down to—and I quote: *you [I—Anna Egleston] don't know nothing about where I [she—Griselda Santander] been.* I'd stood silently until she finally left, announcing her withdrawal from the course to our class, and then I'd taken a deep breath, blinked back involuntary tears, and explained the two beautiful ways to use a semicolon.

"Arbitrary—ah, capricious, wanton, or, just a decision that's random." I extend the fingers of my left hand, the way I plant my palm and my knuckles into my yoga mat, to feel the ground radiating through me as I settle into downward dog, pedaling my feet, breathing into my hips. I would like to pedal my feet into this woman's spongiform stomach. What is so charming about simplicity? Plain speech? A clear answer or path? Sometimes, I think I'm in the wrong profession. "It's up to you, up to your personal choice, which may as well be random—how long the essay is. Does that make sense?"

Barbara shakes her head. On the first day, she announced that she's almost retiring but for now she's still a nurse. I would hate to be on her floor. "Whatever you say, hon."

I scan for hands. "If there's no one else, we'll start. You have the next seventy minutes to complete the essay. Feel free to outline on a page, just label that—"

"What do you mean, outline?" Barbara says.

"Plan. Free write. Take notes." I hear my voice sound curt. "Brainstorm. All right. Seventy minutes. If you finish before the period ends, you're welcome to leave early. There's no homework this weekend."

The knock startles me—and the class. The students cock their heads, chew their pencils, swallow, tuck hair behind their ears, make a show of studying the prompt. I want to believe. Through the door's window, the crosshatched glass, I need to believe Rot's clover-green puffer coat is out there, the hot pink ski tag shouting off the zipper. My head swims out from the purge. I remember when students said excellent, radical, tubular, right on. When they wore jean jackets, Starter jackets, windbreakers, color-block blazers, flannels, canvas coats with Keith Haring scribbles. Lately, the trouble looks respectable. That green coat—was there even a knock?

"You gonna get that, hon?" says Barbara. "I think there's someone at the door."

"Get started. I'll be one minute."

..

Context, I teach my students, is everything. Use slang in a white-tablecloth restaurant, and there's a good chance your request will be viewed as uninformed, inappropriate, at best overly casual. What you say changes depending on where you're saying it, to whom you're saying it, what you're trying to accomplish by speaking. At hypothetical, white-tablecloth restaurant, say, "Yo, get me a spork," and, if your aim is to receive a utensil, your request will likely be met. However, if, as the speaker, you were trying to demonstrate that you understood the mores and conventions of fine dining, you would be unsuccessful. "Pray tell a fork may be procured for thine hand," isn't any better, I assure my students, lest they confuse challenge with competence.

What I don't cover in ENG 101 is the power of surprise, of defying expectation to achieve an effect. This is the sort of subtlety I appreciated in Rot when he knocked at my office, when we first partied, that Wednesday before Thanksgiving.

Even though I knew he was coming, I locked my door. The brass aperture, the right-turning key. I waited five hours, sitting at my desk, back to the door, a cramped crucible for my wants. I wanted a rapping, his knuckles on the ruddy blond wood, the sound that would dislodge my heart from my chest, a yank and a tooth. Bad move—that day, it was fifty degrees, higher than the Chicagoland average. The heater was cycling on, and I couldn't get my window open.

I drank two liters of Evian before noon. Ate a half-pint of raspberries for lunch, mashing them against the roof of my mouth with my tongue. I wanted my lips to look bled. Prepped for violation. Raw, sore. I reread some Plath, apropos: "I come to one bush of berries so ripe it is a bush of flies."

At 3:13 p.m., two minutes before his conference slot, I heard footsteps. There are perks to infatuations with students: teach writing, and you learn everything for free. Air Jordan Bred: those were Rot's Nikes. *Because black plus red?* I'd kept myself from asking in the margin of his essay, where he'd used the shoes to talk about bonding with his father last winter, when they'd had a season of courtside seats at the United Center. If nothing else, I could hide the fact I'd been sizing up his feet.

And then his knock came: a prim one-two. A knock in an academic building is startling and interruptive, a wordless reprimand. Or perhaps this reaction is only mine. There was high school, when I'd be in bed, chewing off my fingernails and spitting the white arcs into the crevice of *The Abortion* or whatever I was gobbling, and my father's pounding on my door would terrify me. (He'd barge in, ask why I'd let my brother Marky cram his chubby cheeks full of Maurice Lenell pinwheel cookies for dinner.)

My heels clicked on the tile as I walked to the door. I wore a black pointelle sweater dress, scoop neck, bare legs. Suede mules. My thought was easy access, like a Skinemax romp: pull up, kick off.

"Hey there," I said.

Rot's backpack hung from one shoulder. His flannel was half tucked, unbuttoned. He wore a white V-neck, baggy jeans, those red-soled sneakers: they gave him inches. Usually, being a professor made me feel bigger than students, but Rot eclipsed me.

"Am I too soon?" He glanced at a black-faced watch with a fat gold bezel.

"Perfect time. C'mon in."

I clicked toward my desk. He lingered at the door.

"Mind if I shut this?"

I took a deep breath.

"Fine."

Context: the smell in the office was vanilla, musk, and dust: vust? Even pushed against the outside wall, stationed beneath a window, the three-drawer desk crowded the room. The chair's cushion: orange-red weave; its wheels, silver; the ball bearings, thirsty for oil; the entire undercarriage, laced with rust. On the wall opposite from the desk, army-green metal filing cabinets flanking a black bookshelf. Hardcovers, anthologies, textbooks. That's where Rot stopped.

He picked up the one visible personal effect (my Butter Blasted and desperation Camels and bottle of ipecac and current journal inside the desk): a 4" x 6" snapshot in a sterling silver frame.

"You're married?" he asked.

I took a few steps backwards. My ass bumped the desk. "I guess."

He laughed, his eyes on the photo.

Why that family? Bourbon and Salinger, couples racquetball with Rolf and University of Chicago, pizza and Poppin' Fresh, ticking biology and flares of impulsivity and weekends in Door County, nursing champagne hangovers with banana walnut pancakes.

Why that picture? I looked my thinnest.

I knew what he saw—me in a lavender shift (early '90s foray into polychromatic dressing), black eyeliner, hair dyed Winona Ryder dark, clasping my elbows like doves about to flap off. There's Elliot, age five, blue pinafore and rabbit ears, bunny nose and wavy whiskers painted on her smiley face. I guess we're happy here. Rolf stands between us: blue-and-purple pinstripe button-down, short-sleeved, his arms so toned they rankle me, Anna Egleston, bearer of a body that refuses to tone, even when said body is maximum rail. The Lincoln Park Zoo Easter egg hunt: the backdrop is trampled magnolia petals; pink, orange, green plastic eggshells clamped around loose Chiclets.

The frame dinged against the bookshelf when he set it down.

"So you were always clutch?"

"Very funny." I gestured toward the spare chair against the wall. Students sat there—a classroom castoff, complete with bars for books beneath the seat. "What are we meeting about? Your documented essay?"

He set his backpack in the chair and, facing the wall, started rummaging around. I watched him. His flannel had a gray hood and, below that, the red and blue flannel. He had broad deltoids, swimming muscles, butterfly. I was water, ready to be thrashed. My pussy ticked. A zipper whinnied, a cork popped. It was loud, unmistakable, but no one was in Building 13: the holiday break had begun yesterday after 2:45 classes.

He faced me, holding a bottle of Dom Pérignon. "I thought, my essay's pretty tight. You're probably sick of looking at our shit."

I scoffed. "Who carries champagne in a backpack?"

Between us, the air seemed like regular Cook County air—muggy, stuffy, scholastic—but really, it was trembling. Flammable. One match away from blue licks of heat and soul-evanescing fucks. He reached a hand into his jeans' front pocket and pulled out a baggie.

"Better?"

"And what might you be serving here?"

"Remember when it used to actually *snow* on Thanksgiving?" he said. "This blows. I'm, like, hot."

I swallowed. "Well, feel free to take your shirt off."

"Hold this?" he said, passing me the bottle.

I took a swig, another gulp, and knelt down on the cruddy floor before him. I unzipped his jeans and took his cock in my hands. It was like I remembered from college—a virile dash, not a comma like Rolf's. It tasted like body wash, citrus and amber.

"Yes," he said in a voice like defeat.

Maybe that was all I had wanted—to hear someone say yes to my mouth. The sound of Rot's sigh—that hitching breath—when he came on my breasts, after he'd fucked me on the surface of the desk, tabled me and ate me; the nothing we spoke of; the coke we AmExed into wormy lines; the champagne, drunk, drunk: in the context of *my* office, on a sweaty November Wednesday, that was everything to be thankful for in the world.

··

A minute later, I smell pretzels.

"Sorry to interrupt," says Glenn Decklin. *Prop. COCC* is stamped on the flap pocket of his pea-green parka. "But we're getting reports of a leak, some people, they're saying smelling gas or a busted water main about here. You notice anything like that in your room? Floodwater? Weird smell."

I sniff through post-purge congestion; I inhale loudly, unflatteringly—a snort.

"I don't think so." I glance down the hall; I might catch some trail of Rot. But there's no one. Why would there be, in the middle of a period? There's a red trash can. Hairs corralled into corners. A purple Magic Glove, the kind you buy for $.99 at Walgreens, the kind that fits anyone. "I'll keep my eyes open."

"Serenity now! I'm joshing—that won't do you much good." Glenn laughs. "Get it—eyes open, gas?"

"Ah—well, water. But, right."

"We're at extension 4444. If you smell something, say something."

I nod. I have never been comfortable being a mandate reporter. If I smell something, I'll let my students burn. This time, I'll be bolder: I'll snort myself stupid with Rot's coke.

Just the thought of him gives me pause. I relish the dumb hallway. Sweat tattoos my neck. Each second, I expect something to happen, and each second, nothing definitive does: womanhood.

I wait. I blink. Sniff out the tinder. Breathe. Blink. Behind me, the classroom door that filters quiet out of quiet. I try to listen for the click of pens lifting off paper, the exhale of pages turning, an ebon spark, but my heart pounds too hard in my ears.

6 ·· ELLIOT

MISS TROUBAUGH YELLED SO MUCH her voice was a scab. "Wrap it up, folks! Balls in bins!"

Spikes and serves rocketed across the gym. I ran toward the supply closet, holding an orange Wilson to my chest. My face was plastered with hardcore grit. My legs seared. Franz Ferdinand had been the day's lesson in Social Studies, and with Mrs. Harper's cello voice, I learned nothing except that he was almost royal. Now my wrist throbbed from the paper clip cut. The pain cleared my mind.

"Let's move, folks, we're not sitting down for cream cheese sandwiches, you cupcakes! Show me how fast you're gonna move during the Pacer tomorrow! Git!"

And Miss Troubaugh kept shouting, presidential fitness trials tomorrow, day of reckoning, blah, blah, blah, everyone's favorite skinfold test.

I paused by the pull-up bars. The skinfold test? I dreaded that more than anyone. Regardless of the three years I'd been *flaca*, I didn't want grown-ups to freak out over my size. I was alone with my weight. Extra alone, now that Lisa faked fevers so Junior Carlos could slink through the sunroom, crouch like a bulldog, and play hide the bone. Well. By now, he was probably mouth to muff.

"One, two, three, four," Coolio bumped over the sound system.

Ignore this, I told myself. I felt back to usual, nearly: I couldn't have *Coolio* making me miss my best friend! Still, denying Lisa's talents was like claiming I hadn't been obsessed with Carmen Sandiego: for a white girl, Lisa could rap, and when she sang Whitney it was like *she* was Dionne Warwick's niece. She was good at things you wouldn't realize could be valuable life skills, like droning with Montell Jordan—*this is how we do it*. Ever since Marissa had wrecked *Real Talk*, the day had been so up and down: Ethan Suva talking to me one minute, Lisa hanging up the next.

Well. Now was fine. Volleyballs banged into their cages. Boys stampeded, hopping, swishing the net, diving like mosh pit limbo, and the few walkers shuffled, shorts sagged to flaunt Marvin the Martian boxers. Park guys, even nerdy ones like Chase Pritzker and Zach Dend, announced themselves through ostentation: grease-painting their faces with Wite-Out or feeding pencils eraser first into the electric sharpener. My feelings about these behaviors depended on who I was looking at. Ethan Suva galloped backwards, his eyes shut, a scuffed volleyball balanced on his greasy blonde head. My glower softened.

He'd touched my wrist.

Most girls trudged. Not me: I darted, a firefly in a Gatorade jar, taking the least direct route to depositing my ball. These were steps, every one of them. I zigzagged across the gym, darting through the throng, and though my patellae were liable to bloom purple bruises, wound chic was my forte. When my heart felt like a Tamagotchi ready to hatch, I launched my volleyball toward the bin. It fell short.

"Whiff!" Nick Pastorino yelled, but I shuffled on, head down, palmed the ball, dropped it with its brothers, and searched for my girls.

As usual, my clients were dragging. Fortunately, I only had three this period; I slowed down and jogged up to each of them.

"Hey, Sheena! Have you talked to Marissa Turner, by any chance?"

She scowled at me.

"Well, okay then! Don't throw in the towel! Hustle, aight?" She shook her head and ran off. Well, her arms were thinner. She was my oldest client, if I didn't count Lisa, proof that, no matter how long you committed to *flaca*, you could still benefit from a friendly nudge, a boot off the cliff between normal eating and real dieting.

"Just a few steps, Jessica, sprint 'em, and then you've put in the work! Yeah! Dang, girl!" She was a great eater—watermelon and cucumber were her faves, she told me at our initial consultation; granola, her guilty pleasure—but she was a Nickelodeon buff (she'd taped every episode of *Clarissa Explains It All* and boasted she could watch four seasons in three days, with only bathroom breaks). That meant she liked to sit. Just for her, two *Real Talks* ago, I'd written "10 Easy Ways to Burn Calories During Commercials."

(Leg lifts, running up and down stairs, pretending to search for the remote.)

"I'm crumblin', El," she said. "I just ate carrots for lunch."

"Sounds like you're missing protein."

"Ughhh." She stared at the ceiling. Huge black overhead fans hid inside black grates. Between the rafters, a white volleyball was wedged like a giant snowball. Jessica's glittery purple eyeliner dripped toward her cheeks. That's why I didn't wear makeup.

I hopped from one foot to the other, a drill we did with tires. I smelled the grossness of the gym: socks, cheesiness. I clamped my fingers around my waistband where my mom had markered my name on my red uniform XXS shorts. Jessica could be motivated. I knew my stuff. For these girls, I had a knack.

"Jessica." I rested my hand on her arm. The heat of her skin reminded me how small I was. She had to know: she belonged on a horse farm, not in a gym. Her body made you believe in the myth of *big-bones*. My father had called me that pre-*flaca*.

I aimed my gentlest voice at her Peace Frog earrings. "I'm about to check up on Rocyo—see? She's not official yet, but we're meeting today. After school. Like, in literally fifteen minutes. She really needs to lose . . . she'd be so beautiful! I want her to know how much my coaching helps you guys, yah know, how *Real Talk* goes, etcetera? So, like, *ándale!* Show her how good you feel. Sprint to that locker room! And have, like, seven almonds, ASAP."

Jessica sniffed. I held out my hand. She slapped me five. Then she sped off, parting lackadaisical boys singing—or trying to sing—Tupac.

"That's just the way it is!" someone yelled operatically.

I spun around. Rocyo was hunching, hands on her hips, huffing against the bleachers. Ugh—what a sight! Elastic bric-a-brac banded her neck, kinda medieval, and her hair was still cornrowed from a winter break trip to the Bahamas. Her improvement potential was sky high. I tried out the phrase—Rocyo, *my newest girl.*

"What's up, babe?" *Babe* made girls feel special. Hot. Sexy. Sexy reminded them of bodies. Who didn't picture her sexiest self at least ten pounds thinner?

"What up? You see my spiking? I was da shiz." She raked her fingers through the sweat on her forehead. "You coming over today?"

"I am indeed, but that doesn't mean you get to putz. This is a transition. *Real Talk* rule: don't bomb your transitions. You're moving between one place and another. From activity to relaxation, school to afterschool. Whatever! Regardless! Gym to locker room! Make something of this! Make it count!"

"How you have so much energy, Elliot? Aren't you tired?"

I smiled, triumphant, mega-all-star. "There's no time to be tired! I'll see you on the bus. Run!" I lunged at her, throwing my arms wide. "Or I'll chase you, beeyatch!"

"Woah, woah, hey! Okay, I move! *Locasita*!" She unpeeled herself from the bleachers and ran off in that do-I-have-to way, dragging her heels.

The gym was empty except for me and Miss Troubaugh, a pear-shaped caution cone in her tangerine spandex. She was harmless, unless she had fitness test results. The last thing I needed was her calling Nurse Golombki, Dr. Kluk the principal, a pair of ever-changing guidance counselors, and my parents for a "strategizing session." Lisa had been subjected to one of those. *Gang flagellation in a grody conference room*, she'd told me last May. Her session had resulted in in-patient. *You sit there, people talk about you like they understand what's right for your so-called* well-being, *and you try not to cry/look for any blunt object with which to bash your brains in. And FYI: there are no blunt objects in the conference rooms. Just water lily prints. Monet.*

There were three minutes left until the bell. Under the volleyball net, I dropped to my knees. The floor smelled like rubber and dandruff. Type O waves crashed in my head; my arms burned. *Los deportes son bien ejercicios*, said my volition. I heard my name. I started pumping.

Miss Troubaugh could bite me. My breath was precious, like certain metals or white AirHeads. Kids were on their way out from the locker room. They needed to see my push-ups. I pictured MJ standing on my back, wagging his tongue, twirling a basketball on his pinky like one of the Harlem Globetrotters. That reminded me of the porn I'd watched with Lisa, the fishy way the first sister had tasted the second sister's nipple. I shivered and shut my eyes. My legs felt crossed (they weren't). Depending on the body butter, a nipple might taste salty, milky, fruity, caramelly—.

"Knock, knock. Egleston? I'm turning off the tunes—"

Bone Thugs-n-Harmony were singing, *Watcha gonna do?* Miss Troubaugh's faded Reeboks were an inch from my fingertips. I poked a purple pump.

"Hun. B-ball practices here in ten. Elliot. Quit overachieving and change."

I hopped to my feet and threw my arms into a wide ta-da. "Now laps! Be happy I love fitness!"

"Happy Gilmore," she said dryly. Then she raised one feathery blonde eyebrow toward the rafters, where felt banners sewn by pathetic PTA moms blew in the gusts of industrial fans. Anna had been a room mom in first grade, and quit when she had to pack plastic pumpkins with kernels of poison (candy corn) at the Monster Mash.

"Elliot, honey. What's that on your wrist?"

I jogged in place, shaking my hands like maracas.

"I don't know!"

"Let me take a look, sweetie."

"Gotta go," I yelled and then I zipped off, sprinting, full-blast.

"Elliot, come here!" Miss Troubaugh shouted. But she was too old to chase me.

I ran. The gym bleared. My cuts were for Lisa. I felt robbed, angry, deflated, sick. I hated school. The vagina-shaped pennants, angular Pollocks of puffy paint and glitter. Fuck. The mahogany bleachers, brilliant with thick wax. The dormant scoreboard. Fuck, fuck, fuck. The pull-up bars that smelled like iron and salt. The blue floor mats in the corner next to the closet where the balance beam and pommel horse and parallel bars lived. Miss Troubaugh had seen. That was bad. Bad bad bad. I pumped my legs. Spewed my navel up my esophagus. Light as a laser, eighty pounds, alive, Lisa-less and fine—well, for who knew how long. She could suck an extra-large egg. I didn't need her, I would show everyone. I was Skeletor, *flacisimia*, Below Average according to my biweekly BMI calc. I felt epic, fascinating, the only real person to ever walk this earth. And I bet you're creaming to know how I skipped breakfast, lunch, and dinner; how I whittled my victuals down to white rice and black olives; how I sprinted strip malls; how I fit into an eight at Gap Kids, where everything ran small to begin with, how I safety pinned my panties. . . and they still sagged, how—

Miss Troubaugh's face sharpened with annoyance. "Elliot Egleston, stop acting like a maniac and get over here!"

The doors to the locker rooms opened and, clothed, my classmates emerged.

"Shoot, I'm late!" I disappeared like a blown kiss into the class of 1999.

I was one of them, for a second, part of the school's clamor. Chairs screeched out from and clattered upside down on top of desks. The talk was relentless: elongated vowels, sentences rollercoasting through ditz voices and stoner sputters and ghetto slang and nerd code and—*and and and tonight and tomorrow night and Saturday night and Sunday night, what's the homework, whose parents are out, when's that show, who's got what, it's the best, the worst, I'll die*. The herd migrated. Lockers slammed like metal pats on the back, and kids loaded their JanSports with notebooks binders pencil cases books workbooks sketchpads art boxes graphing calculators. Was there a conspiracy to break down the adolescent's spinal integrity one one-hundredth of a vertebra at a time per cubit pound? According to Dr. Phil and Sally Jessy, yes. Sneakers squeaked and clogs clomped. Girls peeped their Leo pics and peered into sequin-trimmed mirrors, accurate as aluminum foil, and pinkied on their gloppy lip gloss and then licked it off. Girls giggled and pouted and squealed; boys goosed them or pinched them or did the old-school bra strap snap or even whispered at them, *hey*, the same trick they pulled during recitation of the Pledge. The pot-bellied security guard and the turkey-necked security guard pretended they didn't hear Chase Hampel call Andrea Mizzuski a ho. For good reason: Chase's mom, a lunch lady, gave away the Otis Spunkmeyer inventory, those soft chocolate cookies—special, because they had *chunks* instead of *chips*—and the guards took home for the weekend, called them breakfast, and anyhow, us kids, we were loud, noisy, spoiled brats, but not so strange, not so much more unusual than they—adult men—must have once been, boys with eczema and cowlicks in a good-ole America when no one talked about sex on TV, when kids didn't joke about the nation's leader getting BJs or smoking stogies, when who'd even heard of internships or sixty-nine, and us kids: the last thing we needed, according to an older generation of adults senior to our parents, the last thing we needed was more adult breath steaming down our collars or whatever.

Among the masses, I sought specialness. My clients, my girls, I cared, I wanted for them. They were so—ugh! They sucked in their stomachs under angora sweaters and baggy sweatshirts, tying cardigans or flannels around their waists cuz grunge; they chewed off their nails and coated them with Hard Candy or Wet 'n Wild, baby blue or pitch black; they doodled up each other's arms, slung their necks with friend-ship necklaces on ball-bead chains from Claire's, charms bobbing between budding breasts, thin as puzzle pieces, two jagged halves of a perfect heart.

..

I had no one's necklace. I wanted so badly not to want one.

Butterfly clips spiked the nerdy Nellies' hair.

Athletes wore sports bras on and off court.

Sopranos arpeggioed down the halls, unabashedly ador-ing *The Sound of Music*.

The popular girls were foxes, which is how I knew I was destined to never fit in. Their handsome fathers had names like Jim or Todd or Chris, and flirty mothers who'd given birth—without labial rupturing or anal fissuring, horrors we'd heard in Health—to adorable, just a touch under-weight, soon-to-be cliqued girls whose spit glistened more

Mr. Bubble than anything secreted by a salivary gland, girls who'd grown up into my classmates, with un-acned fore-heads and long legs and Barbie-shaped feet and the ability to look natural in any wash or cut of Guess jeans.

The popular girls sat at a lunch table closest to the emergency exit, as though the APR's feng shui had posi-tioned them where they would most easily escape fictional threats—bullets, bombs, gas, flames—once they were on the blacktop, underneath the basketball hoops, beyond the parking lot, a good kickball-kick away from Flagg Creek, the femur of water separating our school from the park district's trails, where, per rumor, Mr. Kasparek, everyone's favorite Keyboarding teacher, toked.

Yes, the popular girls would get out. Would they take me with them?

I mean, despite their Candies shoes and Limited Too tops and Calvin Klein microfiber bras, they worried about paunches and pooches and saddlebags, too. Upper-arm wings. Under-eye puffiness. Cellulite. Ab flab. That's why I'd be riding the bus with Rocyo, any minute. Even popular girls worried about their unbridled love of Sour Cream and Onion Pringles, Pizza Goldfish, Double Stuf Oreos, Fruit Roll-Ups, Cherry Clearly Canadian (definitely sugar water). They'd shredded cellophane. Done carbo-damage. Sometimes they dissed one another or stole each other's boyfriends, but most times they were unfathomably nice, as though nothing in life could warrant one eyedropper of stress. All the popular girls were guilty of was not giving unpopular girls like me a second thought, unless we could be useful to them.

Well.

Six of them paid me five dollars a month.

7 ·· LISA

AFTER, I EAT ANOTHER DREAMSICLE—IT tastes like Starburst Blue Tootsie Rolls French Vanilla Ice Ice Baby heaven. Junior Carlos has one, too, which relieves me, because then I'm not compensating or balancing or rewarding myself or having behaviors. I'm eating because my mouth is hot stale phlegmy. I'm eating because I want to—and I do what I want. I'm not eating just because I burned calories, some—I don't know how many—being fucked. Obviously, there's lot about sex I don't know. Like, should I move more or less when Junior Carlos thrusts? Should I buck like hula hooping and Skip-It? Should I put my hands over his eyes? I say stuff, like, "Oh yes, big bad wolf," but should I try more? I'll ask him sometime, but whatever happens in the future, I'm all right now. *Perfect baby*, he told me, afterwards. I love that—how I sound like someone from a red-hot, seven-guitar, teased-hair power ballad. *Perfect baby.*

We sit at the island in the kitchen. Our stools are spun so we can see the TV. The conclusion of *Clueless* plays. It's always abrupt. This movie should be longer. Sometimes, I feel like everything should be longer. Skateboards skid up and down ramps, wheels clack and whizz. Tai and Travis Birkenstock (I only *just* this time got that reference—*Birkenstock*, like the fugly shoes) are happy, together. It reminds me of *Stripes*, which I watch with my dad, a diehard Bill "Chicago Boy" Murray fan, where the second half is a weird separate entity, a leathery gray arm bulging out of an infant-soft, skin-toned elbow. We're in Russia now? There's a tank? No more creamed corn wrestling? What?

I suck the milky sheen off my popsicle stick and chomp the wood. Junior Carlos is still on the orange layer.

"Hey." Hearing myself is reassuring. I sound chill. I don't sound like I told off my ex-best friend or had sex with a college freshman or even like I have a cold. I don't sound like someone thinking about her grandma. I sound like my mantra, embodied: hanging with my boo, doing what I want, reading hokey popsicle stick jokes through my bite marks.

"'What do you call a chicken with a crown on?'"

A few strings of Junior Carlos's hair stick to his forehead. His cheeks are flushed. "This movie is already, like, so dated. You know? No one even uses computers, like, at all. This is pre-AOL. Doesn't that seem like so long ago?"

"What do you call a chicken with a crown on?"

"I don't know, Lee. But your life is going to start seeming vast one of these days, and then get back to me. King Pollo?"

"All right, Mr. Serious. *Chicken* a la *King*."

Junior Carlos shakes his head and slides off this twisty bar stool upholstered with dusky peach ferns. He decapitates his Dreamsicle. It reminds me of how he pulled his penis out before he came, how he joggled it in one hand while he put a pinky in my vagina, and I felt like a firecracker, praying to erupt, and he flounced hot semen on my stomach and wiped it off with the Last Supper blanket. I'll have to do wash before my mom gets back from the hospital. My life doesn't seem vast, just snared, like every action, below the surface, comes with 103 million invisible consequences.

"'I'm outie, Cher.' Your mom's gonna be here any—"

"Where are you going?" I twist in my chair. This would've been an oblique workout last year. "Stay. Please please please. My mom's visiting for like another hour. Last rites. You don't wanna make me get sad, do you?"

"I mean, of course not. I'd stay all day if I could."

"You can! You have a car! You don't have to say goodbye to *your* dying mother."

"I have afternoon classes," he says. He grabs the underside of the bar stool to stop my twists. "And you need rest, baby."

"I don't want rest. And no you don't. You said, Monday Wednesday Friday—"

"My schedule changed."

"Why didn't you tell me?"

"Why didn't you ask how classes are?"

I stare at my chest. *Why didn't you ask* me *how school is*, I think. But I pick a long blonde hair off the black fabric over my left ribs instead.

"I have to clear everything with a fourteen-year-old? Roiiiiiiight."

"C'mon. Don't just fuck and duck, Austin Powers."

"Don't go postal. I've been here, like, a long time. We've watched *Clueless*, we've talked, we've laughed, we've . . . honestly, I would've skipped all that if you'd told me about your grandma, because, as you know, I'm not a tool. I have lame shit to do."

"My grandma's not on my mind. Don't make excuses." I bat my eyelashes. I am very good at this, even when I'm sick and my head feels mummified in wrapping paper. I was a tap dancer. "Or, or, or—or, if you really, really, really wanna be lame, stay here! Do laundry with me! There, lame squared!"

"Is this because you hate the basement?"

"As if!"

Downstairs I've seen two rats. One possum. A gagillion ants. One brown leather photo album containing a picture of my parents naked except for bucket hats and friends of theirs I don't recognize, who are also naked except for bucket hats. I do hate the basement. But there are limits to what you can ask your older boyfriend to accept.

"If you want me to put the blanket in the wash, I'll do that for you. I'm that kind of guy, Lisa, remember? Very responsible. Thoughtful. Stand-up. But then I've gotta bounce."

"Don't!"

Junior Carlos opens his mouth and seals his lips over the remainder of the Dreamsicle. He looks like he's preparing a joint. Concentrated and borderline bad. He leans close to my face. There is the start of a soul patch on his chin, like church ashes.

"No. No kiss. Do *not* even think about that."

I see his stubble swallow. He legit gulps. "Think about what?"

He shows me his mouth, his Bazooka tongue, his burnished silver fillings on the bottom left molars. I'm not really angry with him, but I keep staring, to make him think I might be. Black lagoon darkness. Mouth fog. No hangy ball.

He kisses my forehead. "You know I love how fiery you are, right? I'll chat you. When I get home from the pool. Feel better by then, will you?"

I jut my bottom lip and stare at my lap. How did he manage to get cum on my pants? It's yolky. Dirty white. I scratch at it with my nails, but they're too short.

"Whatever. I might die. Or something. But, yeah, until then."

"Don't be overdramatic, L. It's in bad taste. Talk to your mom if you're really upset. It might help you two. Don't you think? Dealin' with your grandma."

"It's *my* grandma," I say, sniffing. "I'll deal how I want." I stomp behind Junior Carlos, his lost shadow, one step too slow. Maybe I'm the definition of bad taste. He leaves through the garage and I punch the keypad to open the door, and there he goes. He backs his dark-green Bimmer out into the snowy suburban world, all the houses still gemmed with Christmas lights, twinkling as dark settles over their too-much lives.

..

There is laundry forever until you're dead. Then there's still laundry. Down here, canvas sailor bags strangled with twine are filled with my grandma's stuff, carefully, some might say neurotically folded, by my mom (*no, Lisa, you can't help*). They line an entire wall next to the water heater. They still smell like her house: baby powder and ammonia and day-old apricot streusel. Butter slumping under a white ceramic bell. Thinking of her with nothing, no clothes, intubated skinny arms and powder sugar hair in that hospital bed, struggling to blink, waiting to die, I get antsy. Panicky. What does she want to say to her parents, dead decades? What does she want to say to her daughter sitting next to her—that she can't? Or won't? What does she regret? What does she want? Is there anything she can even do? This is a time when relaxing into starvation would be all right—end of life, when you have no choice, you need nothing, you can't convince yourself otherwise. When you can relax into the ache. When you're almost gone.

I shove the Last Supper blanket into the washing machine, my cummy flannel pants.

Then it starts: I hate crying. Burning like microwaved grapes, my eyes, I hold my eyelids open with the backs of my palms, my skin stretching like a sunburn. I focus on the noise. The washing machine is loud. A torrent, an explosion, ten thousand shoes tumbling over a waterfall.

I feel sulky, stupid for being sulky. There's nothing wrong with Junior Carlos. He left when he needed to leave. I know what Dr. Ogbaa would want me to do:

Confront the truth.

And here it is: I'm scared of my grandma dying. And I'm scared of Elliot not being able to let go. I'm nice; I can be mean over the phone, but what happens on Tuesday when I'm back at school, after MLK Day? I don't want her roping me into a forever Russian roulette with my own death. No one cares once you're gone—okay, parents. I've never been suicidal, like nabbing razor blades and Ring Pops from Al's Hardware, but when doctors call not eating a slow suicide, I can't argue. That's crystal. The most exciting part of dying is *everything-but*—key difference between sex and death.

I pour a capful of detergent into the washing machine. It smells like airy ecru dresses, lofting linen on a sunny clothesline. I run upstairs, into the front room, where all the furniture is white. My family only sits here on Christmas day, when we open presents in front of the fake tree, me, my mom, my dad. I throw my body on the couch.

I hold my legs out straight and concentrate my abs. I remember old games Elliot taught me: magical thinking. If my toes reach the mantle, I won't die. If I hold my stomach in while drinking lemon water, I'll burn more calories. If I don't think about my friend from the hospital that died, she'll come back to life. Poor Georgette. She hated vanilla Ensure and loved Jonathan Taylor Thomas. And I don't think about her, not usually—it gets too intense. So why should anyone think about me? How long will I think about my grandma?

I stare out the window for ten seconds. One: desperate. Two: I want my mom, to see her huffing up the driveway in her long gray coat and her absurd seal-fur hat. Three: Sigh. Four, five, six, seven, eight: I jog upstairs to the bedrooms—in my striped panties, no bra. Nine: I scream, like I'm about to get hacked to death by Freddy Krueger. Ten: My yell makes my boobs bounce; action beats inertia.

Exhibit A: seventh-grade me. She was action incarnate. Starving required so much energy all meals became negative calories, not just celery. A Rubik's Cube, every bite, each thought, every notebook margin for tallying numbers and choices. If there's a God, He's tempting us on the regular. There are so many choices to get wrong: Do I just jam my feet into my All Stars—or bend and tie the damn double-knot? Will I let the elevator hoist my fat ass? Will I penance-lap the Jewel, after eyeing the sample lady and the yum-plush of a mini bagel schmeared with cream cheese?

Elliot brainwashed me. She's convinced this is the best life could offer.

I look down the hall, toward my bedroom. Now I sprint like I'm trying to blast through a wall, and on the other side is Junior Carlos with open arms to Kevin-Coster-in-*The Bodyguard* me into adulthood, huzzah, immortality.

Seventh-grade girls are an audience: they love habits—their own, other people's, the better to compare or steal. They love braiding friendship bracelets, painting nails, and polka dotting them magenta. Color-coding school supplies, decorating lockers, coordinating scrunchies with scrunch-up socks. Loving the same Ginuwine songs, one spoon of pink yogurt for lunch, one bite of one strawberry: your golf-club elbows (sixty-five pounds), your blue lips (sixty-three). So kewt.

I run harder, down the stairs, into the living room. In seventh grade, this loop burnt calories; now it torches my anxiety. Screw the sixth-grade girls of the world: they'll grow up into the eighth graders, high schoolers, smarmy adults, clubby women, menthol aunts, grandmas. The day before I went in-patient, my grandmother told me I looked better than ever. Women will rain down love on your habits until you're such a sucker for the praise you drown in compulsion. Until you absent the habit and croak. Then, you're the kid who moved. The new girl in the afterlife. Um, who?

I crouch behind a curtain. If the mailman walks by, he won't get an eyeful. I peer out the window. Panting. The Thompson's, three houses down, still haven't cleared their driveway from last weekend's blizzard; their magnolias are porcelain weather vanes. Can you feel everything at once? The trivial and tremendous? I do what I want because I know what I want. I'm so proud of not wanting to be dead.

I want my mom to get home so I can tell her I told Elliot off. I want her to buy me a present, hot cocoa, extra whipped cream, even though I hate wanting, and especially wanting from her. I like having. I should've told Junior Carlos.

But my mom is nowhere when I want her. Outside, our neighbor Mrs. Scott, in a red poncho and waders, shuffles down the sidewalk with her Scottie. The dog wears its '70s orange sweater; its nose is a horn, long as my shoe. Across the street, the Malussas haven't removed their crèche: blue-robed Mary, swarthy Joseph, the shepherds, and the wise men fawning over a baby Jesus stand-in in the manger (this year, Tickle-Me Elmo; last year, a Cabbage Patch Kid).

Elliot is a hazard, says my mom. These days, after appointments with Dr. Ogbaa, she says, "another step away from Hell." (She means me dying from anorexia.)

I wonder when the finality clicks, or if my grandma is holding out for heaven. Is it that I don't remember Georgette, or that I don't *want* to remember? I don't want to remember the ward, either: a gang of dying-to-die girls in cotton ball PJs and Dopey slippers, swathed in cloud blankets, clutching Strawberry Shortcake dolls and Care Bears, stuffed seals and tigers. Slumber party purgatory: die or get fat. And all you do is talk: *Which* restaurant when your mom chucked a dinner roll at you? *What* were *you* eating? *How many* times did you set down your utensils between bites?

My mom's gray minivan pulls into the driveway. Panic whacks my forehead: *idiot, where are your pants?* I don't wait to see her long coat as she opens the car door. I rush to the living room, run the ice from our drinks down the drain, cups in the dishwasher. My feet pound like at a Park pep rally, when we stomp the bleachers to the opening bars of "We Will Rock You."

I try to lock my bedroom. But the lock is six-months gone. Anyone can barge in.

Junior Carlos is right: I *am* a baby: I don't want to know if my mom's been crying. I'm scared. I want to do what I want. I want to brush my hair three hundred times like my grandma taught me, and never have visitors when you're not in a clean blouse. Bra, too. (She had an exhibitionist baby sister.) My grandma didn't have an eating disorder— at least, not a diagnosis. She was picky. Precise. She knew what she wanted, too. Does she still know? Are our wants the last things to go? I remember us, two Christmases ago, at the Signature Room: she put her cold hand over mine and helped me scrape thick red dressing off a wedge of iceberg.

8 ·· ELLIOT

THE WINDY, BUMPY, IMMEDIATELY-AFTER-SCHOOL BUS was Route 107. I sat next to Rocyo.

She'd gelled her cornrows into a whale tail that hung over her shoulder. Inside the translucent Discman she clutched, the "Ghetto Superstar" single spun. Rocyo mouthed the words and bobbed her head: whenever she got to the part where Mýa sang "charms," her jaw dropped like a marionette's. I kept noticing the gap between her top incisors. Her grapefruit-pink braces were disarmingly similar in color and texture to her gums, like she was all mouth, one big, gross undone chicken breast, taking up more than her share of seat, making me squish into myself. I wouldn't have room to think about Lisa now.

I bounced my knee, scanning the writing on the brown leatherette seatback in front of me:

PENI5.

HAVE A K.A.S. (BUT DON'T HAVE A C-O-W).

U CUT W DAWGZ !!!!!!! (AND COWZ).

YO MOMMA DO! (COWZ).

Then, a drawing of a bulbous hand, captioned: TALK TO THE.

Rocyo touched my shoulder. "*Aquí.*"

I stood as the bus slowed, bracing myself on the top of the seat. Melted snow swamped the floor, and I slopped through slanty puddles. I didn't make eye contact when I saw Ethan Suva. He probably thought I was a spaz after what I told him in the library. Around boys—and especially this boy, who I like-liked—I wanted to be invisible, a passing shadow. Ethan professed to love *Full Metal Jacket*. He said he'd tasted acid rain. At least he had shoes on now—black-and-white checkered Vans. Otherwise, he was no hat, no gloves, no scarf, no coat, an open red-gray flannel, whipping his Kurt Cobain hair out of his eyes, chucking a Koosh ball back and forth as I walked by him. The ball flew right into the aisle.

"Sorry, mang." His hand dipped down and grazed my calf.

My heart somersaulted. Was his touch on purpose? I felt a seedling of joy.

He's so genius, I'd say, if I were talking to Lisa. *I'm like slayed. Dead-dead. He's so—.*

So what El? Tell me what about Ethan Suva makes you wet. Ew. I don't know.

Did he touch you? Lisa'd say. *Elliot. Don't be modest.*

Probably not on purpose.

Probably definitely on purpose! One of his brothers was at the same rehab as me; he could score us some pot. You better believe he taught baby bro the moves. I know he touched those candy-cane calves!

What!?

"Suva, hey! Watch it!" Rocyo's words sounded diagonal when she talked to boys. She tap-tapped my back, moving me down the aisle. "E-thone! You lost your balls!"

..

I hadn't been to another person's house since Christmas. My father had been in Europe, Anna's grades had been due on the twenty-fifth, and our family's sole plans had consisted of me making gingerbread cookies with my Uncle Marky and his boyfriend Fernán. (Marky's arms were tattooed and, with fine-tipped brushes, Fernán and I had been trying to give our gingerbread men ink sleeves of royal icing.) I hadn't been skipping festivities when Lisa invited me over the night Mrs. Orlowski-Breit would be at the hospital with her grandma. *We can do presents or watch something, but it's fine for a sleepover, if you want.* I'd pushed myself on her, sent AOL chats, *where are you, it's been forever, are you there God/Lisa it's me Margaret/Elliot? It'll be so amazing to see you!*

The truth was the exchange sucked, even with Lisa and I the only people in the house. It hadn't been the breezy perfect of reunion I imagined: we had been awkward, stagey. Lisa had been mowing chocolate-covered almonds, her eyes radaring me, especially after I gave her a Ziploc bag of the Fen-Phen, the old-school diet pills my mom didn't know I knew she'd been addicted to. I'd pilfered the pills from her sewing box. Lisa had given me a black mesh top she'd worn last year, back when she got so skinny her voice magically leapt up an octave.

I be fly, I'd rapped to Lisa's closet mirror. *Check-a-check out, my cubital fossae.*

Lisa had rolled her eyes. She'd tossed the Fen-Phen in a drawer. Cleared her throat.

El, you're a nerd. Questions. One: Do you want a club soda? Two: would you be down to smoke pot? And three: have you ever seen a porn? Okay, four: are you interested in watching *one—like, now?*

..

Rocyo lived in the most fabulous home in Ridgedale, the only subdivision besides mine that wasn't gated. Kids at school talked about going to birthday parties at mansions with indoor swimming pools and movie theaters with red velvet seats and old-fashioned soda fountains; I'd never been to one of those parties. Everything I knew about these homes I could see from my seat on the bus. Four- and five-car driveways, turrets and balconies, gazebos, and swing sets that made the Park playground look puny. Hedged alcoves. Guest houses. Landscaping with elaborate Stonehengy rock gardens.

In the lawn next to Rocyo's, I counted three fountains, their bases garlanded in Christmas lights. Still, Rocyo's house was the stunner. Under a beret of snow, her red roof wore scalloped bangs. White stucco pebbled the walls, the Disney version of a villa Señora Lurke had shown us in Spanish on the day we discussed La Sagrada Família.

Inside, our boots echoed on the biscuit-brown tile. Sun flew down from the skylight, nestled high in the cathedral ceiling. Rocyo's pet parrotlet flapped on its wooden perch. He was so bright, he looked backlit. His chest was marigold yellow, his tail feathers blue raspberry, his wings Slimer green.

"*Putita*," he cawed.

"Ugh, that's Anthony," Rocyo said, chucking her fur-choked boots into a closet crammed with shoes. In my experience, messiness and fatness were often good friends.

"Big name for a little bird."

"*Culo, culo. Lamame el culo!*"

Rocyo smacked the cage. "Shut up, Anthony! You get what he say? *Lick asshole?* Uck. Gross."

"Ew." I squinched up my face. "Pretty sick."

Rocyo wasn't crafty enough to highlight my ignorance. My mom, on the other hand, would pause a film to be sure I understood innuendo. *Yeah*, I'd say, and Anna would be like, *okay, El, plainly now, what does he mean, eat out*, and I'd fumble the hot mortification potato: *they're not cooking raviolis?* Then, Anna: *all right, El, let me explain.* So *culo?* I'd taken Spanish since first grade, but my vocab stopped at *Bienvenidos!* and the *palabras extra creditas* Señora Lurke wrote on the board in her hieroglyphic print.

I followed Rocyo upstairs. On the walls, Frisbee-sized glazed plates painted with blue and green and orange flowers hung between family portraits. I could see why she needed me. Compared to her mom, a Mexican Heather Locklear with croquembouche hair and a Vaseline smile I recognized from Park awards ceremonies, Rocyo's five-foot-four-inch, 158-pound body was Ursula from *The Little Mermaid*.

I dragged my hand along the iron railing, taking my time. The metal twisted like cursive. Soon we were on a balcony overlooking the foyer.

I touched my left wrist. Even the memory of pain made me feel like a true sufferer. The abrasion squealed through my coat. If Lisa never wanted to talk to me again, I'd schedule another meeting with Rocyo, come over, climb these stairs, swan dive off the railing and plummet, dropping to my death, a scream and low, rolling moaning slurps of brains pooled like crushed casket velvet behind my skull. Beautiful.

And so perfect, with the house fragrant like withered roses. I cringed at the thought of my consciousness rubbed out, bam, an instant. Death: a clap-on, clap-off light.

"You have your own room, Elliot?"

"Huh?"

"This is mine. My sister's there. My parents—you go the other way. They have their own everything. Bathroom. *Cocinita. Todos.*"

"Woah."

"Mine's biggest, though."

"Well, as you know. Biggest isn't always better, right?"

Bruce Willis's sun-soaked face beamed on an *Armageddon* poster that covered her door. Inside, the room was predictable, childish: faux fur zebra bedspread; centerfold of Usher shirtless, his nipples like black checkers; blue furry rug, where Rocyo plopped. I leaned against a white desk and crossed my arms.

"What do you like about your sister's room?" I said.

"Her boom box. It's louder to break your ears."

"So, yeah! There you go: size isn't everything. And, what I want *you* to know is that *numbers* aren't everything. Everyone fixates on numbers," I said. I was confident, prepared, a bullet whistling toward a temple. "But numbers are fake. I don't mean like in math with real and non-real . . . wait, never mind. I mean, numbers are *markers*, they help you track progress, but you shouldn't make them your all."

I paused. The heat was too much. Rocyo's room felt like ninety humid degrees, a greenhouse. Four indoor fruit trees the size of dollhouses grew out of turquoise pots and hard-looking lemons hung from the feeble branches. My turtleneck stuck to my armpits, the skin striping my spine, but I didn't want to be rude and ask to hang my coat. I stood, unmoored, suffocated, breathing in air that smelled like Lysol and Surge.

"Why don't you undress? I'm gonna measure you and take your Before pictures. You'll have a comparison—who you were before and after—a lot better than weighing."

"Everything nude?"

"However much you're comfortable with. Bra and underwear are fine. Seriously. I've seen lots of girls. It's like the same as gym. I'll turn around. And then I'll get numbers on your hips, your waist, your thighs, your wrists, your upper arms."

"Good."

I unzipped my black, patent leather backpack, and removed my kit, bulging with the Polaroid, Listerine strips, a chain of safety pins, paper packets of salt and mustard—there was all the usual stuff, but not my seafoam-green tape measure.

I glanced at Rocyo's desk. I sorta wanted all its girly fun, even though I always thought fun was a stupid, dangerous concept. Fun? Fun kept you dumb; fun kept girls from success. I mean, look at her stuff. A pink-and-black lava lamp. A sequined picture cube that showed Rocyo and two cheerleaders holding hands as they sprang off a high dive, floating in sky. A heart-shaped bulletin board with a roll of red tickets from Enchanted Castle, a headshot of Freddie Prinze Jr., an All-4-One stub, a Bart Simpson key chain, a 7-Eleven napkin with a lipstick kiss and a note: "Ur next Mountain Dew Slurpee = me." Not a book in sight. Not even a pen. What a waste.

"Do you have a tape measure, by any chance?" I turned. Rocyo's hands fumbled around her back, hunting the flesh folds for a bra clasp. "Need help?"

"Hey, don't look, Elliot!"

"My bad."

I snatched the 7-Eleven napkin and crammed it inside my backpack.

"Ready now."

Rocyo was naked. I tried not to gawk. Her arms hung like sausages at her sides. Her nipples were the menstrual brown we'd learned about in fifth-grade health. She wasn't really fat but plump and what Anna would call *nubile*, like Lisa last year before she lost weight: mature, too voluptuous for Park. A good body to mold. Usher and I studied her, a Renoir nude we needed to eye-chisel into a Giacometti or whatever. I smiled. If I helped Rocyo enough, she might be hospital material one day.

"All right, thank you. Let's chat, babe. You can get dressed."

Instead, she flung herself on the Grover-blue area rug. She started to sob, banshee yells interrupted by wheezing. I shielded my eyes from her butt. The smooth bronze boulder of flesh wore its crack like a Y-necklace. I wasn't worried but certain she would feel way better thin, without the bust of a *Baywatch* babe. I let her wail away the half-pound I always shed from a good bawl.

After a few minutes, I rested my hand on her shoulder. Her skin was soaked.

"Don't touch me. I'm disgusting. Get your hand off me!"

"I'm sorry! C'mon. Girl. Get dressed. Or don't. Either way. Let's do this. Hey, hey. You made the move of setting up an appointment, so we'll get down to business. Rocyo? Okay? Let's play nice and have a little talk . . . a little *real* talk."

"Elliot, I'm fat."

"No, you're not. You're working on becoming thin. That's awesome. You should feel like the best person in the world. You're making progress!"

"Am?"

"Yes, you am . . . you are."

Rocyo sat up. She wrapped the edges of the rug around her, like flower petals.

"So tell me what you eat," I said, pen to a sheet of loose-leaf. "On an average day. Yesterday. Was that normal?"

"I eat the bread with jam. That's breakfast. Lunch—"

"Hold up—what kind and how much?"

"Strawberry, a butt-load."

"Okay. Good. Be as specific as possible so I get to know what you like, what you crave, all that jazz. So lunch . . ."

"Lunchable, ham, cheese. Afterschool, Fruit Gusher. Great White. That fruit?"

"Barely. Sugar. Dinner?"

I pressed harder into my paper. My clients' food diaries disgusted me: I might never eat anything but apples and lemon water ever again. Rocyo rolled over and stared at the ceiling, one hand cupping her head, the other resting on her pooch. Her pubic hair whorled like the hard sugar nests my Uncle Marky made.

I felt something, alert and sensitive between my legs, zingy. I was aroused, even though I was also legit grossed out. Ever since Lisa and I had seen *Pleasantville* last summer, I'd been trying to masturbate. I hated that word. Why did something that supposedly felt good enough to change black and white to Technicolor sound so much like a LEGO kit? I called it *avocado*. The next time I tried to avocado, I decided, I would finger all my energy into weirding myself out.

"Dinner," I repeated.

"Is the worst. I eat with my mom and dad, and eat again with my sister."

Unless you were me, and Anna couldn't down a demitasse of espresso without laying one palm on her stomach and another on her forehead, dinner *was* a slog. Mom or dad masterminding the whole shebang: if someone decided the fam was slumming it with Arby's for dinner, you'd better buck up for a Beef & Cheddar, extra Horsy Sauce. In this sense, my parents were complicit in my emaciation: Anna would rather tweeze hair off her toes than cook, and my father ate steakily in Europe on business or spartanly in his office at his desk when he corralled a menagerie of animal crackers on a sheet of graph paper.

"So what *was* dinner?" I said. "No judgment."

Without making eye contact, Rocyo said, "Different stuff."

Girls were so vague. If nothing else, skinniness would hone Rocyo's thoughts.

"Okaaaaaay . . ."

"Okay, rice with, rice with salsa and shrimps."

"That's not bad! Protein is really important. Especially for your brain."

"But twice? And when I also like dessert?"

I tried not to sound demoralized. "Ice cream?"

With both hands, Rocyo drew a circle in the air above her body, her ring fingers and thumbs touching. I imagined sticking my head through and crashing into her lap.

"But sugar-free. Sugar-free, fat-free, cookie and cream."

I'd heard enough. "I have one last question—it's going to seem random. But bear with me. What do your parents do?"

"They own a restaurant."

"Perfect! What's it called?"

"Guadalajara."

"Okay, so you go to Guadalajara and you want real dessert: what do you get?"

"Flan. It's like *tan rico*."

"Mmm, I bet. That sounds good."

I was such a creep! I was like our science teacher Mr. Reid, who'd ask Kristina Parsell to remind him how to distinguish pupal from larval stage insects when he obviously had the correct answer tucked in his pleated chinos along with his yam-ish boner. I knew Rocyo's family owned Guadalajara. We'd gone there on a third grade field trip to the car tower, that spindle of junked jalopies that cameo in *Wayne's World*; I'd handed a hostess the slip with my entrée choice (*enchiladas con queso y cebollas*) and, after *la almuerza*, I'd *eaten* the vanilla flan. I remembered the eggy, caramelly burn, remembered putting a finger on the custard's surface and considering my blurry print. My existence revolted me. Between flan and Anthony's *culo*, I was lying about what I knew or what I didn't know: it was like trying to hop on one foot and carry a glass of Hawaiian Punch across the Atlantic Ocean.

"Your body wants flan, something real. Not fake sugar, fat-free whatever. You can't eat an entire thing of flan can you?"

"No."

"So, get your mom to buy you good, real-deal ice cream. I don't know, Moose Tracks. Ben & Jerry's. Whatever lights your candle. Then you eat that, but only a little—measure it out for yourself, like, say, a quarter cup. That's half the serving size, FYI. But if you love dessert, and you want to lose weight, you should eat that, slowly. You should enjoy every spoon."

"Yeah. Sounds better too."

"Duh. Now, let's take your Before. Then get dressed and I'll do your plan."

..

We'd been standing in the foyer fifteen minutes. Already, I'd demonstrated proper V-up form, explained the notational difference between teaspoon and tablespoon, and given Rocyo a week of menus and exercise sequences and the last issue of *Real Talk*. There was a new five-dollar bill in my pocket.

Rocyo stood on tiptoes, looking through the liver-shaped window in the front door. She didn't know it, but she was watching for a boxy Saab driven by a matchstick woman wearing black sunglasses, the gold arms etched with a quilted pattern; matte maroon lipstick, camel hair coat; black leather gloves.

"Where's your mom?"

"She's an artist—she's late a lot." I was impatient. I didn't have a rapport with Rocyo, and we weren't friends enough for silence. Anna was always on poet-time, but lately she'd been worse. After my pre-Christmas sleepover at Lisa's, my mom had forgotten me. Lisa had gone to church, leaving me alone with her dad, who'd been slamming the double-brewed coffee and heavy cream mixture he called sludge. *Thirsty?* Mr. Breit had asked, skimming the *Trib* as I stared out the living room window. *No thank you. Too strong? Trick is, you just swallow,* Mr. Breit had said. I'd nodded, wishing Lisa had been there so I could make a "your dad" joke, which we'd invented since her mom was so awful you couldn't even put her in the same sentence as something funny. Instead, I'd imagined Mr. Breit's long, skinny-chubby body naked, hairy, slapping against . . . my mind stopped there. The porn had been the only thing I could think of; the girls swallowing a guy's semen had looked the same as swallowing their own spit. Finally I'd trudged home, snow banks past my non-hips. I'd found Anna in her black silk robe: her knees were tucked mermaid-style and she was scribbling in her journal with a glass of red wine in front of an unlit fire.

"Just remember," I said to Rocyo. "You can do this. You need anything, I'm here for you. Call me, pass me a note, whatever, hit me up on AOL: ElleGirl80."

"What's 80?"

No one had ever asked, even though my interestingness was a scarf wrapped around my neck for anyone to compliment. I blushed.

"My weight."

"You don't look like eighty pound. I weighed that in third grade."

"Well, that's a ho thing to say! I *weigh* eighty pounds—" I saw the rabbit-pellet shit I'd expelled that morning. "Probably less. If you factor in gym class and walking during the day and going to the bathroom—"

"All right, psycho. Calm down. Aren't you here to help me? *I* need to be that thinny. We don't go on vacation if I'm fat. My mom says."

Mrs. Vazquez—Ethan Suva had called her *plastica* to Rocyo's face once—fake boobs or not, at least she knew what was best for her daughter.

"You'll be as thin as you need to if you follow the plan. Hey, speaking of . . . are you friends with Marissa Turner by any chance?"

"The plan, the plan," squawked Anthony, his red wings beating. "*El culo* plan!"

"Huh?" Rocyo said.

I ran a finger along his cage. His black bead eyes, fish-egg eyes, viscid with clear goop and admiration or disdain, watched me. I smooched my lips, kissy kissy.

"Tch, tch, tch. Could you teach him to say Elliot? *Ell-ee-it?*"

"Maybe? He gonna bite you."

Her eyes clouded. I wanted her to stroke my calves, lick my ankles, taste every inch of my lightness; instead she opened the door.

"Bye," she blurted. She let me out to wait on the porch.

9 ·· ANNA

I AM A WRETCHED MOTHER. This I think at 4:42, twenty-two minutes late picking up Elliot, when I've hit every red light between the college and the greater kneecap of suburban Chicago that constitutes our school district, when I've rushed from Building 13 to the faculty lot behind the old carriage house turned snow blower corral, slipped, fell on a patch of black ice, walloped my knee and road-salted my pants, limped to the Saab, its leopard hauteur—and I'm no animist—extra haughty and judgmental as I dauntlessly descended disheveled into the driver's seat and listened to my voicemail. Fuck. And this, after I sat in my office, turning through blue books, skimming recollections of the places where my students feel most content: Gram's iguana room— its white wicker, Uncle Jerry's deer camp before dementia ate his brain, Mom's yeasty kitchen when she bakes honey-eyed white bread, the Sears cabin at Lake Beauty, the ferric springs coiling under the bunk beds at church camp. I waited beyond the last minute for Rot, with the door closed, one hand between my legs testing my sensitivity (I was tingling), then door ajar, then door flung open after I left to gulp two Styrofoam cups of tepid, tea-pale coffee in the across-the-hall faculty lounge. I was hoping like I hoped— only for a moment—during pregnancy to lose the baby. A hard and wrong hope, like hoping to return and walk in on Rot, his feet kicked up on my desk, his Jordans dripping like red-and-black popsicles, hoping to catch him in wait, waiting on me. Dumb trumpery of my wants. And I am a bad mother not for what I have hoped, but for postponing El's evening. I am keeping El waiting, and after I have received a doom-mongering voice message from Miss Troubaugh. I am bad because my daughter cut my apples, and conscientious, perfervid El has told me nothing about cutting herself.

.‎.

Here, the on-ramp for a tollway out of Illinois. Badness incarnate, I contemplate veering across traffic, letting horsepower and acceleration stamp out all my heart's base obligations (I should care more for my family, less for my fancy), disappearing into Indiana, where on Weko Beach I have twice felt the sort of inner peace and all-knowingness some readers seek in literature, why, yes, contentment, ENG 101'ers, listen here: Dr. Anna has, if not *the* answer, at least this one answer. I have meditated on Weko Beach, eyes closed, no mantra, lips parted, no makeup, palms sunward on my knees, a breeze lifting my hair like blackly gray Maypole ribbons, the clap of Lake Michigan frothing the beach, stones and twigs beneath my leggings, feet bare, Elliot launching herself into waves with her father, Papa, in this memory, rufous fur on his face and his chest, our family up in Michigan for a day, six hours, five years ago, when my daughter was a little girl.

My daughter matured when her body stopped curving: I appreciate her subversion.

And now she's shielding me from her behavior or she's afraid of my reaction or she's not thinking about me. I have operated under the delusion that Elliot is me, and now, for the first time, truly truly truly she is not.

I do not turn onto the interstate. I leave COCC's county and enter Park's. The Montessori where El attended preschool winks at me. White Hen. McDonald's. Hardees. Wendy's. Kmart. Venture. My pathetic path. I am a dog turning around and around in its bed, appalled by my limited options, no place to burrow.

Burrowing defined my middle-thirties: down comforter burrowing, white burgundy burrowing, *Mrs. Dalloway* burrowing—I was a bad mother five years ago because I indulged in so, so, so, so, so postpartum depression. Nine years partum. Nine years when I felt, not only was I a scourge, but I was a scourge unto others. That year I began running; that year, I shallowed up, let my deep waters settle. That year I gave up on sadness and said *what the fuck?* En route to El, I am a bad mother not only because I have burrowed, not only because I am late, but because I have burrowed and kept quiet, because I am late and have not let her know.

I withhold my whereabouts, Elliot. And you don't even know about my mobile.

The car drives forward; I do not. Acknowledging I am a bad mother does not ease my passage. I am a poet and an adult, alive and thinking in 1999. Overanalysis is my kith's Kool-Aid. We stir our red sugar and slosh the pitcher, steep and stew and store, turn over terms, infuse them with hard spirits, truckle them until they swell with imprecations and implications and incantations and glamour, the archaic, witch work, magic. I study badness until it becomes me. I am bad, I am late, I am so late El has come up with some nickname for my lateness—*the aubade hour.* Something.

Do my tardies thrill me? No. Will it kill my daughter to stand in a foyer? No. In my courses, partner projects always suffer from unbalanced efforts.

At a red light, the afternoon sun lists through the windshield, its Sémillon honey tipsying the day into night. One blade of the wipers drags its rubber, a black leg against the snow, falling again, those wet, pelting prick-your-skin flakes. I reach to the console for the ugliest gift Rolf has every bought me: a Nokia 5110. He gave it to me for my last birthday, six weeks ago, at the Sybaris Pools in Northbrook, first day of December. He had booked a couples' massage and hot tub in the Chalet. That was when I knew we'd really bombed marriage: the suite, its white-leather globular armchairs, its cabana with Mr. Coffee, its waterslide, its twenty-two-foot pool, its king-size bed with tufted headboard, its nightstand full of red, white, and blue flavored lube, how none of that led to anything but good, old-fashioned, college-style talking, in armchairs, with plastic mugs of crappy coffee. I appreciate the ugly phone on which Rolf and I talk, but I don't appreciate the ramble I received from Miss Troubaugh.

"Hello. And I'm sorry to be leaving this on an answering machine. But, this is Jill Troubaugh, I teach Phys. Ed. at Park, and I'm calling because, I wanted to speak with you about your daughter: Elliot's been exhibiting some unsettling behavior. You might want to take a peek at her wrists. The cuts are . . . visible. Of course, we don't like to see any girls—any students, for that matter—in distress, and well, not to discount your daughter's problems, but we don't want her starting a trend at Park. You never know which wildfire will spark Salem, if you know what I'm saying. We call this—a cry for help, Mrs. Egleston."

Mrs. Egleston: that's Rolf's mom.

..

"How many minutes since now?" El's first question: she was two. Good mothers remember first words—bad, first questions, the original opportunity to respond wrong.

"Now's now," I said. Newborn, holding my daughter in her pink infancy while I inhaled chapters: that brought me peace, a deep breath of talc and toast. At two, Elliot toddled and talked. I crouched, knelt, hunched, prostrated, an index finger marking my place in whatever book I refused to put down. I set a hand on her shoulder, like I was checking her temperature, though I was trying to slow her, settle her, still her into a nap. "No minutes since now."

"Now. Now how many minutes since *now*?"

A million, I could've said. Time is a net we fall through. To know now is to strain stars through mesh. Now is a trapdoor. A dream. Now is the imaginary friend adults keep around to jounce the stodge of life. But motherhood frustrated me, even before the job fully began. I straightened my knees and loosened my glance from hers, looked at my book, resigned myself to letting her wander off.

"I don't understand what you're asking."

..

Good mothers would be grateful for Miss Troubaugh. I know good mothers, though when I first began teaching Cook County's impecunious populace—impoverished not only of financial resources but those other wells sapped by compromised monetary freedom—foolishly I assumed I'd instruct Jerry Springer derelicts cast to the Island of Misfit Toys. I was wrong: plenty of my students have fantastic mothers, mothers as upright as Rolf's—the real Mrs. Egleston. A truly good mother. If only Elliot had known her grandmother: carrot muffins with buggy Sultana raisins, hot cocoa scumming a saucepan on the stove, maybe Miss Troubaugh wouldn't be calling. Rolf's mom—her quiddity drove me berserk. Giver of thoughtful, wholesome gifts that would orienteer her son: when he was eight, a map so he could follow along on car trips to the Badlands. Hair unflashy, bobbed, teeth solid as dice, cavity-less, eyes on her flesh and blood until she, taciturnly, closed them. Stolid and jejune sound opposite, but in Ellen Egleston's case, they were a spondaic match.

Good mothers, as with good teachers, appreciate when children, their pupils, entrust them with secrets. Good mothers like good teachers who, when pupils have outsourced said secrets, reveal those mysteries to perhaps-oblivious parents. Good mothers are good teachers, preparing their progeny to plumb the mines of life.

The student with a bad mother: teachers see her demented shadows, vagrant nightmares. The student who knows she has a terrible mother: teachers see her pounded pummeled putrid hell.

But Elliot doesn't think I'm a bad mother. *That* is why she worries me.

The Saab's blackness pours through the afternoon—the sky turns as fast as a Polaroid, the day darkened, dusky, corvine in January, a nocturnal beast that beats its wings after three. The tires slick the streets, and *tsk: where are you going, why, why*. I am off-course, demapped, delinquent. The tragedy of ignoring better judgment is that the gift of better judgment is yours to unwrap any instant, the cigarettes, whose carcinogens you curse every day, you still pay for and smoke. Why? Why do we wolf our hearts?

I am not heading to Rocyo Vazquez's house, where Elliot is working on a project, something that will probably necessitate the purchase of a tri-fold board, the practice of blunt motor skills. Cut. Paste. So my daughter may become a computer. No, though the Vazquez's gauche terracotta roof blights a five-minute-away sky, I turn into Saddle Drop, one of the few remaining ungated subdivisions, immediately beyond Park, past the creek.

Families new to the area don't want to live so close to the woods, not quite forest, but trees, enough of them, oak and willow shaded in the daylight, dense treachery at night. Owls noise and possums lurk. Coyotes have been reported, Pekinese maimed. New families are frightened of natural threats more than the old woes: Christian daycares, arsenicked Snickers. It's a shame: the Saddle Drop homes are solid and stately, like the judicious older man I picture whenever any of my students— against my preference—call me *professor*. Stone griffins guard the drives, and, up until the first frost, in the lawn of one, peacocks wandered like Latinate words on a flat blank page.

Rot lives next to the peacocks. His home—his family's home—I aim to spot. Ten or fifteen times, I've driven here before, alone always—to crawl by with Elliot would be to ask her to replace the batteries in my vibrator. I have, only once, dropped him off.

Though I've never been inside, I have imagined the grounds—namely, the backyard, invisible from the street: a cache of catkins; an unruly scrub from which Rot has fed the next-door birds tiny, wild raspberries; the large in-ground pool in which Rot, with much friction, eradicated his virginity ("water sucks" he told me, after our first, frenetic fuck, and I, ever inquisitor, asked him about his deflowering), where these days he enjoys smoking or sniffing and sipping—vodka and Squirt.

Today I don't think *swimming*. I want to return the coke, see where that leads—an excuse, a reason to make contact. I feel adolescent, lawless, and, frankly, wonderful.

I park on the shoulder along the peacock's lawn, an escarpment dressed in snow. No birds now. Somewhere on the grounds, warmed by an artificial sun, they must coop in fulvous hay, resting, necks crooked like swans. Do they dream of strutting in glitz the way I select clothes? Fetishize isn't too strong a word, Anna the *Pavonine* on Michigan Avenue: how much sumptuous black can one woman own? Baby alpaca, Cucinelli cashmere—how much guilt can one woman stomach?

"Beauty will save the world," said Dostoyevsky. Frippery won't save El: I began her college fund—now I deplete it. She's smart, capable, in COCC dialect, "scholarship material." Other mothers have done worse, I think—a home renovation—and then I remember our bathroom. Rolf and I have never aired the laundry about money.

"If the ill spirit have so fair a house"—well, Rot's home is nicer than mine.

The black leather glove on my right hand, $275 in that orange box: I unsnap the cuff, pull it off, open my palm and reveal, keen as a scimitar, Rot's home phone number.

This is a development. A step. An alteration to which I refuse to assign value: not more or less, better or worse. I witness. I call a thing a thing: our communication up to this moment has been restricted to Rot's pager. Simply: I am creating change.

What you do matters, my yoga teacher preaches, and, Pavlovian, my knee aches from slipping in the lot. Tomorrow, I won't run: I'm getting on the mat, moving through *vinyasa*.

I turn off the Saab's lights. The mobile phone is gray, cold from all-day in the glove compartment, Game-Boy-ish in my hand. I dial and wait.

What I want is for him to pick up. To cut me off before I can finish hello. For him to run out to the street, no coat, to tumble into the passenger seat, to grip my shoulders and press me back against the seat and clamp his mouth over mine, to knee my legs apart and, after I've gulped hard and tipped my neck and wound my hand around his back and up and around and cupped his cock, after that I want him to slit the baggie with a razor and line the torus of my collar bone with powder and snort me up and up until my skin numbs, and in the Saab, all over my body liquefies just thinking about him. *Clench fists glutes calves toes eyes jaw ears cheeks stomach shoulders biceps—more, more—okay: let it go,* this is yoga before down go the lights and out comes the lavender oil to anoint our temples, before we are permitted corpse pose. I am stuck outside final rest in the hiemal clench of cold as the phone rings.

A woman answers, alacritious: "Rottingham's, who may I say is calling?"

"Is Carlos there?"

"Carlos?"

"Carlos Rottingham?"

Anna, stalking tyro: perhaps I miswrote the number.

The woman sneezes wetly. "Ah—excuse me. Are you looking for Charles or Chip . . . Charles Senior, by any chance?"

"My apologies." Had I time for reflection, I may worry at how quickly I accept this appellation adjustment. "Yes, I'm calling from the registrar at College of Cook County, in response to Carlo—Charles's transcript request. Is he available?"

In an oriel window on the peacock house, a light goes on. Peacocks, I think, when no figure appears. I keep an eye on the window, a feather, Carlos. His lie debouches me from my cramped fantasy. Bold and capable, liberated from motherly, wifely duties to which I have never fully subscribed (yet even unborne burdens require shouldering), I could never go home—the thought pulsates my chest. I, too, could tell people I'm someone else, Carlos, build a future on mistruths.

"He's at the pool until eight. Should I tell him you called?"

"Oh, no," I say, meekly, opening the car door. The cold smarts. "I'll follow up. Easier to be in touch with him, his professors tomorrow. Thank you."

Outside, my knee sears as I stand. *Charles* I whisper. *Rot. Rot.* Slowly, I circle the car, a lion tracking its hunt. I run my bare hand along the cold black surface, waiting for the green plumage of a man or a bird to appear, my fingers shivering up the wet, burning cold until I realize I don't know why the hell I want what I want.

The louder the volume, the slower my speeding feels. I want to outpace traffic, to lift off. This is how I get annual tickets. I pass a school zone, the white metallic crosswalk stripes dazzling beneath a streetlamp. The sky is turgid with burgundy clouds, like hell is ascending.

Anna. Really. Slow down.

I hate to. Decelerating, the panic might set. What am I doing, where do I go from here, what will tomorrow be,

tonight? I press rewind and drum the steering wheel, like
rapid arm movements can keep me from despondency, like
action will lighten me, like young people in a band will bring
me youth. They do, so I sing.

Elliot tells me I'm a year late on *her* music, but this is the
girl who didn't understand the notion of *now*. Current, this
minute, this very instant: now is relative. Because singing
now I remember glee, joy, twenty-five years ago, learning to
drive, blasting The Stooges and David Bowie when I took my
dad's red Chevelle, alone, and every mile, "I Wanna Be Your
Dog," the odometer wasn't a mortal countdown—how many
more miles were there to drive in a life—but a challenge,
"Fame": how far could I go? Chicago Ridge Mall? The Fox
River? Starved Rock? Rot, Carlos, Charles—*Fata Morgana*:
how does he do this to me, show me another way—alive in
fantasy, reconstituted by desire—how limitless life could be
without . . . without my family.

At a blinking red light, I spit in my palm. *Au revoir*, Rot's
number. I cup my hand to my nose. It is a woman's hand, up
to no good. Fetid, foul—that's my saliva. So I will retrieve
my daughter, with delectation and noise, my gorgeous gloves
back on.

10 ·· LISA

FOR AN HOUR, MY MOM doesn't come upstairs, doesn't even look for me or huff into my room shaking the thermometer (I'd bite to tempt mercury poisoning). I stay under the white down comforter, in bed, holding my breath and feeling the one good trick Elliot showed me: the heft of thousands of goose feathers sewn into neat little squares heaped on my breasts.

I'm crying lightly about my grandma. I stop. Sometimes, to feel real, you need other people to see your sadness. *Acknowledgment is vital*, Dr. Ogbaa says, and she's right.

I try to picture Junior Carlos's sex face, but all I see is fangs like those ones kids whose moms aren't anti-Halloween let them buy from Murray's Party Supplies.

Then memory bats me. I remember: I'm at my grandmother's house, in a bed that once belonged to my mom, and I refuse to nap. I must be three. *Zoobilee Zoo* beckons from a Beta tape, but my grandma has insisted "everything good waits." I didn't know words like *refrain* or *mantra* then. I knew mad. No. Want now. A tumble of bleeding feelings (injustice?). The afghan covering my face is striped with wavy seas of avocado green and cream, flecked with hairballs from dogs I never knew. I breathe my sour air. If no one finds me, I might disappear. I might plunge through the mattress, into another dimension, a bizarro my-house or my-grand-ma's-house, where I can run my hand along the ballet barre on the wall, without anyone telling me to stop.

This hope belongs to being three years old, my first memory. It was a glimmer of an idea—I had power—before I found a voice, according to Dr. Ogbaa. She's shown me how repressing my appetite and shrinking myself may have origins in what I'd learned from Catechism, CCD, the Church's elaborate investment in self-denial, its propagation of afterlife myths.

Today, under the covers, hearing my mom open white birch cabinets and slam very organized drawers and turn the television on and then off, shouting at my dad on the phone and finally turning on the Oreck, I realize I *don't* want to disappear or be invisible anymore—what once served me no longer does.

Instead, I open my eyes and mouth my dramatic monologue for Speech Team.

The monologue is so depressing I've blue-ribboned off it twice. It's told by a woman, who—sorry, spoiler—reveals she's actually dead. The windshield wipers, she says, the wipers, the wipers. Like that scary-not-scary joke about the Russian guy saying, I *vant* to *vipe* your *vindows*, this lady keeps talking about wiper blades, that's all she sees, and you think she's crazy, until you learn through her first-calm and then-frazzled narrative, that one night, as she was driving through a thunderstorm, she couldn't clear the rain fast enough and she couldn't see a red light and she sped through an intersection and into a head-on collision with a Mack truck. The theme is mistakes haunt you or, maybe, death is insanity.

I practice in whispers. When I act, my brain disappears. I am all face and body, inside a set of borrowed feelings, like thrift shopping at the good Salvation Army on Clybourn with Junior Carlos: toss me that mink stole and I'm two seconds from Joan Rivers. My voice quavers until desperation and terror fondle every word. I scrunch my nose to choke my vocal chords and pinch my sentences until my mom opens the door and I stop.

Kim Orlowski-Breit has a mushroom cut, which does her wispy corn-silk hair zero favors. Right now, she's in a state of half-dress. Her brown, seal-fur hat sits on her head like a shaggy box. She wears John Lennon glasses and shapeless blue jumpers with appliqués of women and dogs or fruit and squirrels. Six-pointed snowflakes and snowmen are today's patches. The snowmen are eyeless. Those naked photos in the album in the basement: I wonder what her babeself would say to her now. I wonder why some women suck when they become adults—so much more than men.

Would I be so harsh toward my mom if it weren't for Elliot?

Before she miscarried with my brother Paul (we celebrate his would-be birthday each August by listening to Eric Clapton's "Tears From Heaven" and walking over to the cemetery with a bouquet of baby's breath), and fulfilled her womanly duties with me, before she decided to devote her life to stacking dented cans of Campell's soup at the Cook County Food Pantry and spreading Wonder Bread with Miracle Whip and Velveeta at St. Catherine of Siena's women's shelter, my mom taught first grade on the South Side, at a school where kids were always fairy-godmothered by social services, the sort of place where little boys would accost little girls, touch their pee-pees and tell them about where they'd put their wees. That time endowed my mom with an unparalleled death stare. This is what I get now. She pulls off the covers and glares, a look that growls, *Lisa get up.* She yanks open my bottom dresser drawer.

"Where are your pants?" Her yell sounds like it's traveled up from underground to attack me. "Do you have to be flaunting your body all day long?"

"What are you doing?" I shriek. "Stop! You're going through my stuff!"

My mom turns, hands on her hips, so big they bump our minivan's parking brake. Honestly, I'm pissed on principle; it's not like I'd be dumb enough to hide anything after my mom became the Stasi in sixth grade. Junior Carlos keeps a topless Polaroid he took of me in his wallet; he supplies his own glow-in-the-dark condoms.

"I'm not going through your stuff. I'm getting you ready. Your grandmother wants to say goodbye, and you—Lisa, I need you to be dressed five minutes ago."

"I don't want to get Grandma sick. Er. Sick-er. And I hate hospitals. You ruined them for me."

"You ruined them for yourself. Don't take your issues out on your grandmother."

"Don't rush me," I say, stretching. I stretch my arms wide like wings. I let my fingers traipse through the air like a ballerina's.

"These are God's minutes, on His clock. You pray, missy. Let's both better hope He's not running fast, or you'll—this will be your burden. You'll regret today for a long, long time." She flings a pair of sweatpants over her shoulder. Up and down the legs, they say, SPEECH DOES | IT LOUD.

They land on the foot of my bed, where only Junior Carlos's feet have ever reached. "Your—what in the world are these?"

She holds the freezer-sized Ziploc bag of Fen-Phen. Diet pills from Elliot. That stupid, stupid Christmas thing.

Above my mom's eyebrows, her forehead sprouts two bulging knobs. Fury lumps. She looks like a devil—God, she'd loathe that. She shakes the bag once, like she's weighing it, and the bottom bursts and pills pour everywhere. The first thing I think of is the clatter they'd make getting sucked into the vacuum cleaner, a lotto machine of candy.

"They're Elliot's," I say, sitting up rigidly. "Elliot's pills."

Now I kneel on my bed, so my mom and I are closer to the same height. I channel the part of the windshield wipers monologue where the woman gives her shakiest confessions.

"They've been here since Christmas," I say, trying to keep my voice from punching up. "She gave them to me, I think she thinks I'm still into that, all that stuff, which, no, I'm not, because I know Dr. O told you I'm doing really goo— well. Really *well*. I've been meaning to give them back, or throw them out or whatever, but I don't really wanna talk to Elliot anymore because I know you don't want me to and, she's, like, the worst, so they're not mine is what I'm trying to get at, Mom, okay?"

The devil horns on her forehead flatten. Her skin eerily smoothes; it's like the ice that kids on the news plummet through while driving snowmobiles. Her eyes close. She sniffles: she's a person whose breathing belies her mounting tears.

"You're popping right now," my mom says. "You're lying to me."

"Popping? What? No, like, not even. I'm trying—I'm being honest, Mom, I swear, this—"

"You think you can lie. That all of this is nothing. Your grandmother is dying, so you think you can lie to me. 'My mother's mind is elsewhere so she must be gullible and ready to be the fool, to be the mourning, God-fearing fool.' Are you addled now? Should I have your stomach pumped? Is this what you do when you stay home sick?"

"I watched TV, Mom! I drank warm 7UP! Hey, relax."

My mom dumps the contents of my pink backpack on my desk. Pens and paper clips and wadded up gum foil and pennies and some random chalk I stole (I don't know why) pour onto the big, flat calendar that covers my desk. It's a mess. I really hate her right now. Maybe forever.

"What happened, Lisa, to Colossians, she 'laid aside the old self with its evil practices.' Psalms, Lisa: 'he who practices deceit shall not dwell within my house.'" She pauses, grabbing pajamas and cramming them in the backpack. "We can't have this, this relentless insistence on lying—is this . . . how long has this been going on? Do you have a schedule for your deception? A diary for me this time?"

"Mom, you're scaring me. I don't know what you're talking about. You're freaking—maybe you're upset about Grandma, which—" my voice breaks here, for real, in a way I always wish I could do on command, which, someday, I'll master if it kills me—"and I'm upset, too, but I swear, I swear to God, and you, and Grandma, and Dad, that I'm not taking diet pills, I haven't even opened that bag, I'm not lying—"

"This disease, like a serpent in your brain—what is it offering you? What is it saying to you? Why is it lying with you? And you subscribe to it. Why do you keep hiding your-self from God? You need—oh, Dr. Ogbaa is so wrong. So, so wrong. Poor, imbecilic, ineffective woman. You've deceived her? That's—Lisa, the heavenly Father told me we might come to this. That. Pack—finish packing. We're going back to the hospital."

I pull the comforter over my head. Inside my chest, fear smears itself across my lungs until I can't breathe, I can't think. I start to cry, and then, embracing the temper tantrum, I pound my fists into the bed, pummeling the mattress, its response like a timpani.

"*Kill me!*" I scream through the blankets. "Just kill me now! You want me dead! Stop pretending you don't. You wish Paul had survived and I'd died."

That's the jugular. The knife twist. The clinch. My voice sounds ripped up, and I pause when my mom leaves the room. The door slams. I'm quiet then, cool and relaxed, apathetic and alone, which is the eternal aftermath of acting.

11 ·· ELLIOT

"We need to talk, El," Anna said, then two seconds later: "What do you want for dinner?" Before I could reply to anything she cranked the volume and started singing.

"Who-ooh ever you are!"

She belted Geggy Tah so hard I could tell she was bullying herself into a good mood, the sort I'd force if I ever bombed a spelling quiz. Another kid would've been blasé or pissed—my mom didn't say *hi*, just flashed me a half-smile and led me to the edge of the cliff, from the depths of which I might chew up hours obsessing over food choices, calories vs. fat vs. what remained of my taste-budular preferences—but I was glad to be off Rocyo's porch. In the Saab's spazzy heat, headed home to my room, where I'd chill on AOL and try to catch Lisa, I was thankful for my mom. She treated me like an equal, not a child to baby and coddle. Compared with doomsday Mrs. Orlowski-Breit, my mom was a godsend, the one person in my life who made me feel like I could win, even when something weird was definitely eating her. Someday, I would grow up and wear gloves like hers, black and tight, catsuit gloves, gloves that protected my writerly digits, but I wouldn't holler out alternative music like a sped.

"I don't know about dinner," I said during the song's trancey bridge. "Anything? What do you want to talk about?"

But the chorus was back. Anna sang, throwing her hands off the wheel. My questions floated, bubbles unpopped by response. That wasn't unusual. My mom was a poet, with an enjambed temperament, thin beautiful focused, so focused that, once, on Thanksgiving, her break as much as mine, she'd been writing a crown of sonnets and was so absorbed she hadn't heard our fire alarm. That was fifth grade, when I'd slathered a twelve-pound turkey with butter and sage: the alpha and omega of my culinary endeavors, after which I augured that food and I would never be friends.

Her question was pointless, anyhow. I knew what we'd be eating—Lean Cuisines, the vegetarian meals, the same dinner we'd had every night since we were downtown at Uncle Marky's loft for Christmas, when he'd served *ropa vieja*, i.e., old clothes; Fernán, Marky's partner, was *Cubano*: the peas and carrots I'd stabbed out had been delicious. Sometimes, I wished *they* were my parents. When Marky talked, I could tell Fernán actually listened, the way he nodded and made little *mhm*-noises, covering his mouth with one hand. They did cool things, like go to plays at the Steppenwolf, and they were both so effortlessly handsome in their dark jeans and Gucci loafers. Really, the only downside would be the food. Uncle Marky was a pastry chef—the only pastry chef in town who actually *liked* dessert. (*Lil' Bit,* he'd say, which, according to Anna, was what he'd been calling me since I was in utero, *most of us are just too anal to sauté.*) My willpower would have to be airtight to resist the no-big-deal pecan shortbread he kept around. Well. I couldn't remember the last time Anna had cooked: apples, lemons, and a Brita pitcher were the contents of our fridge; our freezer had ice cube trays and

glossy white boxes covered with hi-def photos of oxymo-
ronic meals like low-fat fettuccini Alfredo.

In the passenger seat, I sank into my coat. I sucked in my
stomach. Decoding required subtlety. I tried not to stare at
Anna: Her mouth stretched, blurring at the corners of her
lips. She was hard to look at, the way she was so unashamed
of her face.

The song changed, and Anna stayed quiet, waiting, ready
to pounce on the next lyric. I took it as a sign that I should
be quiet, too. A good silence was friable, ground into particles of disparate awkwardness. Anna and I—whatever she
wanted to talk about—we were too together for that.

We drove through the neighborhoods under Park's pur-
view while Anna merged her voice with Shirley Manson's.
School was the body, and the gated communities and subdivisions were the racemose glands and muscles and tendons, each responsible for its own function, producing its
own type: Soccer players mindlessly heading out in Willow
Glen; Girl Scouts in Lindendale dusting their old collectible
Beverly Hills 90210 Brenda dolls; rich brats chucking croquet mallets come summer in Saddle Brook. What architects
could've overseen such trends? It was amazing, like life was
built according to a grand mastermind design, all these hubs
in our chunk of Illinois, not Chicago, not the exurbs, an
almost-white suburb, where nothing was walkable.

Out the window, the Flagg Creek Motel advertised
bargain nap rates in the same lot as Georges' Flowers:
VALENTINE'S DAY BOUQUETS ORDER NOW ROSES $36.99/
DOZEN. Affair city! Park's new marquee reminded me of the
upcoming three-day weekend: MONDAY, JANUARY 18 ***
MLK ***. Anna sang harder and the heat got hotter and the

Saab smelled like all the grody bands my mom adored— Blind Melon, Guster, Alice in Chains—were rotting in the backseat, nodding off next to my black backpack and her black tote.

"Can we stop at Walgreens?" I asked, leaning forward in my seat. My question abutted our neighborhood—sidewalks, river birches, cotton candy mirror balls, cedar swing sets a Frisbee's arc from granite patios: that's what shaped Lisa and me.

The Saab veered onto the shoulder and the music abruptly stopped. I braced myself, pressing my boots against the salt-crunchy floor mats. Anna's prettiness diminished without music: her bloodshot eyes wore shadowy bibs, and she looked staggered, as though driving two minutes to the drugstore were scaling the skyscrapers in Kuala Lumpur that were *supposedly* taller than the Sears Tower. We were stalled, inches from a ha-ha that bricked off the cemetery touching St. Catherine of Siena Church, where once I'd attended Mass with Lisa's family.

"Woah—okay." I watched cars whiz past us. A blue Maserati I recognized laid on the horn. "Um . . . we can just go up to the next light."

"What do you need at the store, babe? It's been a day, arduous, catastrophic. A gas leak in my office, traffic, I've been hungry since my run. You know I hate to be steering our ship by the stomach's prow but I'm just . . . I'm ready to relax."

I never knew with Anna: maybe she'd fasted or anticipated this meal like a date with Robert Downey Jr. I felt guilty for bothering her, even if I didn't want to postpone copying *Real Talk* pics.

"We have Band-Aids and Neosporin, you know," Anna added. Through the lenses of her sunglasses, I saw her squint at me.

"Band-Aids? What are you smoking, crackhead?"

"Elliot. Really? Why talk like that."

"Sorry. Rocyo was tellin' me about this movie *Friday*. But actually, don't worry about it. I can go this weekend. Really. It's just a thing. For Bio. What Rocyo and I were doing. We're making a diagram of a tree, like, showing the parts. Hey, this is cool: did you know the trunk is called the *bole*? Like, b-o-l-e. Not um . . . like soup bowl. Isn't that word weird? I thought of you."

"It's always something, isn't it, El?"

Anna eased the car onto the road, her neck drooping. She patted my shoulder. She'd been doing this my whole life: we didn't hug or kiss, but I depended on her touch, gentle, like I was an heirloom being passed around during show and tell. Lisa was jealous of my low-key mom, and though it hurt the scratches on my wrist to stretch that way, I squeezed my mom's gloved hand. Beneath our tires, snow gristle crunched. A grimy, gray-brown film of wiper fluid and ice shadows painted the windshield.

..

"What do you want to eat?" I asked my mom, after I'd stomped upstairs. I'd unpacked my backpack, arranged my books and Trapper on my desk, a dark cherry antique with two bottom drawers and a narrow top shelf and a locking cabinet (minus the key) that my dad bought me in Dresden. I'd tried to start a *Real Talk* column based on my meeting with Rocyo, titled, tentatively, "Don't Fake It."

I was meeting with a new client one winter day when she offered me a snack. "These are healthy," she said. "Fat-free cookies." I declined—but this poor girl proceeded to eat—in front of me, her diet coach—eight vanilla sandwich cookies.

"Do you always eat this many?" I asked.

"I mean, what's the big deal?" she said. "No fat."

The reason this poor girl needed to eat a downright obscene number of cookies is because they're FAKE. None of us want to be posers in life. I mean, seriously: would you still want a pair of underwear that said 'Calvin Klein' if it was a knockoff? No.

But my brain hurt. I didn't know where to go with the article. I signed onto AOL, and fruitlessly scrolled the chat list for Lisa and Marissa Turner, while being bombarded with messages:

RoHo1984: waz better, chicken or beef

RoHo1984: pasta or rice

RoHo1984: to be fat or retarded hahahaahahha

ElleGirl80: depends on the chicken . . . . white > dark, lean beef > drumsticks . . . . rice is better no question more filling, get brown rice if you can or wild, lots of fiber . . . . and that's way offensive, take that back.

RoHo1984: wat you eat for dinner

ElleGirl80: good question . . . .

"Mom," I said, standing over her on the couch. "Anna. Hey! You said you were hungry. And you wanted to talk. C'mon. Let me help. You're supremely zapped."

The centerpiece in our living room was a Danish three-seater, donkey gray. My mom lay on her stomach, rubbing one hand over the suede, changing the saturation of the color with every stroke. On the coffee table there was a twig-stemmed glass filled so to the brim the red wine made a meniscus. On TV, in tonight's *Seinfeld* rerun, George stood next to a garbage can. A chocolate éclair practically leapt out of the trash, its bite mark smiling up at him.

"You wouldn't do that, would you, El?" Anna said, to me and the upholstery.

I sat by her feet: her heels white and rough, her toes milky blue like mine. That hue, on adults, turned my stomach. It was as though, in her oldness, my mom had gangrene.

"Eat an éclair? As if, what do *you* think?" I said, playfully. I didn't assume anything about her Band-Aid comment because Anna was straight with me: she accepted I wasn't an eater.

When my dad first started traveling for business, one night he was gone she'd told me how his opinion of my body was . . . different. We were splitting a bag of Caesar salad (minus garlic croutons and dressing packet—those sat in the fridge until my dad, a democratic snacker, returned). Anna said, *A father always sees his daughter—and I don't mean this perversely—as a miniature of his wife. You're a girl and woman, a woman who has the potential to be me. Not a terrific fate. But there are worse. Your father thinks you have a problem. He's suggested doctors, or, what he fed you as a toddler: oatmeal and peanut butter.* "Bulk her up," *he still says.* "She won't grow." *Of course, El, it's clear to me—and, I gather, to you—there are more nuanced ways to grow. One might grow by subtraction. A sculptor begins with her or his block of marble and chisels to find shape. This is true of poetry, too. All writing, at that.*

"Would *you* do that?" I said, using a light tone. "Take food out of the garbage—not eat an éclair."

Anna considered, blinking, her eyes staying closed longer than open, like the lids were stuck, flypaper or death mask. She looked stoned.

"I would do both."

I laughed. Anna wouldn't even share a straw.

"Yeah right. I bet Dad would, though. Did you hear from him today?"

"Mhmm."

"Mhmm yes or mhmm no?"

"The latter. Your father's busy-busy."

I hugged my hands around my mom's icicle toes. Pink peppermint lotion—I remembered my dad dribbling that into his palms, massaging my mom's feet as she sat on the pale-green tub in their bathroom, a few years ago, when she was all blisters from starting to run. Dusty pink roses, left-overs from Charlie Trotter's, calf-hair BB pumps: he was so romantic when he was here.

"You should try to find a time," I said. "He misses you. Don't *you* miss him terribly?"

My mom laughed. "Are you reading Edith Wharton, miss?"

"What? Who's that?"

"Oh, miss him terribly, I don't know. She was a writer. A novelist in the early twentieth-century. Beyond well-to-do family out east. She'd draft manuscripts by hand, from bed, and toss off the pages as she finished them. For her amanuensis."

"Amanue—"

"Typist, secretary, scribe. Skilled slave? Your call."

"That's so spoiled."

Anna laughed and nodded. "Your spoiled is my idea of *the* life."

I hopped off the couch. "Well, *this* is the life! Your loving daughter prepares your meal, madam! What would you like?"

Anna sucked air through her teeth, like she was inhaling a cigarette. If I asked her if she smoked, she'd probably be insulted. *As if,* she'd say, like a girl, my age.

"Ah. Ugh. Um. Something . . . red?"

..

My mom and I were sewn together, a black double stitch in the hem of life, one big gnarly knot without a man, so I copied her, minus the wine. I forked the cellophane on two black trays of cheese cannelloni, pasta tubes the size of toilet paper rolls, shoaled with marinara, furred with ice and specks that could've been herbs or gnats.

I set them inside the microwave to spin, side-by-side, on the turntable. X-rays didn't frighten me: In front of the dark glass, I tabulated my day. Two Listerine strips, 13/16 of an apple, one unpeeled carrot, and the Lean Cuisine, 240 calories: 350 calories, rounding up. Under five hundred—that was par.

If my dad knew the computations I did, he'd have to be proud, despite my *flaca*. I missed him. I missed him so much I would've eaten garbage to make him laugh, I would've gobbled an éclair (okay, spitting in a napkin) to prove I remembered family-vacationing in France, before I was *Elliot Le Petit*. No, his travels hadn't prevented him from centering an MJ poster on my closet door or teaching me to program the

VCR to record the Bull's sixth game in Phoenix, when I was too drowsy, chicken pox-y to catch John Paxson clinch the three-peat, but his absence reminded me that daily presence, consistency, showing up, was important.

With a minute left on the timer, I did curtsey lunges, one leg a radius out behind me, like an ice skater. My knees shook, and I held onto the counter for balance.

Now my dad was probably asleep, a big, red-headed yeti of a man, in Venice. I never remembered time differences. He was a dad: I didn't understand what he did. My classmates' fathers had one-word jobs, careers landed in the Game of Life. Accountant. Lawyer. Chef. Even Lisa's shady Pops: WBEZ reporter, political beat. My dad analyzed Global Markets and Supplies; he was a mechanical engineer who collected passport stamps the way Ethan Suva collected bruises he got from moshing at the Fireside Bowl.

Monday, when we last talked, my dad told me what he ate and how Beachy Head in England, one of the most famous places to commit suicide, had crumbled tons of chalk cliff into the sea. A bad season crashing with waves and rainstorms had been one cause, decades of global warming another. *That's an issue for your lifetime, Smelliot. Your generation. Politicians say verdict's out—and then? It's like, all right: man makes ruin.*

The microwave *beep-beep-beeped*. Beachy Head, schnitzel: my dad's world contained so much more than words. I'd imagined flinging myself off Beachy Head when he described it. The world seemed so much more immediate, so much more consequential than literature. Last quarter, when we'd read "The Necklace," I'd felt nothing. Sometimes, I wondered if I was even meant to write *Real Talk* or if all I was truly good at was devising beautiful ways to die. Words were just Lean Cuisines, approximations of rocks and dumplings.

I carried a tray with forks and knives and batik napkins into the living room. Our house felt empty, even with my dad home. Of the five bedrooms (my father had confided: he'd wanted a *real* family), most days only two heard gasps and laughter, the yawns of our wants. In his continentalism, my mom and I were cloistered, informal, clairvoyant. How else to explain her question?

"Do you want to stay home from school tomorrow?"

Anna was still supine on the couch. I set the trays on the coffee table and sat on the floor and peeled off the soggy cellophane from my meal. Cannelloni smelled like Park's caf, pizza day. With my fork, I loosened a curl of part-skim mozzarella.

"Is that what you wanted to talk about?"

I set the cheese on my tongue and waited: how long could I hold the first bite in the first stage of digestion?

"We have PE testing tomorrow," I said, swallowing. "But I hate that . . . I'd skip. Are you going to the spa?"

It was a hope, far-out but not impossible. Usually Saturdays were spa days: we'd bunny downtown in velvet leggings, get our hair done, meet Marky and Fernán for brunch. Even though he was a pastry chef at a Gold Coast five-star (that served what my dad called "frou-frou" food) who probably should've been fed up with restaurants, my uncle always made eating special: he'd take us to Sunny Side Out, the 312 queer intelligentsia's most exclusive club. His loft in an old Nabisco plant, his mauve macaron tattoos, his black-framed glasses, his sugar plum dimples—Marky was cool, not an artist but—when we'd meet him and Fernán on St. Clair, take an elevator to a dining room beaming with sunlight and Lucite, his ditzy voice outdazzled the others. He sounded like a valley girl, but Anna's kin? Duh, he was a brainiac—Quill and Dagger before moving to Chicago to work pastry and sometimes-teach Confectionary Arts. That's where he'd met Fernán—Ben Stiller's clone but buffer, brown, one of ten adults who wanted to learn from my uncle how to weave chocolate baskets and spin sugar swans.

"Oh, no," Anna said. "No. God, I wish. My roots are Cruella. No, I've got one of those awful professional development days. All G.D. day. Diversity training, mental health and comp, retirement over lunch, lord, if that won't be sad. Speaking of pastries, El, do you know how pitiful a frozen food-service croissant tastes? Provincial liparoid death. And, oh joy, the assessment task force on at-risk youth. Can you see your mother there?"

I couldn't imagine "Anna in classroom." I couldn't see her as anything but ornament or oracle.

"That sounds gross. Like, that last assembly, did I tell you about that? Where the Vietnam vet came and talked about, like, the dangers of drinking, and he brought in a paper bag and got in trouble because there was, like, for real an empty beer can inside. The security guards came and interrupted the speech, and he was all, hey man, hey what gives, and everyone in the audience was freaking out . . . I mean, in a tizzy because no one had the brains to evacuate us. But still, who even likes all-school assemblies? I don't get it. If you're not into, and I'm not into . . ." Her eyes were closing. "Hey, Anna." I snapped in her face. "Hey! Sit up. Up! Don't you want to eat?"

She blinked. For a second it looked like she didn't recognize me. "Elliot, don't rush me! Dinner yourself. I mean—fuck."

"Do you want more wine?" I said. "I was going to get some water, I can get you wine or a tissue. Mom, it's all right. The day won't be so bad. You always joke about them afterwards. You'll get through it. Why don't you write . . . what's it called . . . a found poem? Is that where you take stuff people say and make a poem out of that? You could start with, like, I don't know, what you said: 'at-risk croissants.' That's funny."

"Just worry about yourself!"

She let out a breathy cough. A hand steepled her eyes. Then she started to sob.

I swallowed, lost in our living room: the black chain mail curtain hiding the fireplace like a dungeon wench's tunic, the gaps between the floorboards cruddy with mysterious hairs and fuzzes and bugs. My mom's tears annoyed me. The burning behind my own eyes made the food vomitrocious. I swallowed some cheese: it tasted like phlegm.

"I'm trying to cheer you up." It sounded lame, a line I'd lifted from an old, cheesy movie like *Pollyanna*. Today I'd made two people cry.

"Well, you can't, El," she said. She flicked a finger against the cellophane on her meal. "You don't know everything, so don't make light of my situation. It's not flattering to patronize your mother. Avoidance will come back to haunt you. Enough. If you're dabbling in self-mutilation, take a day and think about it."

The ground shifted beneath me. "What?"

"Take a day," my mom said. There wasn't room for disagreement. "That's all I'm asking. If you're not going to let me in on your oh-so-shocking secret, can you think about it yourself? Figure out what statement you want to make before your gym teacher leaves me 'I'm-calling-DCFS' messages. Are we clear?"

"Are you punishing me for something you don't even know?"

"Elliot. Just take a day to collect yourself."

"What are you even talking about?"

She didn't respond.

"Fine." My stomach crunched itself. One measly piece of cheese. I felt fat. And even though Lisa had told me that her therapist told her that "fat isn't a feeling," I knew that was b.s. I felt like a dirty, sweaty, bristly hog. The *Seinfeld* credits played, burping. "Sure, I'll stay home. That's a great way to . . . to solve this non-problem."

Blackness spun as I stood. My mom's eyes were closed—I couldn't remember her ever acting so immature, and the behavior was contagious. Two could be tired: I was tired of this day, which had made me desperate and grabby. I wanted to sleep, wake up in tomorrow. There was so much *Real Talk*. Tomorrow, I'd be productive. I'd walk to Lisa's—she hadn't ever missed only *one* day of school for a cold (her sicknesses came in waves) and we'd talk, at her house, in her room, since no one ever wanted to come up to mine.

"Good night, Anna," I said. "Enjoy your dinner."

I threw my napkin over her food. Underneath the steamy plastic, the cheese was congealed.

FRIDAY

1 ·· ANNA

To wake thick-headed at four in the morning without stirring princess-and-the-pea from Xanadu, do not stumble to the kitchen, where gray lumps of snow tumor the windowsill, moonlight inks hulking appliance and pendulum sauté pan shadows across the floorboards; where the coffee pot timer ticks the seconds until 5:13, thirty minutes before you should leave for yoga; where the oven frowns in disuse, its racks stacked with cookie sheets, a pizza stone birthmarked in char. Leave your body on the couch. Let Rot or Carlos, Charles, whoever, break, enter, demoralize your organs; let him tongue out your tar. Goodbye, Anna, offed by wooziness, can't-find-your-ass drunk.

Your eyes climb out of sleep, acclimating to lightlessness. Russet outline of last log in fire. Carousel of ash-tipped iron tongs and pokers on jade tile before mantle. Wine glass on coffee table: when did you slug the dregs? You blinked, saw *Family Matters*, hated fat people, returned to sleep, heavy, dreadful, apt.

You dreamt about your mother.

Uppy: that's what Elliot used to say. Up, up, you tell yourself, though sitting is a ruse. The living room whips, a percussion between your temples. The yeast of wine is on your tongue. Your spine aligns and your head, reluctantly, steadies

on your neck. El must have turned off the TV. Did you see
her, hear her pad downstairs in red sateen pajamas, reedy
as a mantis underneath, as flyweight as *your* mother, cold-
cream cheeks, set jet curls, amber brooches, apricot blush,
Gallic nose, wiped-up mouth—but lined like a Latina in the
casket (assessment courtesy of your El Salvadorian nanny,
Estelle)—you were fourteen, in a black jumper, a poplin
Peter Pan blouse—a color called *noir*—and you felt French
at the funeral, your mother's skin cold as marble.

Marble-heavy, a bag full of God.

Plath again? Christ.

Second-person, what a gag.

You can't escape myself.

..

On the coffee table, a napkin hides one tray of cannelloni;
on another meal, the cellophane is still attached to the plastic container: that must be mine.

Quaaaack—it's so fucking loud when I pull it off.

I hook a pinky in the tray, trace the perimeter of the inte-
rior, suck sauce from my finger. For being the body's largest
organ, skin tastes an awful lot like a corner. The cold marinara is acidic and salty, sharp with garlic powder. It could use
black pepper. A lot of black pepper. Eating pizza at Salerno's
with Rolf, we'd go through a dozen pepper packets, raining gray-brown onto *quattro formaggi* pie on a dinged-up
tin. That was twenty years ago, when everything was tin:
the serving spade (tin), the paper plates (equivalent of tin),
the Poppin' Fresh French Silk (in tin) at Rolf's mom's, meet-
the-family dinner (tin conversations), University of Chicago
tin; first gasp of grad school and a deadly man, steady ready

tin, booking it to seminar, Old Milwaukee's tinny hops in my mouth; backseat of his Cobra, ashtrays and tin cigarette holders shaped like caterpillars, tin yelps when he ate me out from behind, fucking, then, tin confines of cervix; clamped-down red-checkered tablecloths, pizza sauce stains like phantoms in period-panties; napkin dispensers, two tin modes: slice your fingers or release a stack the thickness of *Heart of Darkness*.

Twenty years ago, twenty tins.

Now everything is frozen or plastic. I squeeze off a hunk of pasta. The noodle is gummy, peeled-feeling, like a skinned grape. The cheese tastes like cottage cheese with Mrs. Dash. I'm still drunk—otherwise, what excuses this feculence?

I pinch my next mouthful before I swallow the first. Regret, the shaky mule I rode after drinking in college, when I let anyone bed me so long as he'd listen when I told him what bimbettes the editors of the lit mag were, hay-haired Todd Rundgren groupies, chubby cheeks, wrists sprayed with Charlie: I expected motherhood to pasture that beast. Not like I saw myself as Mrs. Brady, mending Jan's why-aren't-I-Marcia blues, but I believed fewer occasions would present themselves for me to foul up.

False.

I gulp a hunk of cannelloni. Yes, I regret speaking harshly, rashly, grossly to Elliot last night. I regret that I did not calmly broach the subject of her self-harm. I regret that I trusted the sort of woman who becomes a middle school physical education teacher. I regret, I realize, much of life—and I regret that regret, a fruitless worry, a recursive loop, like getting the TV stuck on PBS, forever airing the pledge drive.

I regret fourteen years ago. Drugs ragged my head with turpentine, and Heathcliff, Hester Prynne, and Holden Caulfield, a ragtag cavalcade, marched through me, muddled me under the nuzzled-soft lavender blanket in the Mother Baby Unit at Rush. Elliot was in the nursery, her footprint stamped. I drifted through pain pills and IV drips, asking anyone who'd listen: *have I had her yet?* And then home, chafing achy nipples, sandbag breasts, one postnatal morning. Already I was bored of rocking. And Rolf told me about his mother—I'd *become* his mother when the Percocet torched my brain: "You sounded like her, dying," he said. "It was losing her all over."

My eyes don't focus on the living room. This is one of those times minutes fizzle and you realize you're not seeing. Mindless eating—or drunk-girl resuscitation. I lift the napkin off the second Lean Cuisine and repeat: sauce noodles fingers.

"Hello, fork, you silver snake," I say. My voice sounds like a spent wish.

The house's quiet chides me. I sniff, giggle, and continue clawing my food.

I regret five years ago, though, then, I was better than this (crudités, Foreman Grill chicken breasts, Diet Rite, I never barfed). I almost acted on my impulses—yes, I was depressed, but at least I was driven, five years ago: *Dear Rolf and Elliot, I have never expected myself to be writing a note, and I reflect on the virtues of last words over . . . this. The written husk. Last words are so personal. I'm thinking Oscar Wilde—"This wallpaper and I are fighting to the death. Either it goes or I do." For all the voice in an epistolary, there's no voice in a note. The windows in my office open, you might not know. Looking out through glass, one follows shapes and forms. But, pane removed and there's a girl, her royal blue backpack, her auburn hair parted left of center, her ivory sweatshirt hitting her hips, the glint of sterling silver hoops as she finds her neck and scratches a long itch; this is the second floor, and I doubt it's high enough. But* Moby-Dick *is on my desk, and I leave you my mantra:* "I am in earnest and I will try."

Well, I hadn't tried. Not really. I fit my fingers, my elbow, my shoulder out the window that January afternoon, almost five years ago from today. You'd think I'd remember, would've jotted it in a planner or hidden it on the back of a take-out fortune in the Rolodex: *January X—suicide attempt.* But I didn't.

Memories jigsaw: My back-to-normal breasts, flat empty chest, wedging my torso out the window, angling sideways, the way I did at libraries, when I needed to share an aisle. I was halfway out when I realized there wasn't a ledge: I'd have to dive, headfirst.

Fear had pinched my trachea. I'd turned my face. I plunged my fingers in the snow capping the windowsill's bricks and that's when I felt something material, warm. Air stung the bridge of my nose. I hated the sky, the building, my timidity, life. I dug at the snow, baring the bricks, clawing the ice until I'd bled off my nails and found the struts and waterlogged feathers of a crushed black wing.

Around the lips of Italianate Lean Cuisines, sauce crusts the tray; I scrape that with my teeth. I savor the fierce bites, like a Butter Blasted bag. Intensity, flavor, maximal taste: Nacho Cheesier crap marketed to moms.

Better nothing for Elliot than that.

My stomach protrudes against yesterday's sweater, baring its vacuity: it wants more of this breakfast. My stomach says, what do you mean you ate? Gobble up, cunt.

And I say: Body, enough. Food is a ghost. Time to get on with this.

I rise. Activity routes me out of the hangover. The floorboards creak as I walk to the stairs. My knee joint cracks: which? I can't tell left from right right now. One hurts.

"Owwww," I whimper. My head or my knee or my neck, which I kinked sleeping on the couch, or my back pocket, stinging with Rot's coke—what hurts? Want hurts, I could scream, until an object responds: the TV zings, the sun explodes, Elliot screams, *Mom, what's wrong?*

Yes, Mom. What's wrong? taunts the cold floor under my cold feet.

Here. I want Rot to break the screen door, overturn the coffee table, snag my arm, drawl: *What's wrong, bay-beeee?*

The question shackles my ankles, roots in my pelvis, firecrackers my shoulders. Brain stem: that's where my hope gets stuck, a failed rocket.

Winter withholds Friday's sunrise. I extend my hands, searching for the walnut railing, like Audrey Hepburn in *Wait Until Dark*. I saw that with my mother, at the movie palace on Lake. One by one, the theater's lights went out. The faster I inhaled Junior Mints, the surer I was that I was dying—and dying alone. I was eight years old.

What was Marky then? A teardrop, a kumquat, a zygote? Had my father screwed him into her? My mother baked him birthday cakes until he was five, until his first day at Edison, when she sprinkled her Cicero Rye with Ajax, and Stell found her doornail dead, blood-veined vomit on the *petit déjeuner* Color-Flyte and her daffodil charmeuse dressing gown.

Here's the funeral: me crying into the collar of my black crepe dress, Marky gumming a chocolate Tootsie Pop, flattening the wrapper against the pew in St. Pious, trying to find the shooting star.

I don't miss my mother as I climb upstairs. The shadowy portrait of the Egleston family, a trio of dark bodies, the parents themselves orphans. No, it's not my mother, but her myth I miss, who she could've been—nurturing, patient, alive. I must be better, kinder, more assured than her, more sensible than my father who tasked me with packing Marky's bologna and pears. I want to maintain Anna, not push away El.

Suddenly, it's an emergency. I must see my daughter. A scene from a children's movie El watched comes to me: a Victorian girl with sausage curls and a sad face, plump figure pinafored and white stockinged, levitates above her bed, on which an olive-skinned goblin tramples, his every jump lofting her higher. The girl neither screams nor stirs, poor thing. She rises higher and higher until the tip of her nose grazes the pale blue ceiling and then she dissolves. A cut. She has slipped through the roof and is lofted on the soughing wind, a speck above the craggy English countryside, the grass the same green as the goblin. Eighties movie: his face appears, superimposed over the landscape: silos, lambs, brook, rocks, silt-sky, shape of girl.

My heart bumps. I turn the doorknob and walk into Elliot's room.

Light through black pantyhose dims Elliot's world, and there I am: the windows reflect me—my daughter forgot to pull the shades. Even though she's tucked in, sleeping on her stomach, one arm crooked behind her head, her brown hair a rat's nest, her bed seems fixed. Elliot's so thin her pulse doesn't rumple the covers.

She snores: this breaks my heart.

I survey, stepping softly. Snooping rarely woos me; I don't frequent my daughter's boudoir—in fact, I can't recall the last time I was here without El. *Listen to this*, she'll say, and read dialogue from a play she's writing. Then I lean on some wall while she paces, notebook in one hand while the other darts, grabbily conducting words. She gets so excited to share herself; she keeps suggesting we swap, that I show her new poems. *Sometime, summer*, I say, *if we go on vacation*. I'm thankful that, at her age, she forgets anything not immediately relevant to her own life.

The truth is I haven't written a poem in two years, since New York.

See El's effects: a down comforter stuffed inside a white duvet. One pillow for her head, the other between her knees. A cherry dresser, hip-height, with brass drawer pulls; a cheval mirror in the opposite corner. *Untitled (Painting)* by Mark Rothko: she bought the poster from the Art Institute gift shop in third grade with report-card money. A smoldering orange rectangle hemmed by a yellow stripe: the walls' only decoration, though I'd wager Michael Jordan still tracks El's height, in the closet.

My daughter impresses me: Her order. Her quiet, persistent aesthetic—tidy furies like Rothko. Her hygiene: no clothes on the floor or hairball tumbleweeds. The vibe is light, transitory, Heaven's Gate, except for the desk.

That desk: what an ordeal.

Unlike my office, my daughter's workspace is neat. Chaste, on first glance. I shuffle to the desk. Chill and menacing as a safe, there is her computer, stenciled rainbow rhombuses crossing the screen.

I pull the copper chime and on goes the moon shell lamp.

She might stir. If that happens, I'll say, *sorry, about to leave, yoga, have a good day, stay home or go to school, either. About last night, I'm sorry. El. I love you.*

But, save for snore-rattles, she is serene beneath the eiderdown.

On her desk is a Trapper and a book. *The Diary of Anne Frank.* An index card salutes. I turn to Elliot's page and read:

"Once when I was spending the night at Jacque's, I could no longer restrain my curiosity about her body, which she'd always hidden from me and which I'd never seen. I asked her whether, as proof of our friendship, we could touch each other's breasts. Jacque refused. I also had a terrible desire to kiss her, which I did."

Before winter break, Park's Language Arts faculty circulated a letter to parents, warning that Anne Frank's diary contained "mature passages"; that "past classes recoiled"; that sensitive students could "opt out." The cautions twisted my stomach.

Comfortable, familiar, paperback, faintly warm: I imagine the worst of Elliot's classmates, snickering over a dead girl, the word "breast."

My daughter has said nothing about the book.

(Of course, in fifth grade, I took her to see *Kids*.)

Her Trapper is closed, not zipped shut. My daughter worked before bed, I think. The image—her costume-bead spine hunched over her work; her chapped lips parted in concentration; her eyes narrowed, crumbs of sleep crusting the crooks—touches me.

I'm healthily curious, I tell myself. Just a peek, like Miss P.E. suggested. I open the binder, where a pencil holds place.

El's cramped cursive slopes up. At first, the writing seems to be stage directions, a scene's start. "Be Your Own *Paramour.*"

Good word, I think. I keep reading:

Maybe you're expecting flowers from your crush. A fuzzy red box of truffles and bonbons. Maybe you've got plans to arrive early for At First Sight so you can get your freak on pre-previews. (Kissing burns 300 cal/hr!) But whether you've got a date or not, be your own sweetheart by showing your bod some extra l<3ve.

Standing abs are a cinch in the shower: you'll feel xxxxxxtra-bendy with the steam! Try 2 sets of 20: side bends and torso twists. In bed, kick those pillows aside! Lie flat, being sure to engage your abs. (This supports your back!) Then, scissor your legs, keeping them a couple inches above the mattress: I do sets of 25, until I hit 100!

But nothing's more important than eating lovely lunches. Bonus points if you score red fruit (à la raspberries) and a red veggie (bell peppers!) in your midday munch. Be sweet to yourself; go for pretty noshes. You and your valentine will thank you!

I laugh. If nothing else, I've taught my daughter to pack a lunch. I wonder if Park is starting a humor magazine, something *Lampoon.*

I turn the page and lift my head. Did I hear something? My blood thunders so loud in my ears, Elliot must be faking. I pause, waiting for a hitch in her breathing. A decrescendo to her snore. But there's just my heart harrumphing, my guilty reflection, soap-scum skin in a dark window. I read.

"Dear Lisa, everything has been weird since before Christmas, I don't know what more I can do" is unconvincingly crossed out. Below, in block letters, round letters, crosshatched all-caps, lowercase polka dots, in sweeping cursive and analog print is one word, a hundred fonts: Lisa.

..

My own bedroom is a sty. Tidying doesn't entice me. Why? I clean before Rolf returns, when we share the sleigh bed, our backs and feet reacquainted. I pull off my sweater and unclasp my bra. My eyes shut and I force them open. I am weaker than I thought; I need to get out of the house.

I pull on a singlet for yoga. I smell my sweat, potted, stewed.

I'll shower at the studio.

I know what to do with bad news. Analgesia is a tool. I can turn a blind eye to Elliot's problems: probably anorexia, definitely comorbid dysthymia. I haven't had her admitted. I haven't suggested meds. But I read *Prozac Nation*.

Is a girl crush so awful? Elliot is obsessed with Lisa. Can I worry over that when I'm obsessed with Rot? What *is* a day without obsession? *Jane Eyre*: "I have little left in myself—I must have you." And the *Cosmo* diet? I tell myself it's prewriting for a play or parody, one component of a worthless project assigned by her Health teacher.

I take off my work pants from Thursday, pull on my black yoga Spandex, pack a gym bag with a dress and pumps. My mind is on-task and resuming proper functioning when I remember the coke.

My nails are not long enough for a bump. What I have is a necklace, an ugly thing that predates Reagan's first term.

There, in the jewelry box on my dresser. A strip of buffalo suede and a gold, tubular bead, like a Kraft Macaroni noodle.

I've used that before. I use that now. I tap out the powder onto my vanity. I draw out my sniff, let my eyes flutter, exaggerated, like someone's watching. I love watching: do I constitute someone? When I'm fucking, I love finding the cock as it enters me, seeing me in action.

The burn is pleasant. It restarts my heart. My sternum sweats.

Coke, I'm not bringing it back to campus. If Rot finds me, we'll sober-talk. I open the closet, scoot aside a fleet of garment bags. There's my old sewing box: I've had it since my mother died, when I inherited it from her. Hideous, 1950s shade of brown. I hide the baggie under a stack of denim patches, beneath a plastic tray, beside a tomato-shaped pin cushion. I used to be a girl who darned stockings and hemmed men's pants.

I grab my yoga mat. Stop in the kitchen to write El. Precipitation wasn't in the forecast, but snow has started falling, lightly, glitzily, like the bright spots that arrive behind your eyes when they've been squeezed shut in terror.

Wake up and smell the coffee, I almost write. What a note. I slap my hand.

Now I wouldn't dream of mending. I spend wantonly. I ignore signs. I relish the slow drip that mounts in the back of my throat.

2 ·· ELLIOT

I WAS BRAIDING THE BABY hairs of 1999, the Friday before Martin Luther King Day, home alone, considering how I'd make a better adult than Anna. Did I spend the morning bed-hopping and red-cup-clutching with *The Real World*? Did I watch a single pop-up video on VH1 or one of the Top 20 countdowns Lisa had given me an appetite for, choke-sobbing to "Candle in the Wind," "I Don't Want To Miss a Thing," "My Heart Will Go On," or any of the sad anthems from 1998, another year that had proven the decade cursed, steeped in celebrity death and misfortune: Christopher Reeves and Nancy Kerrigan and Kerri Strugg— utter tragedies—Princess Diana and *Titanic*, Tupac, Biggie, Kurt Cobain, John Candy, Phil Hartman, Audrey Hepburn, Jackie Kennedy, Krissy Taylor. Did I dog-ear the dELiA*s catalog, long for skater skirts as I blasted B96, cackling at Eddie and JoBo's pranks, breakfasting on Toaster Strudels, nay, worse, mainlining the foil packet of gluey cream cheese icing, squiggling it on my tongue like the semen I'd seen in porn? No! I slept in and did my Spanish so I'd have a clear scholastic conscious before I avocado'd.

I'd dreamt the stupidest dream: Jim Carrey, in his clothes from *The Truman Show*, smooched me. Antic clownish puckers on both cheeks, the way the owners at the salon kissed me and my mom. Jim Carrey didn't peck once and say *hola*. He pivoted at the waist and kept kissing, left cheek, right, again, again, and the more he kissed, the more of me I wanted him to kiss, my face, my hair, my neck, my throat. I wanted him to kiss my ribs. My hipbones. I woke squirmy and inspired: an orgasm would wow Lisa.

I'd come.

Go to the Breit's.

Where she couldn't hang up on my face.

My thoughts flitted in the kitchen, where I perched on a stool at the island. I wore glam red PJs and felt luxurious, a hand cushioning my kneecaps, sipping green tea in a gasp of snow-bleached sunlight. The snow had been falling all morning. Anna's note—"Home by four. Will call if reach boiling point w/croissants. Sorry about last night"—implied she wanted to move on, forget the empty wine bottle and iced tea spoon in the kitchen sink, but I was whatever. Mom, Marissa: insolence bored me. *Real Talk* didn't need a dumpy body and my life didn't bad vibes. I'd find someone else.

I flapped my Spanish book, *Bienvenidos!*, open to the tense charts. I began fill-in-the-blanking a worksheet on the difference between *ser* and *estar*, irregular verbs of being. The pages smelled like chicken nuggets. Below the conjugations was a random picture: two girls in splatter-painted sweatshirts tossed their crimped hair in a convivial exchange over *refrescos*. I studied their faces; were they actually fat, was the angle bad, or what? Afternoon light blushed their skin Bubblicious pink, and whoever'd used the book before me had blackened their eyes so they looked like UFOs. Despite being socket-heavy, though, their expressions were too nice to be for real: Lisa and I'd never looked like that. I wondered if the photographer had asked them to kiss, more tongue, yes, take off their terry tops and caress each other's breasts once the textbook portion of the photo shoot had wrapped, if there was a second, sordid aspect to every job. I wished teachers at Park would make kids have secret orgies so I could be forced to do . . . stuff.

This was the sort of thing I thought now that I'd seen *Terrible Twos.*

In other news, my worksheet was cinchy:

1. *Los niños* _____ *estudianties.*
2. *Sammy Sosa* _____ *guapo.*
3. *La chica estúpida dice: el padre* _____ *embarazado.*

"*Ser* describes a permanent condition or feature, like height—unless you're Tom Cruise," Señora Lurke had told our class in her sheetrock voice. "*Estar* is temporary. Say I have a cold. *Estoy enferma.*"

We were rapt, unmoving, zitty, greasy, everyone except for Denzel Washington, Señora Lurke's screensaver, who was ping-ponging across the computer. *To be or not to be* wasn't just an existential question or a T-shirt slogan. That blew some kids' minds, minds that struggled to remember Benjamin Franklin had never been president.

Por supuesto, Ethan Suva yoinked the silence.

"What if I'm a sick*o*?" he said. I heard my pulse tick, like chalk touching slate. "*Soy enfermo.*"

Suddenly the room's focus seemed to have shifted. I half-expected the red-and-purple maracas Lurke kept under the overhead projector to start shaking in excitement. Ethan's protests—their warped logic, their futility—were beautiful in the damaged way I loved.

Behind her square glasses, Señora Lurke's eyes were suspicious. She shook her wooly hair *no*.

"*Sí*," Ethan insisted, stridently. "*Soy* muy *enfermo. Para* siempre."

..

I piled my schoolwork. The stove clock's green numbers read 11:11 a.m. Make a wish: I asked for an easy orgasm (I'd read they weren't automatic for girls like for boys) and an amenable Lisa, who'd join me on my quest to stay thin forever.

I opened the refrigerator and stood in its uric glow, shivering. I thought about eating: the five bad apples banging around the crisper, spoons of the Edmond Fallot green peppercorn mustard unopened from Marky's Christmas basket two Decembers ago, shakes of Tabasco. But the chasm between eternity and now wasn't bridged by slacking; anorexia and I had to be till-death-do-us-part. Repetition transformed a quirk into a habit, a symptom, dogma: in fifth grade, I'd skipped lunch for 142 days before I could say *soy anorectic*, before I could use my favorite word, *flaca*. Since then, I'd spent more hours ogling food than eating.

Outside, the snow fell in clumps like wads of Play-Doh. I was chilled down to my toes. I wandered upstairs, ready for a hot bath and avocado.

The halls were dark. Lisa's house was better—she had a white TV/VCR in her room, a popcorn-colored loveseat—but she'd been over, a few times. *What's the word*, she'd said, *sterile? Does that mean something?*

I didn't bother switching on the light, especially passing the one portrait. The photo made me gag: me with Anna and Dad. Anyone who saw old-Elliot (fourth grade, obsessed with shower-singing "Circle of Life") and the girl I was today wouldn't call us cousins. In the picture, fat softened my face: I looked less haggard fifty pounds heavier, regular, a bison, unibrowed, rectangular. It wasn't even a good shot of Anna; she wore a crushed velvet bodysuit and a crocheted vest, a style you could call *gypsy frump*. I tried to only see my father's brilliantined mustache, his fisherman crewneck. He didn't look outdated. His clothes were fine.

On another wall, a sheet of sad brown paper hid "Enter Key," a poem by Anna that'd been listed—not published—as an honorable mention in *Best American Poetry* three years ago. My dad had hired a printer who used a letterpress and pulped rose petals into homemade paper; there was a painter who built birch frames. *Juxtaposes your critique of Microsoft as some kind of twentieth-century manipulator—or masturbator!* —*with the artisan's what I was thinking*, my dad had said. My mom had pounded her own nail and hung the poem backwards. *Thanks*, she'd told him, *But I'll play my piano in the closet.*

I lifted the frame off its fastener. The rectangle of wall was pale, like a finger after an old bandage is peeled off. If I was going to avocado, I wanted to read the poem, especially if it was about masturbating. I flipped the frame. But where there'd been a sheet of glass all that remained of

Anna's broadside was the feathery fringe of torn handmade paper.

..

The master bathroom was all sex. Basil and eucalyptus reeds herbed the air from a diffuser that looked like a beaker. I flipped a switch: a swarm of heat lamps buzzed.

A few years ago, after *Interview with a Vampire* came out, my parents had remodeled their bathroom. *I'm thinking austere*, Anna had said. What they got was a drably erotic torture chamber. Slabs of slate for floor. Bare lights, edgy cylinders. Half-boulder towel hangs mounted on velvety gray walls.

The perfect place to avocado.

I'd tried before: in my own bed, through white cotton Jockeys, listening to a cassette tape of Mariah Carey singing "Dreamlover"; once, on the living room couch, a few days after watching *Terrible Twos*, home alone, the Leo *Romeo + Juliet* playing, slipping my hand under the waistband, finding wispy pubes. I'd been too shy to legit finger myself in the same room where Anna indulged in *Seinfeld* and *ER*. I'd never had hot water pelting me in the tub. This orgasm, I knew, would ripple through my body like a crowd at the United Center doing the wave.

In glass apothecary jars on the counter, Anna's soaking salts and bath confetti, pistachio-green and pink crystals, paper-soap cutouts of hearts and stars, were lined up like candy and sprinkles. Bathing burnt calories or at least sweated out bodily impurities. I ran the tub. In the floor-to-ceiling mirror, I saw myself. I pinned on a scowl.

I could never find my pretty parts. At least, not pieces girls would want. I had searched. I was resigned to the fact that I was a rawboned aberration, something for the Mütter Museum I'd visited with my parents in second grade, where I got an anatomy coloring book and saw 139 nineteenth-century skulls, each a calcified treasure chest that had once protected an individual and perverse brain.

I unbuttoned my pajama top, the collar a deep V that revealed my stumpy neck. My eyebrows stood out too—at least they'd been plucked into eyebrows-plural now—shingles over my face, Byronic, parched-dirt brown. My skin was pimpled. My nipples, dime-sized: I knew because Lisa dared me to empty her piggybank on my boobs at our first sleepover, and of course I'd submitted.

I untied the floppy bow at my waist and let my pants drop.

Here's what I liked:

Two ocular moles above my left hipbone.

The coastal margin of my ribcage, showing through my skin like a dark girdle.

My iliac crest, protruding as if I'd swallowed a shoebox.

The goosebumps that stippled my upper arms.

Decent as those details were, they couldn't erase my thighs. From above, my legs were timber for Paul Bunyan and Babe's hoisting mirth. I pinched my butt.

Cold flesh = fat.

I toed the water, hot but not scalding. I dumped in bath confetti. It skimmed on the bath's surface, dissolving as it floated, leaving a trail of oily orange slugs. I stepped in. Heat was shackling my calves when the phone rang.

Whatever: I descended into the water, chin glued to my sternum. I was always cold, and the heat felt itchy, but I liked discomfort, how it made me fidget and ball up my body, so no one could touch me. I dunked my head. In a sec, the phone would cease, and gentle lapping wavelets would accompany my first bliss. I shut my eyes.

"You have reached Anna, Rolf, and Elliot," answering-machine Anna said in her poetry voice, each word cradled with space and enunciation. "Clearly leave a message and a number, and your call will be returned."

The beep always sounded too long to me.

Then I heard my dad.

"Hi Smelly, it's your dad. I'm calling from . . . well, you know where I am. About, oh, six or a little after here. Your mom told me you weren't feeling hot, so I thought I'd check in. I hope you're getting some rest, taking care of yourself, doing the chicken soup and chamomile thing. I'll—"

I jumped out of the tub. Naked I ran into my parent's bedroom, where the phone and answering machine sat on a capillaried marble planter.

"—catch you later. Love you, honey," my dad said as I grabbed the portable.

"Dad? Hello?" I said.

He had already hung up. But I wasn't mad at my dad. Headphones would've avoided this, unplugging the phones. I hadn't prepared and now I'd wrecked my avocado session. I was mad at myself.

..

In the big mirror, through a column of fog, channels of wet shone on my legs. My dime-nipples were bullet-hard. I twisted one: it felt like an Indian burn, not sex.

I turned off the water, sloshing over the tub's brim. Most of the confetti had sunk soggily to the bottom, but a few pieces sailed on the surface like melting Pop Rocks.

Now I understood ruining the mood. Lisa had accused me of this after we watched *Terrible Twos*, when we were half-asleep, playing Truth or Dare. *Put a finger in every one of my holes,* she dared me, and I'd said, *sure.* I knelt down in front of her couch. *Open your mouth,* I said, and I touched her tongue. *Let me see your ear,* I said, and I touched her canal. *Do you pick your nose,* I said, and I poked each of her nares. I'd paused. *How about my butt?* said Lisa. *Junior Carlos wants to put a finger in. How about you, El? Would you? Sure,* I said. Lisa got quiet. *Okay,* she said, and pulled down her flannel pajama pants. *Through your underwear, right?* I asked. *Sure, whatever,* she said. *All right,* I said, *but I'm afraid there's going to be . . . shit. You know.* Then she'd snapped, like whatever spell we were under had been broken. *What the hell is wrong with you, Elliot? You were actually going to do that?! Why are you so sick? Do you have to make everything disgusting?*

I walked to the mirror, pressed my nose to the glass and locked eyes with myself. I licked my fingers. Sexy desirable vixen minxy: I wanted someone to go *hot dang.* I wanted Lisa in awe. I reached my hand like a flipper and rubbed my puny clit. It felt like a sliver of hot dog. Clitoris: the word sounded like a disease. I'd learned it from Anna, who explained during the Mulva episode of *Seinfeld*. Mole-ish George confronting the éclair reentered my mind. I smacked the mirror.

"Dumb cunt." I pinched my nipple again, angrily. This time, it felt better.

I took a deep breath. Work on *Real Talk*, finish a play (I was a scene-girl, perennially stuck), I told myself; drain the tub, try again. Lisa's not going anywhere.

Then, suddenly, I had an idea. Forget Marissa. I'd impress Lisa; I'd remind her what she was missing without all eighty pounds of me in her life. If my clients wanted a picture of us together, they could do the Xeroxing. They could tape their Polaroids next to mine. I'd give them measurements, my dimensions. I'd lay down the gauntlet. Enough dillydally inspiration. Elliot Egleston, they'd see, was the real deal:

"Ser or Estar? A Photo Essay from the Editor."

..

The Polaroid Spectra had a self-timer. I set it and scurried to pose. I never knew what to do with my eyes when I took a picture of myself, so I turned my face. I took one shot close-up, getting the gleam of water on my collar bones, the crosshatch of my clavicle. A mid-distance shot, where my torso's contours—like an obscene hourglass, wide at the shoulders and my favorite iliac crest—would shut up anyone who said I was too narrow. And one with the door open, inside my parent's bedroom, so everything—from my blue toenails to the flaky crown of my scalp—would be in the picture. Full-bodies were my fave: I took one straight-on, another in profile.

The bathwater was scuzzy now. The drain burped. I wrapped myself in my mom's thick white robe. It fit, more snugly than I'd expected it to. I was bigger than I thought or my mom was smaller.

In my parent's room, on the heap of white sheets atop the sleigh bed, I laid out the Polaroids to develop.

My body emerged like a concentration camp snuff film in those squares, going from ghostly gray to Technicolor. I was pleased. My clients' bodies weren't even the same species as mine. Now all I needed were measurements.

My hair fell on my back like a wet rag. Somewhere my mom kept a sewing kit. Back in elementary school, she'd mended my acid-washed Lee's, the denim inner thighs I'd worn away. There were skittles-colored pins, spools of blue and black thread, coffee-colored velum patterns, a gallimaufry of scraps: I could picture her supplies—and her pale pink tape measure.

I needed that.

I opened the closet and paused, admiring Anna's wardrobe. Someday, when I grew up and sat front row on opening night, watching my actors perform, maybe I'd be her. She was too stylish to be a teacher. At Park, adults chose corduroy and tapered chinos, plaid jumpers and billowy-butted jeans. My mom looked like Posh Spice. Through plastic sheaths from the dry cleaner's or garment bags, I saw black, a runway of chic mourning, the sharp collar of an Anne Fontaine blouse, a boiled wool sheath, calf hair belts, spare leather gloves. Black ponte leggings with silver ankle zips, ribbed stirrup pants, pleated skirts with leather buckles. Knits loose enough to waggle a pinky through, turtlenecks chiffoned at the cuffs. Everything smelled woodsy, like the vetiver perfume she sprayed on her throat.

On the floor there was an empty cellular phone box, probably my dad's. In the corner, beneath the hems, the sewing box.

It was ugly. No wonder she kept it so far out of sight. The box was plastic, embossed like a wicker picnic basket, the color of a brownie.

I unclasped its metal hinge. The lid squeaked as it fell backwards. You could tell it was old because things didn't open like this anymore. Now, boxes had plastic clasps; they were color-blocked, like the blue-and-green Kaboodle in my closet, where I kept vials of Chanel No. 5 that the Fields perfume ladies pressed into my hand with a wink.

The inside of the sewing box was compartmentalized like a Lean Cuisine, but everything was chaos. That was Anna. Loose pink string and flathead pins in three separate spots, notions that smelled like skin and must. No tape measure. I lifted out the top tray.

On top of a stack of denim patches, there was a baggie of white powder.

"What the heck?" I said.

Once, while running the mile at the Park District during gym class, Zoe Rozich had found a used, bloody condom on the wooden bridge that straddled the Flagg Creek. Everyone's time was messed up: Who could resist stopping to stare? Even most girls—they pinched their noses and fake gagged. That's how I felt now—fascinated and disgusted— by Anna's drugs.

Heads or tails. Boys or girls. Truth or dare, Lisa. Heroin or coke?

I saw Anna's clothes. Her affection for *Panic in Needle Park*. How, she'd been playing Geggy Tah in the car yesterday, Nirvana and Blind Melon the months before.

Whatever drug this was, I picked it up.

The powder was heavy like when you fit an empty balloon over a faucet and dribbled in water. Fear was pointless. Jerry-curled Officer Angie had awarded me a D.A.R.E.

completion certificate, like everyone else at Park, just for learning that, around adults, I should say no.

Rules were different with girls.

"Oh my god."

When I wrote, I talked out my dialogue. Now, I was too excited to be quiet. My life felt more dramatic than any plot I'd ever invented. It had to be heroin. Coke was so boring. My mom would never do coke. "'K, here's what I do."

I gathered my Polaroids and ran into my room. I shoved everything except the baggie inside my desk drawer. The heroin, I held tight.

I moved the mouse at my computer. "You've got mail," said the invisible man who welcomed me to AOL. There was nothing from Lisa. Only:

RoHo1984: can I tell you the breakfast how bout bacon just bacon ok???????

I shut off the monitor and went downstairs.

"I get dressed. I go to Lisa's. No, yeah, bundle up. It's negative ten. I walk over. Knock, knock, 'oh, Lisa, oh, how are you *dooooing*,' nothing about Junior Carlos. Very smooth. I say, 'hey, you still wanna get high,' like, marijuana or whatever, duh, yes, she'll say, oh my god, Elliot's like down? Chill. And then I'll be like, 'well, wanna supersize that high, chica?' 'You have balls?' 'Loser,' I'll say, 'whatever heroin is.'"

I zipped my puffy black coat. I put up my hood. Coyote fur sealed me in an Elliot bubble. I grabbed my keys from the brass hook, on the side of the closet with my dad's jackets (they smelled like him: cigars, coffee, brown sugar).

Outside, snow surfed on the wind. Even bundled up, I was cold but I felt warm, just picturing Lisa and me, finding veins in each other's arms, tapping the flesh, using old Scrunchies for tourniquets. I skipped the injecting and imagined the aftermath: we'd nod off under the snow leopard fleece blanket, drift to sleep in each other's tresses, Herbal Essences deluging our dreams.

3 ·· LISA

VITALS

"I'M THIRSTY," I SAY TO the nurse hovering at the foot of my bed. Her maroon hair is corrugated with a bad crimp, her expression is pinched in her face's bloat: you know she just works here to torture pretty girls. She's cracked open the door, and EDP's sodium fluorescence spits into my room. Am I dreaming? My head aches, thick and congested, from last night's fried chicken. Leave it to my mom to bring me to hospy in time for dinner.

"Weight and blood pressure. No liquids until, Lisa. You know the drill." She consults her clipboard. "Right?"

The nurse walks to the window and pulls a cord that raises the blinds. The sky is as blue as Easter egg dye and snow falls by the fistful. The nurse's body is a cobbler, lumpy and bubbled, poured into an old-school uniform dress, white and tight, like Jenny McCarthy might wear. Her butt, Junior Carlos would call a *badonk*—ew. I wish he were popping out from the shitty tack-board bureau next to the one stiff-backed wooden chair, reaching a hand under her skirt, mouthing, *Watch this, Lee. Hey: watch*. I wonder if this vision is a sign that he's read my note. Yesterday, with LeeLEE_69, the AOL screen name I made solely for him, I messaged

RotTheCasbahJr, right before my mom grabbed my elbow and tugged me down the hall, down the stairs, down the driveway, into the van: "She's psychoer than we think. Back to Carousel Gardens. SAVE ME, SEXXXY!! `_` Rescue ur bb girrrrrrl!!"

"Have you seen my chart?" I try affecting *chummy*. "I'm not even supposed to be—PHP, intake told my mom. Day—IP is *un*necessary. You should have, like, a sticky note, all caps: PATIENT'S MOM INSANE. BE GENTLE W/ HER."

The nurse stops at the foot of my bed. Her hair is the maroon-black that makes women look Wiccan. With daylight, her orangey foundation, a bad match for her dye job, is visible. Ugh. In another circumstance, I really might pity her, but here I hate her smug, queenly attitude. If Elliot wore makeup, I bet it would be equally hoochie.

"Hello? Are you listening to me? How long have you worked here? Protocol is, 'well, sweetie, I hear you but . . .' So what's your *but*? Why can't I have water?"

"Noncompliance?" the nurse asks, her tone flat. "Early start. But, I suppose, when you're only in for a week, you've got to make the most of it."

I clutch the thin blue blanket to my chest. I sleep naked—someday, Junior Carlos will appreciate this, I think. Even in the hospital, I do what I want.

SHOWER

"Count or flush," says the woman who's introduced herself as Marjorie, not the skank vitals-snatcher from fifteen minutes ago, but an older woman in kitten-gray slacks and lace-up black leather slippers, like tap shoes without the taps. Marjorie has white, Bill Gates hair, and she's whatever's not a nurse and not a doctor: the toe wedged inside my bathroom door.

"Neither?"

I can't pee. Every time I try, my urethra squints shut. Going to the bathroom while someone monitors you—I didn't even get used to that during my sixty days here last summer. Then I was the Unit envy: along with multi-vites and SSRIs, I got laxatives.

"I can barely hear with the shower, honey," says Marjorie. "I know it's hard. Think waterfalls. Lakes. Rushing rapids. Puddles. Melting glaciers and polar ice caps. A monsoon. Raindrops on roses, whiskers on . . . Hon. You drank all that water, and right after Bethany recorded you, those numbers. We figure out whose system's working diuretics, you know. Right as rain, and there's another drop in the bucket. Count or flush? Either I flush the toilet for you or you count so I know you're not purg—"

"Obviously, Marjorie."

"Is that a tinkle? Count or flush, hon. Otherwise, I'm coming in."

Steam rolls out of the shower stall. I squeeze my eyes, trying not to feel self-conscious. I imagine my soul, gaseous, evaporating from my body, the way the weasels die in *Who Framed Roger Rabbit*. Except, in my vision, I don't die. Soul Lisa (in a white baby-doll dress instead of her speech team sweats with the drawstring locked up at the nurses' station) swirls like a vortex over Body Lisa's head; Soul Lisa's nighty starts clinging to her cleavage, the silkiness crumpling with sweat. Soul Lisa swishes her blonde hair in Body Lisa's face and says, *get your ass out of here.*

I don't have to pee. The white toilet seat, chipped on the part of the circle I can see between my legs (Exhibit A for some previous patient's purge-and-pass-out), is freezing. My bedroom, its private bathroom is freezing. The unit, the snack room like a White Hen for fattening frail girls, a fridge full of Vanilla Ensure, cabinets of grahams and pumpkin-or-ange cheese-and-peanut-butter six-packs, classrooms A and B, like Park without Señora Lurke's cardboard sombrero bor-der stapled above the blackboard, with two Caboodles full of glue sticks, without scissors (sharps—our collages are hand-torn triangles and trapezoids from *Highlights* and *Scientific American* and other magazines that remind you of your smallness in the universe's hugeness while trying to make you forget Portia di Rossi and Calista Flockhart are diet-ing-to-the-death on *Ally McBeal*), the clanking stand-scale where Skank Bethany led me and spun me backwards and slid the fifty-pound incremental and the one-pound incre-mental and bared her incisors (brandywine lip liner on her teeth—someone missed Cindy Crawford's *Basic Face*), her stethoscope pressed to my chest and her pointy violet nails on my wrist: freezing.

I'm too cold for more protests. I count. I try to sound as bored as the cousin tallying McAllisters in *Home Alone*. "Two, four, six, eight, eleven, fourteen, thirty-two."

"Hooray!" Marjorie calls. I'm waiting for her or another EDP staff member to says, "Phone," to curl an arm around my shoulders as I lose hold of the receiver as the news of my grandma is relayed. I want her death over with. I want to be one tragedy closer to adulthood. Too bad my grandma hadn't decided to die in the suburbs, I think, wiping. I could've gotten a pass to the next-door hospital, if she was in ICU.

Instead, I have Marjorie, humming "My Favorite Things," her shoe's black toe taptaptapping.

BREAKFAST

Two proteins.

Two grains.

One fruit.

One milk.

Two fats.

I'm the last one in the cafeteria, which isn't even a for-real cafeteria. It's like a gym or something. The tables are circles. In the middle of each, like a bull's-eye, is a red basket of paper napkins. FYI if I wanted a napkin, I'd need to ask permission, even though the only people sitting here are me and Connie, a Marjorie in-training, wearing a purple fleece zip-up.

"Lisa, what are you doing with that packet of peanut butter?" she says.

I don't feel like eating and I don't feel like talking.

"Hello." Connie waves at me and juts out her head. "Still not seeing it."

The peanut butter is in my hand. I scratch my torso like I did when I had a feeding tube. (They itch.) I scratch, scratch, lower, lower, and let the peanut butter fall.

"Not buying that Kitchen short-changed you. Don't think Kitchen does much skimping in EDP. As much as— What's that?" Connie ducks under the table and comes up with the packet of peanut butter.

I shrug. "Fell?"

"How come 'fell' seems an awful lot like 'was tucked in hoodie'—what's that—COCC on the back? You know, no zippers, no ties, no drawstrings, no triggering depictions: that calls up to your DP, but sounds like food-code to me."

I sigh. I don't want the yogurt, the peanut butter, the Cheerios, or the banana. I want Junior Carlos. A syrupy make-out session. Whatever goes into the drink called Sex on the Beach.

"Why are we here?" I say, sneering at the empty gym. Talk about triggering: off in one corner, there's an old exercycle, the kind with a fan in the front wheel.

"Why we're in the rehab room isn't relevant right now."

"It sucks. Carpet?"

"I don't care if you don't like it."

I ask some questions; Connie answers them:

"No, you can't go underneath and see if Georgette's signature is still there. I doubt it. Our facility's staff is very thorough."

"No, I don't think it's weird to have breakfast in a room with a stationary bike."

"You can talk about that with Dr. Ogbaa when she gets in."

"No, that doesn't mean fat."

"I don't know if it implies that."

"Lisa, my tone was no such—"

"If you're an expert because you've won some speech team, then I'm Mrs. George Clooney because I worked in the ER."

I smirk. "I'd like to be Mrs. Clooney. Or, like, the babysitter. The sexy one. The one George drives home and—"

"Inappropriate."

"What am I supposed to talk about?" I say. "I'm a sexual being."

"Lisa, we're not here to talk about anything when there's still a yogurt, a banana, a box of Cheerios, juice, one packet of peanut butter on your tray and no evidence of eating."

"When in Romania."

"I think you mean when in Rome."

"Romans eat and puke." I take a swig of juice, gargle it around in my mouth, and spit it back in its Styrofoam cup.

"Inappropriate."

"And you're who—my mother?"

"Someone's Mary Melodrama today."

I bang my fist on the table. The yogurt jumps. "*Is your grandmother dying?*"

"I'm sorry to hear about your grandmother. As soon as you finish up, I'm, uh, I'll, the nurse's station would have any messages. And I'll check. In the meantime, I suggest you stop scratching your initials into that cup and—"

"Isn't it your job to, like, be nice?"

"No. Your grandmother isn't an excuse either, and I'm sorry this interaction has come to this, but you've got, I have to make sure you—"

"Fuck you, fuck Elliot Eggleston, fuck everything," I say. I drum my fingers at my temple. Even though the room is empty, it feels swarming. I don't think doctors get how being in the hospital, EDP, unleashes a hive of killer bees for girls like me.

"I don't know who Elliot Eggs is—"

"Stupid shemale."

"Well, I'm sure he doesn't deserve your curse words."

"Do you even have any idea why I'm here?" I say.

Not-Marjorie fiddles with the zipper on her fleece. "I think you should talk about this in Group."

STRATEGY

Marjorie presses pause on the cassette player in the center of a ring of chairs. The silence is wooly without Chumbawamba. Skank sits in a folding chair next to the entertainment center. Her knees are wimpled with thigh flesh. She fans herself with a clipboard, and it whooshes the air. The room is what you'd expect: ceiling popcorned with pasty bird-turd kernels; carpet like TV static.

Our circle is nine patients. If the group is a clock, I'm at eight forty-five.

"All right. So what does this song bring up for you all?" Marjorie says, nodding her beaming face at all of us. Skank scribbles something.

I lean back in my folding chair, until the legs tilt and I teeter. Then I let my weight go forward and come down with a clang. I hold up my hand, like the Loser sign.

"Pissin' the night away?" I say. "Drink a whisky drink, a vodka drink, a cider—"

A birdy woman, at 7:35, in black leggings and a hunter green sweatshirt giggles. She has plain gold rings on three of her eight fingers, a steely rock glommed to her left nostril. *Phoebe*, she said, a few minutes ago, during lightning round introductions, which turned into how long you'd been at Carousel Gardens. Lisa, one day. Phoebe, four weeks.

Marjorie's eyes crinkle like accordion folders. "Perceptive, Lisa. Anyone else?"

Without Marjorie or Skank, all of us combined probably don't weigh six hundred pounds. I size up their silence: Brown hair, tulle-bowed headband, gray circles and teeth too big for a mouth too weak to speak. At three o'clock, a girl with Pepto-pink blush and gold body glitter dandruffing her hair closes her eyelids in a languorous curtsey. At six, a blue pointer finger slides a white ID bracelet up and down a furry jaundiced wrist. I'd forgotten how beautiful a broken body can be, like an oil-slicked seal or a pelican wearing a soda-ring choker, hurt and wild. I'm envious. For the first time since I've been in eighth grade, I ignore Dr. Ogbaa's cognitive reframing jabber. In my mind's eye I bubble-letter: I Feel Fat.

The room is so awkwardly silent I worry my head is transparent, a fish tank for my illegal thought. I clear my throat.

"Um, also a message of triumph over the day to day," I say, folding my hands in my lap to look earnest. "Like, you're beaten down or something, but there's—you're still resilient. Slips or relapses could happen, but what they're saying is you persevere. Ultimately. Even if you have to—"

"Drink through," says Phoebe. She sounds old, her voice blistered and wry. "Drown your face in Everclear, I mean, blank substance. Sorry. Shit."

One of Marjorie's hands leaves her lap and she flashes two fingers, a peace sign, to Skank, who scratches the paper on her clipboard like a scab that's coming off.

"Rules. A reminder, for anyone new to this circle. 'We abstain from names and the profane. We use nurturing words to express our hurts.' No numbers. And keep behaviors—self-deprecating thoughts included," Marjorie says, catching my eye, "unspecified. So as not to trigger anyone. Speaking of anyone . . . you're all so quiet."

"Pancakes," an Asian girl in a Purdue sweatshirt whispers. I frown. Suddenly, I'm thankful my stay—one week, intake conceded—will be short.

"But Phoebe and Lisa make good points," Skank says. "So let's defiantly note them. You guys!"

"Definitely," I say, under my breath.

"Huh?" Skank's eyes are two sizes: one quarter, one nickel. She compensates with catliner. She sounds too flabby for girls like us, girls with fly wrist bones, arrowhead chins, flinty noses, tiara brows. Then I remember my boobs, how Junior Carlos suckles my nipples and between my legs goes buzzy and tight, like I'm crossing my fingers to break a promise. There *are* reasons to embrace fat—*phat*—parts.

"You said *defiantly*," says Phoebe, lifting her chin. "That's a different word. Than *definitely*. Which is what we think you mean."

"Common mistake. Let's see if we can't pick up more by listening again," Marjorie rushes. "This time, think about what you're struggling with. Try to relate."

I lower my head to listen to the music. Phoebe's ivy eyes are twin lasers pointed on me, I can tell. Moments like these are grommets that can be threaded with friendship. This is what I could've had with Georgette, what I once had with El: a partner to finish my sentences. The problem was that I was tired of being fed my lines.

APPOINTMENT

Dr. Ogbaa is from West Africa, and even though she grew up in Houston, and likes to use words like Amarillo and armadillo, there's some something about her voice I go gaga over, no matter how many times I've heard it. Now it's just me and her, sitting in a closet—seriously, Elliot's mom's is bigger—a school desk, a folding chair, a trash can, fancy Plus-Aloe tissues. I smell Dr. Ogbaa's latte-breath on her accent: not British, but Joan Crawfordly quavering, powerful, dame-ish, which is the same operatic reverb produced by Eric Hudson at Park when he nails a slurve with a metal baseball bat.

"—and after four messages from your mother, each, I should say, a notch angrier than the next, I'm worried about how you're handling this sudden reversal of fortune, if you would. Tamales in the bucket—"

"Wait, what does that even mean?"

Dr. Ogbaa's laugh is loud, a deck of cards being shuffled. "Seeing if you're here, Lisa. And glad you are. Very glad to have you in the room. Perked up. Tuned in."

I sniff. "Tuned in, all right. Tuned in, turned in, turned up, turn-tailed. Like, being turned around with a blindfold for, what, pin the tail on the donkey? Except somehow I'm both the person pinning the tail and the ass. I mean, sor—"

Dr. Ogbaa covers her smile with a hand. Her nails are round and polished the color of baked plums. She flutters her eyes (tracking gaze, mascaraed lashes): the opposite of EDP girls'. Would I rather her plump apple cheeks or their cored cheekbones? Duh: I feel guilty for even thinking the F-word. *I do what I want,* I remind myself—*not what the eating disorder wants.* It's scary to know I probably would've relapsed if my therapist weren't a woman who shows me beauty is not a house of bones.

"Anyhow, I *am* feeling very angry," I say.

"I bet. What else?"

"Um . . . triggered?"

"So, more. Take me to that rodeo."

I snicker, get serious, stare at my red Converse; they're floppy on my feet without shoestrings. I miss the flat laces, Sharpied

JC<3LB, JC<3LB, JC<3LB, JC<3LB, JC<3LB, JC<3LB, JC<3LB, JC<3LB, 4EVAEVA. I didn't do that doodling. Junior Carlos did, at Brookfield Zoo the night after Thanksgiving. Our second date. We were at Holiday Magic, and we skipped the Christmas lights on the cages and the Clydesdale carriage rides to drink watery hot cocoa on a sticky gray boulder in South America, the first room in Tropic World. We didn't even talk; we just sat there, with my legs in his lap. Above, the quetzals and cockatoos wove under vines and misting nozzles, cawing at the gibbons hooting like primate carolers. I was wearing my leopard print earmuffs, my leopard print polar fleece vest, my mom's nerdy Isotoner gloves, my Converse—and I was covered with goosebumps, totally in love.

"I'm going back and forth around these girls," I say, heaving the words so I don't wuss out. "I'm jealous, even for my G-tube, that phantom limb thing? I'm feeling it. I—I miss the feeling of being the worst one. The best one. You know that thing. And at the same time, you know, the . . . stuff with Junior Carlos is very good for me, despite what you say about um . . . our sexual activities or whatever. He's kinda, he's like the person that makes me love my body. I feel gorgeous around him."

Dr. Ogbaa nods, ever so slightly, and interlaces her hands in her lap, over the mustardy suede skirt. "Mmm," she murmurs, meaning: go on.

"And . . . what else? I'm, so there's the fence of this place, you know? You have to decide where you are in relation to it."

"What's the fence?"

"The fence is ah, like, um, your will. Your choice. Or—wait. One side's the eating disorder, the other side's recovery or just, like, not having behaviors if you don't want to commit."

"Do you not want to commit?"

"I didn't say that. I want to normalize without becoming boring. Can I have that? I wanna be okay enough that I still look skinny, but I'm not thinking like a crazy-skinny person. I want to be the sort of girl who someone . . . say, Junior Carlos . . . would, like . . . love."

"Verified. And that's what I wanted to hear, Lisa, because I wouldn't want you to take this—maybe less-than-thought-out move by your mother—as a punitive gesture."

"Like a punishment?"

"Exactly. I'm tremendously pleased with your progress. And retribution would be a fool's motive for relapse."

"Like getting back at Elliot?"

"Your mother was the person to whom I was referring. What about Elliot?"

"That's how come I had the diet pills," I say, louder. "Like, seriously, what the hell. I mean, whatever, I'll be here, probably when my grandma dies and yah know, weirdly, I could see a benefit to that, this, here instead of home, but at the same time, c'mon! Effing Elliot! I don't mean to be paranoid, but it's like she's . . . she rigged me to get caught or something, like so I'd get sent back here."

"That is a little unfounded. I'm not quite sure you've the evidence to, well that's not exactly probable. She's you're friend," Dr. Ogbaa says gently. "Don't you think?"

"Seriously? No. Did I tell you—yeah, the Ouija board thing, all the times we were dialing each other's numbers at the same time, we'd wear the same . . . whatever, she's ESP enough that it's like, c'mon: she's the person who needs a lesson. Puny . . . punit—sorry, vocab blanking. Punition?"

My heart thunders under my bra. The red marker in my mind appears again: I want to make Elliot pay.

Dr. Ogbaa twists her fingers in front of her chest, like she's shielding her heart from my malice. The room is hot, stuffy, an incubator. She meets my eyes.

"Now you're lassoing octopi, Lisa. Reel it in."

SNACK: A HAIKU

Goldfish crackers mush
On my tongue like Communion
Why why why no fins?

OT EXPRESSIONS

I'm scribbling red crayon over the body on the coloring page in the art room, at same long table where I've colored this same empty body twice before, when I remember a random thing with Georgette.

Here's an in-patient perk: no one cares if you space out. Being here healthy-ish reminds me of CCD at 9:15 on Sundays: easy worksheets, like "_____ and _____ were expelled from the Garden of Eden," or "create a Godly design for Joseph's coat" (while Donny Osmond sings).

There are six of us in the art room. The blinds are down; the light is shuttered and low. Staff is another woman whose name I've forgotten, whose most prominent feature is a bristly head of gray hair shaped like a broom. When you can't see the snow, the room is warmer: with this placebo, the thinnest shiver less. Phoebe and two other girls were pulled for appointments. I'm disappointed, kinda; I

want to talk to Phoebe. I want to talk to someone, anyone, who's not being paid to help me. Instead, we listen
to a Beethoven sonata. The task: scribble inside the body,
where you feel the most stress.

(I've worn through the paper on the humanoid's chest,
the spot where I used to place my hand to recite the Pledge
of Allegiance.)

I'm remembering being here over the summer and my
friend who died, Georgette. The week before her final trans-
formation—emaciated body to emaciated corpse, flat-lining
heart monitor—she was as fine as anyone with an NG tube.
Then, I was thirteen, the youngest in the unit (now, the record
is nine: regular nine-year-olds munch boogers—EDP girls
puke in pencil pouches). I was decapitating Teddy Grahams
when I saw Georgette's red head of curls on the floor.

Big girl, little hair, she always said. Staff hated her sar-
casm, but I bet they were jealous: her Neiman Marcus nose,
her French blue eyes, her creamy skin dappled with tawny
freckles, her family's chalet in Davos. She would've inherited
a shampoo fortune.

I went over to her. *What are you doing?* I asked. Her forehead was on the carpet, like she was all ready to be buried.
You should get up.

Less than a year ago, I sucked. I was orderly, by the book,
ruled by the same bullshit that constituted my sickness. You
can't recover if you're not willing to shake those principles:
try hardest, be the best.

Georgette didn't move. If I hadn't been watching her
vertebrae through her pink sweater, I'd have thought she'd
fainted. The more emaciated a girl, the more insistent her
skeleton. Georgette's bones breathed through cashmere.

She turned her head, the way we did neck and shoulder stretches in Movement Therapy, twisting to detoxify our systems. She hooked a finger at me. *Secret, baby?*

I leaned in. Sucked the headless torso of a Teddy.

Georgette smelled like brown iceberg lettuce and rancid peppermint tea. She doll-winked. *I'm doing what I want.*

I raise my hand, holding the red crayon.

"Liesel?" the woman with broomstick hair says. "May I help you?"

Through their bangs and patchy hair, the other girls eye me as I walk to the front of the room. I would eye me too. That's the ED unit. Whose body can you use? Whose thighs would you want? (Trick question: no one's. Legs would be better if they were all calf.) Whose body is so hardy that you have to speculate on the hidden magnitude of her behaviors' fucked-up-ness? Broomstick knits a long green sock into her lap and guards a short stack of manila folders. I crouch, so our faces are together, like family.

"My grandma is really sick," I whisper. "I'm waiting to hear, like, an update on her condition. Can I go to the nurses' station? Marjorie told me they'd have messages there. And I—I need to call my mom. I haven't heard. Anything— and. I want to check."

"You need a chaperone." That information comes out like a boast: newbie.

"Ooh, okay. Can you get, like, the nurse? Bethany?"

The woman presses a doorbell in the wall and a minute later, Skank is at the door. The white collar of her dress is streaked with foundation, like Tang. I smile.

"Dr. Ogbaa said I have phone privileges. This is an—"

"I know how phone privileges go. You already had a caller. So. Here's the message." Bethany hands me a pink slip of paper. "Looks like one of your little friends. I'm sorry it's not about your grandma. But maybe it's a no news is good news sitch?"

I nod. I fight the urge to squeal and shriek and sing happy happy joy joy, to backflip down the hall. "JC visit this afternoon." It's hard to read such sweet words in ugly penmanship. Her handwriting is so predictable: round and ugly, like a row of swollen grapes.

4 ·· ELLIOT

WIND SHRIEKED THROUGH THE RIVER birch, its branches bare, its bark Dalmatian velvet. Three-week-old snow frosted our lawn, and sheets of ice pleated the roots of the oak at the edge of our driveway. The sidewalk was a skating rink. I concentrated on my abs, steadying myself, trying not to be a wimp, as I walked the block to Lisa's house.

The air smelled bleachy, sharp, like inhaling swimming pool water. I'd forgotten my gloves—but I didn't need gloves! I warmed my hands in my pockets, squeezing my mom's heroin. I was dangerous, powerful, stronger than the tasering windchill. I could demand anything of Lisa.

My own neighborhood looked changed, suburban but whack. I saw all the weird stuff that other days I missed: The branches of the Valenta's magnolia capped with jade-green bowling balls. The vine of bronze garland swinging from the Novak's gutter. A nondescript black mailbox that had once belonged to a woman who'd given me and my dad king-size Hershey's with Almonds the Halloween I went as Strawberry Shortcake. Another mailbox wrapped with a rainbow-bright plastic lei. A brown deer, paused like a cake topper, in the street. Lisa and I used to spot families of them—does and fawns—in her backyard, in sixth grade, when her mom wasn't home. We'd take the Ouija board (*demons*, according

Kim Orlowski-Breit) out to the garden, spread the snow leopard blanket a few feet from the Melrose peppers, near a petrified alder that supposedly marked the grave of a pioneer child. We'd lay our hands, mine on top of hers, the pads of my fingers kissing her sky-blue nail polish, icicles, on the planchette:

Is your soul in purgatory?
(F-R-O-M B-A-B-Y J-E-D-E-D-I-A-H I D-O N-O-T K-N-O-W)

Who's your best friend?
(E-L-L-I-O-T)

When will I die?
(4-3)

When will I die?
(F-O-R S-P-I-R-I-T T-O D-E-C-I-D-E)

Why is Hanson so popular?
(M-M-M-B-O-P)

A thunderous revving startled me. The deer paused and then bounded, the spade of its tail vanishing into a snowy grove of evergreens. A heavy bad feeling came over me: where would the deer go and who would take care of it, and who did it have? And what if that was the last deer I ever saw?

The source of the sound was a red blur. The Jeep sped by, its tires slicking slush. The driver was going too fast for our neighborhood, where streets canted and forked, and on weekends parents led toddlers in their snowsuits to coned-off blocks that were prime for sledding. But I would have recognized that car at Oakbrook Mall on Black Friday. In my subdivision, if they didn't have sedans, people drove Land Rovers, the spare tire covers decorated with a line drawing of a pachyderm. This was a salsa-red Jeep sponsored by Tabasco Sauce: a green-and-white decal flanked the gas cap. I knew just where that car was headed. From a million visits to Lisa's, I knew her dad's license plate by heart: WBEZ769.

I walked up their driveway. Their garage door was open like a yawn. Inside was the Jeep, parked next to a soot-colored lawn mower and a barrel of croquet mallets. Lisa's mom wasn't home. I was relieved. Ever since she sent me the note stuck to Lisa's calculations of our proportions, I'd been a moving target for Mrs. Orlowski-Breit. *Your mom hates me*, I'd said to Lisa. She always replied the same: *You're right. It blows. She does.*

Diamonds of sandstone led to the front porch. They glimmered with blue melting salt. It was weird not punching in the garage security code with Lisa, hefting our backpacks loaded with textbooks and binders and diet pills. We'd go to her room, swallow a Fen-Phen each to be festive, light a brownie batter votive, flip between Q101 and B96, making fun of Will Smith—*he rhymed Miami with Miami!*, stressing about equations, jiggling our ankles, messy buns drooping, Lisa's Urban Decay speckling the tender skin under her mantis-green eyes with Smog. I missed all of it. Without Lisa, I was friendless. Other than the night of *Terrible Twos*, I hadn't even been to her house since Thanksgiving, when Junior Carlos had asked Lisa out or proposed or whatever.

I rang the doorbell. *Trick-or-treat! Drugs!* I thought. I cracked myself up.

Mr. Breit opened the door. His status quo was pretty rough, and today he looked downright wretched. Maybe, one parent at a time, the adult world was disintegrating, the first pebbles of America's own Beachy Head: jobs vanishing, gas prices skyrocketing, Chicago crime bleeding into the suburbs, moms hoarding smack. Lisa's dad's facial hair seemed to be scrambling off his skin, like it was ashamed that it comprised a patchy chinstrap. *Low-grade merkin*, Lisa called it. Deep purple circles half-mooned his eyes. A mysterious tooth-pasty substance had dried in his philtrum. He had the long, lean body of the skinny-fat: a population of girls I would never reach. (One day, though, they'd be Twinkie-tubby women, Larry Breit's age, who'd need me to whittle away their postpartum pounds.) He was wearing a red flannel. He was tall, but he had hips— the kind that, on women, guys called *phat*.

"Would you look at this? Girl of the moment!" he said. He was holding a highball of sludge. His voice was deep and easy, like sliding your feet into slippers.

I tried laughing. It came out like a neigh.

"Is Lisa home?"

"Elliot."

My name hung between us, a loud fly hovering over a puddle of honey. Bansheeing at my back, wind flicked snowflakes that pricked through my black jeans.

Mr. Breit raised an eyebrow. His nostrils were chalked with that same stuff as his lip. Mucus or dry skin or drugs: I couldn't tell the difference.

"Elliot, Elliot, Elliot."

"Don't wear it out," I said. My teeth chattered. I could see the Breit's foyer, where heat radiated up through the floorboards. I looked down. Lisa's dad was barefoot. His hairy toes were as long as millipedes.

"You want to come in." Mr. Breit shook his glass. Ice rattled. "Don't I have any friggin' manners?"

"I don't know. I mean, about. Not your manners. I could come in—"

"We'll talk like adults, Elliot. Enough with the yadda yadda."

I followed him through the family room to the kitchen. Something felt wrong. The lights over the island were off and the television was dark. The radio, which typically droned WBEZ all day long, was silent. Something smelled like toast.

Mr. Breit pulled out a stool. I didn't recognize the cushions: winey and mulled pink, upholstered sunsets. I patted my pocket. Even if everything had changed since I last saw Lisa, I could do it, I told myself. I unzipped my coat and hopped up.

"I just wanted to see if Lisa was home." I balled my hands in my lap. "She wasn't in school yesterday. You, so you know that. And I figured she might still be sick today. She's usually—she gets sick for a while."

I waited for Mr. Breit to interrupt me. I didn't know why he'd be home if Lisa wasn't sick; even if she was, his presence didn't make sense. *Three a.m. to three a.m. shifts—means sometimes you shower at the station*, he'd told me the first time I met him, when I asked what he did. He'd talked to me like he was reading Richard Scarry to a tyke. Now he stood across the island, staring. I was someone new.

"Lisa's not here." He spat out the words like a bad mouthful. "Do you want something to drink? Coffee, tea? Hot cocoa? Scotch?"

"Ha-ha. If Lisa's not—"

"What's so funny? I was thirteen when I had my first drink. At my Papouli's cabin in Michigan. The UP. Beautiful country. Makes you see the *truly* fungal nature of Chicago. Anyhow, I loved that place when I was a boy. And we're camping, fishing. All my uncles, my cousins. And the thing to do was, real slick, you go to Canada to get—cheaper. I don't know, someone has a sixty-pounder of LCBO. Just *annihilate*-your-mother, piss-poor rum. And my uncle Vick is like, here, hands me a bottle of Green River, tells me 'take a swig,' and then he fills it up with booze. He puts his thumb over the top, shakes her up . . . next thing you know, I'm puking a leprechaun."

"That sounds revolting," I said.

"You girls need to lighten up. You and my daughter—enough with the rules. Be kids. Fuck up."

"Very funny."

"Who's laughing? You'll all be dead by thirty if you don't learn how to relax into the screwed-upedness of life."

I shrugged. "How many calories in Scotch?"

Mr. Breit smirked and peered into his sludge. "How many calories in *who cares*?"

I liked the wolfishness in his eyes. I saw the magenta lips from the "Macarena" music video in my mind; they lip-synched that robo-femme voice: "I am not trying to seduce you." Was Lisa's dad flirting with me? If she wouldn't be my friend, was this the next best thing?

"Fine," I said. I hadn't eaten anything yet. Usually by this lunch I was two hundred calories. "A little."

He left his glass on the island and opened a cabinet above the sink. He turned to look at me. His eyes glistened.

"You seem like a neat girl. Am I right?"

"Um . . . yes?"

He handed me a shot of amber liquid. I could smell it, like nail polish remover or the fixative spray we used in Art that we had to go outside to deploy. It was thick in my throat before I opened my mouth.

"Cheers," he said, retrieving his sludge. He stood at the other end of the island, his glass raised, like we were royalty commencing a banquet. "To Lisa."

"To Lisa."

I took a sip. The Scotch burned my lips, cracked from the cold; it burned my gums, pink and tender; it burned a canker sore I couldn't shake; it stung my tongue and numbed my heart. I let out a choked *eughhh*.

"Thoughts?"

"Honestly, Mr. Breit, I don't know if I can finish—."

"Larry. Hun. Elliot, Larry. Larry, El."

I coughed. "Larry. I don't know if I'm finishing that shot."

Laughing, he walked over to my side of the island. I could smell him. *He* was the toast. Wholegrain. Dry. Char-slapped. He dumped the remainder of my shot in his drink.

I spun on my stool to face him. I had to look up to make eye contact.

"Is Lisa at school?" I didn't know why I was whispering.

His eyes tracked something over my head. I tried imagining what he saw: the sliding doors, the sage-green curtains tied with turquoise ribbons and pinecones, the Breit's back-yard, the deck bogged down with snow, the annuals slumbering in the frozen garden, petals of dead mums, thorns from long-gone roses, the pioneer baby's ghost beating its calico wings and shaking its bison moccasins, Lisa in a slip dress and her suede snow bunny boots, the furry pompons bouncing as she twerked her hips. The "Macarena" was stuck in my head now. Dammit. I saw Lisa wink and toss her blonde hair back; it rippled in the winter sun, whipping in tune to the song: "You all want me, you can't have me . . . Ay! Ay!"

Mr. Breit put a hand on my shoulder. I couldn't feel anything through my coat, but I knew he was touching me. I was like a book that had been ripped open. I stayed very still, trying not to breathe.

"Elliot. Did you know Michael Jordan retired two days ago?"

Stagey nodding.

"Okay. Good. Sweetie, it's a dark day in Chicago. End of an era—and I don't even wanna forecast what's next for this shit stew of a city. Cops condemning dibs, all other vestiges of civilization with the '90s winding down. So no more three-peats, no more Hummers. I'll tell you. Following the Lewinsky business? It's a bad sign. Apex of our nation's problems? Not even. We've got 'em here, in spades and clubs and hearts and diamonds, the full deck of corruption. Jesse White appointing his own daughter to Accounts and Revenue, George Ryan with his perpetual psyching everyone out about that airport on the South Side, Daley's publicist chump—Ahgh!" He clawed the back of his neck. How much Scotch was in his sludge? "What I'm telling you is, I'm sick of the buddy-buddy show. City of onions and cowards and cons, Capone's Chicago, that's still the story. Call those folks in Edinburgh. Forget Dolly the Sheep. Tell 'em to clone Mrs. O'Grady's cow, and burn the 312 to the ground again."

He paused, took a sip. The Scotch burbled in my stomach, rubber-banded my brain. Mr. Breit was making zero sense. Or, for the first time, I was drunk.

"What I'm trying to say is there's enough corruption on my desk. Elliot. Egleston. Don't lie to me about my daughter."

His hand squeezed my shoulder.

"Lying about what?" I said, weakly. "I asked a question. Where's Lisa? How can a question be—"

"Okay, not a lie. Christ, you and my wife. The fact-checkers. Men are from Mars, Women play semantic games. Jesus. Don't be sly or go all coy or act innocent. Does one of those work for you?"

"Mr. Breit, I still don't know what you're talking about," I said. Suddenly, I felt scared. Trapped. His hand clamped my shoulder tighter. Crunch a bone, I wished. Just do it.

But he relaxed. I tried to speak slowly and calmly. "I'm legit looking for Lisa. I thought she'd be here. She wasn't at school yesterday. I'm home today—"

"Doing what?"

I coughed. "Sick?"

He didn't respond.

"Half-day?"

"This is what I'm talking about, Elliot. Lies. Don't you have a father who's told you never to tell a lie?"

"I'm not George Washington. My dad travels a lot." I wriggled out from under his hand. I slid off the stool. Beneath me, the floor spun like a maelstrom. "It's fine. If

Lisa's not here, and she's not at school, it's a mystery. So
. . . whatever. Thanks for the drink?"

I shoved my hands in my pockets. I was trying not to
cry. This was useless. A waste of time and calories. I began
to leave the way we'd come, back through the living room.
Then Larry started.

"You have my daughter in the hospital. In-patient redux.
Congratu-fucking-lations. You have my wife furious, petrified, at wit's end, terrified about my daughter, as her own
mother is dying. Let me clarify: *that's* dying. Deathbed. Life
of struggles and Great Depression survivor meeting her
maker. Not teen-girl necking with death hysterics."

I turned, holding onto the black leather couch. "What
are you talking about? What happened to Lisa? What's going
on?"

"You wanna tell me how many of those pills Lisa was
taking a day? When Kim's driving her once, twice a week to
this doctor, *that* group. Like we need another M.D.? Elliot
Egleston, Dr. Feelgood with the Fen-Phen, everybody!" He
slammed down his sludge. The ice jumped. "What's the
script? Two pills? Four?"

"Those were a Christmas present," I said. "A joke."

"A five-pound bag of funny. Good one, Ellen DeGeneres.
When can we see you at Second City?"

"I didn't tell Lisa she had to take them or anything, okay?"
I sound insistent, whiny, like a child. Detestable. "She was
the one who asked me to steal them from *my* mom. Don't go
blaming me for what she did. Lisa has a mind of her own.
Okay? She does whatever she wants and she doesn't listen to
me or you or Mrs. . . ." The tears shook out of me now, and
they wouldn't stop. "She doesn't even want to talk to me."

The room spun. Black leather, brown sludge, white snow, gold Scotch, sky blue fingernails, gray Berber. I sunk to the floor and leaned against the couch. Aloud, there were no excuses, no pretending everything was copacetic with my best friend. There was no best friend. I shoved my chin into my coat. I punched my ribs.

Larry's toes were there first. He waved a white tissue embossed with seashells at me. I dabbed my eyes.

"That was zero to sixty," he said. "I apologize. I'm stressed as hell."

My heart wanted to shrug everything off, but I sat stiffly. Inside, I was all sloshy and frozen.

"Up you go." He held out a hand. His fingers tapered into wide, rough-bedded nails. What did that mean for his penis?

I let him pull me up in one swift tug. It was like fifth grade, during Outdoor Ed, when we'd practiced trust falls in Wisconsin, in a meadow, surrounded by prairie grasses, a blessing, knowing someone had your weight.

I hung my head, trying to drain the tears from my eye sockets.

Larry put up my hood. I was looking at him, but, with the coyote fur I could only see his chest. He was like a giant teenage boy; his flannel had come off. "NO FEAR" said his T-shirt in red and black graffiti letters. I wanted a slogan like that, something to believe in.

We were both standing, but he was so much taller than me. Lisa was tall, too. He bent his head down and kissed the top of my hood. His lips rustled against my coat.

"I don't think Lisa'd be hanging onto those pills if she didn't want to be your friend, sweetie. Don't cry. You're at that age when shitty is the accepted currency."

I nodded.

"Call her when she gets home. She's at . . . well, she should be back in a week. Maybe don't call. Her mom's pretty pissed . . . at you. At everyone, for that matter. Not the best time to be a parent."

"Thanks." I wished the Scotch had suited me. I wished I were forty. That I could relax on the couch, talk politics with Mr. Breit. That he'd kiss me, my face, his mouth, his tongue. His chinstrap scratching my neck. "I'm sorry to barge, to barge in."

"I *invited* you in, honey," he said. "Let me drive you home?"

"Okay."

I sniffed. I wanted him to say something conciliatory, sexy.

He passed me another tissue. "Blow your nose, would you, kiddo?"

I did. He opened his palm and I handed him my snot.

5 ·· ANNA

HELL IS CONTINENTAL BREAKFAST. PINIONS of pineapple and melon, bendable silver, Styrofoam plates, bran muffins the size of golf balls, awful American mini croissants. Silver vultures of Regular, Decaf, and Hot Water. Orange pekoe tea, pastel rainbows of fake sugar.

I am seated behind Chalet DeGroot, who drifts like a jellyfish, stinging with simper, table to table. Now she's small-talking Alicia Aurelio, the Dean's Secretary, whose mulberry turtleneck is so tight the flesh above and below her bra line protrudes like a bolster. I have a mug of Regular. Every sip is a burnt reminder that I'm in Laughlin Banquet Hall, room awash in collegial blather: blond wood floors, a screen on stilts to accompany the overhead projector, fireplace of aubergine stone guarded by twin metal serpents, their two forked tongues the ledge on which balances a poker. The buffet—white-tableclothed, legs hidden beneath the shirring—abuts the back wall.

Noted: Location of exit (four bounding steps from coffee).

Queried: Location of Rot: unconfirmed.

Chalet DeGroot is my colleague, proof that our profession doesn't privilege the privileged. Chalet is workaday; her eyeballs swell like olives afloat in a tired gin martini shaken for someone sated by Zima's; her nose is piggy. She is a mysterious deep sea species who gets genuinely excited to flap her gills about Comp Rhet. She wears a lot of coral—a maternity blouse billows over her puffer fish stomach but clings like seaweed to her breasts. She is the same as all my female colleagues, flaunting her condition with JC Penney pregnancy portraits magneted to the faculty lounge fridge and offhand remarks—thirty-eight weeks, she mentions now, at 11:27, three minutes before the forum on writing and mental health begins.

I can't tell if Alicia is eating it up or annoyed. She has a Cheshire grin on her face. She's sketching a pair of fuck-me stilettos on a legal pad with a hot-pink (Fruit Punch) smelly marker, keeping notes for the Dean in absentia.

Chalet kisses Alicia on the cheek and half jogs to the podium. "Two minutes," she announces, waving her hands like a Bollywood dancer, her upper arms jiggling. "Seats, everyone!"

"How's it going, Anna?" says Alicia, craning her neck. Her tone is lizardy, suspicious, though I've worked in the department for ten years, and she's the one who has slicked her hair back tighter over time. Dandruff rests on the gelled black strands. A mite of mini muffin is stuck in her brown lip gloss. "How's your semester?"

"Same, same." I beam in on a mole under her left eye to avoid her scalp. I nod toward her plate. "They did a good job with this, the food. It's a nice spread."

"Aren't you gonna eat? At least, hey, make a plate, take it home."

"My brother's a pastry chef. My family's spoiled—"

"How do you stay so thin with a brother who works in a bakery!? I'd be a truck and a half. You're so skinny."

If I ever become an administrator, I will outlaw refreshments at public, professional, and social campus events. *Well, I ensure that roughly one-third of my daily calories are eradicated by purging or distance-running, so that keeps me in the shape you see.* Or: *Well, actually, Alicia, you should see my daughter.* Or: *Well, truly, I'm not thin, you're just chubby.* Or: *Well, my mother was weight-conscious and after she died my father prime-ribbed himself to an early death, so food's never really compelled me.* Instead, I shrug.

"Should be starting soon," Alicia says. She crosses her legs at the knee and waggles a mauve suede pump, the toe stained white with salt. Then she leans in. "Pretty out-there topic for ProDev, at least in my opinion, that's what I think."

(Revision: Hell is continental breakfast and chitchat.)

"Mmm." I open my notebook, shopping for something to occupy my attention. After yoga, after I'd felt viscid in my body, after I'd showered in the locker room with rosemary mint hippie soap, after I'd stopped for a dry skim cappuccino to foster comity in my morning, I sulked in my office. Dinked on AOL. Skimmed student essays, trying to iron out Barbara's knotty blue cursive, fixating on Rot. I'd drafted nothing.

"The creatures of idleness/are pure speculation," writes Paul Violi, whose book I eventually took off my shelf. My eyes played connect-the-dots with lines: "cold coffee" "nope" "lick my watch." I emailed Rolf: "El's home sick. Hope you're well. Miss you. A." Waited for Rot, wrote Rot: "~~I want you please want me I'll take you.~~" Wished for coke (idle creature), waited more. Until 8:59, and Setting Measurable Outcomes had already begun by the time I stomped to Building 9, my boiled wool coat shouldered with snow.

Nothing in my notebook is legible; I stare concertedly and try to make sense. The room gets louder before it quiets. Coats unzip, rustle their nylon, sigh their weight over the backs of chairs. Tables fill. Mine, too: a woman with corn-rows I recognize from professional development events over the years, (maybe the math department?), sits down across from me, with a plate of pineapple. I almost smile.

"All right!" Chalet says. I wonder why it's just now dawning on me, after all the years we've been colleagues, that she was cheerleader. "Thank you everyone, so much, for attending COCC's first forum on Writing and Mental Health, especially on such a cruddy day. Ick, right! El Nino all over again. I know it's not easy for all of us to get bundled up on a Friday—" She pats her stomach. "But I hope you'll find these activities, these slides, and this conversation very worth your while. Yours—your *whiles*. Sorry—preggers brain! Anyhow, to begin, let's do an exercise. On your table you'll find handouts, enough for everyone. Now this, here's an essay—it's anonymous—but it's authentic, meaning I took this from one of our Composition classrooms. What I want you all to do is read over this, not worrying about grammar or anything—if you can, I know it's hard." (Pause for chuckles.) "But take a peek—see if it raises any red flags, you know, concerns about the student-writer. And note when those flags go up. Whatever color flags, actually. Orange or yellow. Okay? Two to three minutes then."

The math professor slides me a facedown essay. I flip it over.

It's short, only two pages. The same font as all college documents. No name, no department code, no section number. Vaguely I remember a call for papers.

WHAT DRIVES ME

Everyone lives with motivation. Sometimes, that's the clearest thing in life: the goals you set for yourself (or the goals other people set for you). I have been told that, through visualizing what I want, success will be my only option. Clarity will guide my every move, each of those moves will be working in service of some motivation. But what I want is ephemeral: as soon as I have it, the script changes. I'm a thrillist, an adrenaline-junky. I want the high, the next high, the next next. No, not necessarily drugs. I'm looking for whatever's deleterious enough to destroy me.

Stomachs don't gulp—or they shouldn't—but mine does, like it's forcing down a wad of croissant. Of all the passive-aggressive stunts: brandishing my own mistake in front of me, in the company of a hundred teachers? Tar and feather me, Chalet. Make an outcast of me. Tell faculty, and administration via Alicia Auerelio, who will surely convolute this message, that I have put a student at risk. I fucked up. Dammed the proper channels.

Of course, I could be paranoid. She could have acquired this essay a hundred ways. Seized it from a recycling bin, a duplicate in the writing center, a stock paper. Schizo much, Anna? *Rot* could be the problem, the plagiarist, a thief, a cheat.

I wait to become the target of narrowed eyes, but everyone's head is bent, studying the paper. Pages turn. The math professor draws a big bracket around a paragraph. Chalet has projected the essay on screen and, in blue overhead marker, written, "Forum Notes."

The tap on my shoulder almost makes me jump.

"Sorry to startle you," Glenn Decklin whispers. His campus security uniform parka smells like pretzels. 7UP. A goodtime guy at a billiards hall. Men almost my father. "You have a moment?"

Chalet bolts her mouth and lifts her eyebrows in my direction: if I were in her classroom, I'd abhor her. Thank god we've never been paired for observations. Alicia's head tips. She's listening to Glenn, her black bun jutting over the chair.

I grab my tote and jacket, follow Glenn into the hallway.

"Yeah, sorry, but I've got a student outside your office—217, Building 13, right? Looks like he's writing the next J. Peterman catalog."

"Ha."

He cringes. "But anyhow. Says he has an appointment with you. Something about a rec? I can mic the custodian, tell him you're here."

"No, I'm there," I say, my heart trilling.

"Snow's wicked right now. You sure? Want a lift?"

This is the power of desire. Suddenly, I'm no longer a professor, in a black blouse and a black cardigan and a black skirt. I'm seventeen, twenty-one, shredded jeans, blushing knees, skin softer than pudding. I feel effervescent. Flirty.

"You're too kind. What do I owe you?"

"A big salad? The witchy woman dance at next year's holiday party?"

"You're crossing the line between man and . . . okay, not bum," I say. "That was lame too. I didn't sleep. Try me next week."

Outside, the sky is ominous, the color of the dull side of aluminum foil. The snow is higher than the heel of my boots. I leave a trail of exclamation points all the way to the curb, where Glenn's campus golf cart, shielded in all-weather plastic like the popemobile, waits to taxi me across the quad.

··

On the floor, cross-legged, in that enormous bright green coat, the pink lift tag no one's bothered to snip, Rot looks gangly and scarlet-mouthed, like a pouty child. He shuts a soft navy notebook. I remind myself he can buy cigarettes. Pornographic videos. Lotto tickets. He can vote. He can gamble, with our nation, with himself, with me.

"You have something of mine?" Rot says, getting to his feet.

I sniff. "Doubtful."

"Anna, don't parent me."

What the hell, I think. *Stupid, stupid, stupid. Mommy and her mistakes.*

"I don't have it . . . here. Can you stop by on Tuesday? I'm sor—"

"You dig in?"

I smile.

"Yessss." He sounds pleased with himself. "I love that."

"But Tuesday," I say again. Another time, another date. "Okay?"

"We're all good. What now? Did I rescue you from pure Kafka or what?" Rot says.

The hall is vacant. Echoic. Cold. I wonder if yesterday's thermostat problem persists or if facilities were told not to heat #13 Humanities on a day the college isn't in session. Across from my office, the windows to the faculty lounge are dark.

"Have you even read Kafka?" I ask. "Or did you just get that from *Congo*?"

"Anna! With the way-back score. Dayum."

"That's not an answer," I say, unlocking my office. I flip on the tentacled pole lamp, rosier than the fluorescents. "You wanna come in?"

He steps inside, courting liminal space. How do you define a door frame? Half-in or half-out? How do you define adult? Eighteen? Twenty-one? Fourteen? Forty? Half-alive or half-dead?

Rot unbuckles the wrist straps on a pair of black nylon gloves. He pulls them off, holds them like a bunch of black bananas.

"Everyone reads *The Trial* in high school," he says. "'The Metamorphoses'? 'The Hunger Artist'? Actually, we spent more time on that dude than I thought."

Usually, I let a student sit first. Power is a stickler for height differences. When I was first married, I tried on antifeminism, settling my head lower on the pillows than Rolf's. Did I want subservience? (Not with him.) Now, I perch on the edge of my desk. Let Rot tower.

"I didn't read Kafka until graduate school," I say. "In high school, we read *Moby-Dick*, if you can believe that."

"Avoiding the easy jab there, Anna. Cuz . . . yah walked right into that one."

My jaw relaxes. "What can I say? I don't fear the obvious."

Rot drops into my desk chair. "I can't believe you saw *Congo*."

"My daughter's in junior high—that was, what, eight years ago for you? Seven? You know the extracurricular drill.

It's not like I'm getting to Godard retrospectives at the Music Box every night."

"Yeah, but your kid? She's gotta be smart. Eighth grade, seventh?"

"Elliot's fourteen."

"Yup," he says. "Time to plant that Jean Seberg seed."

"And what makes you the Dr. Spock of fourteen-year-old girls?"

He pauses. Rubs his nostril. "Sisters?"

"I didn't know you had siblings."

"Have and—had. My older sister passed away."

I look at my lap, my crossed legs, the crest of my knee. Apologizing for someone's loss: I've hated that, now, for more than two decades.

"It was over the summer. Kinda crazy how that feels like another lifetime already. Not that it lessens the loss, but—she—she was pretty sick."

I try not to pathologize or narrativize or analyze, but I can't help it. I close my eyes and see Rot younger, shoulder muscle sheared, shadowy facial hair Wited Out, trying to read Kafka on the bus. He can't concentrate. He pictures his pretty sister, so sick. The last time they were familial and wholesome, holidays, cider bobbing with cinnamon sticks, sneaking tipples of boozy eggnog, skiing. He senses disintegration will repair his heart. He bums a cigarette, trudges home, raids the liquor cabinet and pours tequila in a water bottle, wanders the grounds, getting dizzier and dizzier until the peacocks' feathers blur into a NASA-shot of Earth.

"You have another sister?" I say gently.

"What?"

"Sisters. Plural. Now—"

"Oh. Yeah. My little sister. She eats movies up. How many times can a person watch *Clueless*?"

I laugh. But the juncture in our conversation is visible, begging, like a fort of empty cardboard boxes we need to kick through.

"So what's up? We resolved the . . . confiscation."

"You wanna chill?" Rot says, swiveling in my chair. His legs are spread wide.

My heart runs into a brick wall: it feels so good.

"Not here." His voice is clipped. "Is that okay? Can we go someplace else? Do you have another one of those session things?"

I grab my tote. "Not until two. We break for a late lunch—that's . . . Sure. We can go. Where did you have in mind?"

"Will you follow me?" he says.

"What?" I blurt. "I mean—Of course."

"Probably best to take two cars."

He is sensible, too. How many ways can one man be meritorious? Did I ever have reservations?

I slip off the desk and land between his legs. "Sure. Right. Good thinking."

..

Carousel Gardens is fifteen minutes from the college. The fifty acres of land comprise an arboretum, behind the eponymous county hospital. My students visit for landscape architecture or horticulture or nature drawing classes: I know from letters, form excuses penned by professors, detailing absences, duration and purpose. The drive is a straight-shot, past the glassine river, over two wooden bridges unphased by snow: me in my black coat in my black car trailing Rot, green in green.

The Wednesday before Thanksgiving, his boxer-briefs were black, ARMANI in silver. Two Saturdays after, navy and hunter.

"Open to the Public" reads a placard mounted on the wrought iron gates. Inside the arboretum, the unplowed road wrenches and curves, unmarked by signs. Rot steers without hesitation. I slink behind. To be following, staring at the blue-and-white BMW insignia, in wait, suspended, wanting, approaching, closing in on an encounter—I love this. This rush. My drive. My gamble: At a freight train, I debooted, wriggled out of my tights, tugged off my panties, stuffed them in the glove compartment over that childish phone. Husband walkie-talkie. The crossing dinged. I only had time enough to jam my driving foot back in a boot before the candy-striped arms raised.

Rot turns into an empty, kidney-shaped lot. My tires sniggle over his tracks. He parks close to stairs leading to a conservatory. There is a glasshouse, like a Victorian fairy palace. The building is wet iron and verdurous window-panes licked with frost, a mansard roof Mohawked with snow.

I roll down my window, without touching the heat. It blasts my bare legs. I spread my feet and tilt my pel-vis forward and open my knees and the warmth blows up my skirt. The air is all windchill in Chicago. It burns my cheeks.

The snow on Rot's window smushes as it lowers. "Oh hey," he says. "Didn't I take, like, a class with you?"

"Me? I don't know."

"Yeah, weren't you in that lady's writing class in the fall. You were the super brilliant babe everyone was intimidated by."

"Right, right." My voice loosens. "Gosh, I had no idea you felt that way."

"It's too cold to do this!" Rot calls. A gust of wind blows and snow chords his words and flies inside the BMW. "Wanna come in?"

I pocket my keys and pull on my other boot.

He leans over the parking brake and opens the passenger door. I'm inside. The car snaps like a suitcase.

"Is this awkward?" he says, facing me. His coat is unzipped and his cheeks are flushed. I glance at the cup holders. There's a soda from McDonald's.

"Because of yesterday? Believe me, the stuff will be back in your possession before—"

"We're cool, I told you. Just awkward 'cuz . . ."

"I'm old? If it's awkward," I say, "it's me. I made this . . . this. I changed the record."

"What'd you put on?" he asks.

"Something horrid. The Partridge Family? Cheese, when I was your age, the sort of thing total Stellas would listen to."

He cringes. "Don't say that."

"Say what? Partridge—"

"'When I was your age.' Don't go there, all right?"

"Well it's a fact."

"Facts are overrated."

I nod. "Touché."

Rot presses the volume button. "So I'll deejay, old lady."

My bones reassemble themselves: The Clash. "Death or Glory" barks. We sit until the bridge, our listening knitting the windows with woolen fog. It is so different from what I remember—the rush of youth, the expedience of action, the drive to grope, ashes piling in ash trays. This car smells clean, lemon and leather. We wait, breath bated, until the final drum kick. Rot turns down the volume. Nature raises an eyebrow: outside, thunder unfurls.

"Wanna drink?" he says, flicking the McDonald's. Hazy through the lid, I can tell it's not Coke. "Not quite Dom, but hey—my parents burned through the last case on New Year's."

"Orange soda?"

"Absolut and Crush. *Così deliziosa*." He takes a sip. Touches his lips. Puckers.

"What the hell. It's like orange juice. Breakfast."

He holds the cup and grabs my bare thigh, twisting his fingers on my skin. I lean over, but he's moving, his chest covering mine, his mouth on my lips, his tongue sugary and orange. I close my eyes. I try not to cry.

"What?"

"You're not mad about yesterday?"

He snorts into my neck. His voice is lower now, croaky. "I'm not squirreling some pathetic nut. I have as much as I want."

"Mr. Cartel," I whisper.

"It's not that. You're such a teenager, yah know? For someone, like, twice my age, you're really . . . arrested development? Is that a thing?"

"Thing's a thing," I say. I tongue the star of his chin. "Chin's a chin."

He combs his fingers through my hair and turns up The Clash. "Spanish Bombs" goes off on the radio, vanishing us swift and melodic. I close my eyes, pull at the straw. The sky around us brightens. Snow packs us inside the car, like kids buried in sand, and he's moving my skirt and I'm kissing his neck and he's reclining my chair. The world disappears inside a chamber of our heat. Languid, sighfully, oohing, I say to his head in my lap: "I like how you gnaw me." A second later, I yap.

..

I straighten my skirt and swish soda in my mouth, open the door and spit in the snow. An orange splotch shaped like Illinois.

"That," I say.

"So that." Sweat cribs Rot's face. His tone is plowed.

Rolf was the sort of lover who made me do the moving, the insipid bounce and thrust, grinding, riding until my hips ached, my back was textbook lordosis. All the while he stayed cool. Unmussed. Hair moussed, hands manicured. I never want that again.

"What is this—that? A conservatory?" I say. "I'm assuming you've been here."

He nods.

"My family, um, donates to the arboretum. Especially, this. The glasshouse in particular. My sister loved it."

"It's gorgeous," I say. I imagine the winter away and picture us, two miniscule bodies, roving around a greensward. "Show me around."

"I wish I could. But the weather's supposed to get bad-bad. We have to get you back to school, missy."

"Let me ditch," I say. "I like to be your teenager."

"This is fun. You're fun. Let's keep it that. I don't mean to be an ass. But—"

"But nothing. Whenever it happens, it happens. Whatever whatever. I wish I were a teenager."

"I think you should say what you mean," he says.

I can feel my shoulders inching toward my ears. "What *do* I mean then?"

"It has nothing to do with not being a teenager. You're like every girl who wants to grow up and become someone else. The problem is, you're there. You're grown up and you're not who you want to be."

I scoff. Joe Strummer wails on "Rock the Casbah." And it's like the noise of our fucking has been squelched under ice. The windshield is poxed with snow.

"What makes you the every girl expert?" I say. The wine-sleep of last night hits me. I'm tired. "Who do you—"

"Fine, not every girl. My little sister's not like that."

"And how old is she?" I say, ready to spar.

"Fourteen."

"My daughter's age. Give her time."

"That's a pretty shitty way for a mom to think."

"Maybe I'm a pretty shitty mom."

The CD stops. The more serious Rot gets, the harder his jaw squares.

"You can dispute that," I say, trying to laugh.

"I'm not into lying to people's faces."

"Noble of you. What's your sister's secret?"

With the heel of his hand, Rot rubs his left eye. He grimaces, like he's suppressing a stretch. Then he's cackling, laughing, a wafery huff.

"I crack myself up," he says. "Sorry. Sorry. My sister? She does what she wants."

I wave my hands, at the car and the greenhouse and the snow and the soda and the skirt, at Rot. "Isn't that what I'm doing?"

"If you are, you're not very convincing."

"I'm forty," I say. "You know that, right?"

"Whoop de fucking doo. A couple months ago, John Glenn—at seventy-seven—took his old balls into space. Tell me again what's so special about age? What does how long you've lived on this earth matter? John Keats, Mozart, Charlie Fischer?"

"Bobby Fischer."

"Whatever. Who cares how old you are?"

"I don't know."

"I do," Rot says. "Forty isn't old at all. Forty is when you have enough shit under your belt that you can actually make a go at your dreams. Forty is when you take that hard look at your life and say, damn, I'm a zombie. Or, fuck. I hate who I've become—except, oh wait: now I'm smart enough and, like, capable enough to change."

"I think you're young." It's so depressing. "You have a beautiful hopefulness. And I'm sorry if I—"

"What do you want?" He's in the driver's seat, his body angled toward me. "And don't say *a bad boy*."

I shake my head. I want to tell him how naïve he is, how responsibilities alter everything, that marriage and children demand time and remand aims, how the ways out dwindle, but I can't. I don't want him to hear me lying to myself.

"I don't know." I open the door. The cold lashes my skin, the sweat. "Life is funneling you through, squirting you out empty. I just want to be left with something."

He gets out of the car and comes around, puts one of his green jacketed arms around my back. He ushers me into my car.

In the side mirror, I glimpse myself: snow in my hair, on my eyebrows, my bare hands. The heat is still blowing. He holds up a finger.

One moment.

A sumptuous minute. I close my eyes. Orchids and ferns garlanding stone cupids, I picture, vines and tendrils, verdure inside the glasshouse, trellises and gardenesque fascinators. You can fantasize without a specific object. Flange me, Eros. Then, a rapping on the Saab's pane.

Rot bows, his arm behind his back. For madam, let me slake thee: a half-drunk Crush.

6 ·· ELLIOT

WHAT'S SCARY ABOUT LIFE IS how clearly you remember the bits. Reposed on my bed, on top of the covers, in my coat, baggie of heroin on my sternum, a tableau *muy elegante* with spindle legs and white stuff and black fabric, my Larry bussed hood, I wore headphones, like indoor earmuffs. On Repeat, the Smashing Pumpkins murmured "Perfect."

Billy Corgan's voice was a wishbone: pull, pull, split. He sang *purr* like a raft to float away on, Ophelia down the I&M Canal, and his every word sent more of my heart to Lisa.

Stuck in my head was a phone call from more the start of the school year, the night I talked to Lisa after I stumbled into another client. One sec Sheena Sharma and I were in her basement, coloring a poster for Science, drawing the prairie dropseed we'd sniffed (it smelled like popcorn); the next, Sheena was pivoting in her pointelle undies, sobbing that she needed to be smaller for beam if she wanted to make state.

Now, from my bed, I could see the computer screen. The music was soft, knitted inside me; it could've been my own breath. I listened through the lyrics for the creaky door that meant someone new had signed on to AOL.

She wants me to help her diet, I'd told Lisa that day with Sheena. *Isn't that so random?*

Not really. Lisa's tone was game-on, not judgy. *Dr. Ogbaa says anorexia kinda wrangles girls. Sorry.* Everyone *wants to be thinner. Even the president—he's fat, one day he's jogging, the next he's condemning heroin chic, the next he's got a Big Mac. We're a yo-yo nation: size six to zero, Hardee's to Snackwells. And you've been anorexic since fifth—you're like the Doogie Howser of EDs. Sheeney probably thinks you're a mini celebrity.*

You too, Miss Hospitalization. Miss Feeding Tube. You got thinner than me.

Yeah, but, how long did that last? Your parents let you maintain a weight of . . . what—?

Eighty, post dinner, I'd said.

Damn. Not crushin' on that, believing my body is beautiful at any weight. Actually, hear that? There's like two of me: ano-rexic-me, who wants to be like you, and fighter-me, who's doing all this therapy. If there's a recovered me, she's like . . . one toe in that lake.

Lake Michigan?

Um . . . more like Goose Lake, Lisa'd said.

I'd laughed. *Oh, the manmade drainage ditch thingy in our subdivision?*

Yeah, and it's a shaky, unpolished toe that's totally freaked out about getting a staph infection from all the goose poop in the lake.

But also, it's a very small lake.

Right, Lisa had said. *One toe in, and before you know it, I'm walking on the other side.*

"Perfect" was starting again. I buried my face in the pillow: it smelled like my dad's mousse, like apple pie jellybeans. When I started with Sheena, Lisa didn't think coaching was so sick. She didn't pose ultimatums. Refeeding, Monday night LoveThySelf sessions, family therapy with Kim the Harridan—*recovering* was her deal, not changing me. What had changed her? I wanted Larry Breit to be right. For the diet pills to have been more than something she forgot to trash. I wanted to believe I knew Lisa, even though, in my heart, I wondered. I wondered who I was, too. And I wondered who I was waiting for on AOL.

A ding interrupted the song. I squeezed my eyes, my brain tumbling in an ocean of Scotch. A ding wasn't a door. A ding wasn't Lisa pleading, *Ellie. Rescue me. Use your $$$ to send me a limo.* Did ED units even let girls use computers? A ding was a client: other than Lisa, those were my contacts. And I'd wager all $370 of my *Real Talk* profits on which one. After Mr. Breit dropped me off, I'd logged on to a chain of messages:

RoHo1984: u help me w sumthinnnnnn

RoHo1984: 8 pizza 4 lunch but no cheese bahhahahhaha

RoHo1984: pepporon = proteeeeen?

RoHo1984: . . . why???? Mr. Kasparek wrote MOM = WOW on the whiteboard

RoHo1984: ELLIOT!!! u have time 2day? i can pay

I'd sent my phone number and address, and asked to be picked-up; *RoHo1984* obliged.

Park's bell would toll in fifteen minutes. Right now, the unfortunate heifers were hurting, the skin caliper clamping their thighs. Maybe Rocyo had anticipated her despair. I'd started swearing in fifth grade, when I last got tested: if your body fat percentage were 29, you'd say *fuck*, too.

I sat up. The heroin was on the comforter, patient as a rock. *You're not going back—don't look that way*, I'd read on a Zen tire shop's sign. I liked that. Rocyo would be here. I needed to get my *Real Talk* binder, my diet kit, my black mini backpack.

I stood, stretched, bent left and right. Did fifty jumping jacks to defog my head. My mouth tasted dry, fumbled, disgusting. I went to my desk.

I moved the mouse and my computer awoke. Thank God: no more chats from Roho. Instead, a pop-up window blinked. I'd never seen this one:

GROUPS
XX JUST AS BORED X AS ME
NO FRIENDS IN COMMON
MALSUVIALMOLLOY IS ASKING YOU TO JOIN A GROUP

Join   No Thanks

I stared at the choice. The day had swallowed me, and I felt like I was reading the invitation from inside a distended sac.

Join?

I wanted to click and click and click.

I bit my lower lip, a petal of dry skin. Tasted iron and blood. Around boys they liked, my clients worried about every blink. They couldn't raise their hands in class, for fear of pit stains and armpit stragglies. I watched the box, expecting it to *Poof!* Disappear. Could Ethan hit "Undo" in Chat?

I had to stall. I opened my closet. In his red and whites, Michael Jordan was grinning. A basketball hugged to his hip, an armband wrapping his wrist, clean socks, fat-tongued sneakers, his muscles were so defined, he looked stuffed with tubers. What would he do with my life—what lay-ups, what dunks? Beside him a yellow ruler measured six inches. But in the poster, inches equaled feet. I had a long way to go. I only came up to MJ's chest, his jersey, the letter B.

I grabbed my backpack and shut the door. The last thing I needed was another adult looking down on me.

Ethan's message was waiting. I stood at my desk, the screen in my peripheral. My computer felt like a camera or something with a conscious, a heart, a brain, recording, capturing. This was new: a boy—a friend—messaging me.

"What the hell," I whispered. I clicked *Join*.

A bigger whiter page appeared. I'd never been in a chat room. How to begin? *ElleGirl80: I'm drunk? Oops—forgot you're XXX straight-edge?* I typed. I held down "Delete."

A car horn squawked at the same instant that the phone rang. I scurried to the window. Stalled at the foot of my driveway, a yellow convertible had its top down, like a school bus for pimps. I couldn't make out the music, but the bass shuddered up to my glass. I dashed for my parents' room, to the closest phone.

"You see us? I saw you," Rocyo said. "Ready?"

"Yeah, grabbing my stuff."

Back in my room, I hovered over the computer. I would check the chat, without peeking. I shut my eyes, let the heat build, opened.

MalSuvialMolloy: What's up, Ghouliet?

MalSuvialMolloy: You weren't playing Texas Chainsaw Massacre by yourself today, were you?

The horn honked again. I X'd out of the chat. My heart thumped. What did I need? All I could think of was how

badly I wanted to be wanted. By Ethan, by Lisa, even by my
Mom, even by Rocyo. I looked around. The drugs: I shoved
them back in my coat pocket. From my underwear drawer,
I took the envelope of my client cash. It was fat, fives and
singles, jingly—Marissa'd paid with quarters. I might need
options. Who knew how late my mom would be today.

..

Rocyo's sister was one of those girls whose hands look good
in gloves. Feather-fingered, graceful, not tumefied into
Minnie Mouse mitts. Hands like Anna's—that's what I saw
from the backseat. Static crinkled Power 92 "Number One
in the Streets." The extended remix of "California Love" had
been in heavy rotation ever since December, when Tupac's
Greatest Hits dropped.

"You sick?" Rocyo craned from the front seat. Her feet
splayed on the dash, windshield-wiping to the music.
Grubby pink fuzzies dotted her white socks. "Or you, what?
Skip a test?"

"Nah, I'm fine. My mom's cool with me home. Taking a
mental health day."

"That's so bitchin', I'm jelly. Cool you still help with our
project!" She winked at me. "What we do today? Shoulda
been a four-day weekend. We listen to Harper talk about
World War. Kasparek was so wasted! Mom? Wow? *Dios*—"

"How is that even educational?"

"You guys need to stop criticizing everyone and be students," Rocyo's sister said. Her hair was like Selena's, on the
cover of "Dreaming of You." I still had the single, from pre-
flaca days, before I discovered radio beyond pop. "I loved

Park. I'd go back in a minute. You got stand-up people looking out for you. Trust your teachers. They're there for a reason."

"This one," Rocyo said. "She think she's Mommy Number Two. Like, what I gotta be there every day?"

"Yah do," said her sister.

I was waiting to be introduced. Rocyo's sister hurried through yellow lights, revving past Park. Already, the parking lot was almost empty, nearly vacated for the long weekend. I felt invisible.

"Otherwise, you'll be talkin' to some net scrub. Or conversating with Anthony."

"As if," said Rocyo. She gave me a crazy look.

"Girl. I wouldn't put it past you to bird flirt—with a lil' sum-sum on the side."

Rocyo buzzed her lips. "How 'bout you, Elliot? Who you like? Anthony?"

I paused, flattered. Rocyo was interested—or good at faking. I searched for an answer. A fleet of black shopping bags from Express shared the backseat with me. The car smelled like evergreen air freshener. A green cardboard pine tree dangled from the rearview mirror. Snowflakes stuck to the floor mats. Oh yeah, I remembered. The top was down. I held up a hand and touched the sky.

Only Lisa knew about my crush. The second you told girls anything, Park caught fire like a popsicle stick project. But the Scotch had lowered my inhibitions. *Why not*, I thought. *What the hell.* "Actually, I do—"

"Oh my god! Turn her up! I love this!" Rocyo screamed. "Brit!"

The way she said *Brit* sounded like Breit. I shoved my hands in my pockets and hugged the drugs. I could never truly confide in a girl like Rocyo. She and her sister swerved their heads to the beat. During the chorus, they rallied off each other's lines and swung their ponytails, chanting along to "(Hit Me Baby) One More Time" like it wasn't about sex.

..

"You wanna snack?" Rocyo said. We were inside the red-roofed house. Her sister—still nameless—had vanished. "We got juice box."

The car ride had sobered me. I was hungry. No breakfast, no lunch, and last night's dinner: a shred of Lean Cuisine cheese? I wanted to eat, but I couldn't do that with Rocyo. I only ate when I outlined that in the client's plan: *Elliot will model diet-paced consumption.* Then, I'd place my Casio on the table, set the timer for twenty minutes, and show a girl how slowly to deconstruct a clementine.

I conked my head and rolled my eyes. "Do *you* want a snack?"

"I don't know. I'm hungry."

"Did you follow the meal plan?"

(Half a bun, no butter. Carrot, meat from whatever Lunchable. Gulps of $H2O$ from the good fountain by the upstairs boys' bathroom during passing periods.)

"Mr. Rhodes ordered pizza at lunch—for Martin Luther King's *actual* birthday. You know he have an affair?"

"King or Rhodes? You ate that?"

"No cheese. Three squares."

"Did you blot for grease?"

"Whuh?"

"Never mind. No, no snack. What's the dilly?"

Rocyo put her hand on my back and guided me toward the stairs. I was nervous. Her touch radiated through my coat, up my spine, a hot poker stabbing my skeleton. Or maybe that was the Scotch. I lingered at the cursive railing, the metal cold beneath my palms. I leaned.

"*Puta, puta!*" Anthony squawked, suddenly behind us.

"*Chode!*" Rocyo said. "C'mon, Eel-ot. Sorry."

Her room was warmer than yesterday. Heat made me feel fat. I unzipped my coat and scratched my ribs through my black sweater. Rocyo and I sat on the Grover rug, facing each other, knees up. My backpack slouched like the IV bag Lisa had gotten during her first hospitalization, creepy clear calories hanging from a pole. Lisa had worn it like a Miss America sash.

The room was soundless, except for a distant thudding.

"My sister, she doing Simmons. Sweat to the Oldies. Nerd."

"You ever join her?" I said, tensing my abs. I would've loved a work-out bud.

"As if!"

"Hm. Maybe think about that. But anywho! What's going on?"

Rocyo reached into a pocket of her cargo pants. She unfolded something pink on my calf.

The Post-It was heart-shaped; on it, her handwriting was Tetris-blocky: *Miss Troubaugh knows.*

I pushed up the sleeve of my coat and held out my arm. "Dork. No kidding! She saw yesterday. She's, like, the pinnacle of overreacting."

"Saw what?" Rocyo said.

I glanced at my wrist. The scars had calmed into nothing. "The—"

Rocyo's mouth gaped. "She see *Real Talk.*"

Somewhere in the house, hands clapped. I envisioned the pretty, nameless sister doing jumping jacks or knee lifts or hammy curls. Her hair going wavy with damp. Why wasn't I with her instead of the *grossera*? I took a breath. Rocyo was dim. She'd probably gotten this wrong.

"What do you mean, babe?"

"I go for body fat. So, Troubaugh say, leg up. She clips my thigh. Okay. And she does my arm. And then, boom, okay, 24 percent. Good, not bad. Except . . ."

"What?"

"Except you write in *Real Talk*. 'Over twenty is . . .' No good. What did you write?"

"'Bogus,' is, I think, the word you're looking for."

"Well I start crying *y* Miss Troubaugh asks what's wrong? And I say, I can't be over twenty. It's pizza. And she says, why can't you be twenty? And I say, *Elliot says*."

I raked my fingers through the rug's blue tufts. "Elliot says what?"

"Says . . . says in *Real Talk*. I show Miss Troubaugh."

My hand was all fist. "You what?!"

"The one you gave me yesterday."

"No. *Why? ¿Por qué?* W-H-Y? *Comprende*, dummy?"

Rocyo stood. "Don't talk like that in my house. You got me in trouble. Now I meet with everyone, the nurse *y* counselor, principal. You, too. Tuesday."

"What are you talking about, me, too?"

"Miss Troubaugh says. You're outta line."

"And what did you say, stupid?"

"*Perdida*. I said, no, she help. Elliot weighs eighty pounds. She's good at skinny."

My stomach hung over my head, like I'd plummeted on Giant Drop at Six Flags. Soon, I'd be tunneling, strapped into a molded seat, plunging through crust, mantle, inner and outer core, the hot pit of death that was the nucleus of teen shame, absolute mortification, sayonara, cowabunga, dudette. I was screwed.

Rocyo knelt. Tears glazed her sausage-colored eyes. She put her palm on my knee. Her thumbs were chubby. I imagined those fingers mining my vagina. Barf.

"I'm sorry," she said. "I fuck up."

She stuck out her lower lip, like a ledge she was saving for my apology.

"You sure did." I jerked my knee away from her touch. "We're done."

"But I pay!"

"As if I care!" I was furious. I groped in my backpack for the envelope of cash. I slipped out a five and threw the bill at her. "Take your money."

Rocyo blinked. "Elliot, I don't want it. Please. Let me help." She stretched out one arm, like she was spanning a lunch table. Then, she threw her body at me.

The dizziness that came whenever I stood hurled me into blackness except now I was falling. I toppled. My brain was space junk, orbiting out of our solar system as Rocyo pinned my wrists. She smelled like Gap Om, Pepsi, Fritos. She pressed her cheek to my chest.

"What are you doing? Get off me, molester!"

Rocyo was straddling me, her weight a steady pressure, heavy on my hips. I twisted and twisted but I was stuck.

"You help me. You gonna make me beautiful. I need the rules. I don't wanna go fat to high school. Please!" She brought her face up to mine, an Eskimo kiss away. Then she tackled me with her lips.

"Ugh!" I donkey-kicked into her stomach. I scrambled to my feet. I grabbed my backpack. "Leave me alone! Gay rod!"

"Wait! Please, Elliot! I need—"

I ran. The iron railing looked like a cage, melted down and twisted into bars of music. I didn't need to fling myself over any edge. People like Rocyo were everywhere, ready to do the flinging for me. I pounded down the stairs.

"*¡No me molesta!*" screamed Anthony. "*¡No me molesta!*"

I struggled with the deadlock. I needed to get out.

"Whatcha do, Ro-Ro?" said a voice behind me.

I turned. The pretty sister was standing there in bike shorts and an oversized T-shirt knotted with a white scrunchie.

"Elliot!" Rocyo called, running, her cargo pants unzipped. "Don't go!"

The sister laughed. "You gettin' after cooch again, *Chiqui*?"

"*Cerdita!*" Rocyo spat.

With a yank, the door heaved. There was the world, gusting snow and wilted tinsel onto the front porch. A shriek of wind lurched me into the streets.

7 ·· LISA

EVEN PRE-ANOREXIA, THE STUPIDEST RULES controlled me: Hop over cracks in the sidewalk. Let Eucharist dissolve (no teeth) on your tongue. Finish every book you start—even *The Babysitters Club: Kristy's Big Idea*. I used to think microwaving ice cream was cheating. Before my Year of Sadness (seventh grade, the realization that starvation turned real life into your very own epic drama), I was a bowl-a-night girl. From my grandmother, I learned a pantry makes vanilla exciting. Marshmallow Fluff. Honey-roasted peanuts. Strawberry jam. Hot fudge. (I wonder what her last flavor will be.)

But after talking to Georgette, I realized doing what you want means disregarding rules. My first change when I got home, between seventh and eighth grade? I started microwaving pints. Fifteen seconds right-side up, fifteen seconds upside down. I stopped believing in right or wrong. No one could define my standards for me. My food, my stomach. If I wanted to zap my Cherry Garcia, big whup.

We're on Munchies of Menace: MoM according to the schedule. We're back in the room where we listened to "Tubthumper." Today's frightening food . . . drumroll please . . . ice cream.

Marjorie posts up in the corner with a clipboard. Skank is taking princess steps around the circle of patients, like this is all whatever, like it's snack day, like she's leading a pony or playing Duck Duck Goose. Everyone is tapped on the head with a choice.

Ice cream sandwich or Drumstick.

My other times at Carousel Gardens, MoM coincided with AM or PM snack. Today, scheduling it on the kitten heels of lunch is cruel. Okay, not for me—I'll do ice cream *as* my meal (like those dorky shirts my dad wears, *NO FEAR*). But some patients straight-up panic at MoM. It's gotten ugly: Johnny Depp trashing the hotel. The male nurses with canvas restraints are on-call. I feel bad for girls who are scared of Twinkies or Sun Chips. I remember their terror from last summer: touching the crunchy skin of a fried chicken breast; the gagged feeling of crying over a mouthful of dry white meat.

"Drumsticks?" Phoebe says. "Are you shitting me?"

I snicker. At lunch, I sat next to her, too. Why hadn't Elliot been cool about writing? Fun fact: Phoebe's revising a novel. Her hospitalization—aside from being research for the book that necessitates she escalate all possible confrontations—is, she said, a mistake. *Me too*, I said, trying to ignore Skank and Marjorie twirling their sundried tomato linguini. *Mistake, not novel.*

"Language," says Skank. "What is that: violation number two?"

"Ew, you violate your number two?" Phoebe says.

Skank thrusts a Drumstick in its white plastic at her. Phoebe pincers it, thumb and pointer, like it's wet toilet paper, a dead rat.

"Can I have two?" I ask. "Or, like, one of each? Decisions make me ralph."

Skank narrows her eyes. She probably thinks because we walked down the unit together, because she gave me a message from J.C., we're best friends. She probably thinks my sass is a betrayal, like I'm breaking some Patient-Staff Code. As if.

"That would be a behavior. We haven't portioned for seconds."

"Yeah you have," Phoebe says. I know exactly who'd she be in school: that girl who doesn't shut up. The girl who teachers pull aside, pleading: give other kids a chance. Well, why should she? Her answers are always right. "You've *clearly* portioned for seconds—*each* of those boxes have eight. There are nine of us. Two more if you and Marj are modeling. So. *Why* can't baby girl have two? Miss Thang? Miss Sun-In?"

Skank's nostrils flare. "Um, that's a second violation. You can call me Bethany."

Marjorie pads over. The more I watch, the more I see she could lose weight. Her hips, her haunches: she waddles. Her expression is ruffled; her forehead, ruched.

"What's happening, lassies?"

"Woof. Woof, woof," says Phoebe. "Timmy. Get out. The well. Oh no. He's drowning. Drowning. I'm melting. He's dead."

"What's your problem?" says Skank.

"Um, have you read T.C. Boyle? Oh, I forgot. Miss Defiantly definitely has the skillz of a third-grader."

Skank claps her hands in front of Phoebe's face. "Are you retarded?"

"Bethany, that's enough," says Marjorie. "Pass out those things before they—"

"So do I get two?" I ask.

"No," Marjorie says. "And I think we both know belaboring the matter is a waste of everyone's time. Lisa, biscuit—not every John needs Paul, George, and Ringo."

Skank/Bethany scowls and her nose gets puggy. She looks pleased, like Marjorie reprimanding me tastes delicious. She deposits a Drumstick into my lap.

"What's in your craw? Balls?" I fold my hands across my thighs and flick her two middle fingers.

Skank/Bethany's eyebrows reach for her hairline. "Marjorie, is retardation contagious on this Unit? Is this—"

"Bethany, talk to Station. Right now. Give me the treats."

Marjorie takes the boxes. As she's distributing ice cream to the other girls, Phoebe shoots out her palm, face up, even with my hip.

"Side five," she whispers. "Operation Remove One Staff Member complete." I slap her lightly, like my touch weighs nothing, the way Cher and her crew toss their hair in *Clueless*. "Your departure is *so* bagged."

"I hope so," I whisper.

"All right," says Marjorie, gesturing with a Drumstick. (Note to Dr. Ogbaa: no way for Staff to eat with EDP girls that isn't Urkel annoying.) A peanut flies into the center of our semicircle. Eight pairs of eyes hone in on it. "So we begin. As feelings come up, raise your hand so we can process."

Marjorie takes a big bite out of her Drumstick. Old ladies have that bulletproof thing. How does she withstand brain freeze? She covers her mouth and chomps.

The room is pre-marathon mute, the moment before the speech team judge starts his stopwatch, but the starting gun never sounds and minutes stand still. Some tongues pop out, puppyish, licking lines of ice cream, the sides between cocoa wafers. Drumsticks are more complicated. Phoebe breaks off the bottom, where we all know there's a chocolate nugget. I hold my cone, waiting until veins of vanilla start oozing out the shell, waiting until the inside is drippy and melty, waiting until everything is so soft I don't need to chew. I can practically suck out the insides of the Drumstick like a tube of Fla-Vor-Ice or a langoustine or—*swoon*—Junior Carlos's D.

..

Tell El: By the time we go to the visiting room, Phoebe and I are BFFs. I imagine, in another life, she's my big sister. She's attending an impossibly urbane college in a city bigger than Chicago, and she's trench-coating me into Goth nightclubs where guys in black eyeliner clasp leather bracelets around our wrists, marking us as their skinny slaves. She's taking me out for fifteen-inch slices of pizza that we fur with parmesan; we tear off the crusts, sniff deeply, give the waste to homeless dudes. In the morning, she makes coffee—not the sludge my dad brews—but delicious, foamy skim cappuccinos in big bowls like they use on *Friends* at Central Perk. She's *my* Phoebe, but Courtney-Cox-sized (I'll be Rachel). We coordinate Joe Boxer jammies. I'm reading her drafts and voicing her dialogue. Who can believe what a mature little sis that Lisa is?! She sits in on fiction workshops, comments sagely, and no one blinks an eye.

Marjorie leads a line of us to our visits. Only four girls have parents or friends or boyfriends coming. If I weren't so excited to see Junior Carlos, I'd feel sad for the other patients, the ones stuck in the unit with the dietician, watching a video about the merits of carbohydrates. Eating disorders are lonely without regular people. I know: My mom convinced my dad that visiting me at Carousel Gardens would be like rewarding me, making me a celebrity, giving me an undeserved prize for bad behavior. In the three months of that first hospitalization, I only had one visitor: Elliot.

The six of us walk past the intake office. The door is closed, its half-moon window partially obscured by a ruby red tinsel wreath. Inside is a girl who doesn't yet realize she's about to get my bed. I know I'm in recovery because I don't even wonder how her body compares to mine. Mentally, I wish her luck with Skank.

Three cold fingers tiptoe across my neck. I fall in stride with Phoebe.

"You ready?" she says. Her eyes are pregame, flinty. She looks pumped.

"Obviously. This is what I want."

"Marjorie." Phoebe's tone is over-the-top. "Why did Bethany call me a retard?"

Marjorie pauses at the double-doors that separate the locked unit from public areas. Her ID card dangles on a pink lanyard. She rubs the card, then claps it between two fingers, like she's killing a flea. Her hands shake.

"It would be easy for me to say you were annoying her, wouldn't it?"

Phoebe shrugs.

"Yes, you were. And I'm not sure why you seem proud of that. But, emotions aside, I see no circumstance . . . no reason for any—patient or staff—to use that word."

Marjorie hunches close to the sensor. She doesn't remove the lanyard to swipe her ID. When the two doors pull apart, like ghosts in a supermarket, we follow her.

"I definitely was annoying," Phoebe says.

To get to the visitation room, you cut through the lobby. Today, except for at the front desk, where a receptionist is reading *Bridget Jones's Diary*, the room is empty.

Noise is the main change when you cross the border between committed and free. It's quiet. For fourteen chairs, there are four TVs on Mute: Jerry Springer, some soap opera, Jerry Springer. *Pinky and the Brain.*

Phoebe pauses in front of the cartoons and starts humming the theme song.

I fakesy-punch her ribs. Through her dark-green sweatshirt, I feel her bones and her muscles, wiry, breakable, a stretched-out Slinky. "Geek."

"Geek's a chicken eater."

On the tube, the Brain wears an ACE bandage around his head like a turban.

"Huh?"

"Geek—it's like a guy at a carnival who bites the heads off live chickens."

"Ew! Why do you know the randomest stuff?"

"Well, that's what writing—"

Marjorie shakes her wrist: no watch. "Eating into visits, girleens."

If they could, other EDP girls would probably love that: eating time. They're like me—terrified and exhilarated by counting down to the end. If someone said, *super power: you can gobble the minutes until you die*, who would binge and who would starve?

I observe everything, like catching clues on *Ghostwriter*. White wall, two placards: Chapel to the left. Visiting to the right. Which means, in moments, my escape route will be

Exit, turn right, left into Lobby, beeline for Junior Carlos's Bimmer.

Marjorie and the other girls keep walking. But I'm nervous. I pause. I don't know why I'm so scared. With every beat, my heart burrows deeper and deeper into my chest. I wait for it to break through my back, hatch from me like an alien.

..

Hardcore PDA is frowned upon in visiting rooms: now I know. Sure, we're told not to accept gifts or foods without running them by staff, but no one's said anything about making out.

Junior Carlos clutches a bouquet of hot-pink roses with one hand, my waist with the other. He tastes like orange soda and aftershave and breadcrumbs. He kisses me. We're in a play, live-action, one-take, all-in, now or never. Tongue, tongue, tongue.

"Ahmmmm," Marjorie says. "Greet and move on, Lisa. Please."

I float down from tiptoe. Two pairs of parents are shooting death rays from their bovine eyes. Phoebe, blank-staring at her mother (equally skinny, thicker blacker hair, no nose ring), flashes me a thumbs-up.

"That's my friend," I say to Junior Carlos. We walk over to the table closest to the door. It's set like this is a luncheon, with vases of daisies and ivory lace placemats. The room *would* be more civilized if it were like the Oak Room, downtown, where my grandmother and I used to get tea and popovers. He pulls out a chair for me. I lift my chin in Phoebe's direction. "The pretty one."

"Lee-Lee. There's only one pretty one in this room. In this hospital—"

"You're gonna make me hot."

He nods, all sexy and skeezy. "Then you haven't forgotten what I like."

Junior Carlos twists the pink ski tag dangling from his zipper. The paper comes off in his hand. He looks at it, crams it in a pocket, and unzips his coat. Underneath, he's wearing a T-shirt—under that, I can tell from the collar, another T-shirt. This is something boys, who don't have to worry about the bulkiness of layering, can do.

"So . . . what's the weather like out there?" I eye Marjorie, who's seated in the far-most corner of the room, diagonal from the door.

"Not stuffy like in here."

"Yeah . . . stuffy in my brain."

"Your parents call? Do you know what's up with your grandma yet?"

"Hah. Ha-ha. That would involve them being conscious."

"Conscientious?"

"Whatever."

"Well, no news is—"

"So is it snowing?" I say. My voice is slippery. "Will I need a jacket?"

Junior Carlos stretches his arms out wide. His eyes are glued on me. He wriggles out of the coat and puts it on the table, a bright green heap between us. Without it, he looks vulnerable. Halfway undressed.

"Dude, your fly is open," I say. I kick his chair leg with the heel of my shoe. The metal thwacks flatly. "What's that say—*Ar-man-i*. Is that a phoenix?"

He flushes. His black stubble is more subtle when his skin has some color.

"It's an eagle. These are cheap. Emporio."

The girls and their parents talk in low, guiding voices. I can't hear anything specific anyone says, but I get vibes: doubt, concern, hope, horror. With my fingernail, I scratch a black fuzzy on the placemat. I glance at Phoebe. She's pressing her pinky into her nose, screwing her nose piercing. In the corner, Marjorie leans against the wall. An Agatha Christie novel is open on her clipboard.

"Wanna take off?" I say to Junior Carlos.

You only need codes if you care about what other people think.

He nods. "After you, beautiful."

I stand up and push over my chair. It clatters against the floor. Junior Carlos pops up.

"You okay, baby?" he says. He sounds stagey. He's a bad actor.

"Oops." I smile at the room, like a curtsey, thank you, thank you, enjoy the performance. I pick up the chair. Make a show of pushing it back into the table until its maroon back pad is an inch from the lacy placemat. I grab J.C.'s green coat. It's heavy. I tuck it under my arm and saunter toward the door.

"Lisa," Marjorie says. "Where—"

"Skank, bitch, fuck, shit, shit, dammit, cunt!" Phoebe yells. I hear her fists pounding the table like it's a bass drum. "Oh hell! Fuck! Christ sandwich! Balls!"

I scurry into the hall, shuffling, my red Converse loose and annoying without their laces. Junior Carlos is behind me.

"Don't lose a shoe, Cinderella." He rushes ahead, pushes open the door to the lobby, and we bolt. The receptionist's eyes land on us.

"Left the car running," Junior Carlos says to her. He doesn't stop moving, but he grins, and it's one of those looks that can totally bust a woman's kneecaps. *Smooth.*

"You can't just go outside with a patient, young man," says the receptionist.

I run through the automatic doors, and break into the cold. Snowflakes dump thick and heavy from the sky.

"Fuck!" I say. "Where are you?"

Junior Carlos grabs my elbow and pulls me with him.

"Right by handicapped. It's open. C'mon!"

"Lisa Breit, get back here," a woman shouts. Her voice quavers like a viola. It's Marjorie. But only idiots turn to see who they're leaving behind.

Junior Carlos's BMW is flicked with snow, parked between a white van and a red pickup. I open the door and throw myself in the passenger seat. The car is warm and damp feeling. It smells like chlorine and locker room. He opens the driver's door and slides in.

"Oh shit!" he yells. "Why don't I steal more often?"

I laugh. "Let's go! Go! Go! Now!"

I slap the volume on the radio. "Rock the Casbah" starts. I press ">>" and ">>" and ">>" until I get to "Lost in the Supermarket." Junior Carlos backs out. The car swings, and we're heading toward the parking lot's perimeter. Somewhere behind us, an ambulance siren yowls.

"Oh my god!" I sweep my hair into a ponytail. I feel giddy. Alive. Like every vocab word: Resplendent, adrenalized, enraptured. "How did that just work?"

"Mad props. That was like *Speed* or something. Un-believable."

I settle back into the seat and buckle up. Something bunches under my butt. Flippers, goggles, towels, trunks: I've sat on his swim stuff. This time, though, I reach around and grab a set of black leather gloves.

"Swank." I smell them. They're perfumey. They feel like brushing against a baby's cheek. "Whose are *these*?"

Junior Carlos's glance goes akimbo. "My mom. She told me she lost those. She'll be . . . relieved relieved. Stupid expensive."

I toss the gloves from hand to hand. "Nice. I mean, she might not miss 'em."

"Oh no. You don't want to know what those bad boys cost."

"'And if you don't know, now you know, nnnnnnn,'" I sing. "Don't you have any Biggie? We're, like, in my dad's CD tower."

"Hey! Don't knock—"

"Gleep!" I spread my fingers and start to try on the left glove. I do what I want—except when the leather won't go over my first knuckles.

8 ·· ELLIOT

THE CUL-DE-SAC WAS AN OMEGA. The house I headed for was the apex of the extrados, the keystone, a crumb from Ridgedale's table—but the only crumb I knew. Being friends with girls would have been über-convenient. The only person I could randomly ask for a ride was Anna, and the only person I randomly could ask to use the phone was my crush. I braced myself against the cold and speed-walked up *Mal-SuvialMolloy*'s driveway.

So this was boyhood. Super Soaker pistols, colorful as honked party horns, littered the white-blanketed yard. Droplets of dog pee pocked a vector at the base of a snowman with a carrot pecker. I'd never been to a guy's house; I'd never surveyed my crush's lawn. In another circumstance, I'd marvel at my bravura, but this Friday was so weird I expected pigs to flap across the sky, to rut around in the clouds.

More than anything, I wanted to talk to Lisa. I wanted to tell her about the drugs and Rocyo, even flirting with her dad. A whole day had piled on to everything I'd wanted to say yesterday, but I couldn't talk to Lisa until I got home, to a phone, and only then if she was desperate enough to accept a call from me in the hospital.

The steps to the Suva's front porch were shoveled down to concrete. I climbed up. There was a stoop, but no walls or awnings or railings to block the wind. I shivered. The cold honed in on the shreds of black denim that revealed my knees. *Rodillas*, said my volition, cake to remember: your knees were the rods of your legs, held you ramrod straight— but also aided your bends. I worked holes in Señora Lurke's pneumonic devices to feel smart, worked holes in my clothes to show off my body's largest organ. Skin: mine was velum or muslin, mottled or moiré.

Jalousie windows framed the front door, but I couldn't see anything except the broad strokes of my reflection. I was nervous. The sun was already setting, a cracked orange glow stick. I couldn't go back to Rocyo's. If Ethan or one of his brothers or his mom didn't answer, how would I get a hold of Anna? And when I did reach her, how would I not accuse her of being a junkie? I felt like an ingrate, a brat, a bad daughter: I hadn't even been thinking about her addiction. I pressed the doorbell; it shined yellow when it chimed.

I bent down, picked at a string in my jeans. I ripped it off, rubbed it between my thumb and index finger until it balled, and set it on the back of my tongue. The string tasted like a dull thought. I couldn't decide if this habit was good or bad, but when I was beyond hungry, I chewed or twisted thread into a knot, like Miss Hiday had done with a cherry stem on *Late Night with David Letterman's* Stupid Human Tricks.

With a butter knife clamped between his lips, a fla- menco dancer *con rosa*, Ethan opened the door. His flannel was unbuttoned; underneath he wore a twilight-blue T-shirt with *Nirvana* and their dead-eyed yellow smiley. The collar was frayed with tiny, minus-sign-shaped slits. He jerked his head and flipped away a few strands of greasy hair. The knife stayed still.

"Um, hey," I said. "What's up?"

The blade scraped clean between his teeth as he pulled it from his mouth. He smelled like peanut butter. He looked at me with his green eyes. Every second tripled.

"Do you like . . . did you want me to join some . . . chat group?" I said.

He squinted and waved the knife in the direction of my chest, like that one old sub, infamous at Park for jousting at a pull-down map of the USSR with a pointer.

"Yup. Exactamundo. *On-line*," he said.

"Oh. Well, I was in the neigh—"

"This is better. C'mon in."

He held the door. I stepped onto a mat with an image of a grouper wearing a Santa hat. Inside, the tile was printed with muddy-brown fractals. On the wall, three bright-blue parkas hung by their hoods. The house smelled like mac and cheese.

Ethan motioned to a nimbus of street salt surrounding a plastic tray printed with shoe grooves. I recognized his black-and-white Vans—they looked like they'd waded through pond scum. It was weird seeing them without his feet.

"Can you take off your boots?"

I nodded, balancing against one red wall. Door slams, brothers, parents, guitars, cartoons, TV, deejays, punks, ringing phones, sportscasters: I heard nothing. We were alone.

"I'm just finishing up a snack. Then we chill. Tight?"

"Tight." The word sounded like a frog hopping out of my mouth.

We walked into the kitchen. There was something frightening about being so close to someone I didn't really know. From the door frame, I watched Ethan. He stood at an island. It was covered with packages of all the stuff I told my clients to avoid: Corn Nuts, Fruit Roll-Ups, Fruit by the Foot, Gushers, Oreos, Chips Ahoy, Dunkaroos, Rold Gold buttery pretzels, Doritos 3D. I could feel my eyes bug.

"My mom just raided Sam's Club. My bros like their food big and boxy."

"Hah."

He was spreading peanut butter to the upturned edges of a flour tortilla. He poked the same knife into a jelly jar printed with a cartoon of Roadrunner. The metal clinked glass. He hocked a loogie of grape onto the PB, folded the tortilla in half, and held up the knife like it was another finger.

"You wanna wrap?"

I rested my palms on the counter. He waved a plate, printed with balloons—"Happy Birthday at Discovery Zone!"—under my face.

"Nah, your snack." I shrugged, trying to act like we were two buds, friends, hanging out. But we *were* hanging out, there *were* two of us; maybe friendship was simply a product of repetition.

"Hey, I got a whole pack of tortillas here." He mispronounced the word intentionally, in the ironic way smart but cool, non-jock boys spoke: Tore. Till. Uhzzzz. "And, like, a couple things of Jif."

"Is that vegan?"

He nodded, shook his hair out of his eyes, and took a bite.

I liked watching him chew, the busy way his mouth worked, as if it were fetching out the knot in a kinked-up necklace. I liked him in my jaw and my pelvis and my stomach. I liked his eyes, traffic-light green, go, the long lashes fringing them, go, fawn freckles dappling his nose, go, Elliot, collect two hundred dollars, go. I liked his face, sorta lupine, especially around the chin. I liked how, like me, he had a diet.

"You sure you don't wanna bite? This is one sick PBJ."

With my tongue, I poked around my mouth, looking for the thread. It was gone. I tried not to ogle the snacks. Ethan's brothers had to be stoners. I touched my coat pocket. Maybe they'd want to buy my mom's drugs, if I couldn't figure out how to replace them in the sewing box.

"You're hungry, dudette," said Ethan. "I can tell. I mean, no offense but. You've got that 'gimme some grindage' look."

"I—yah know, that does seem like . . . um. A pretty good wrap. Any chance I could get half . . . a tore till uh?"

"Yeah, mang." He opened a drawer and took out a clean knife. "I'll split ya."

He halved his tortilla and passed me the unbitten part.

"Thanks," I said.

I held the plate under my mouth as I ate. It was an oozy roll-up. Grapey peanut butter dribbled out. I'd forgotten the sweet, cozy rush of a sandwich; it tasted so good, I almost cried. I remembered things, from when my diet included more than apples and Listerine tabs and Lean Cuisines: chocolate ice cream sandwiches with vanilla in between (the ice cream melted, the cookie stuck to your fingers). I remembered fork-and-knifing cheese enchiladas, winding up with a greasy, saucy corn tortilla loop. I missed the fullness that followed those meals, a heavy satisfaction like a giant kneeling on your stomach. I chewed methodically, my mandible creaky from disuse.

"Yum to the O," said Ethan. "Am I right?"

I nodded. He didn't know how right. I looked at the floor. I wore black anklets. Ethan, Umbro socks. Friends hung out sans shoes. Barefoot, belly down, on snow leopard rugs, eating whatever. Friends said: make yourself at home. Wanna watch a movie? Wanna snoop around? Wanna snack? Wanna go upstairs?

..

Ethan's bedroom smelled like celery and felt like a cellar, even though we were on the second floor. It was dark. The burlap curtains were mostly closed: I could see a squint of the snow-blustering sky. I lumped my puffy coat on the porridge-colored carpeting to cushion my tailbone. Ethan was finessing Kurt Cobain's volume. The only part of the song I knew was about will being good.

My eyes were everywhere, exploring the unknown territory of a boy's bedroom. The wallpaper looked like isometric graph paper I'd seen on my dad's desk. On the bookshelf, Beckett showed up thrice (*No Exit, Waiting for Godot, Molloy*) next to other comrades, Nabokov and Burgess and Burroughs. I recognized two shiny hardcovers: Ethan had twice aced About the Author, Park's annual writing contest that resulted in the winner's story being bound and displayed in the Beanbag Bookworm Lounge in the library. (Third and fourth grade—I'd been so mad at myself for not winning. I was supposed to be good at everything.) His bed churned with wrinkly sheets.

Was Ethan's will so good he didn't jack off? Was he better than Lisa's dad? Or me?

I heard the hissy click of a lighter, and two wide pillar candles on a nightstand sizzled. Ethan slid down the side of his bed.

"Woah, this floor's like prison-cell hard." His face twitched like he'd gotten a mini electric shock. "You wanna sit on the bed?"

The house suddenly felt endless. I was nervous.

"Um. . ."

He stood up and yanked on the sheets, sorta straightening them. He leaned a saggy black pillow against the headboard.

"Seriously, mang. More comfy."

I sat down on the bed, knees tented. I covered them with my coat. For an inhale, I was nervous—Lisa and I didn't even hang out this up-close—but if I wanted to make a phone call, I needed to get over that. After all, Ethan had chatted me; I was the one brazen enough to show up at his house. And anyhow, he was sitting at the foot of the bed. Everything was fine enough.

I leaned back. The headboard squeaked from the force of my bony back. "Your parents don't care about you having a girl in your room?"

"I mean, maybe?" He ran over to the CD player, started the song over and lowered the volume. Then he slid down the bed again. Our feet were an inch from touching. "Should they care? Shit, is that like in the manual? Dr. Spock, does he say—"

"Live long and prosper." It was everything I knew about *Star Trek*.

Ethan flashed me the Vulcan V. "I'm talkin' about the guy who died last year. The psychologist or whatnot. Does he say, so, to make your kid normal, care this much?" He held his hands apart. "What, would your parents care?"

For a moment, the song was just guitar, a plodding strumming. The room was murky even with the candles, but I could still see Ethan. His eyes, in the dim, had become hazel. They were glued on me, like we were both under the same covers. It felt good to be watched.

"I don't know . . . I honestly have no clue. My mom wouldn't. My dad? Um . . ."

"Well, even if caring were on the Unit's parental agenda, no one's home."

"No one?"

"Mang, they've got their twenty-four seven on lock. Crib be mine. My moms is at Market Day 'cuz District 107 kiddos gots to get their French toast sticks. Dad plays money at the Merc. My brothers—rolling with Mary Jane and Molly. Dude."

"Dude?"

"You know . . . not girls. Drugs."

"Yeeaah. Gotcha."

"Right, so, they're consumed with their own consumption, like what can we sell or sell to ourselves. We allllll gotta be better off. 401K, Roth IRA, payday? *Comprende*? It's that slave to desire shee-it. They're purchasing their own indentured servitude, nailing in the post and locking up the cuffs. Ipso facto, they can't care about me, at least not that much, because what can I sell them? A nice retirement? I don't sell. In fact, nard the sales. I'll check out my *Ad Busters* from the library, spank you very much. Do you know how much the government makes in tax revenue? You hear about all that mail the post office is hoarding? Dude. Buy Nothing Day times 365. So, whether my family cares . . . well, it's not like they've got this place under surveillance. So what I do or don't do, what's it to them?"

Boys dizzied themselves into these referential games of intellectual Twister on the daily, especially gifted boys, and those were the moments when Other Girls sucked the most. They were intimidated; they were dumb. I remembered my favorite quote from *A Clockwork Orange*; we'd read it together in the dystopian unit in Headways last quarter.

"'But what I do I do because I like to do.'" I tried to sound sure, like everything Ethan touted made sense, like it all boiled down to one slick sentence.

"Not quite, Alex, my brother. What is Locke? My body, my property."

I laughed and rolled my eyes. On the ceiling, neon sticky stars constelled Ursa Major and Ursa Minor and Cassiopeia. Nirvana was thrashing, loud.

"I get that," I said. "I don't want other people telling me what to do with my body. How to govern it, I guess. Like, let me maintain it however I want. My parents don't get on me about that."

"*Muy* decent of them."

I thought about Rocyo, then, about what she'd told Miss Troubaugh. The room seemed gloomier. "Most adults, anyhow."

"Well, you're not worried about the Suva grown-ups then, Elliot. AKA, you're not meetin' my parents. What's the visit for? I mean, yeah. It's a little out of the azure."

I shrugged. "You chatted me?"

"Mangette. Don't even."

I sighed. "I'm really bad at being smooth in situations like this, so I'm not even gonna try. If I show you something, can I use your phone?"

Ethan laughed. His whole head hinged, like the lid of a can. "Yah coulda asked to use the phone first. I'm not gonna, like, hold you hostage on behalf of Illinois Bell."

I took my coat off my knees and felt around for the right pocket. I tossed the baggie into the center of the bed like it was as innocuous as a hackie sack. It landed between Ethan and me.

His nostrils flared. "You swear you're not some narc?"

"How does that even make sense?"

Ethan picked up the heroin. He tossed it from one palm to the other, like an apricot he was waiting to nosh. I watched the bones in his hand; they were as flat as the laces of his sneakers, but not markered GO VEGA.

"Where did you get this?"

"My house. More specifically, my mom's closet."

"That's screwed up."

I was surprised to feel, like the premonition of a sneeze, defensive. "Didn't you say your brothers were out doing drugs?"

"Well, yeah." Ethan sat the baggie next to him. He glanced at it. "But my brothers are in high school. Your mom is . . . a mom."

"She's a writer. Like me. Those clichés about artists are sometimes true."

"Like they're starving?"

I bristled. "She's temperamental."

"Are you sure not just *mental*?"

"Do you think your brothers would wanna buy this?"

"Exsqueeze me? Dude, I'm not, like, a middle man for them. They can rot their own brains. Do you know what straight-edge means?" He pushed up the cuff of his flannel. Three Xs and his creamy wrist stared at me. This time, I couldn't help seeing those same Xs in the Nirvana logo, those eyes that were all blotto.

"I know what hypocrite means, Kurt Cobain."

"Woah, don't get psycho, okay?"

I felt my face scrunch into a scowl. I forced myself to breathe. Eating that wrap had put me on edge. I was disgusting, the opposite of the song: I had no will. "I'm sorry . . . fuck. I'm acting like an idiot and I have, like, no clue. I should just, like, bounce."

"It's all good. Dude. Relax. Slow down, okay?"

I nodded.

"So, this is H?"

"What else?"

"I mean, I guess lots of stuff. Coke?"

"My mother isn't that boring, thanks. If she's into drugs, she's hardcore."

"Aight. So, these drugs in exchange for a phone call? Is that the gist of this transaction?"

It didn't make much sense to me either. "I don't know. Actually—" Suddenly I felt overwhelmed. What was I doing? Why was I here? "No, I definitely should go. This was a mistake and you don't need to be dragged into . . . whatever this is. I'm sorry."

I stood up, leaving Ethan sitting in a skewed lotus pose on the bed. I didn't need distractions like this, the generic, hetero-boringness of my clients. I needed to get home, work on *Real Talk* or call Lisa. But nothing was propelling me back into the January cold. Kurt Cobain was singing about wings. Then like "touch yourself" or "fuck yourself." I looked at the ceiling. Right above Ethan's one, thin black pillow was the North Star. I wasn't leaving. I was just standing there.

Ethan kicked out a foot and jabbed my torso. His socks' soles were brand-new clean. "Hey. We're hanging out. Relax, mang. You wanna try?"

"Try what?"

Ethan picked up the baggie. He unknotted the top.

"You know what this stuff is supposed to smell like? You taste it?"

"I don't typically go around tasting unmarked substances." I sat down again, but this time I didn't lean back. I sensed the CD-case distance between my spine and the pillow. Our bodies were that much closer. I wondered if Ethan could feel it, too. "Anyhow, don't you need a needle or something? Those, like, broken looped rubber bands?"

"I think this is the perfect occasion for a sample," said Ethan. He unknotted the baggie and held it under his nose. He closed his eyes and inhaled.

"What does it smell like?"

"Kinda nothing? I don't know. You tell me, Heroin Chic."

He held out his palm. I scooted into the center of the bed and leaned over. My hair grazed his hand. I extended my nose above the bag. "Like medicine? Hold on—"

I sniffed deeper. This time I tried to find Ethan's skin beside the drug smell. Peanut butter, some whatever hand cream: putting my face on his hand was ten thousand times more intimate than having anyone's dick down my throat.

Stupid Lisa. Stupid porn. "Yeah, like. Have you ever accidentally sucked the coating off an aspirin?"

"Not really a hospital, but nasal spray?"

"Or vitamins, their aftertaste. Think it's vegan?"

"Dude. Very funny." His cheeks dimpled when he smiled. He mimed a chortle. "Why you gotta hate?"

"I don't hate," I said. "Just seeing if you're seriously game."

"Are you?"

I opened my mouth and made a show of biting my pinky. I tasted grape jelly.

"Don't you think there's like trace calories? Isn't that your can of Pringles?"

"Huh?"

"Elliot. Mangette. You know what I mean." He sucked in his cheeks and fluttered his eyes. "Ghouliet. Kate Moss. Lead Sister."

"Lead—?"

"Karen Carpenter?"

"What?"

"Dude. Never mind."

I sighed. "Consider the towel thrown in. I've already eaten a sandwich—"

"You mean that piddly wrap attack?"

"Yes. The *gimongo* wrap attack. Heroin calories aren't gonna kill me."

I put my pinky in my mouth, pushed it back to a corner. The skin inside me was wet and warm and smoother than inside my vagina. I stuck my pinky in the baggie. When I pulled it out, it was white capped, like Lik-M-Aid Fun Dip. Ethan's eyes were big, green again, spattering, on me. I gave him a look that said, *nudge, nudge.* Then he was sucking his index finger, dipping it, too, and we were right there in his bedroom, getting high or stoned or strung out together, for facts or science or whatever.

"'E.T., phone home,'" I said, wiggling my pinky.

"Nerd," said Ethan.

"One, two—"

"*Uno, dos, tres, cuatro . . .*"

"*Cinco, cinco, seis!*" I shouted.

"Really? Offspring?"

"*The* Offspring," I said. It felt good to be right. "And . . . yeah. I know, I know. Somewhere, Kurt's cringing."

I put my pinky in my mouth and closed my eyes. I tasted bitter black coffee like Lisa's dad's sludge, something vinegary, anti-sweet. I swallowed. The taste stayed, like a phlegmy cough. I opened my eyes. The room rocked and swayed, and Ethan's head was cocked.

"Grody on a stick."

I nodded. I felt queasy. "Can we get messed up from this?"

He shrugged. "I don't know. D.A.R.E. skipped this part." I watched his tongue prodding behind his upper lip. "I don't feel anything. Do you?"

My mouth opened, but I couldn't answer. I couldn't tell if my heartbeat was speeding up or slowing down. My eyes closed. When I tried to open them, blackness tarred them shut. For a moment I panicked and then I let myself go. Time was inflating, the opposite of what adults ascribed to growing up: nothing was faster, each second was inflating, quadrupling. I saw a field of minutes, a thousand balloons, a wish inside each one. And what I wanted, even with Ethan

Suva offering up his Friday evening to me, *Flacisima*, Heroin
Chic, what I wanted was Friday sleepovers under the snow
leopard blanket and mornings resisting Larry Breit's bagels
and playing Ace of Base, "The Sign," three years after it was
all that and a bag of chips and talking about what life would
be like after Park, after high school, after college, how our
friendship, like our skinniness, would span a lifetime. I
wanted nothing but everything with Lisa.

..

I blinked. I was lying on my side in the bed like I had decided
to take a nap. The bedroom was brighter now, almost glow-
ing, and something smelled vanilla and cakey. A third candle
burned next to the others. The music had changed to something I didn't recognize: there was a xylophone, a plaintive
voice singing about arms and surprises. I looked around:
Suva the youngest had left.

The door opened. Ethan walked in, carrying two tumblers, the kind that had held the grape jelly. The Breit's
reused their jars, too.

"Water?" he said, handing me a glass with a beaming
blue stegosaurus.

I sipped. The water woke up my whole body. "Did I pass
out?"

"Yeah, dude, you just nodded. Drink up. No calories,
I swear. Just good ol' Lake Michigan H-2-O. You probably coulda eaten all that tore till uh. Not just half of a half.
Mangettes need more than nibbly nibs. You wanna make
that phone call?"

"Whatever," I said. I was bummed. I'd always expected
my first blackout to mark the end of a marathon fast, some

stack of five or seven days when I'd keel over after ingesting nothing Darjeeling and lemon water. Fainting from heroin sorta discredited the faint. "Are you high?"

"Nah. My mouth tastes like butt, though."

I propped myself onto my elbows, looking for my back-pack. It was on the floor, a million feet away from the bed, in another galaxy. "You wanna Listerine strip?"

He shook his head. "Gelatin, right?"

"I don't know." I paused. This music sounded like a mor-bid lullaby. "How would I know if I were high?"

"Here." He pulled something off the bookshelf and sat perpendicular to me. Now we were both on the bed again, our bodies processing the same air. I wondered if, like Lisa always said that Cher said in *Clueless*, proximity to certain furniture (i.e., beds) made him—like it made me—think about sex. "Can you read this?"

It was a booklet, a zine, thicker than *Real Talk*. There weren't any daisy chain Clip Art borders; instead, the entire front cover swarmed with Ethan's printing. I flipped through. Each page crawled with the same crabbed hand-writing. Between a list of Clear Channel radio stations and a stick figure cartoon, a Xeroxed Calvin Klein ad's models had their eyes blacked out. On the next page, a pasture of cows sported devil horns, and on the next, receipts from the Gap and The Limited and United Colors of Benetton were packed with all caps, block-lettering: STOP CHILD LABOR STOP UNLIVABLE WAGES STOP JUST DOING IT STOP NIKE STOP THE GAP DON'T FALL IN STOP CONTRACTING YOUR "SELFISH TV DEATHWISH" (STD) TAKE OUT YOUR TUBES STEP AWAY FROM THE GOVERNMENT AND NO ONE

GETS HURT PUT DOWN THE VOTE SAY NO TO
MOBILES GIVE UP YOUR GAS AND WALK LISTEN
TO YOUR KEANU GET YOUR MEMBRANE INSANE
BE HUMAN BE MASTER OF YOUR OWN DOMAIN
GIVE NAME TO YOUR NONPERSON.

"Woah." I was impressed, but embarrassed by Ethan's
unabashed interest in these topics, way deeper than anything
I ever thought about outside of Social Studies. Suddenly, my
concerns seemed petty, insignificant, like cheap stick-on earrings that belonged to, like Gwen Stefani said, "Just A Girl."

"I mean, yeah," I said, staring at the text. "I can read
parts—there's a lot of writing in . . . this. What is . . . or who
wrote it?"

Ethan looked at the zine. At the roots, his blonde hair
was almost black. I liked his head, too: in sixth grade, he'd
shaved it down to the skull. "*Nonperson*, issue two. I'm tryin'
for twenty-five volumes. I don't know. Four issues times
twenty-five, that's a hundred chances to disrupt the system
before college."

"That's ambitious." I tried to sound cautiously respectful.
"I bet you totally, like, shift paradigms."

"Keep it. I've got the master."

He took the issue from me and set it on the floor, on top
of my mini backpack. He scooted toward me; his hips were
touching my side, just below my ribs.

Now my pulse was pounding. Ethan was so close, I could
smell all of him: peanut butter, something grainy (oats?),
and the blue masculinity of cologne, like the Stetson Lisa
and I used to spray on each other's wrists at Walgreens. I was
excited and terrified: that he might touch me, that when he
pressed my shoulder my bone would dissolve, slo-mo, the

hard cortical, the spongy cancellous, and his hand would push and push all the way to my marrow, and he'd discover I was not vegan friendly, I was all animal, bred by, tested on, living amongst. I was not all there; my heart was in another field. I was so animal, I would've chewed off my own arm if it meant getting Lisa's attention.

"Um, what's it called?" My voice shook.

"Dude, *Nonperson*, you just asked. Double-der."

"Duh. I'm sorry. Wow—I think . . . the smack messed me up. Can I make that phone call now?"

"Hey, what's the rush? We're just hangin' out. Finish your water. Yo, whoever you need to talk to is gonna get a better Elliot if you're hydrated."

I nodded. I felt spacey and, suddenly, swamped by sadness. I was no closer to Lisa. I took another sip and squeezed my eyes shut so I wouldn't start sobbing.

"Hey, Heroin Chic," Ethan said. He pivoted. With his thumb, he drew little infinity signs on my thigh, right above my knee. Then he craned his body and faced his face toward mine. "You're super pretty."

He kissed me. He was not so pretty—he had blotchy skin on his forehead where zits had been undid—but his eyelashes were long, wet, thick fringe and his eyelids were so smooth, blank, calm that I couldn't take it. I closed my eyes and felt his mouth on mine. For a fat second, I sunk into contentment. I was the great '90s abstraction, all the slow songs Park played rolled into one, "Truly Madly Deeply" and "All My Life" and the one about love suicide. Ethan's tongue wrested my lips and I tried not to think about those old dances, the ones where Lisa and I would fake–slow dance together because neither of us was going out with anyone. I tried not to think of how it felt when she wrapped her arms around my neck and I clasped my hands behind her ribs, how she felt like crushed velvet, how the disco ball strobed the floor with pink and red lights, how our veins ran with Diet Coke. I tried to be with Ethan.

He leaned back, paused, breathed deeply. A small smile started in the corners of his mouth. Then he stood up, reached for his fly, and unzipped. Peeking out the flap of his Space Jam boxers was a flushed red boner.

He put a hand around my neck, half a collar, and pushed me toward his waist.

"Woah! Hold up," I said. I scrambled backwards. *Be* cool, I told myself. Other girls could handle this. I tried to pretend I wasn't seeing his penis. It had that blinky hole in the tip, like a balloon with a leak.

"I'm not pretty," I said. My ears rang as I said it, like a siren was going off inside me, blaring *Elliot, wrong, Elliot, wrong.* "Do you know Lisa Breit?"

Ethan's shoulders slumped. He looked down and pulled up his jeans and zipped them back up. His face was confused. "I mean, just from school."

"She's my best friend." Suddenly, I really was about to weep, and I couldn't control it at all. "I have to go. I need to call my mom. Do you think your brothers would want that? I mean, the dru—"

Ethan knuckled his hipbone, which jabbed against his jeans. "I don't know. Um. Elliot. Hey, mang, was that bad? You know? I'm—I've never done that before. It just . . . felt or seemed . . . right."

"Oh, no, I just—" And for a second, I wanted to fling myself onto his bed and let him trounce me like in my old stupid fantasies. I wanted to join him in something and fall asleep forever.

I grabbed the baggie and my backpack and stood. All the organs and muscles and veins swooshed inside me. I would never stop being dizzy, like I would never stop loving—like a sister or a best friend or the person who recognizes your every blink and breath—Lisa. I leaned against the wall.

Ethan backed toward the door. Red flared on his cheeks, nervous and sweet, but all I could think of was that D. In my head it was still staring at me, like a cyclopean mole rat. "You wanna make that phone call at least?"

"Nah, I'm taking off."

"Hey—how are you gettin' home?" he said.

I opened the door. The rest of the house was dark, too. I felt like we'd broken into a construction zone. My footsteps banged down the stairs. I slipped on my boots.

"Elliot! Wait," he said. "Seriously. Don't spaz. How are you—?"

"I'll walk, okay?"

"Yo, my mom's gonna be home any minute. Just chill. Dude—you see that cardinal sign thingy? Yeah, that's a thermometer. It's twelve degrees. We can watch a movie or something. I bet you'd love *Pulp Fiction*."

I opened the door. A lingering strand of Christmas lights gilded the snow. It even smelled cold, red and gold glitter raining down on the world. I zipped up my coat.

"See you Monday," I said.

"That's MLK. Dude, c'mon—"

I waved goodbye and rushed down the stoop. My entire body cowered at the change in temperature. Home: it was two miles from here.

"Hey!" Ethan yelled. He was standing in the doorway, in socks. In the foyer light, I could see his cheeks, still on fire. "Heroin Chic! It's like lose a limb cold!"

9 ·· ANNA

THERE ARE ADAGES I REPEAT to students: Writing is a process. Trust your reader. Revision is a door.

There is ornate Italian: *Villanelle*—from *villanella. Stanza* means room. *Volta,* the turn a sonnet takes, vaunted time, vault of heaven.

Corpo, body.

Hate sits like a warden in the passenger seat, watching the slutty woman mouth.

How relentlessly I detest my body. Open as an anemone! Hungry as a sea dog! Thirsty as a leech!

In the Saab, I suck soda. Steer.

Rot was right: the snow is thickening. The wind is tempered and flakes felt the windshield. There are no other vehicles on this path, a corridor mossed in white. I turn the wipers off. The polka dots cluster. I lift my boot from the gas and let the car creep. My eyes are closed, resting. *So I may do the deed/that my own soul has to itself decreed,* wrote hunky Keats. Let the auspices have their say.

For five seconds, it's me and my breath. Beth, meth, death. Brain death. Crib death. Death death.

"Oh Anna," I say to the soundtrack (tires, motor, snow). "You chicken shit."

I am about to exit the Carousel Gardens Arboretum when I notice words. Café. The Grove. On a glaucous sign, a wavy arrow jabs: Welcome Center, Restroom, Orchid Temple.

It's one forty-five.

This is what it looks like to forsake a job. This is what it looks like to give up.

The Saab mushes toward a new lot. Here, no clandestine meet-ups. No befogged panes. Only nice cars, parked not so long ago. Their windows haven't yet iced. Their blunt noses sniff the sidewalk. Sabayon and ecru and ivory, powder blue and platinum: these are lady-lunching Lexuses. Lexies? They slumber like snow leopards.

In the Saab, full-blast heat chats with my vagina. *I* feel rather *un*ladied. Let my crevices scent the world. Anna with the easy gibe: smells like Rot.

I leave my panties in the glove compartment and put on my nylons. My scaly legs snag the hose. I examine my calf: a run the length of a banana, thin as a cannula. Could be worse.

I'm missing my gloves.

I shake the Crush and stab the straw between the ice cubes. I swig a sip. Watery soda and air. A growl pries up my ribs.

Fuck. I'm hungry.

..

I am a woman moving through space, waiting for her thoughts to crack open. My mind is an egg, rolling off a cliff. What do you call an egg in an ocean?

(The joke is I'm hardboiled.)

"Table for . . . ?" says the hostess. Screw her young body. She could like my Rot. Dolphin eyes. Parsnip face. Purple lipstick. Triangle hoops. In another life, she might do hair.

"One." I clench my camel coat around me. Then I drop my hands. My skirt is twisted, my black bra strap knotted. I feel louche. Trampy.

Here is the dining room, the opposite of Laughlin Banquet's white tablecloths. Gold charger plates. Napkins starched into accordions. A somewhere viola. Glass bud vases: vanilla roses, petals edged in chocolate. Three groups of women, two and four and five. Diamonds the size of front teeth. Brooches. Bouclés. Tweeds. Wrists poking out of silk like branches.

No accident that I'm seated in the corner. From my skin, the Crush's vodka seeps (it smells like a skinned knee misted with Bactine). My hair is not a helmet. It is every strand out of place, the crown erupting with bumps. Gray blackened with dye. My back is to the window: I ignore landscaping. Winter gardens. Boxy hedges. Pebbled aisles. Mums or cro-cuses. Plants bore me. Give me women, in whose figures I may lambaste myself.

A pair of ragged claws/Scuttling across the floors of silent seas.

In college I had a trick for meals. I brought no book, no folder, no magazine, no paper. I imagined a compan-ion. Sometimes my mother: she critiqued my fork-and-knife skills. Sometimes my father: he shook his head at my sprouted pitas. Most times, Marky, my brother: his squeaky voice, one big agreement, his proclivity for sweets. With him at the table, we'd reminisce about the cartons of Neapolitan Seal-Test we devoured, root beer floats for breakfast.

A server in penguin separates approaches. On his basset face, he wears round tortoise glasses. His hair is old-fashioned, trim and curling, a moldering toadstool.

"Young lady," he says. His water pitcher is pewter, its white linen a jabot. His pour is a last bow. On good days, I look younger than my age. This afternoon, though, *Herr Ober* is being kind.

"May I see the dessert menu? And the wine list."

"Of course."

Last course, of-course course, off-course course: let dirty women dine in peace.

..

Marky, I say, *rate the crème brûlée.*

Meh. Custard a little liquidy. Should I be able to drink it like a melk-shake? And, c'mon. Aren't we over vanilla specks yet?

True. I lift the scalloped ramekin, where dark spots seed the ceramic. I lick my pinky, lift a field of vanilla.

Like roe, crunch, crunch.

I can't believe you demolished that lava cake, Marky says, raising his eyebrows and rolling his eyes as he finesses the big butterscotch mohair scarf he always wears. I can picture him, his starburst dimples, like a baby that never grew up, how when he's not smiling, his whole countenance clouds.

Not terrible! That tasted like a sexy nap, with the port.

The charade is voice-only, but I picture gestures, too: Marky's hand raised, palm slapping forehead.

The port, in its tulip glass, gave me one hard punch in the mouth. The cake was a strangler. Some food, I eat to feel my arteries' protest. A coward's morbid flirt.

Jean-Georges called. He said he wants that sad cake to strap its molten self into a time machine. Hand over the raspberries and mint leaves. The '80s called—they want their signature dessert back.

You know, for someone so sweet, *you're a real* tart.

For someone so straight, you're a real fruit.

I tip back a flute. No more champagne. Empty. The glass is bird bones. I run my tongue around the inside rim for the remains, a taste, brut sticky.

Brut sticky, by the way, says Marky the clairvoyant, *is the name of my favorite leather bar. Second favorite. Next to Berlin. Remember when you were at University of Chicago? My fake got us into so many clubs. Raise a glass to whoever, that Canuck me-clone out there. God, all those fakes at Grizzly. I could die. Don't you miss those days?*

You ate more of the lavender cheesecake than me, I say. *What does that say about you?* When you've been the oldest your whole life, you don't start admitting what's wrong just because your baby brother baits you in daydreams. You don't stoop yourself. You chin up. Soldier forth. Expire silent. *Don't act like I'm the only one at this table.*

"Anything more?" says my waiter. I blink. I have forgotten him, though surely he hasn't forgotten me. My "every dessert" order. My "keep the drinks coming." My nod to Glenn Decklin: "here's to feeling good all the time." The restaurant sounds blare their fastidiousness. The women are gone. Another server rolls silver. A bar back hefts a rack of highballs. The hostess flips through the reservation book.

"You've been too patient," I say, in professor voice. My talents are squandered in the classroom. *You're prince for keeping your trap shut about the menu sweep. Who are you?*

I want to ask. *What could* you *have brought to this life? You wear glasses—you must be perceptive. What do you see in* me?

"I'm sorry to have kept you."

I hand him my AmEx. When the check arrives, I forget how to sign. The waiter stands at the next table, holding a chardonnay glass to the light—and watching me.

"Can I help you up, Ma'am?" he says.

I throw down the pen.

"Help me—help me by shutting the fuck up. Ma'am. Ma'am."

"I beg your—"

"Grow a pair. Not even my husband wants a man as floppy as you."

". . ."

"If you know better, you'll stutter on your own time."

I push my chair back from the table and the waiter scurries away. It takes me several starts to stand. The room waltzes. My table is busy with remains, glasses and three forks and two spoons. Plates like decapitated, faceless dolls. Only the crust of a lemon tart is left. The filling was smooth curd. Rosettes of Chantilly cream. The crust sucked. It was saltines but too salty, too soggy, like licking the Morton Girl's bloomers. Still. I've had *deux* splits of champagne, a pour of port, Crush and Russian's blood, whatever lingered on Rot's lips, water water water. Forget the fork. I pick up the crust and chomp it like a chicken wing.

..

Every step requires a deep breath. I beseech composure: Stay with me. Steady, girl.

So much snow has fallen, I can't spot my car.

At least not from one step beyond The Grove's door. From the walkway, I see a glass wall (*Garden of Donors*) heaped with white, hedges blinking red holly berries, the half-moon of pinecone on a conifer. I feel for gloves, pockets. Then I remember: I am a woman with hands. Plans.

"'Fair and foul are near of kin,'" I say, under my breath. Nature, dumb mother, doesn't care. I yell: "'Fair and foul are near of kin!'"

I could shout an hour and the world's turn would be no different.

I pull open the door. The music in The Grove is louder. Wilder. Not *my* wild. Phil Collins wild. The hostess props her elbows on the desk. She eyes me, like a sore that's leapt from a vagrant's body and is trying to be seated for—no, not dinner, too late for lunch—linner.

"May I help you?" Her voice is incommodious.

"Where is the, I need to use the . . . the girls."

Even my phrasing is sozzled.

The hostess flips her hair. She has a birthmark like a pinto bean on her scalp.

"The hallway beside the bar. Either door."

Handicapped accessible. Solo stanza. Private stall. Score.

..

The myth of the drunk-puke goes like this:

Once there was a poor, featherweight woman. The woes and whether-or-nots wore her. On any given Wednesday, nary a meal did she eat. A snack here, a nibble there: meager the energy expended by worrying! Our woman remained drawn and dour.

Inside each of us, though, a better self resides. *Multitudes!* Cried the poet. And in the woman, a merry crew of bacchants and maenads munched peanuts. They sent persistent, telepathic, obvious, wobbly messages. Call them naughty thoughts: A little _____ won't hurt. Everyone deserves a _____. Unwind with a _____.

And the woman told herself: you can always go back to work.

One day, the bacchanalian raged too hard for the woman to ignore. Being pitiable and paltry, she was more susceptible than others—or so she believed—to a tempting noise. She stamped her stony foot. And why shouldn't she? She had a little _____. After all, she deserved a good _____. So she unwound and unwound and unwound.

Doused and soused, the woman felt like a victim of the Catherine Wheel.

She rapped on her skull. She pulled her hair. She ground her teeth. Bongoed her ribs. *Wake up!* she hollered. But the maenads and bacchants were face-plant drunk.

A final sad missive reached her: _____ or party alone. The woman did not party alone. She found a closet and did her deed. With each pull, she told herself she was saving her bowels. She was preserving the day's sanctity. She would emerge from her closet gutted, catharsis complete, a functional filly.

The woman's madness was not her folly. Her flagrant avoidance of the day's duties was fine. So too her fun. No, the woman's foolishness was guilt. She acted on her desires—and then purged herself. A perjury. She lied, listened, reneged.

She expected two fingers to sober her.

··

In my boots, my toes say NO. I walk to the Saab, shifting my weight to my heels. This season is so dull: The snow is still falling. The water is still freezing. Now wind lofts it. Now sun melts it. Now it happens again.

The ground I tromp on is steady. It's fast going, trying to dodge flakes. Whether one landing on your nose is a burden or a joy depends less on the flake and more on one's mood. I slap something wet from my eyelashes. Winter's gnats.

I shut myself in the car. I jam the keys in the ignition. Dings ding, a puff of heat. *Wait for the engine to warm up*, Rolf always says. But how long does one wait? After what period? Has the engine been in hibernation while I've been dining? What does exhaust taste like from a cold pipe?

I fold away my fingers. Puking was a two-hand affair, like bilateral breathing. I remember El's preschool swimming. Left, right, left. Heave, ho. Shift into Drive.

There are the foibles. They talk like kindergarten teachers. *Aaaaaannnnnaaa: did you check to see that toilet flushed?*

(No. Sorry, dear hostess. Don't let the pastry chef see the cause of the clog.)

Then there are fricatives. I idle at the edge of The Grove's lot, flub the number twice. I keep punching the wrong numbers. Anna. Fathead. Fat fingers. Get it together.

"Slow the fuck down," I say as I speed forward, back to Carousel Garden Road.

I pause at the arboretum's iron gates. One by one, I press the right buttons to call Rolf. The radio clock reads 3:58. The gray phone feels like a frozen filet against my ear. I turn onto the two-lane highway back into the world.

"*Guten Morgen.*" I sound like the chef on *The Muppets*. I watched them with El. I try my lines: "I want you to have custody. Please. I won't apologize. Better for all."

But there's no Rolf, just ringing and ringing: the call takes a lifetime to leapfrog the Atlantic. I imagine his matching mobile, its ribby side panels flashing deep inside his attaché. He's sleeping, snoring like his daughter, somewhere in the Vienna Ritz, adjacent to the Stadtpark, where statues of Schubert and Strauss collect snow on their marble heads.

Here there's me. Eyes sort of on some road: white, guardrails, bruising sky. I am heading—back to Cook County? But the professionals have developed. Leftover croissants are being refrozen. Building 13 is shut down for the weekend. Home. I'm going home. That's what I have. That and El.

"Shit." Where did 4-a.m.-I-swear-to-be-better-me go? Why can't I stick with one vow? I need a personal trainer for my morals. I hold the phone out in front of me. I look at it, a new limb I've sprouted. I miss the finality of slamming down a handset, screaming into a receiver. Which of these buttons hangs up a call? X or End?

I thumb until the screen blanks.

Behind me, a driver lays on the horn. I look up. The Saab is in the middle of the road, straddling the double-yellow like a tough decision.

"Shit. Sorry!"

I pull over. The car skids over the rumble strips on the shoulder as an Audi accelerates. My head is waterlogged and buoyant. I dial our house.

I am talking. I sound like a patroness: "You have reached Anna, Rolf, and Elliot. Clearly leave a message and a number, and your call will be returned."

"El, it's Anna," I say. Then I hang up. I don't want to hear a recording of me. *This* is me, me on the shoulder; me on the machine, I don't recognize.

I dial the only other number I know by heart. Marky's phone goes straight to voicemail.

"Talk to the machine," he says, "Because neither the hand nor the face is available to hear it."

And here goes real me. She is wonky. Every word like another push on a swing that keeps getting closer and closer to flipping over the top.

"Marky. You're probably—prep and prep and prep. That's life, right? One big almost. I'm on the mobile. Remember when we used to tin can through the walls? When you were a kid? Did we do that? Shit. I . . . it's better this way. Not having to . . . seconds to think. Okay. So. Here goes: I love you. Bye bye."

I roll down the window and fling the phone. I can be cautious. Or not. What matter? I can be myself. I flip my turn signal. Black, black, silver, red: rushing past, a fleet of Benzes. Clear—and I merge.

"Focus," I say. "You're drunk. But not so drunk. How much did you absorb? Not so bad. A drink? Maybe a drink. Maybe two. Okay, so you concentrate. Take this slow. Lights on! Hey. There you go. Lights on because of snow."

My headlights beam into the dusky road. I turn on the radio. Music is waiting. Music will wake me.

What's playing is a song I remember from grammar school. The Saab rounds a corner and I don't decelerate. I hold my breath, waiting to skid on two tires. But I don't. I am stable, bound, accompanied by George Harrison after the Beatles. "What Is My Life." Up-tempo, tambourine clambering, galloping horns, zigzagging guitar.

It's one of those songs that has always reminded me why I write: to feel this lofted. I'm in tears I can't try to control. The volume doesn't go louder. I bob my head and sing along, imagining this trip home doesn't need to end. I imagine that this song doesn't need to end. I imagine that I don't need to decide between caprice and commitment, that I don't have to feel bad for being bad, that I won't keep grading myself. I imagine that, I, too, might write something that moves a woman alone and terrified in her car.

"Fogies at four," says the deejay. His voice is a slide whistle. "Taking you back to 1971. This one got up to number ten on the charts in the USA. Screw you, Yoko! Bring back our boys!"

"Ass," I say.

I Seek, Seek, Seek, scanning FM for something listenable. Then I think I hear the phone. Elliot. I turn down the volume.

The sirens blare with blue and red strobes. They are loud. In my ear. I glance at the speedometer. I'm speeding—but not by much. Five over in a fifty.

Pull over, snaps my mother from the passenger seat. *Anna, honey, be a good girl and you'll get a treat,* says Marky. *Did you wait for the engine to warm up?* Rolf asks. And Elliot: *Mom, weren't you supposed to write me a poem?*

Rot: *Don't you ever do what you want?*

Ahead is the wooden bridge that spans the river. It is small, hardly more than a creek, and frozen solid, argent with ice and mounds of pristine snow. Snow only soils beneath cars. And this tiny bridge, its puny railings wrapped in evergreen garlands, infrequent balusters choked with red velvet bows, the whole construction as old as me, older. I remember my father driving over this bridge, my mother sucking her ivory kid gloves in the passenger seat, me sliding around the back. Good old whatever before seat belts. Sixty or eighty years ago, before there were McMansions in the suburbs, when goats and ducklings pastured and ponded. Horses. My mother rode. When people built cottages. Siloes and dairies and granaries. This bridge. Rickety enough to off a girl.

There must be gradations of siren: the red and blue blink faster. I take a deep breath. I am not sorry, I think. No mess for El or Rolf. Let me freeze to the river bed. I speed up. The blinker all-clears me for the bridge. Days when life was one lane.

I accelerate up the planks. They bump under me, like driving on popsicle sticks.

"I'm not sorry," I say. And sharply I turn. I press the gas and grit my teeth and take my hands off the wheel right before the Saab cracks through the railing. I scream, shut my eyes, and wait for my stomach to plunge.

10 ·· ELLIOT

MOST TIMES YOU THINK YOU feel lonely, you're really not. You just don't know better, or you're lazy—like my girls, listening to their rumbling tumblies when they get home from school: Fritos whistle at them, so they forget the baby carrots in the fridge. Loneliness, like bad decisions, is convenient, but usually, you have choices, people to keep you company—even if only your mom.

I was still hunting for a payphone after hoofing it from Ethan's. The treacherous twenty-minute power-walk had taken me through the suburbs. They were laden with sporadic sidewalks and SUVs, and snow had stung the widest parts of my calves and the backs of my knees, and my fingers had stiffened despite being curled in the deep, fleece-lined pockets of my black down coat, and the brutal windchill had seared the peaks of my face (cheekbones, forehead, nose). There was a dumb, calorie-dense PBJ paperweight in my stomach. I understood how real loneliness could drive a person to abandon all hope.

Real loneliness sapped the joy out of kissing. It was like watching a deflated basketball roll across the court. Real loneliness was the Flu Game—if Michael Jordan hadn't been able to keep up.

I approached the shady Flagg Creek Motel. I hated myself for stopping. Quitting wasn't an Egleston trait, but Ethan was right: the cold *was* lose-a-limb. What if Lisa was that limb? What if, by the time I got to talk to her, she was gone?

The Flagg Creek was next to a florist, a block before Park. Since yesterday, the price of Valentine's bouquets had risen to $37.99; Georges' was dark, but, in their window, atop a stout vase, a pink-snouted stuffed bear mooned over me. I walked through the motel parking lot. It was liver-shaped, mostly deserted. If you found yourself here on Friday night, how would you muster the self-respect to face Saturday? I checked back driver's side windows for decals. Pale green meant Park Faculty/Staff. Teachers, I bet, conducted their Mary Kay Letourneau biz in those nap-rate rooms. If I had to run into anyone, I decided, let it be Señora Lurke. She'd set me up with *Courage Under Fire,* a mug of sangria, and tell me how to get through life.

Elías. (She'd use my Spanish name.) *Obtener a través de esta noche. La vida puede esperar.*

I paused at the marled doormat. I feared for myself; I felt like Sidney in *Scream*, boldly, irresponsibly ignoring danger; hunted but blind to the killer. Only the motel was visible, shaped like a V, sandy bricks and rusty red railings, bereted with snow, strung with silver tinsel, two tiers of balconies. I scanned. I wanted to catch a naked person smoking a cigarette, a woman with a makeup bag filled with hypodermic needles, Lisa's dad, Rocyo, someone who could entertain me if Anna didn't pick up.

She *would* answer, of course. I'd done some Nancy Drewing on the icy walk from Ethan's and had drawn certain conclusions:

1. If, when I finally got through to Lisa, she wouldn't talk to me, I was done. Groveling = Loserville. Two guys—Ethan and Lisa's dad—had kissed me today. I didn't want an idiot girl who wasn't paying.

2. Ethan deserved an apology. My abrupt exit was heinous and weak. Saying sorry would give me reason to talk to him again.

3. *Real Talk* needed to be more like *Nonperson*. My tips had to be more drastic; the pics, of women sicker than me. If RoHo was right, if Troubaugh was gathering tinder to burn me at the stake, then my clients would get an epic issue.

4. My mom, even if she did dabble, was no heroin junkie. *I* was so love-crazy for Lisa—did I really miss her or did I just want to win her back, like a crash-diet challenge?—that I couldn't think of anyone but myself. I was selfish.

I faced the street, my back to the motel. Maybe the Saab was about to pull up, its exhaust panting in the night, one of Anna's catsuit gloves hovering above the steering wheel in a quick *hello*. She'd appreciate the setting; it belonged in a seedy, modern *Canterbury Tales*. But the night was empty.

I hugged my mini backpack to my stomach. I checked: my ribs were still there. The envelope of cash was still there. If the motel didn't have a payphone, I would use a room phone: I could afford a whole weekend of nap-rates with the profits from my clients.

..

The lobby was a stew of classy and trashy. There were pamphlets for a Ghosts of Cook County tour that promised to reveal Resurrection Mary. There were lamps with stained-glass shades; the shards formed the Chicago Bears logo. Blue, white, orange light streaked the aisle leading to the front desk. On TV, a toad-green Marge Simpson flew across a gloaming sky on a broomstick, cape and beehive streaming behind her. I checked the corners: no payphone.

"You waitin' on the moms, honey?" The woman behind the desk stood. Her earrings were Bugs Bunny and her necklace was a foot-long crucifix. When she closed her mouth, she was one big overbite. "We're quiet here at this time-being, but you're welcome to get cozy in the front room. Storm of the millennium out there, said Jerry Taft. I was at the Jewel this morning, and they were cleaned outta bread. Three days of this, someone said."

"It's whatever. Not so bad." I peered over the counter. A pair of zebra-furred flip-flops sat on the floor underneath a swivel chair. On the desk, a facedown Gameboy beeped the Mario theme. "Um, by any chance, is there a phone I could use?"

The woman pointed a skinny finger wearing Tweety Bird toward a slab of silver on the wall. Red wires shot out from the metal, punched with tiny holes that formed the shape of a phone. There was a sticker, slashed in half, that was supposed to say "1-800-COLLECT."

She frowned. "Y2K."

"Oh." I paused, staring. The former payphone reminded me of a picture I'd seen in a book about tabloids (Jayne Mansfield's head on a dashboard) and a term Anna had taught me (*mise en abyme*). "Can you make local calls in the rooms?"

"Shame. I have a mobile, if you wanna. I never use all my minutes."

"No, I can't . . . But thank you very much. How much for, like, a . . . studio?"

I didn't need more than the icky green room Anna and I'd shared in Soho. Suddenly I was exhausted. Shivering my butt off on another hike, only to come home to an empty house and a Lean Cuisine sounded depressing. If I was going to steep in solitude, I wanted to do it entirely, eerily alone.

"My mom's gonna meet me, so I could . . . call her. Tell her I got here safe. I don't wanna miss *Boy Meets World*."

"There's the hourly and the overnight. If you're—"

"Overnight."

"$79.49, plus tax."

I unsnapped the top flap of my backpack and uncinched the drawstring. "May I use cash?" I put on a syrupy voice and started peeling out fives and tens. "That way, my mom's all set!"

"Honey, you pay however you want. Money's money. You sign this register and you're all set. Angel." Nimbly, the woman arched an eyebrow. "Can you tell the Big Guy upstairs to send me a daughter as thoughtful as you?"

..

If I died, it wouldn't be so awful. Michael Jordan's birthday was the seventeenth of February, so room 217 portended well. Between the time I expired and a maid found my body, I'd probably burn off that PBJ. The image of Ethan's peen would become any gross thing, like Rocyo's butt crack or *Terrible Twos*. Maybe there was a God, a Big Guy who'd grant me access to afterlife consciousness, who'd let me know how much my corpse weighed at the autopsy.

I was trying to stay plucky. The room was gross. The bed was narrow and covered with a comforter the color of roast beef; the headboard was a gallows that felt like the flimsy balsam wood we used in IA to build models. Gashes in the TV tube suggested victimization by tire iron. Everything smelled as if Binaca had been used to mask an eternal belch.

I set my backpack on the nightstand and sat down on the bed. There was a tilde of blood on the threadbare white pillowcase. I flipped it over and dialed my house.

"You have reached Anna, Rolf, and Elliot. Clearly leave a message and a number, and your call will be returned."

I thought about hanging up. I could try again later; after all, I'd paid for a full night. But I was so exhausted, my shoulders felt like they were harnessed to anchors, like I was being pulled across a million leagues of ocean. I might sleep a year. If I turned on the TV and dozed off, I didn't want my mom worrying. I didn't want her to think I was running away from her—or encoring my self-mutilation with the emo-cliché of running away from myself. For the first time since getting *flaca*, I was letting life happen. Here I was, finally not being a child. This is how people orgasmed, without overthinking. Today at least boded well for my avocado prospects: I'd stumbled into these drugs, this excursion, this afternoon, this evening.

"Anna, it's me." I twisted the curly black cord of the phone around my index finger until the visible flesh reddened, an isosceles triangle. "I was working on that same project with the girl from yesterday. Yah know, in Ridgedale? I thought I'd walk home, which, in retrospect . . . way stupid. But, anyhow, I stopped because I was literally freezing. So I'm at the Flagg Creek Motel. It's not so . . . well, it's fine. I'm in room 217. Um. Yeah. You should pick me up. It's too cold to walk. Okay. Love you."

I yanked off my boots and kicked them toward the wall. Other Elliots had been cavalier; there was a rainbow of gray-black scuffs.

I toured the room in my socks; after this, I'd have to incinerate them. There were scattershot stains on the pale yellow carpet; it looked like someone had been doing Skip-It while drinking coffee. In the bathroom, two plastic cups sealed in cellophane sat on the sink. I yanked back the shower curtain, the color of Lorraine Swiss. A cockroach, a fingernail, a pubic hair: I was hoping for something revolting, but the tub was clean.

Next to the TV, the remote was Velcroed to a clipboard listing a channel menu and the numbers for three pizzerias. I brought the control with me to bed and flipped. Reruns and news were all the non-cable stations showed until seven: I zipped past *The Simpsons* (now, three characters I didn't recognize were wearing Pilgrim garb and being roped to a pyre) and a commercial for Viagra starring Bob Dole. In California, eighty-four Methodist ministers would be gathering in the morning to marry one lesbian couple. That made me happy. Miss World reported rape: that made me sad. Da

Bulls: Luc Longley and Scottie Pippen were waiting for the lockout to end before they went the way of MJ. Tim Floyd would replace Phil Jackson. Slug-eyed Jerry Krause said, "No other coach has had to step into a situation quite like this one." My heart sunk. I really did feel alone. The Bulls' sea change was no different than a new crop of Park eighth graders entering high school. All the names I remembered from championships, B.J. Armstrong and Toni Kukoc, they'd be here and gone, forgotten, like Lisa and Rocyo and Marissa and Ethan and me. Mr. Breit was right; our world was a mess. If it felt this bad now, how would it feel to be his age or my mom's? Forty-five? Forty?

I rummaged through my backpack and grabbed the baggie. I pulled open the drawer of the nightstand and set the heroin on top of the phonebook, next to Gideon's Bible. I wanted to pass out again. I wanted to fall asleep and wake up to Anna's hand on my shoulder. I wanted my mom to guide me to her car and drive me home.

I untwisted the heroin. I licked my pinky, dipping and sucking the way Ethan and I had done. Leaving his room—what an idiot I was. I'd weirded up the situation, been dumb and cruel, right after he kissed me. It really happened—he'd leaned in and worked open my mouth with his tongue. Fast and vertiginous and good. Not awkward. I'd never seen anyone's eyes that close-up. His skin was soft and oily.

I turned off the TV and grabbed the phonebook. I set it on my lap and felt thin when it completely covered my thighs. If Lisa's dad had been honest, I knew exactly where she was. I flipped to H, for hospital.

I dialed the number and the switchboard operator answered instantly.

"Carousel Gardens, how may I direct your call?" I couldn't tell if I was speaking to a human or one of those automated robots Anna complained about whenever she paid her credit card over the phone.

"Eating disorder unit," I said. "May I be connected to Lee—"

"Transferring."

On hold, I wondered if heroin had psychedelic properties. A flute-heavy Muzak rendition of "Mo Money Mo Problems" played. It sounded like a jig for elves.

"EDP." The woman's accent was PBS. "Marjorie speaking."

"Hi. Can Lisa Breit take a call?"

The woman cleared her throat. "Who's calling?"

"I don't have to frickin' tell you that . . . Her—why?"

"Miss Breit is no longer . . . If you have information about her whereabouts, I'd implore you to . . . well, you can imagine, her parents are very concerned."

"Bull. Shit. Have you met her mother?" I felt cheeky. "That woman doesn't have a concerned bone in her fat-ass body."

I slammed the receiver down. I pinched a tiny mound of the powder and tried to chew; it was like crunching soft snow. That chemical taste filled my mouth. I dialed my last bet and crossed my fingers that Larry would pick up.

11 ·· LISA

"LET'S DO A DRIVE-BY," I say. "I'm tired of wearing sweats . . . with no drawstring . . . that I also slept in. Especially after being in a movie theater. That's just narsty."

"It's not a slumber party, Lee-Lee. That's the beauty of a hotel. 'Holiday Innnnnn,'" Junior Carlos sings.

"Watch the road," I say.

He doesn't. He makes the whites of his eyes more and more enormous until I laugh.

"Lisa. You lock the door. You order room service. They provide the towels. Hey, get this: fluffy slippers and Egyptian cotton robes, too. You've got Mr. Lova Lova here to pay for champagne. Or, yah know, his dad's expense account. No big. You keep your sexy self in bed and kick it. Catch? Real clothes optional."

We're back in the BMW, and I have *Life After Death* in the CD player, half a box of Cookie Dough Bites in the side compartment on the door. Carousel Gardens is in the past; now tonight can be like any other JC+L= 4EVA. A D8. There's Friday traffic, even though we're only ten minutes from my home. When you're not in a sheltered little neighborhood, the world is lit up and blah. Three blocks of fast food, eight car dealerships dickering with giant seasonal inflatables. (Currie Motors has an MLK blow-up. As my dad would say, *Someone call the* Suburban Life; *it's their time to shine*).

We inch forward, stop, start, skid on ice, fake-panic, brake brake brake, stop. The snow has been tromped by the wind, pushing the car like a go-kart; Junior Carlos's jaw is clenched, his hands tense on the wheel. Today they look rougher, speckled with blood. Winter sucks, but I don't care. A thought paused me while we were in the back row of the theater, his arm around me, my hand chilling on his through-jeans cock, watching Val Kilmer and Mira Sorvino, *At First Sight*: Someday, I'll tell J.C. I love him.

"One: I feel gross without having a fresh pair of underwear," I say. "Two: I don't want you taking me to the mall and strutting me around Victoria's Secret like we're in some Skinemax sex movie. Three: I am *this much* curious about my grandma."

"You think your mom stuck a note on the fridge? Grocery list: 2%, Pillsbury crescent rolls, Velveeta, turkey franks. Arrangement of RIP flowers for Lisa's grandma?"

"Douche. No, but, hey! I'm the one who had to *escape* from a mental hospital. Gimme a break!"

"Oh, like how I just took you to, literally, one of the worst movies I've ever seen in my life."

"What's a better movie?"

"Um, *Breathless*?"

"I don't even know what that is."

"196—"

"One made in the last decade."

"*American History X*."

"That sounds pretentious. What's so wrong with *At First Sight*? And how does that affect whether or not you can swing by my house?"

"Insert obvious joke about me wishing I could be the visually impaired one in the theater. I think that's a break. Why do we have to stalk your house for you to get panties? Can't you just call and see if anyone answers?"

"*Great* idea." I sound bratty, sarcastic. It's fulfilling to be rude, to say what I want. Not like I was a saint this morning, but men change my manners. "You wanna leave me at a payphone?"

"Open the glove compartment, Miss 1994. And, no, you're not gonna find *Dookie* in there."

"I don't know how to use a pager, Mr. Mr. . . . Mr. Drug Dealer."

"I am an infrequent passenger aboard the cocaine train. And smoking pot doesn't make me a drug dealer."

"You ever give anyone that pot?"

"Yeah, but not for more than I paid."

"Then you're a drug dealer who's getting robbed."

We come to a red light, and Junior Carlos leans over. I get to be this close to him two days in a row; usually, I'm lucky if I see him twice a week. Riding in the Bimmer, I feel like my skin is magnetized to attract his charge. When he opens the glove compartment, the heat of his forearm diagonals over my lap.

Unlike my mom's minivan, where twin Saint Christophers watch over us, offering pious protection from the visors, and a rosary in a yellow satin pouch is coiled in the first aid kit and Saran-wrapped stacks of Chips Ahoy are available "just in case," J.C.'s car is masculine and practical. In the glove compartment, there's a frosty bottle of *Acqua di Giò*. A pair of green-lensed goggles with chewed-up straps. Two types of eye drops. A folded map of Illinois that fits snuggly in a clouded plastic envelope. A sturdy silver coin, bigger than a quarter. I flip on the overhead light to examine it.

"'Confederate-E-Oh—"

"Confoederatio Helvetica. Swiss five franc."

"You've been to Switzerland?"

Junior Carlos nabs the coin and slams the glove compartment and turns off the lights.

"Here."

He hands me a phone. It's shorter and skinnier than my graphing calculator; its antenna feels about as sturdy as a coffee stirrer.

"Call your house, so we don't get caught lurking. I've heard your dad on air. He sounds like the James Earl Jones of white guys. Pretty sure he'd castrate me."

"I want a cell phone." The buttons illuminate at my touch.

"Why? So your mom can be even more in your face?"

"No. Why don't I know about this?"

"Because I don't want you bothering me around my real girlfriend?"

I'm still wearing his puffy green coat; when I punch his arm, I hit layers of T-shirt. Underneath, the muscle is concrete. "Jerk."

"I never use the thing, Lisa. I'm surprised it even has a battery."

"Okay, be quiet now. It's ringing."

Junior Carlos spider-walks his fingers up my left thigh.

"Quit it. Hey—!"

"Asshole," he yells, at a woman in a Mercedes who swerves into our lane. He honks, so long that I feel awkward just sitting there, like I should be shouting and swearing, too. "A fucking Pomeranian on the dashboard and a cigarette in her mouth? Jesus Christ. Hey, Anna Nicole Smith—someone stole your MENSA card."

The ringing stops. There's a click, the same as when you press Play on a tape. Duh, I think, one of those mini cassettes is inside. My dad's baritone rumbles on the answering machine.

"Score!" I hang up, before the beep can record me. "Okay. I'll be two seconds. You'll call if someone pulls up, right? Park in front of the Malussa's."

"Which one?"

"Um, nativity? Tickle-Me-Elmo in the manger instead of baby J."

"I'm sure your mom loves that."

I jam my feet in my Converse as Junior Carlos turns into my neighborhood. We pass Goose Lake, the surface covered with a screen of ice, and the surrounding beach, a graveyard for headless snowmen and Red Hot candy hearts that bleed cinnamon blood. Elliot's house is pitch black; all the curtains are wide open. I sniff. I hope their power got shut off.

"You know what's so ironic? I bet when my mother finally meets you—you know, in like, a kagillion years, she'll be totally fine. She'll reconcile our age difference with some 666 biblical numerology."

Junior Carlos turns up the volume on the CD player. I've won, by the way. Biggie Smalls is rapping "Hypnotize."

"That wouldn't surprise me," he says. "I've always had a way with moms."

..

My grandma, when she could still speak more than a few words, when she could form acerbic sentences and vitriolic gibes, referred to herself in the first person plural. My dad said it was because she worshipped my grandpa so much she couldn't accept herself as a widow, even though she'd been on her own since I was born. My dad thinks she actually believes she's still wedded to my grandpa, except now he's a ghost. That info, by the way, was between my dad and me. My mom would shit bricks—multiple bricks—if she knew my dad had occult theories.

Along with those nudie pics of Kim and Larry in the photo albums downstairs, there's a section of dogs. My parents, their first years dating, had two: Rocky and Adrian. We've never had pets, so I'm bad at breeds. They could be black labs or black retrievers or black hounds: is one of those a thing? The dogs have floppy, zucchini-shaped ears. Mopey eyes that are more lifelike than most humans. Red-violet tongues.

Sprinting upstairs to my bedroom reminds me of being a champ like Sylvester Stallone and that reminds me of the dogs. In my room, the Fen-Phen are still scattered all over the carpet. You'd think former pet owners would have some "vacuum up" reflex, like my grandma's phantom marriage.

Either my mom is more callous than I thought—or things with my grandma are worse.

Under my bed, I keep a box of CDs. I pull that out and flick to the last row, where I keep the albums I don't want my mom to see: Lauryn Hill and Snoop Dogg and Erykah Badu and Tupac and Faith Evans and the Quad City DJs. The *Space Jam* soundtrack. The *Waiting to Exhale* soundtrack.

The *Dr. Doolittle* soundtrack. From inside the double disc of *Riverdance*, volumes one and two, I grab the stack of bills I've collected for each pound I've gained back over the past year and a half. I crumple a black lace thong in my fist, when the phone rings.

"Shit." Any minute, my mom could barrel through the door. By now, Carousel Gardens must have alerted her and my dad to my getaway. *She met with a visitor*, I hear Marjorie saying. *A brother? Older? Swarthy male with luscious locks?* When my parents can't come up with anyone who goes by J.C. ("*blaspheme*," my mom will howl), poor Phoebe will be treated to an interrogation.

The phone rings again. I shove away the CD box and smooth the bed skirt and, to silence the noise which is about to drive me bonkers, I answer.

I wait. I refuse to say the first word. I wish, on all the pennies I've ever found and all the birthday candles I've ever huffed, on every 3:33 and 2:22 and 11:11, that I hadn't wanted a hot-pink fun fur phone from Limited Too. No Caller ID. No portable receiver. Just me, standing like an idiot, yanking up the waistband of my sweats and staring at my Converse, the tongues sticking out like kindergartners' tongues, kindergartners who've gone to town on cherry Blow Pops.

"Mr. Breit," says a reedy voice.

I would recognize it anywhere. Even today, right now, when, for some reason, Elliot sounds like Alvin and the Chipmunks, or a tape on Fast Forward.

I clear my throat. Have I mentioned I'm a good actress?

"Mm," I growl in Larry-tone.

"This is Elliot . . . Elliot Egleston. From today. I'm at the
Flagg Creek Motel and . . . well, like you said about Lisa, so
I tried Carousel Gardens and they said, they said she's not
available, and I didn't know if you and Mrs. Orlowski-Breit
pulled her out . . ." Her words tumble like a maze of dominos.
" . . . or there was a development with Lisa's grandma, or if
she just doesn't wanna talk because I think . . . I really need to
talk to her and I need to know if she's not gonna or if I should
wait, and I know you said, give her time, but I can't do that.
Every day I don't talk to her, I feel like we're getting farther
apart, we're gonna be old . . . history, just reruns of everything
we . . . and soon, it's gonna be a week, and how are you best
friends with someone if you don't talk to them once in a single
week. I mean . . . hello?"

I close my eyes. I summon Drew Barrymore (quirky, lov-
able, incapable of malice) from *The Wedding Singer*, which
Elliot and I saw last summer. Before Junior Carlos or my
grandma, before I knew better. I know what I want to do.

"Elliot?" I'm earnest as honey. "My dad just gave me the
phone. It's me."

"Oh my god," she breathes. Even her inhalations sound
sick, wheezy, like wisps of tissue. "Oh my god. Lisa! Lisa!
How are—I've been trying to get a hold of you for, you
wouldn't believe what I've been through. Can you talk,
what's going on? I'm—"

"I'm not here," I say, carefully. "Technically. Where are
you? Junior Carlos and I will meet up with you. You said the
Flagg Creek—"

"Room 217. You'll come over? Can you . . . can Junior
Carlos, like . . . I mean, can we have some time to talk?"

"Oh, absolutely, sweetie," I say. "Calm down. Hey, babe. Take a deep breath. You sound pretty worked up."

There's a pause. A zip line of snot. Elliot is blubbering. *Eat something*, I mouth. *For Christ sakes.*

"Okay," she says. Flooded by tears, her words sound bloated. "I'm just . . . sorry. I'm so happy to talk to you."

Do what you want, I remind myself. *You.* Not Elliot. Not Junior Carlos. Not Dr. Ogbaa. Not Mom. "Hey, me, too. Love ya like a sister."

..

I knock on the car window. It's fogged, billowing clouds punctured by one or two random fingerprints. Inside, I throw my neon-orange Speech Team duffel at my feet. With my index finger, I draw a heart in the steam. On one side, I make the feathery, nocked end of an arrow; on the other side, the pointy head.

"That was more than two minutes." Biggie is gone, and even though Junior Carlos turns down the music, the bass shakes the car. "*Boricua*," someone sings. It's a song you hear a million times and know all the words to but never remember the artist.

"Ah! 'Don't stop, get it, get it!'"

"Yeah," he says, raising an eyebrow, " . . . are we taking off?"

I wish the music could get so loud that it overpowered my thoughts. Dr. Ogbaa would call that risky behavior—wanting to disconnect from your consciousness. And I agree. But I don't care. I want to feel gone, with J.C., but I can't.

"Uh-huh," I say. "That's uh-huh yes."

Junior Carlos eases away from the curb. I keep my eyes straight ahead. You can't see much at night, in winter, but we're far enough from Chicago that, up above, the sky is coated with stars, like glittery nail polish. A slice of moon glints through a tuft of silvery cloud. All of a sudden, this babyish song from *Barney* (yes, the big purple dinosaur) injects itself into my brain. I sing along with B96, harder, trying to ignore it.

I stretch out my phrasing and round my vowels to sound angelic; this is funny for dirty rap. "'Punish ah, punish ah!'"

I lean back and move to the beat, leading with my pelvis, crotch out, the way TLC dances in, like, every video. Useless. In my head, Barney is indefatigable:

Flying high in the sky, we look back to say goodbye, as our spaceship is flying away. Past the earth and the stars, look there's Jupiter and Mars, as our spaceship is flying away.

"All right, Big Pun. I'm driving us to the Hyatt in Oakbrook. My dad has the penthouse on forever-reserve."

"No! I mean, not yet."

"What no? What's the plan? Please tell me you haven't cooked up some kind of me-heisting-you scheme. Because lines are drawn—"

"We have to go to the Flagg Creek Motel." I sit up straight and tuck my pelvis. Now I feel respectable. "Elliot's there."

"Who's Elliot?"

I pause. I get how EDP girls who tell stories about hitting rock bottom or asking for help must feel, admitting the grossest things in the world. ". . . she used to be my best friend?"

"Oh. Tell me if I remember . . . Skinny? Weird?"

"Very skinny. Very weird."

"What's she doing out at the boom-boom room?"

"The what?"

"Don't Park kids still call it that? They did when I was there."

I unbuckle and kneel on my seat. I lean over and wrap my arms around Junior Carlos's neck. Right now, I think. I want to say I love you. Instead, I give him a peck on the cheek, a gulf of stubble. I rub my kiss into his skin with my thumb. I say: "You're old."

12 ·· ELLIOT

LIFE IS BORING, A STORY that ends the same for everyone. Girls who call anorexia dullsville have chucked in the towel or been hoodwinked. What's more important than your body? In the last issue of *Real Talk*, I decided I'd poll my clients: Are you *trying* to keep your diet exciting or expecting foods to do the work? Are you happy with your weight or are you just lying to yourself?

My thoughts were optimistic, clear as I decked out the room. Lisa had talked to me like her usual self over the phone; now I wanted her to want to spend the night. We could have a sleepover, a hotel party, like Marissa Turner told me her parents and other popular kids' parents were planning for after the eighth grade dance. She could tell Junior Carlos to scram or at least have him bring us a two-liter of Diet Coke and then scram so we could rekindle our friendship in peace. If she made me read stupid *Cosmo*, maybe I'd even share my own confession (*Suva dropped trou—and it was just, like, watching me!*), and, for the first time, we'd talk about boys' bodies instead of girls' before falling asleep in the narrow bed, our shoulder blades jabbing one another.

I smoothed the whisper of wrinkles in the lumpy comforter where I'd been sitting. I took the baggie out of the drawer and set the heroin on the pillow like a Peppermint

Patty or some disgusting chocolate mint. (Who wanted food where her face would go?) I replaced the phonebook, stacked it on the Bible, and shut the drawer. My heart was gunning. I was ready, ready to get ready, the way Uncle Marky had taught me *mise en place* a few weeks ago, when we made gingerbread men: bringing the butter and eggs to room temperature on the counter, weighing flour and cinnamon and ginger, coloring royal icing in ramekins, piping bags and pastry tips and paintbrushes all set.

There was a clock radio on the nightstand on the far side of the bed. I turned it on: AM announced the hourly traffic reports, black ice incidents, and a rash of accidents in the southwest suburbs. Boring. I switched to the real stations, where pop and techno jams pumped people up for Friday. I skipped too-peppy—Shania Twain and *NSYNC, too plodding ("Sex and Candy"), too sad ("Jumper"), but at "Bitter Sweet Symphony," I stopped. I turned up the volume and sank onto the floor.

Here I was: leaning against a bed that had surely seen fat, disgusting, flesh-slapping boinking, in a stale-smelling fleabag motel, a block from school, no clue where my mom was, the girl who used to be my best friend coming over, my head muddled from drugs, my stomach a blimp from two bites of PBJ. Every time you feel the acuteness of *Now*, there's so much *Then* behind it. I was forlorn and pitying myself, and I felt bad for feeling bad for myself, which was as obvious as emotions get. Why did I have to be the worst? Other girls *had* friends. Dependable parents. Other girls could eat and not spaz. I bit my lip and blinked until I couldn't help it, I was crying again; even when I let my eyelids rest I couldn't calm down.

"'No change,'" I sang, my voice ragged and desperate. "'I can change.'" I turned up the volume until I couldn't hear myself. I stomped my feet. I banged my fists against my forehead.

When the song ended, I took a deep breath. I found B96. K-Ci & JoJo, I could deal with: Lisa was nuts about them.

I rolled up my sleeves and looked at my cuts. They needed work.

I opened my Trapper to the *Real Talk* section and positioned it on the shaky desk. I took a ballpoint that said FLAGG CREEK in gold script and set it at an angle that suggested I'd be answering Lisa's knock at the door *media res*. The blocky, mishmash chair, with padded arms and carved legs, I pulled out, not enough for someone to sit in, but enough for someone to think I'd been at work.

Good.

I tried the TV again. Having background would create a cool vibe, like I'd been hanging out. But the best I could find was *Sabrina the Teenage Witch*. I shut it off. No way I wanted to see Melissa Joan Hart's Mrs. Potato Head face.

I went to the bathroom. For once, I wished I used makeup, even Carmex or Vaseline, which probably seeped transdermal calories, but whatev. I looked *bad*. Under my eyes were gulches of bruisy shadow. My lips were seamed with blood; above the top one, I saw tiny, fine brown hairs. The light didn't help any: my skin was dirty-water gray. I turned on the shower. Maybe humidity would dewify my pallor.

At the desk table, I picked up the ballpoint. I put the nib end in my mouth and tugged until the body came out. Somewhere I'd seen this, but it was still amazing how much eureka you could have alone. I shook the ink cartridge and the spring into my hand and I pulled the spring until the coil straightened. Now I knew the drill: I traced over yesterday's marks, pressing until I felt less than nothing, ruthless. At the end of each scratch, a bead of blood bloomed.

..

Even though I'd seen her in Science on Wednesday, standing outside my door at the Flagg Creek, Lisa reminded me of someone else—an older someone with ratty blonde hair, Courtney Love. Lisa but puffier. Off-balance. Her red lipstick was smeared over her Cupid's bow.

We didn't usually hug, but I opened up my arms. Today was different.

"Hi, Elliot." She sounded like her mom, who used the same smarting tone when she had to address me.

She waved down my arm and walked in like this was her personal motel. She stood with her back to the TV. I positioned myself in her line of vision, leaning against the nightstand. The phone bumped my tailbone.

"Well, yuck." Lisa's glance lapped the room. "Tell me again why you're sleeping here?"

"I'm not, not necessarily."

She picked up the Velcroed remote and put on a pouty face. "Damn. 'Cuz I was, like, gonna gank that."

I tried to get out of my head. The Christmas sleepover had been awkward at first, too. PJs, talking, VH1, music—that had helped us be ourselves.

"What happened to you? I mean, your dad—"

Lisa sat on the bed. She tucked her feet; she was facing me. I could see the bright red of her low-tops underneath her calves. Even if her mouth was bee-stung and messy, even if fat rounded her formerly-angular chin, she was still beautiful, more beautiful than my girls, more beautiful than I'd ever be.

"There are long stories. Then there's the last twenty-four—no, thirty-ish hours."

"Well, I've got time. I'm here for the night . . . or until my mom decides to give me a call." Like I was trying to surprise a rabbit in a field, I inched closer to the bed. I seared my spine to the headboard and hugged the pillow's blood-tilde to my stomach.

"Where's your mom?" Lisa asked.

"Who knows? Who cares?"

"Woah. Harsh-sauce."

I clenched my teeth and raised my eyebrows. "If you'd been stranded at Rocyo's house, you'd be pissed, too."

"Ew. I heard she gave Mr. Rhodes a hand job."

"That is so sick, I wish I were bulimic so I could barf in, like, solidarity."

"C'mon, Elliot. Just—didn't you get what I was saying yesterday?"

"Saying when?" Maybe I could convince her I'd never called during C Lunch, that everything between us was all good, that there was a mysterious misunderstanding risen out of nowhere. The more I thought about it, the more this rift *did* seem like a freak occurrence—one Lisa had witnessed without being thoughtful enough to send warning signs or light caution flares.

Lisa shook her head. She stood up, hiking the waistband of her pants through her coat. "I knew this was a mistake. I knew I should've—fuck."

"What?" I folded my arms across my chest. I tried ESP, to bore a message through her skull: *Go back to who you were.* "What *should* you have done? Who's telling you what to do?"

"Jesus Christ, Elliot. *No one's* telling me what to do. I do what I want. I don't listen to—Oh my god. I'm done."

"Done with what? Done with caring?"

"I'm done trying to, like, help you."

"Why do I need your help?"

Lisa stomped around the bed. Her sneakers slapped on the carpet. I hoped someone would knock on the ceiling or punch the wall so we could laugh at over-sensitive adults. She grabbed me by the arm and yanked me off the bed.

"*Look. At. You.*"

I eyed my body. My thighs were huge, like hunks of black-denim meat.

"I've looked."

"You're sick. Joking about bulimia doesn't make you . . . like, cured. And it doesn't make you better than me."

I pulled out of her grasp. She stunk, like girl sweat and buttery popcorn and cheap cologne. Vegans were supposed to smell, and Ethan Suva—*all* parts of him—had smelled way better than Lisa.

I climbed onto the bed and tucked my knees to my chest. I plucked the heroin off the pillow and tossed it from one hand to the next.

"I don't think I'm better than anyone," I said in an innocent way. My head hurt. Everything was happening too fast and my throat burned and I couldn't tell if I was serious or not. I felt all tripped up. "'I'm just a girl . . . blah, blah. Little old me.'"

Lisa exhaled like a steam engine. Her hands fisted and her fingers stretched long, and she closed her eyes and bared her teeth, and, without any noise, screamed.

"I'm going to tell you what I know, Elliot," she said, her eyes still shut. "Then I'm going. And I'm not playing when I say that I don't want you to talk to me. Not for a long, long time. I'm not a jerk—so I'm not gonna say never. Because I don't know if I believe in never. Death is never—that's about it. Would you look at me? Stop throwing around that—"

"What?" I jutted out my chin. Mine was pointy. "Heroin? You want some?"

"I'm not even going there. Unbelievable. You're, like, really serious about killing yourself, aren't you?"

I waved my wrists at her.

"I don't know if you hear me," she said. "I realize you could be like one of those brain-dead, zombie girls I just spent the night with—because, yes, my mother checked me into the effing hospital because of those stupid, idiotic diet pills you gave me."

"I thought you liked those!"

"I don't care if I once *liked* those. I don't care if I once liked . . . Barney the Dinosaur! That doesn't mean I have to like . . . diet pills or Barney forever."

"So I'm like Barney and diet pills?"

She paused. "All rolled into one. One anorexic, self-important, childish, scared little girl."

I squeezed the baggie. "I'm not afraid of anything."

"You could barely watch that . . . that . . . the porno. You're afraid to *see* naked people having sex. That's how emotionally stunted you are. Or, just, like chronically perverse."

"What? You were the one who was all like, 'Elliot, tell me evvvvvverything—'"

"Yeah, because I didn't want *you* to feel, like, self-conscious or whatever. Oh my god! You think screwing with my head's going to make me forget that you're actually, like, . . . You talk like you're so tough and, what, you're a chicken? Actually, worse. You're a geek."

"C'mon. Seriously. Lisa, you have to—look, I'd do anything. Okay? Really. Anything. Please. Please." Suddenly, I knew she wasn't joking. She *could* leave. An almost-adult was waiting, downstairs, to give her a ride. She didn't care about her eating disorder. In fact, she was the worst kind of girl: her anorexia had been a phase, like slap bracelets or glow-in-the-dark pacifiers.

"Give me a chance. Anything—truth or dare me."

"What is this, fourth grade?"

"Don't be a poser. We played last year."

She rolled her eyes. "Whatever . . . Truth or dare."

Truths sucked. The epitome of lame. No one cared what you said. People only wanted to see what you'd do.

"Dare," I said.

"Fine. Have a three-way with me and Junior Carlos."

"You're gonna rope your boyfriend into that without, like, consulting him?"

"How do you know who I've consulted? This is exactly the issue, you thinking you know everything—"

"Okay, geez. I'm so sorry. Forgive my mistake."

"Even that—you're so patronizing. Unbelievable."

"No," I said. "I'm not patronizing. I'm trying to keep up with you. Lisa who changes her mind about who she's gonna be every year, apparently. *I* haven't changed. *This* is me, like it or not. Me is anorexic. So . . . if you need anorexic me to like . . . whatever with you and your boyfriend, if that's gonna show you I'm not the psycho, robot Skeletor you think I am, fine. Whatever. Get Junior Carlos. Sounds like a blast."

"Oh, this is . . . wow," Lisa said. Her voice brightened, the way in movies crazy people sounded before they cracked. "Sure! Outie!"

··

As soon as the door slammed, I opened the heroin and dipped. I'd developed tolerance; I wasn't woozy like I'd been in Ethan's bedroom. Instead, I felt wound-up, on edge, strung out: expressions I'd heard before. Now I understood. I sucked my finger, getting each bitter taste of the powder, until I calmed down.

The room was stuffy, hot. My stores of resolve had been replenished. Now the last leg of the walk home didn't seem so impossible. I could make it. I zipped up my Trapper. Pushed in the chair. Another twenty minutes and I'd be inside, asleep in my own clean, non-roast-beef bed with Michael Jordan watching over me.

The knock surprised me. I hadn't *really* expected Lisa to come back.

"Elliot?" He didn't look like anyone a fourteen-year-old could date. He was a man, in a bright-green puffy coat. His hair was black and tousled, sparingly gelled. Tasteful, I thought. Cute.

I held out my hand. "Elliot."

His hands were big, warm, and, in patches, scaly. "Weird name for a girl."

"Go in, baby," Lisa said. I couldn't see her. "It's freezing out here."

The three of us stood in the room, actors dumped in a minimal set. On B96, Jay-Z rapped and a girl whoop-whooped; it was awkward being with a couple that was half-Lisa. The room was smaller than the studio Anna rented us in Soho—and it felt tighter with more people. Dingier, too. I sat with my back against the headboard, where I'd been earlier, and Lisa turned the desk chair so it faced me. Junior Carlos took off his backpack and set it at the foot of the bed. If I'd been in his spot, I would have seemed awkward, but he was tall enough that just standing he looked like he was doing something. I liked him.

"Who's Elliot?" he asked.

"My mom's a poet. Ever heard of T.S.? *The Wasteland*?"

"Sure."

"Well, there yah go."

My knee bounced *yesyesyesyes* in time with Jay-Z.

"Elliot's mom teaches at COCC. J.C.'s doing gen-eds there. That's general—"

"I think she knows what gen-eds are, babe."

I wondered if they'd ever had a *ménage à trois*, if they were always this terse with each other.

I half laughed. "The perks of having a professor for a mom. Is it J.C. or . . . ?"

"It's actually Charles, but I go by whatever."

"All right, Whatever."

Lisa glared at me. Junior Carlos smirked.

"Girls, want something to drink?" He unzipped his back-pack and bottles clinked. "I've got vodka and . . . vodka."

"Elliot doesn't drink calories," Lisa said.

"Sure, I do. I drank calories today, even . . . with your *dad*."

There was no need to ruin that joke.

"I have . . . " I hopped off the bed and disappeared into the bathroom and returned. "One cup!"

Tomorrow, I told myself, would be an epic calorie burn. Tomorrow, I'd start a three-day fast. I'd take the Ex-Lax my mom kept in the medicine cabinet and the handful of Fen-Phen I'd snagged for myself and do two thousand sit-ups and two thousand burpees and two thousand lunges, one thousand on each side; I'd study in my bra to shiver off any remaining fat grams. Then, I felt awful: all these tomorrows made me sound like my clients, as badly normally lazy as Other girls.

Junior Carlos laughed. He held up a bottle of Absolut and lofted it over his head like a trophy.

"Fill 'er up?" he said.

I held out the cup. He poured vodka to the rim and it spilled over and down my hand. It was ice cold, like he'd just taken it from the freezer. I brought my hand to my mouth and licked.

Heroin was nothing. Scotch was whatever. Vodka stang. Stung?

Junior Carlos stoppered the bottle. "Come here, Lee-Lee, stop being weird."

"Elliot wants to have a threesome," Lisa said. She pushed her chair further back. It rapped the table.

"You mentioned. *Due bellezze*. Excellent."

"Being sexy in Italian isn't gonna erase how you talk like Wayne Campbell."

" 'cha! Get it through your melon! Babe-raham Lincoln. Over here."

"Yeah, not gonna get me in the mood."

"Cheers!" I said. The cup was flimsy, squeezable in my grip, spilling. "To friends!"

"New friends!" Junior Carlos was taller than me, so he stooped for a gulp.

Lisa shook her head.

I took a drink—and another one, to prove Lisa wrong. I gave Junior Carlos the cup and leaned across the bed to turn up the music. When the guy sang, "Don't stop, get it get," I purposefully avoided Lisa's eyes. I could feel them, burning and furious and itching to rap along. She loved this one.

"I don't wanna be a playa no more," Junior Carlos sang, dancing over to Lisa. "Your turn. 'Punish-ah, punish-ahhhhhh.'"

"Did you know Big Pun weighs, like, six hundred pounds?" I sat on the bed with my legs out straight and bobbed to the music. "He's *morbidly* obese."

"*Fuck me!*" said Lisa. "Should I start telling you my dad saw Chris Farley do stand-up?"

"Are you kidding?" I said. "How big was he in real life?"

"Seriously!"

"Hey, heyuhh." All of a sudden, Junior Carlos sounded slurry, like the tape of a drunk person we'd listened to in D.A.R.E. "You need to un-wiiiiiind. Get it . . . wiiiine? Oops . . . vodkaaaaah?"

Lisa brushed past Junior Carlos, the way girls accidentally touched boys they liked when they were excused to use the hall pass, the way Ethan Suva had brushed my calf on the bus. This brush, though, was a shove.

"I'm leaving. This is literally the stupidest thing I've ever even considered doing. And I did *lots* of stupid things with you over the years, Elliot."

"Baby." Junior Carlos looked at me doggedly. "Uh-oh," he whispered.

"No, you're fine. Whatever," said Lisa. She hiked up the waistband of her pants. Her eyes glistered like nail heads. "My boyfriend can do what he wants. *I* can do what I want. You, Elliot Egleston, can do what you want. Baby—gimme the car keys."

"Lisa, stop acting like a—"

"Don't go there, Junior Carlos. Charles Rottingham Junior. Don't even."

I tweaked the volume louder and tried to disappear into the mattress. Metal coils, dirty feathers, random foam would smother me to death. Not bad.

"Let's kissy, make up. Baby. Lee-Lee, please? My trooper," Junior Carlos said. Their romance made me uncomfortable, like I was wearing a wool turtleneck two sizes too small. I'd never even heard my dad talk to my mom with such besotted passion.

He handed Lisa the plastic cup. She tipped her head back. The mechanisms in her neck still showed, remnants of the body she'd starved herself to have. She threw the cup on the floor. Junior Carlos took off his coat and let it fall on the bed.

I giggled and they started. I'd forgotten I was in the room, too.

"What?" Lisa said.

"Junior . . . you're wearing like . . . four shirts?"

"Now *this* is the good feeling I'm talkin' about," he said. He lifted Lisa up and started walking around the room with her over his shoulder. He must have been *really* strong. When he threw her on the bed, she landed—boing—in the center.

"Now you girls kiss and make up."

I stared at the comforter: maybe it was more the color of raw hamburger or filet mignon. I hadn't eaten red meat since fourth grade, way before I was *flaca*. With my legs out, I could see the beefy fabric in the gap between my thighs. If I died in this bed, I hoped an artist would plant roses there, let my body mulch. The opening of "The Boy Is Mine" began.

"Ugh, I hate this one—" I said.

I turned my head and bumped into Lisa's mouth.

Her lips on my lips were rougher, more rushed than Ethan's. It was a peck, the equivalent of the obligatory high five opposing teams exchanged after softball games in gym. I didn't kiss back. I was frozen, tasting her: cocoa and cherries and cola. I knew what she did: she put Dr. Pepper Lip Smackers on top of her lipstick.

"Ow!" I yelled. I backed away. "You bit me!"

"Good!" Her eyes were darting all over the place. "I hope I did. Now maybe you'll stop calling and passing me notes and looking for me in the hallway and chatting me like a stalker creepazoid on AOL. Is that clear?" Now her words were shaky, too. "J.C., I said, gimme the keys."

She found them from the heap of his coat. "I'll be in the car."

..

I rubbed my lip. There was blood on my finger, bright-Lisa's-Converse red. I put my head in my hands, tented my knees, jammed my face into my thighs, and cried. Sometimes people left the room and sometimes people really were gone.

Junior Carlos came over to the bed. He put his arm around my shoulder, and it felt like a hug from a punching bag.

"Don't let her be out there alone," I sniffled. "That parking lot is so sketchy."

He handed me a handkerchief. It was monogrammed, with the same burgundy thread as my dad's.

I wiped my eyes. "My dad has this. The color, I mean."

"Gotta respect a Brooks Brotha."

I laughed, weakly—like an empty cough.

He put his hands on my shoulders and sat me up.

"Look at me," he said.

I blinked.

His face was right there. "Can I big brother you for a minute?"

I wanted to reach over and grab the heroin off the nightstand, but I just shrugged. "I don't care."

"Open your mouth."

I parted my lips.

He slid in his tongue. It was thicker than Ethan's and his face was rougher and he sucked Lisa's bite, which was in my bottom gum.

"Big brother?" I said. "I think that's illegal in Illinois."

"Stupider shit is legal," he said. He reclined on the dirty pillow. "Deleterious shit is deemed OK in this country. So, . . . So big Carlos slipped you some tongue."

"I guess." I swallowed. *Big Carlos*? I cringed. His mouth tasted gross.

"Advice? Let Lisa come around. Or not. It's middle school, yah know? She's paranoid about her mom and she's tryin' to beat this food thing and I know that's tough, okay? For you—and for her. But she's fighting. Maybe because of her mom. Maybe because of something else."

"Yeah, she saw a girl die in the hospital," I said. "Shit. What's her name."

"So I know people who've been through . . . what she's been through. Who haven't been as strong as her. You gotta respect her that. You do you."

I nodded. He didn't need to tell me she was amazing.

"You want a ride somewhere?" he said. "Pretty gross place to spend the night."

"My mom's coming." I looked at the clock radio. Nine forty-five p.m. "Sometime."

He put on his coat and walked toward the door. It's like we were in a movie: he paused and turned. His forehead gleamed with sweat.

"Can I ask you something borderline inappropriate?"

"Borders are imaginary," I said. I wanted to sleep. "So. Sure."

"Lisa was rambling all kinds of stuff when she came out. She said you had . . .?"

"Heroin? You want it?" I pointed to the nightstand.

Junior Carlos picked up the baggie. He held it under his nose, sniffed, touched his index finger to his mouth, dipped, rubbed his gums and his teeth.

"That ain't heroin," he said. He knotted the top and put it in his pocket.

"Whatever." I shrugged and pulled the covers over me. "It's yours."

SATURDAY

1 ·· LISA

PEACOCKS. I SEE THE WHITE birds, like snowy ghosts. They're Italian, I know, one of those facts that's caught in the syrup of sleep. This is how you have to learn lines for speech: like they're invisible fish swimming under water. This is what I see: swan necks, trim bodies, too-much tails like Princess Diana's wedding train. Patrician birds. Their faces, almonds. Their eyes, critiquing. On the crown of their heads, poofs and puffball-tipped crests. Pipe cleaners and Q-tip tops. Pretzel sticks dipped in white chocolate capped with cotton candy. A headband Baby and Scary Spice would have fought over.

I blink awake. If hospital beds have opposites, that's where I am, a room that reminds me of *The Little Princess*. That movie sucked compared to the book: everything you could think of, every ermine silk mink pearl lace lamé turban, your mind imagined better than what you saw on screen. It's not that this room is diamond dusted, but niceness is its own jolt. I'm in some fancy basement bedroom with gold and marble nightstands and a lampshade like a pale blue tutu.

Next to the bed, there's a high window. I can see out, to the ground line, a ribbon of white, frosting bordering a cake. This is the first year I haven't been excited about snow. Is that what blizzards do to people? It's like recovery, the worst buzz kill for diets. I watch and watch. The wind is pretending we're not outside Chicago. Very funny—not.

No peacocks.

The sheets are warm where I've been curled up, warmer where Junior Carlos lies, still. He sleeps on his back. His mouth is parted. Overnight, his sorta beard has sprouted more stubble. Overnight, I have lost all clothing except my black thong.

Hm.

I pull the comforter around me and cover every part of my body except my eyes. Even my head—I wrap the comforter over my forehead and up past my chin. It's like looking through the viewfinder on one of those old toys, where you load in a card of pictures and click through to see just what fits in your field of vision. I see my new friend Phoebe. I see my dad imitating Bill Murray in *Caddyshack*. I see my grandma gesticulating with a grapefruit spoon. I see my boyfriend through a rectangle.

No Elliot in sight.

His chest rises and falls; at whatever time this is, the fact of this movement—unconscious, automatic—blows my mind.

"I love you," I whisper. Of course it's cheap to say to a sleeper. But I believe in osmosis or whatever, the thing we learned in science that says borders are porous, states of consciousness permeable. The corners of Junior Carlos's mouth turn up. I scoot my body against his torso and, without opening his eyes, he pins me to the bed with his arm.

Probably I fall back asleep. Maybe I die for a sec.

True or False:

Only skinny girls think about life and death.

..

Snow gets in my low-tops, at the tongue and on the sides, where the red canvas gapes. I need laces. It's like running through sand. Solid ground gives way beneath your feet. I'm out the guest door, on a side pathway that, bummer, staff never shovels. (*Staff?* I said. *Yeah,* said Junior Carlos. *I'm warming up the car. Gardeners and . . . stuff.*)

In a circular drive, the Bimmer is waiting, emitting snarls of exhaust smoke. The sky is cerulean, one of those mornings that looks fake.

"Your house is pimp," I say.

"Pimp or nouveau riche, your dice. Ready to face the dragon?"

Junior Carlos stands on the passenger side, an ice scraper in hand. He's dressed like an off-duty Olympian in his swim conference track suit, Hampshire High colors, the same palette all my school duds will be next year: brown and yellow. Like even my dad, he looks new and sexy wearing sunglasses. Wayfarers.

(Very mature: Park wannabes wear Oakleys.)

"No use postponing the inviable," I say getting in the car.

"Inevitable?"

"That's what I said."

He backs out of the driveway and we leave his house.

"Warming up?" Junior Carlos says. He punches the heat. "This car sucks."

"Are you kidding? I love this car."

"Yo, my mom *hit* me in this car. No joke."

"She hit you? How are you still alive?"

"Oh, Lisa." He smiles and pats my knee.

"What? Are you sure you're not like Casper? Am I secretly Christina Ricci?"

"Yikes. I hope not. I'm not into brunettes. Especially not creepy brunettes."

"Really?" I ask. "You don't wanna date Elliot now?"

"Do you know any guys who aren't down for . . . *that* . . . when their girl suggests it? I mean, you've got to be off your nob to think anyone in his right mind is gonna pass that up."

"I don't know any other guys."

"C'mon Lisa. Those Park shorties have totally defiled your yearbook picture."

"Ew. Okay?"

Junior Carlos turns on the radio, where skankalicious Britney Spears reigns. I cover my ears. Her voice reminds me of the stringiest hospital girls, feral and electronic—the exact opposite of the sultry, silky, feline Brandy, Toni Braxton, Mary J. Blige, Aaliyah, Aaliyah, Aaliyah I adore.

The car rolls by Park. *Monday,* JANUARY 18 *** MLK *** flashes the school's upgraded, digital sign. No more janitors using wrenches or pliers or whatever the tool's called that lifts plastic letters off an actual marquis.

"Is this a hangover?" I say. "Like, my head hurting? Desperately wanting scrambled eggs?"

"Are you gonna spew?"

"No, Garth. I'm not. But thanks for reviving me. Just what the doctor ordered. Are you gonna pick me up, Tuesday, after school?"

" 'cha." He smirks and his eyebrows lift over his sunglasses.

..

"Your father is covering the CTA delays," says my mom, once she's finished haranguing me (*who dropped you off—no one—where did you go—Elliot's house—why are you consorting*

with miscreants—good question, major mistake—God is keep-
ing your grandma with us until you can find time in your sched-
ule to visit her—I'll get ready—you better—am I going back to
the—no, Dr. Ogbaa left instructions that you are to continue an
aggressive course of out-patient therapy but the hospital setting
is, and color me skeptical here, is too intensive at this time—
good—so get ready—okay, I'll get ready—are you okay—yeah,
Mom, I am). "We can't listen to him. He sounds . . . take pity
on the man. He didn't sleep."

Now we're in the minivan, heading downtown, toward
Rush Hospital. I grip the ashtray on the door as we go over
the Forty-Seventh Street train tracks. My mom, for all her
propriety, drives like a cowgirl. She's a swerver, a stop-and-
goer, a screamer, yelling invented swears that will keep her in
the Big Guy's graces.

"Frank-*furter!*" she shouts at a red Jeep; she's extra harsh
on those because of my dad. "That's a stop sign."

I smother a smile. I hate my mom, how she's a sloppy
driver, how she wasn't happy to see me but pissed, how she's
bossy, righteous, into bad haircuts—but also I love her. I can
love her, now, at this sec. I love how she wears a fur hat like a
spy from James Bond land; even though I gave her hell about
this hat, like, four years ago when she bought it, now it's her.
She rocks it. It's the only piece of her that I want.

I want her to know: That I like her hat. That I love her.

"Mom." I stretch out the vowel to sound earnest and
hopeful, like an innocent girl in a play. Just talking with a
smile in my voice starts to make me happier. When I do
get married, I'll be the best wife in the world—always sexy,
always fun. "Mom, guess what?"

"Not now, Lisa. My brain can only handle so much."

She turns on the radio, and for a second, she lets B96 play. Was she listening without me? The music tolls in the pit of my stomach. There's Dr. Dre, rapping "Keep Their Heads Ringing," that creepy minor-key chorus that makes me feel like I'm dead: "Ding, ding, dong."

2 ·· ELLIOT

THIS WAS MY FIRST CUP of coffee:

In the cabinet under the TV, there was a machine with a preportioned filter, a paper cup, a wooden stick, a white napkin, Sweet 'n Low, powdered creamer. Who would've expected this hospitality from the Flagg Creek? Like a bombshell, I walked around in just-my-sweater. I'd kicked off my jeans in the night. After Junior Carlos left, I'd eaten five Listerine strips and turned off the lights and slept in my clothes, with Michael Jordan tiptoeing on my back, a tonnage infusing me with power and serenity. No one had called or I hadn't woken up.

Anna used a French press, so I'd never worked a machine like this. The brewing began, and when actual coffee started sluicing the sides of the tiny carafe, I was wowed, like I'd landed a round-off dismount off the balance beam. I could hear Troubaugh lauding me: *Egleston, you're a natural.*

The most trivial accomplishments can make you feel the best. My volition concurred: those first lost *voy-a-la-flaca* pounds.

I opened the waffled curtains. The morning sun flooded the room with washed light. Outside, in the parking lot, all three cars wore slabs of snow. None of those were my rides. I imagined the minivans and trucks and the one cream

Rolls Royce that everyone claimed belonged to Bo Jackson, who lived a town over, adults with licenses hitting it, a quick pound-pound in the night, the parking lot ebbing with horniness. I hadn't heard moaning or bouncing. I had also never slept so deadweight in my life.

It was eight thirty a.m. There was a newspaper and something on motel stationery under the door. The plastic cup that had teemed with Absolut last night was on its side, in a corner. I had another two hours until I really had to check out. And even though my head hurt behind my eyes, like someone was playing my bones with mallets, a xylophone, I wasn't going to call my mom to pick me up. I didn't need her, I didn't need Lisa: I had boys and men. And writing.

I poured myself a cup of coffee and turned to a blank page. Standing at the desk, I started taking notes for a supplement to *Real Talk*.

"Is It Worth the Work?"

1. "No pain, no gain" is a cliché.
2. Clichés can be true.
3. What's wrong with suffering?
4. Does objective suffering exist or can my suffering be your pinnacle of joy?
5. If my pinnacle of joy is starving, does that make me wrong?
6. Should I want everything to taste good?
7. Why do adults care if kids are [insert air quotes] hurting themselves?
8. What about "hurt so good"?
9. I.E. Doesn't sex hurt?
10. Why do I have to be happy?

11. Why do I have to have high self-esteem?
12. What if I have high self-esteem but don't want to be healthy?
13. Can those two things coexist?

I paused for a sip. The coffee tasted burnt and weak; then again, a cup has two calories. Sometimes, you need to lower your expectations. Maybe one day I'd think back on Ethan's penis as the cutest thing ever. I grabbed my binder and hopped into bed. I covered myself with the sheets and the comforter. In LA, Ms. McMahon would put on Yanni and twist the Venetian blinds until the room got dark and tell us, *write without picking up your pens; write anything that pops into your heads*. Usually, I didn't do this. What was the point in scribbling when you didn't know what you wanted to say? But today I wanted to figure everything out. Otherwise, I'd just go around feeling basic stuff, like, this room is cold.

A knock shook the door. I ran into the bathroom and stood in front of the mirror. Had I become prettier? My neck was still fine, pale and corded with the usual tendons, but my pupils were shiny and black-olive big, my under-eye shadows weren't so hollow, and my lips were swollen. I pulled down the bottom one, searching for Lisa's bite. But everything inside was the same: wet, smooth, occasionally veined, pink, healthy.

The knock repeated.

"*Hola*? Hello? *Cariño*?"

"Just a second!" I recognized that voice. I pulled on my jeans and put my foot straight through one of the holes at the knee. The fabric ripped all the way to the floor and the shreds hung like kite tails. The downy hair furring my calves and my contaminated black socks showed. Well. Whatever.

The knocking began again, slower and louder, stern, like a brute's footsteps.

"Okay, okay!" I tucked my hair behind my ears and opened the door.

The two men's bodies were angled toward one another. I'd interrupted a tête-à-tête.

"Holy hell," said my Uncle Marky. His words were floppy: he sounded like, instead of Amherst, he'd gone to college in New Orleans. He wore a wool peacoat with a fat fur collar, the mink earmuffs Anna had given him for Christmas, and his huge camel-colored scarf. Maybe it was a shawl. It was so big it could probably wrap Shaq.

He rushed me with a hug. I pressed against his belly, and in his clutch I felt like an arm gripped by a blood pressure cuff.

Fernán pushed past us and went inside. He put his hands on his waist and immediately untied the Burberry plaid scarf around his neck.

"Theses places should charge for heat. El, did you turn this up?"

"I don't think so."

Marky looked around. "This is so eerie: this could *be* your mom's first dorm room. I'm not kidding. Just the— everything. The ambiance."

"That's creepy," I said. "Do you think that's why she wouldn't come get me?"

Fernán growled out a sigh. He shifted his weight and pointed his hip at Marky and frowned. Fernán was tough: once he'd been rolled in a convertible and an entire windshield had shattered on him. Every time he got a serious look, I couldn't help wondering if part of him was remembering that.

"Time to go, Lil' Bit," said Marky. "You set?"

I picked up my binder and my mini backpack. I opened the closet and grabbed my coat. My uncles watched me. I could feel their thoughts: What does a fourteen-year-old do in a motel room? That girl—skinny as a last chance.

..

"Don't let your mother convince you she's a luddite," said Marky. We were in his station wagon, heading to Jewel's. Fernán was doing the driving, and Marky was ranting, his whole torso more in the backseat than the front. "She had a CD player before anyone I knew."

"She's too young for a cell phone," said Fernán. "Fourteen?"

"No one's too young. You need to be able to call us, no matter what, anytime. Just in case. Your mom and dad need those, too. Do other kids have mobiles at your school?"

I tried to picture all sixty-five of my fellow eighth graders. "I don't think so."

"There. You'll be ahead of the trend. The first. Do kids still say *radical*?"

I laughed. So did Fernán.

"You need to get out more."

Marky moved aside his earmuffs and pretended to plug his ears. "Any-whooo. Do you have peanut butter at home, Elliot?"

I squinted. "Does that sound like Lean Cuisine or microwave popcorn?"

"Food deserts can be anywhere," Fernán said. "In fact, you often don't need to look any further than your own backyard. American's healthiest go hungry."

"Why do we need peanut butter?" I asked.

Uncle Marky swallowed. He shook his head. With his coat open, I could see the top of his chest, where a stab of green belonged to some new tattoo.

"Your mom's favorite cookies," said Fernán. "We've been debating the merits of crisscrossed versus uncrisscrossed since Halsted. Also, someone brought his cookie cutters."

We turned into the parking lot and Fernán pulled up to the curb. Saturdays were bananas, Anna usually said. This Jewel was one of the only stores that still closed on Sundays.

Marky opened his door. "PB, eggs—hell, I'm stocking you up. I'll assume barren. Elliot, you hungry?"

Fernán cleared his throat. I could just imagine the lecture.

"Actually," I said. "Can you buy me some, um, vegan bread?"

..

When we got home, I went upstairs. Marky and Fernán were in the kitchen. They'd told me about my mother's car accident: the black ice, the bridge. I'd cried, finally, but Marky hugged me and hugged me. *She's okay, Lil Bit,* he'd said. *She really is.* We'd take Anna a tin of cookies at visiting hours—and, get me a cell phone.

I put my mini backpack and my Trapper in my closet, and touched Michael Jordan's chest. The poster was cold. It felt like I'd just returned from summer camp or a year-long vacation, like I needed to unpack a million bags and collapse. The me-shaped crease remained on top of the comforter from yesterday's post–Larry Billy Corgan session. My shades were up. A green light blinked on my computer.

I moved the mouse. I hadn't logged out of AOL and I was bombarded with windows. I hinged over the desk and typed.

RoHo1984: Plz don't be mad at me . . . more $$$?
  (*ElleGirl80*: No.)

MasistahTurn612: Sorry I was a brat.

RoHo1984: You wanna come over Monday and show me exercise?
  (*ElleGirl80*: No.)

RoHo1984: $20????????
  (*ElleGirl80*: No.)

MalSuvialMolloy: Are we good?
  (*ElleGirl80*: Yes.)

MasistahTurn612: The *After's* in your mailbox.
  (*ElleGirl80*: Sorry to be so slooooowww. Thank u!!
    You really look gr8.)

MalSuvialMolloy: Are we seriously cool though, Heroin Chic? I didn't mean to play the rapesichord or anything, I just got caught up in . . .. Ummmmmmm. I know it's not cool to chat this, but . . . do you wanna, like, go out sometime? Or come over? *American History X* comes out on VHS soon, and I've been wanting to see it. Think you'd really like it. I mean, if that's not too . . . whatever. Ummmmmmm. They misprinted my number in the directory, but, like, call me. I'm 839-4714.

(*ElleGirl80*: Will U B home in 2 hrs? U hungry?)

In my parents' room, I flipped through the Rolodex in the roll top desk. Anna kept a running list of my dad's numbers in there. Under R, there were contacts for his hotels, in Sintra and Bali and Wolfsburg and Vienna and Shanghai.

I dialed. The receptionist's voice sounded like a rare piece of classical music. I gave her my dad's name. I stood, surveying the bedroom, the way I'd left it yesterday: I'd closed the closet door. Taken all my self-portrait Polaroids from the sheets. I should snoop more often.

I unbuttoned my jeans, waiting. In my head, I saw a list of everything I could tell my father, a scroll that would wind out the door and down the street and into the woods and through the river and blah blah blah. I could become a girl who shared secrets with adults.

Another operator came on the line. *So sorry: Mr. Egleston has checked out.* My heart sank. Then I stepped on the scale. From yesterday, I was minus two pounds. Emotions *were* overrated.

In the shower, I luxuriated. It felt good to get clean. There was always some boy in Health who said he didn't need to wear deodorant in winter, and Ms. Cummins would have to explain sudoriferous glands. He was an idiot. I had been freezing for the last twenty-four hours, and I felt begrimed. Gross. I lathered my loofah, rubbed circles over the walnut-sized bones sitting like epaulets on top of my shoulders, scrubbed the tick-tock of my clavicle. I felt tenderness, love: I pounded the beaks of my hipbones.

I was using the handheld showerhead, wielding its flexible chrome hose, to pummel away the disappointing flesh of my butt, when I remembered the porn. The end. I thought it had been boring, but now I understood. I adjusted the water from scalding to warm. The sisters had bathed each other, gently and sweetly, with shy smiles. First in a bath with a natural sponge; then, in an open stall. They had taken turns, kneeling between the other's legs and moving the showerhead. I had learned something from those girls. You could come and come.

3 ·· ANNA

My body: what of it, prone, in a movable bed? My mind, a cork in a fishbowl. These are symbols. I can't exactly do what I want. Bridled by propriety and braces or bandages or abrasions on my knees ribs feet, the mysteries of spine and spleen, flat mass that is the back. Not—well.

The lights are out, but it's clear I'm in a hospital. I recognize from examinations and childbirth: scratchy Kleenex, a yellow shower curtain topped with a panel of mesh barring me from my roommate, a silent television mounted near the ceiling. Ficus, succulent, some precious plant. If I track my gaze backwards, I can see my pulse: greenly transformed into a spiky graph, pinched and soaring, like a freestyle jazz trumpeter, improvising the hell out of his solo.

Why don't more people talk about the mute? The block that gets shoved in the trumpet. AKA the wife.

I can twist. Wiggle my toes. Wave my fingers like hocus-pocus-dominocus.

I mumble incantations: "I do it so it feels like hell. I do it so it feels real."

Oh lord.

One *year* in every five.

Fucking this up means I rule it out.

Watch ambiguous pronouns, I write again and again on students' essays.

This = killing myself, suicide, self-murder.

So unsexy to say it straight.

This = life.

Dear god. Anna, the clichés.

I wish I could be my daughter. Go back, redo after fourteen, folly with a filly, get off of men. *Au revoir*, Rot. *Au revoir*, Rolf.

He will have clogged the answering machine with messages, or at least sent me a paragraphless email, one big block of prose, lines and lines of *Why*, some meek middle, an optimistic ending: *How can we make this work?*

No, I don't blame my mother, Oprah, but thanks for that question. It's a gas. Filling the big shoes of other book club greats—Wally Lamb, c'mon!—and I wear a 37½. Oh, for the home viewers, that's the French. I'm not walking around on skis. Ha! Not walking around much of anywhere, which is one of those surprising gifts in the life of a writer. I'm like the Jimmy Stewart, Rear Window, *of poetry!*

All right, chump. Enough. The room beeps and breathes with cords and plastic boxes, invisible batteries. The bed smells like old urine and Ralston. The sheets are shitty. I shut my eyes.

This was me, waking in the middle of the night.

..

"I'd like to call my husband," I tell the nurse, who comes to check my blood pressure and clip a fancy clothespin on my finger, at some time, anytime, an hour after hours on hours. Morning.

Her face says: *I'm frightened but I've always been that way, I swear—it's you, but not you.*

Her body says: *Sometimes I exercise—mostly just walks.*

She wheels over a nightstand with a phone; the buttons protrude like warts.

"This is international," I say. "Any special codes or—?"

"Only local numbers, I'm sorry. You can buy a calling card from the gift shop." She frowns at my condition. "I can run and fetch that, on my break in half an hour."

"Kind. Too kind. 'In the very temple of Delight, Veil'd Melancholy has her sovran shrine.'"

Are we in the psych ward? the woman's expression says. *Order a transfer for this kook.*

"Jesting," I say. "I've got . . . calling my brother."

..

"Professor Anna?" says an ebullient woman. "Is that you? I wasn't sure of your last name, hon. Two versions on the chart. Slashed or dashed. What's that?"

Beside my bed, Barbara holds a Dixie cup. Based on the way she shakes it, I expect pills. I hope for sedatives. Tranqs. Painkillers. A misgauged dosage. Something to bludgeon me.

"Hi," I think I say. But this time, waking, I've lost my voice. My mouth unhinges and I croak. And when I check again, the nurse is no more Barbara than Michael Jackson is Michael Jordan. This nurse has a broad nose, a Hawaiian countenance. Her name tag reads *Babette*. She's my age, which, from my vantage, looks—unpardonably—young.

She swings a table out from inside the bedframe; it sits before me like an arm in a sling. She sets down a tray.

"Will you show me you can eat, Mrs. Egleston?"

"Anna," I say, but whatever's happened to me makes my voice come out like the noise one saves for the dentist. *Ahhhhhhnnnnnnnnn.*

With a switch, the nurse inclines my bed, so I'm leaning closer and closer to my food. There it is: a city of Styrofoam. Stewed prunes. Gray-blue yogurt. Raisin Bran. In cups, milk and orange juice. No coffee. A prayer card—maybe that's supposed to revive me: it shows a glossy white sand beach, frothing waves, a sunset radiating yellow, orange, pink, red, smoked purple, black. *Manawa*, is printed in lilac, at the bottom.

I point to the text. The postcolonialist in me cringes. *Dear anyone, please forgive me for assuming this woman can parse an unfamiliar term and offer, in my moment of weakness, "authentic" wisdom.*

"*Manawa*," she says. "I got a whole box of these at a garage sale. It's nice to spruce up the meals, you know? We all know the food's . . . Not exactly regerbilating. If you go on the web, Ask Jeeves or AOL, you can find . . . well. I checked, to make sure it wasn't some satanical, Manson thing. It means, 'Now is the moment of power.'"

I nod. Tantalizing epiphany.

(Not so fast, World. I'll leave you yet.)

The nurse covers my hand with hers, fits a spoon in my grip.

"Can you eat the yogurt, Mrs.?"

Looky. My arm works. The pain is an afterthought, reverbing my ribs. I swallow the yogurt. The tannins parch my tongue. Saccharine. I abhor fruit-on-the-bottom.

"Okeydokey," the nurse says. "You want TV?"

I shake my head and cringe a smile; she leaves. I wish she were Glenn Decklin and I were back in Laughlin, a freak wheeled in for observation. *Try me, dullards*, I'd say to my life-living, worthless colleagues. I'd raise an invisible mug: *Here's to feeling good all the time!*

The room is not quiet. The door is ajar. In the hallway wheels roll across the floor, shoes scuff and squeak, printers—the kind with tear-off edges that medical institutions and the relegated-to-Building-13 administrators at COCC still use—wheedle and drone. Ugly machines. Ugly me. I don't have to see my face to know it hurts, in an empurpled way, that my cheek is not my own. Some chthonic slut.

What else is there? I expect my brother will be coming soon, bearing Elliot. Rolf, flying business class, keeping it civilized with red wine before whisky. Good man. I shake out the napkin until it's one-ply, in my palm. I scoop a spoon of dry Raisin Bran. Take your pick: cardboard or hospital food, all the taste scrubbed off in the feeble name of health. Texture, crunch: that's all that remains. I chew and chew, bring the paper to my mouth, and spit.

4 ·· ELLIOT

So many little things I remember, I miss. Lisa hanging a *Sun-Times* cut-out of Matt LeBlanc in her gym locker, and I'm back in sixth grade. The smell of Gap Heaven on her piddly wrist, and we're at Oakbrook Mall, riding up the escalator, ducking into the Disney Store, trying on costumes for *really* little girls. Cinderella dress, size 6X. Thinking a boy's erection had the permanence of a pipe cleaner, a whole misinformed decade. A childhood of seeing my dad's Jaguar pull into the driveway, the headlights winking twice, like, *Hey, Smelliot! I'm home.*

Then there's all the stuff I remember that I'd rather forget. Those things are blurry, unpinned to my life's timeline. "You go, girl," for instance, is a phrase I can do without. Yet, everywhere, all over the country, I hear adult women launching this bad boy, like it's a fiery missile heading for a wet target.

I'd rather forget the bated breath nervousness of hospital waiting rooms. It never changes. That Saturday afternoon, two days before MLK Day, Marky and Fernán let me out at the triple-doored vestibule at Rush Hospital. The entrance was as a magnificent as one of the modern homes in Ridgedale—glass and transparency was the future. I checked in as a visitor and sat in a rocking chair. On TV, a black-haired man threw a fistful of herbs into a screaming hot pan. "Bam!" I read the closed captions, got hungry, turned to an end table crowded with Kleenex boxes and old magazines. I picked up a *People* and flipped to an exclusive with Calista Flockhart, scanning for numbers. The article, "Arguing Her Case," reported the Ally McBeal star weighed 102 pounds. I smiled. *Flaca, flaca,* I was *la más flaca.* I felt so good.

The unmistakable smell of musk and jasmine wafted past me. I looked up. There was Lisa, wearing the snow leopard blanket like a robe, a fat furry hat sitting on her head like a book. Beneath her eyes were long howling streaks of mascara. A couple days ago, I would've imagined licking those clean.

"Hey!" I said too loud. A man in a Bulls Starter jacket shot me a thorny scowl.

She paused. Her eyes got saucer-big and crazy, the pupils like anime. For someone who claimed to be an actress, Lisa really needed those minutes to rehearse.

"What are you doing here?" she said. She took off her hat and squeezed it to her chest. "Stalker much?"

"My mom's upstairs," I said. "She's . . ."

I swallowed. My mouth tasted like the water I sucked out of washrags in the showers when I was desperately hungry. I so badly wanted to say I was scared. Of course, it hit me: I could still want to say that—and not say it to Lisa.

I nodded, squeezing a grimace into a grin. "She's going to be fine. Watch out, um, or tell your mom to watch for black ice on the ride home. Pretty gnarly. I mean, nasty."

"Good. That your mom's okay," Lisa said flatly. She topped her head with the hat. Her gaze fell onto the magazine in my lap. "See ya on Tuesday, Ellie McBeal."

"Sure," I said. "Whatever."

..

On a whiteboard outside Anna's room, someone had written, in big turquoise bubble letters, "ANNIE." The only respectable association I had with that name was Little Sure Shot, Annie Oakley, one of the many groundbreaking women we'd studied a couple years ago in Headways. Her, Florence Nightingale, Elizabeth Blackwell, Sojourner Truth: that was my heritage, bold and unstoppable.

I stepped inside, willing my boots not to squeak on the tile. The room was dark—my mom was in the half closer to the door than the window. She was separated from another bed, another person, maybe another woman, by a creamedcorn yellow shower curtain on a curvy metal runner attached to the ceiling. That's where Anna's eyes were—looking back and back and back, like she was trying to stare into her brain.

"Mom," I said. I was used to her spacing. She could be hunched over a notebook and not notice me blasting "Who Let the Dogs Out?" at full volume on all the CD players in the house. This time, though, I needed to bother her. My uncles would be up any minute. They'd just wanted to give me some one-on-one time.

Anna coughed and turned toward me. I stepped closer. I kept my face relaxed, the way I'd stayed cool looking at Ethan's crotch, the way I'd let Lisa bite me. My mom's face was swollen, gauzed here, purple there, abraded everywhere, like she'd picked a scab and bruised herself on a boiling cauldron. I couldn't see her arms or legs under the hospital gown except to see their shape: very small. Not much bigger than mine.

"Baby," she mouthed.

"Can I sit down?" I said. Next to her bed was a pine dresser, cruddy, with a red plastic tray like they gave you at

McDonald's. There was a Styrofoam cup with a straw sticking out of it.

Anna tried to move. She let out a moan.

"It's okay," I said. "I'm good. Are you okay?"

"Where's your father?" she whispered. Her eyes closed and squeezed. I expected a single tear or something poetic to appear on her cheek, but nothing did. Her skin just stayed ugly and purple. Even her lips were mangled looking, brown red and shredded.

"Marky and Fernán are coming up. I guess—is Dad coming home?"

"Probably."

"When—when do you think you'll get to come home?"

I waited while she breathed—it sounded like work. I couldn't keep looking at her. I didn't want to be the girl who made her mom feel self-conscious or sorry for herself. I counted the pleats on the shower curtain. Thirty-six.

"A . . . a couple days," she said, finally. "You—do you want to stay with Lisa?"

My mom didn't know. She didn't know my dad was on his way home, that he'd be flying over Beachy Head. She didn't know my uncles had made me food, peanut butter cookies and something called *pernil* that I'd sniffed and disregarded. I leaned over Anna, holding myself up, my hands planted on the scratchy hospital sheets. She closed her eyes again. *Bruises as a natural substitute for eye shadow?* I thought. For all my vegan clients. Now Anna's single tear came—followed by another and another. I kissed her forehead, on the purplest part. She was my mom. She didn't know I had other friends.

ACKNOWLEDGMENTS

ALL MY THANKS TO NOAH Ballard and Alexandra Hess for their faith and savvy, and to everyone at Curtis Brown Ltd. and Skyhorse Publishing who helped give this book a spine.

I am grateful to the academic institutions that afforded me time and welcomed me to their literary communities, and to Kathryn Davis, Kellie Wells, Kathleen Finneran, and Noy Holland for encouraging and challenging my practice. To Barbara Tannert-Smith for teaching me about scenes, and to Glen Brown and Scott Eggerding for their unwavering confidence. Thanks to my peers and readers Dan Bevacqua, Andrew MacDonald, Hannah Brooks-Motl, Tyler Flynn Dorholt, and Amanda Goldblatt, who each practices art with a verve and grace that inspires me. To my family for caring for me. To Shannon Buckley and Courtney Napleton for loving me. And to Thomas Cook, my partner always, in everything.